D0354710

NO LONGER PROPERTY OF
SEATTLE PUBLIC LIBRARY

FANGBONE!
THIRD-GRADE BARBARIAN

MICHAEL REX

G. P. PUTNAM'S SONS AN IMPRINT OF PENGUIN GROUP (USA) INC.

G. P. PUTNAM'S SONS

A DIVISION OF PENGUIN YOUNG READERS GROUP.

PUBLISHED BY THE PENGUIN GROUP.
PENGUIN GROUP (USA) INC., 375 HUDSON STREET, NEW YORK, NY 10014, U.S.A.
PENGUIN GROUP (CANADA), 90 EGLINTON AVENUE EAST, SUITE 700,
TORONTO, ONTARIO M4P 2Y3, CANADA (A DIVISION OF PEARSON PENGUIN CANADA INC.).
PENGUIN BOOKS LTD, 80 STRAND, LONDON WC2R ORL, ENGLAND.
. PENGUIN IRELAND, 25 ST. STEPHEN'S GREEN, DUBLIN 2, IRELAND (A DIVISION OF PENGUIN BOOKS LTD.).
PENGUIN GROUP (AUSTRALIA), 250 CAMBERWELL ROAD, CAMBERWELL, VICTORIA 3124,
AUSTRALIA (A DIVISION OF PEARSON AUSTRALIA GROUP PTY LTD).
PENGUIN BOOKS INDIA PVT LTD, 11 COMMUNITY CENTRE, PANCHSHEEL PARK, NEW DELHI - 110 017, INDIA.
PENGUIN GROUP (NZ), 67 APOLLO DRIVE, ROSEDALE, AUCKLAND 0632,
NEW ZEALAND (A DIVISION OF PEARSON NEW ZEALAND LTD).
PENGUIN BOOKS (SOUTH AFRICA) (PTY) LTD, 24 STURDEE AVENUE, ROSEBANK,
JOHANNESBURG 2196, SOUTH AFRICA.
PENGUIN BOOKS LTD, REGISTERED OFFICES: 80 STRAND, LONDON WC2R ORL, ENGLAND.

COPYRIGHT © 2012 BY MICHAEL REX. ALL RIGHTS RESERVED.
THIS BOOK, OR PARTS THEREOF, MAY NOT BE REPRODUCED
IN ANY FORM WITHOUT PERMISSION IN WRITING FROM THE PUBLISHER,
G. P. PUTNAM'S SONS, A DIVISION OF PENGUIN YOUNG READERS GROUP,
345 HUDSON STREET, NEW YORK, NY 10014. G. P. PUTNAM'S SONS, REG. U.S. PAT. & TM. OFF.
THE SCANNING, UPLOADING AND DISTRIBUTION OF THIS BOOK VIA THE INTERNET OR VIA ANY
OTHER MEANS WITHOUT THE PERMISSION OF THE PUBLISHER IS ILLEGAL AND PUNISHABLE BY LAW.
PLEASE PURCHASE ONLY AUTHORIZED ELECTRONIC EDITIONS, AND DO NOT PARTICIPATE IN OR
ENCOURAGE ELECTRONIC PIRACY OF COPYRIGHTED MATERIALS. YOUR SUPPORT OF
THE AUTHOR'S RIGHTS IS APPRECIATED. THE PUBLISHER DOES NOT HAVE ANY CONTROL
OVER AND DOES NOT ASSUME ANY RESPONSIBILITY FOR AUTHOR OR THIRD-PARTY
WEBSITES OR THEIR CONTENT.

PUBLISHED SIMULTANEOUSLY IN CANADA. PRINTED IN THE UNITED STATES OF AMERICA.
DESIGN BY RYAN THOMANN. TEXT SET IN CC WILD WORDS.
THE ART WAS CREATED IN INK AND COLORED DIGITALLY.
L.C. NUMBER: 2010931550. ISBN 978-0-399-25521-2

5 7 9 10 8 6 4

TO MIKE CHEN,
FOR MAKING ME A STORYTELLER
INSTEAD OF A DOODLER

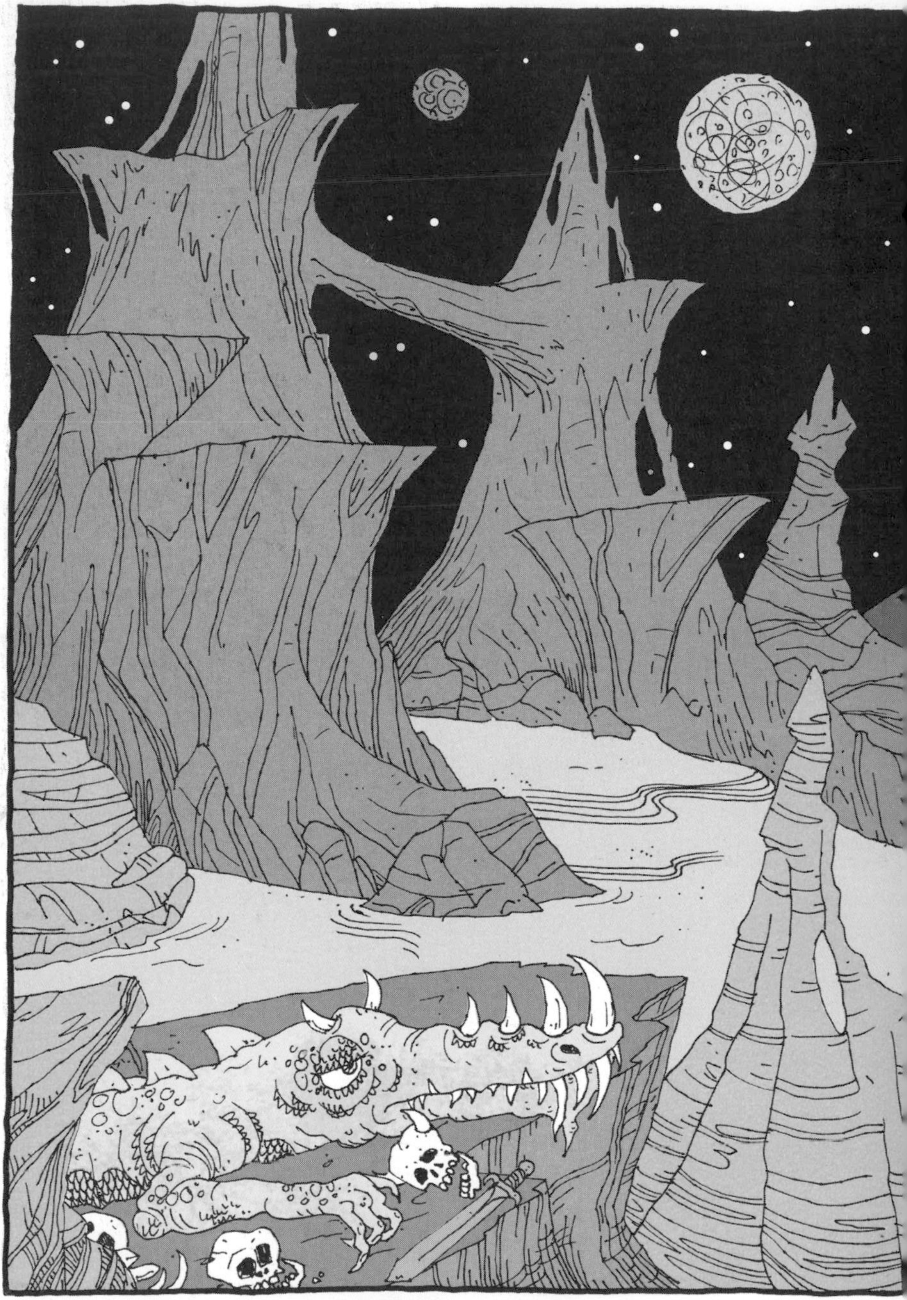

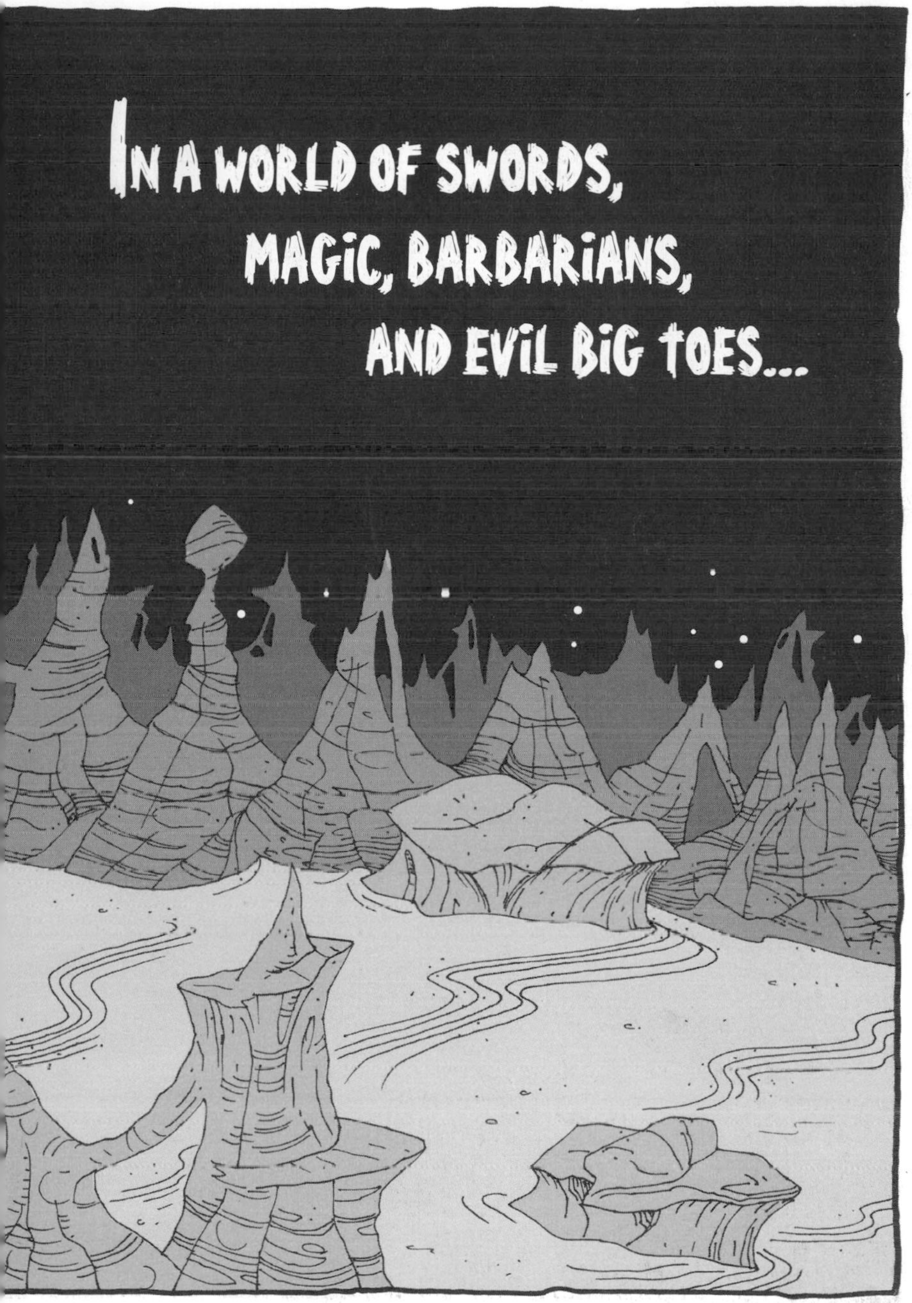
IN A WORLD OF SWORDS,
MAGIC, BARBARIANS,
AND EVIL BIG TOES...

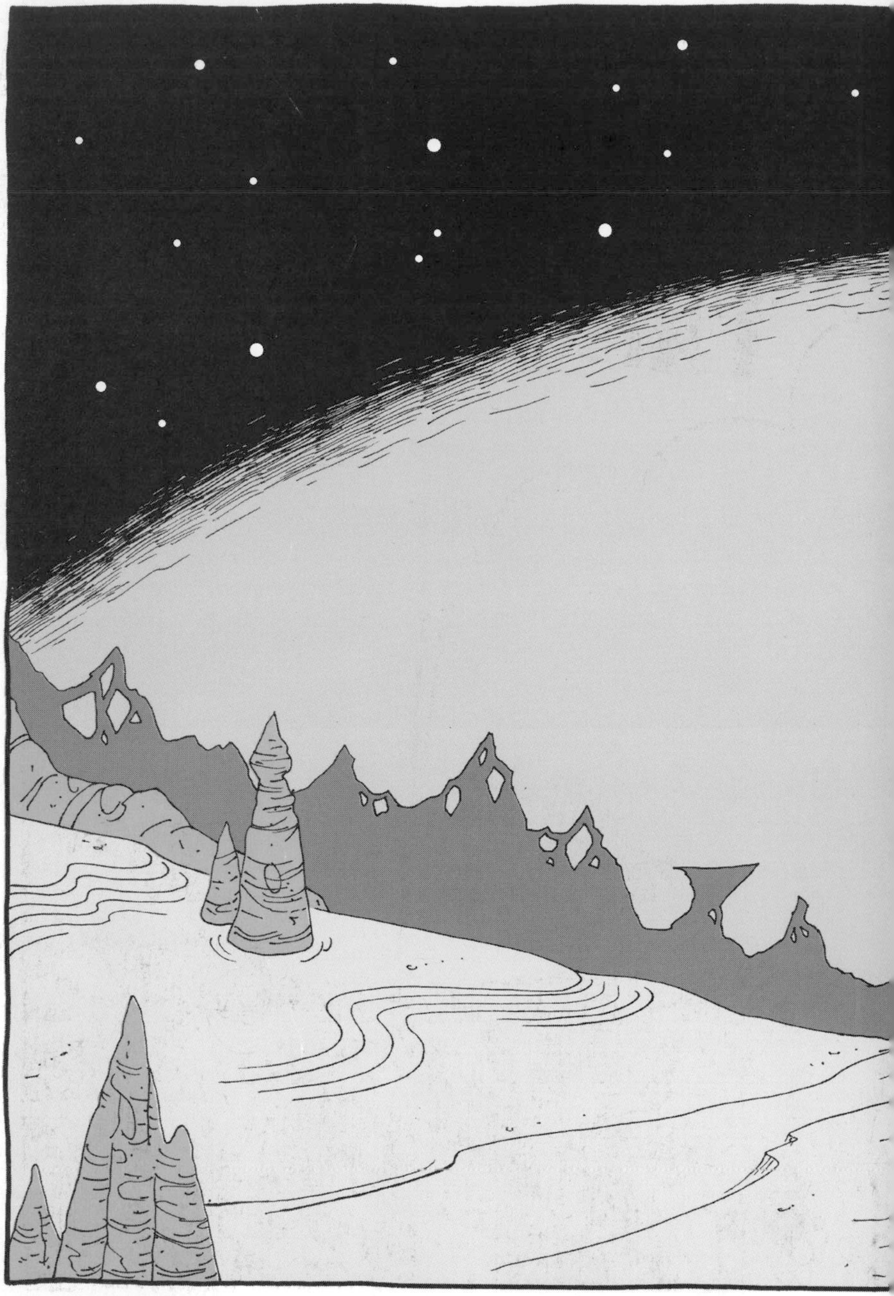

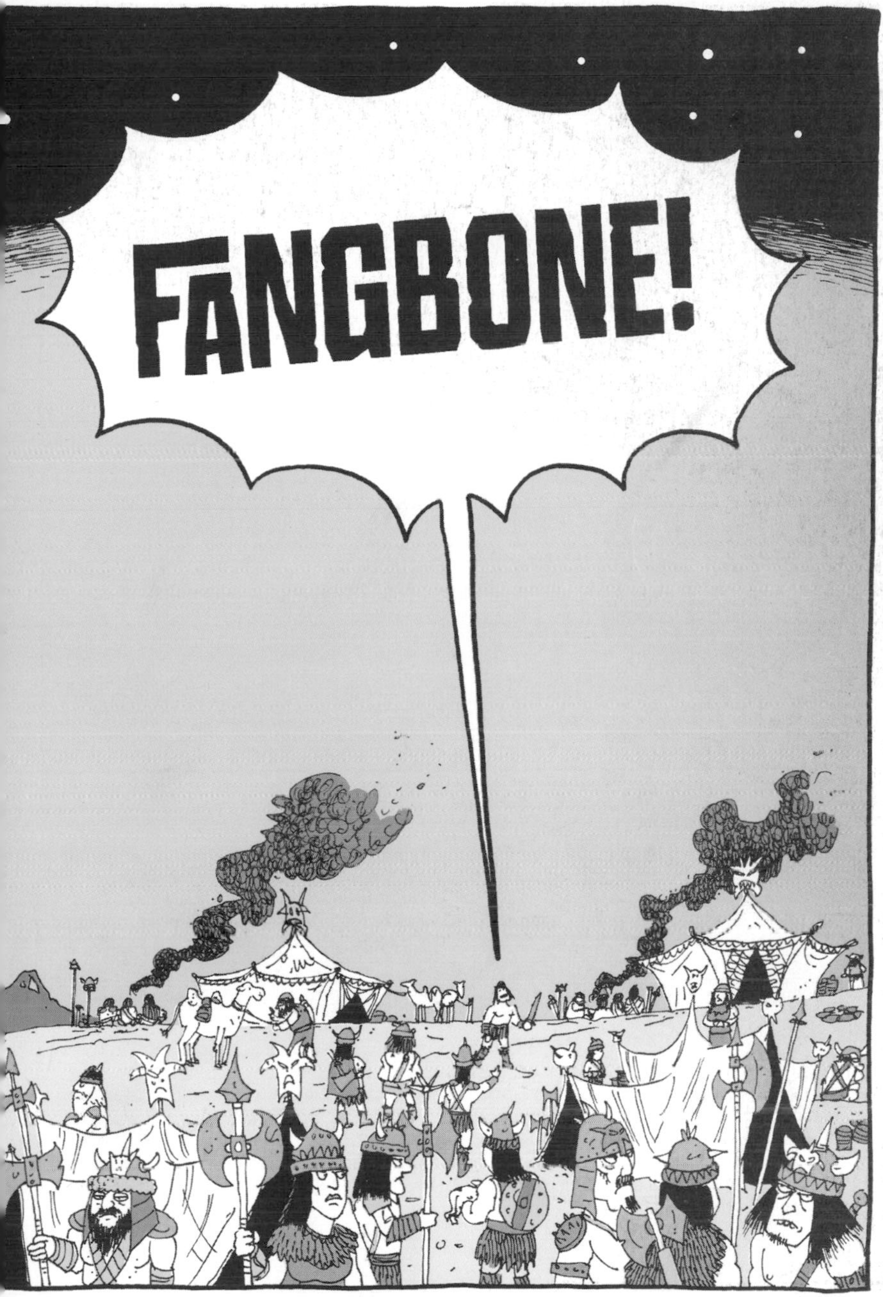
FANGBONE!

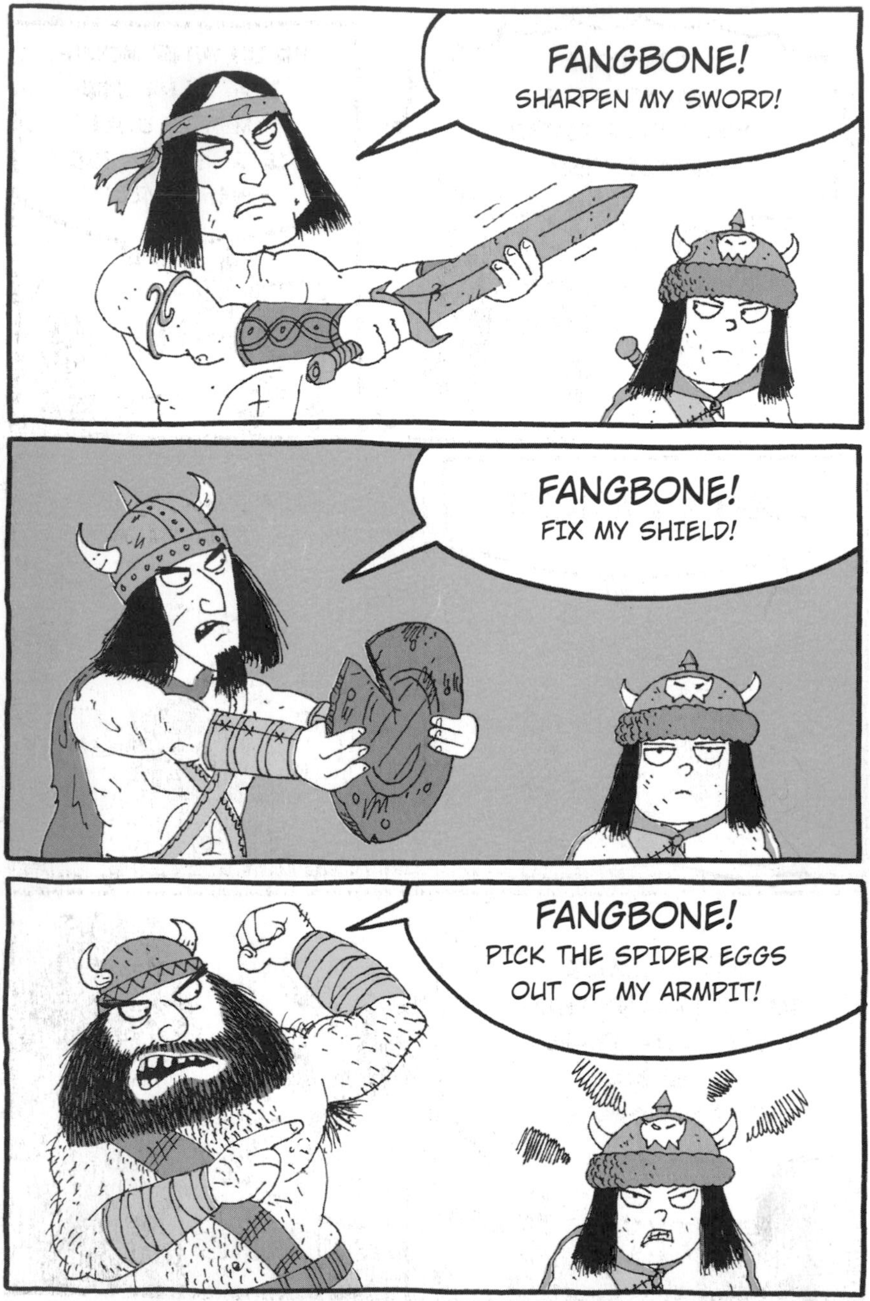
FANGBONE! SHARPEN MY SWORD!
FANGBONE! FIX MY SHIELD!
FANGBONE! PICK THE SPIDER EGGS OUT OF MY ARMPIT!

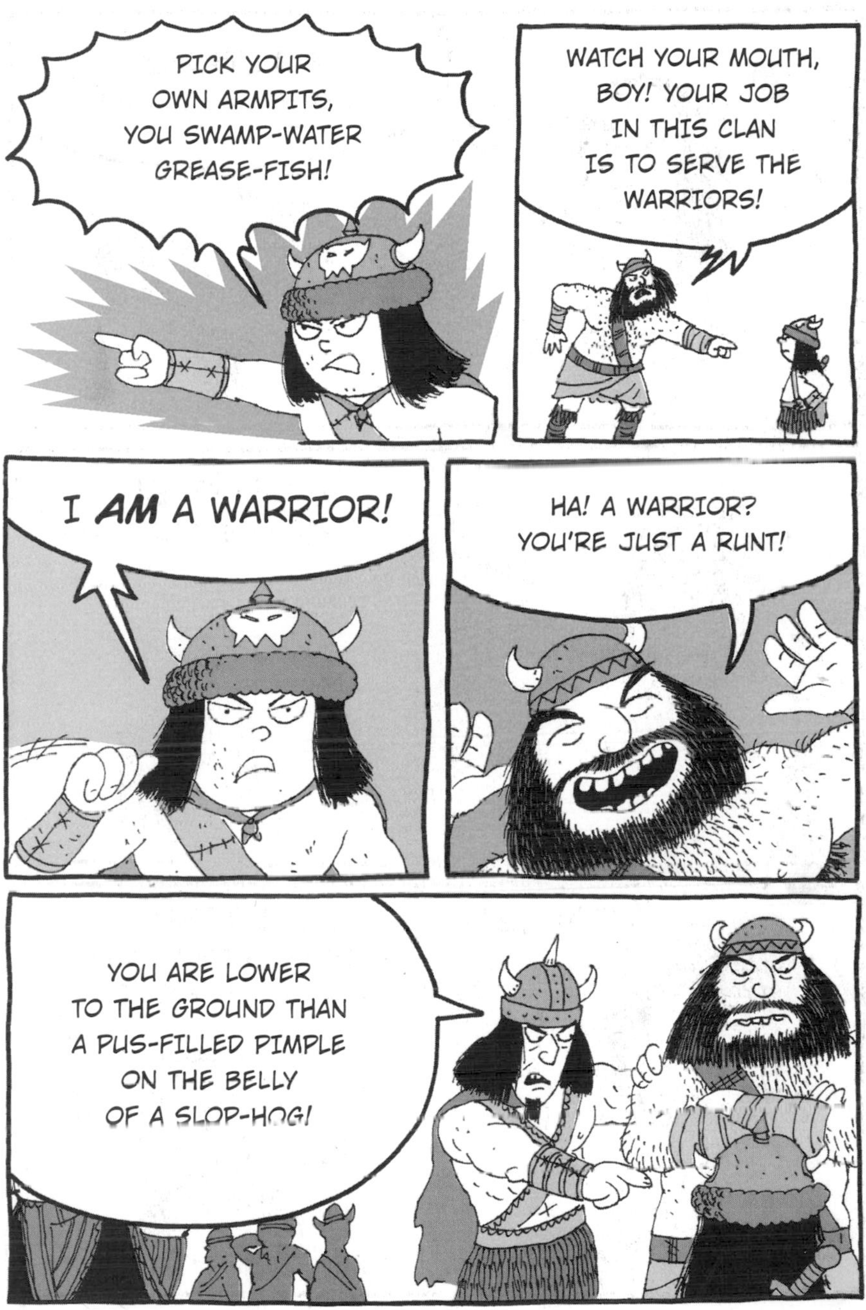
PICK YOUR OWN ARMPITS, YOU SWAMP-WATER GREASE-FISH!
WATCH YOUR MOUTH, BOY! YOUR JOB IN THIS CLAN IS TO SERVE THE WARRIORS!
I AM A WARRIOR!
HA! A WARRIOR? YOU'RE JUST A RUNT!
YOU ARE LOWER TO THE GROUND THAN A PUS-FILLED PIMPLE ON THE BELLY OF A SLOP-HOG!

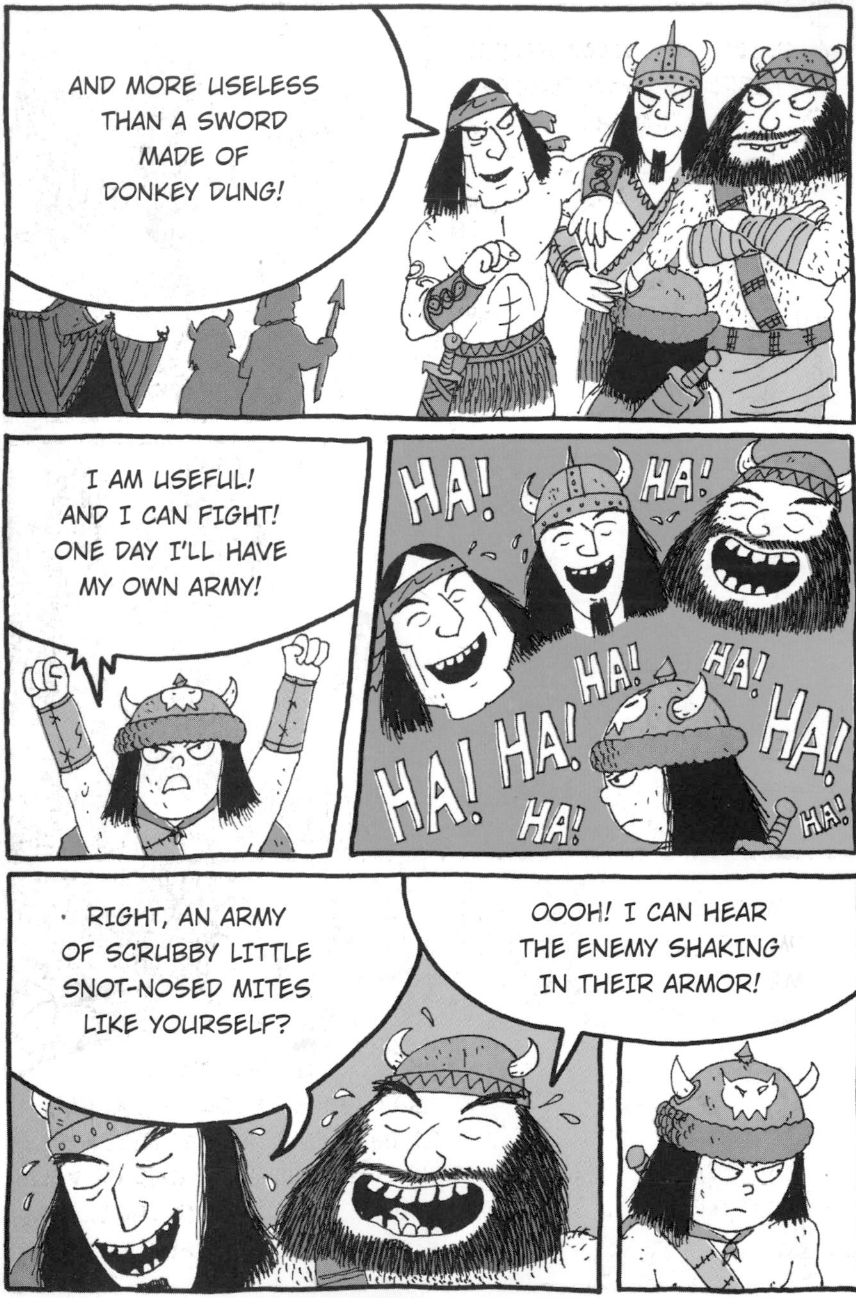

AND MORE USELESS THAN A SWORD MADE OF DONKEY DUNG!
I AM USEFUL! AND I CAN FIGHT! ONE DAY I'LL HAVE MY OWN ARMY!
HA! HA! HA! HA! HA! HA! HA! HA! HA! HA!
RIGHT, AN ARMY OF SCRUBBY LITTLE SNOT-NOSED MITES LIKE YOURSELF?
OOOH! I CAN HEAR THE ENEMY SHAKING IN THEIR ARMOR!

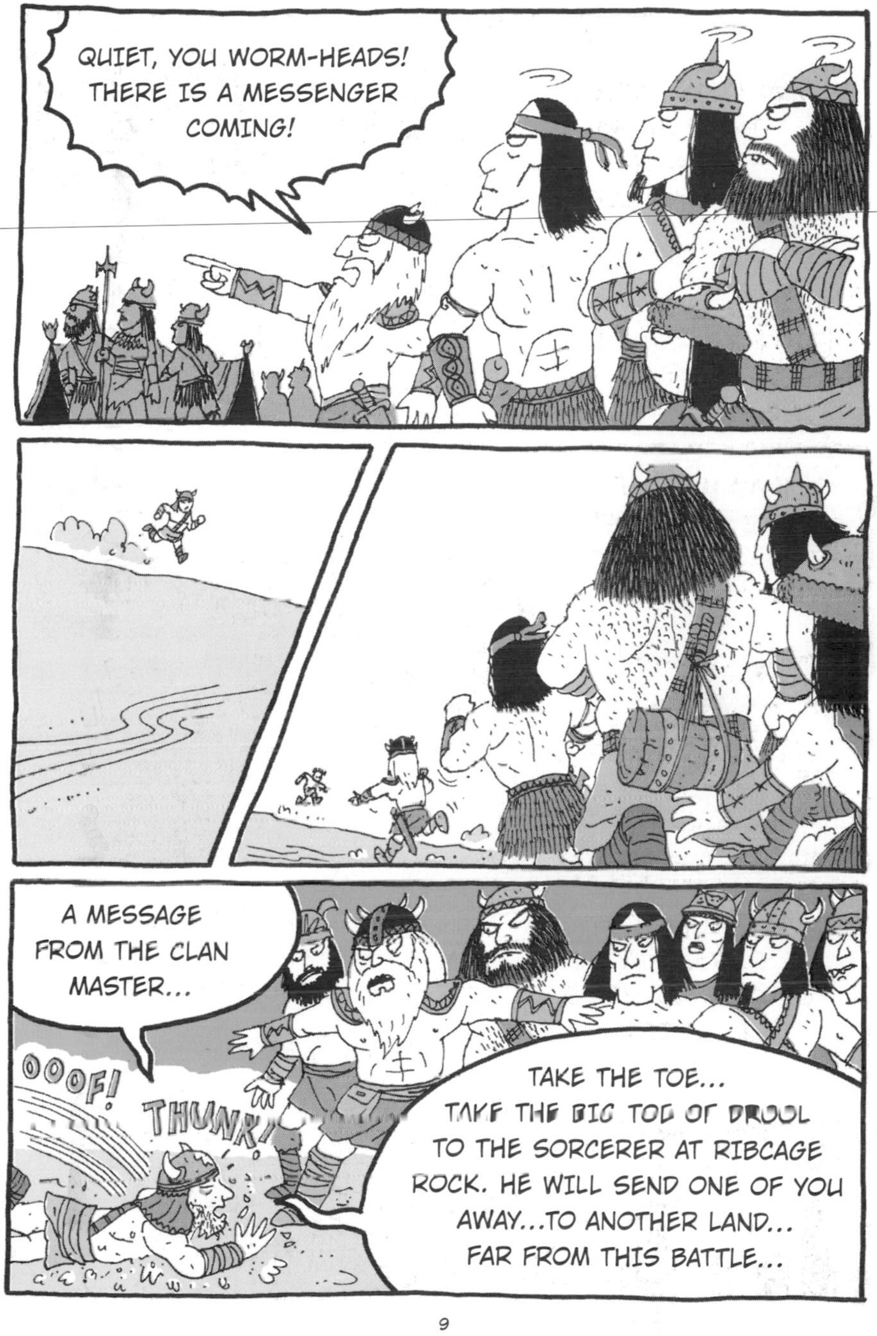

QUIET, YOU WORM-HEADS! THERE IS A MESSENGER COMING!
A MESSAGE FROM THE CLAN MASTER...
OOOF!
THUNK!
TAKE THE TOE... TAKE THE BIG TOE OF BROOL TO THE SORCERER AT RIBCAGE ROCK. HE WILL SEND ONE OF YOU AWAY...TO ANOTHER LAND... FAR FROM THIS BATTLE...

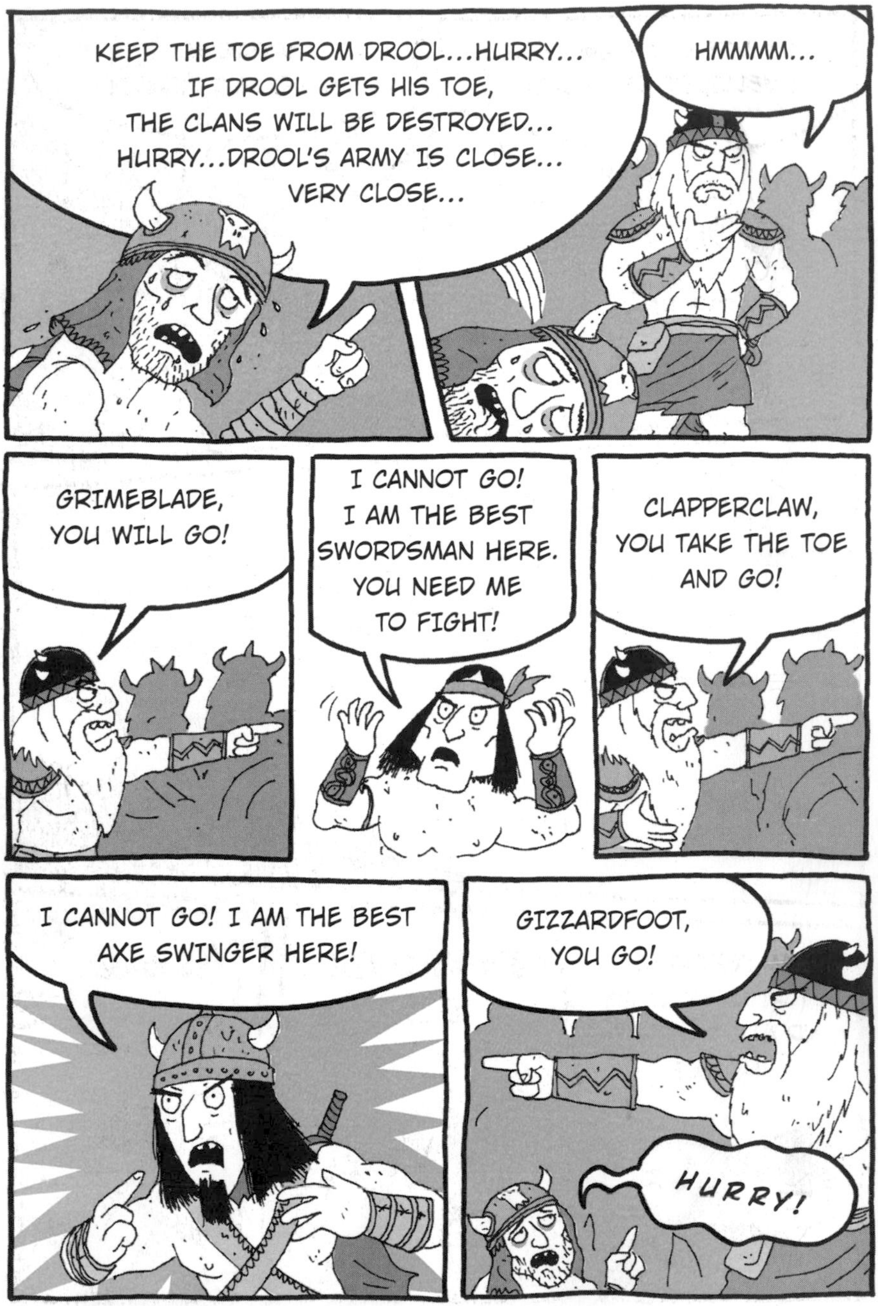
KEEP THE TOE FROM DROOL...HURRY... IF DROOL GETS HIS TOE, THE CLANS WILL BE DESTROYED... HURRY...DROOL'S ARMY IS CLOSE... VERY CLOSE...
HMMMM...
GRIMEBLADE, YOU WILL GO!
I CANNOT GO! I AM THE BEST SWORDSMAN HERE. YOU NEED ME TO FIGHT!
CLAPPERCLAW, YOU TAKE THE TOE AND GO!
I CANNOT GO! I AM THE BEST AXE SWINGER HERE!
GIZZARDFOOT, YOU GO!
HURRY!

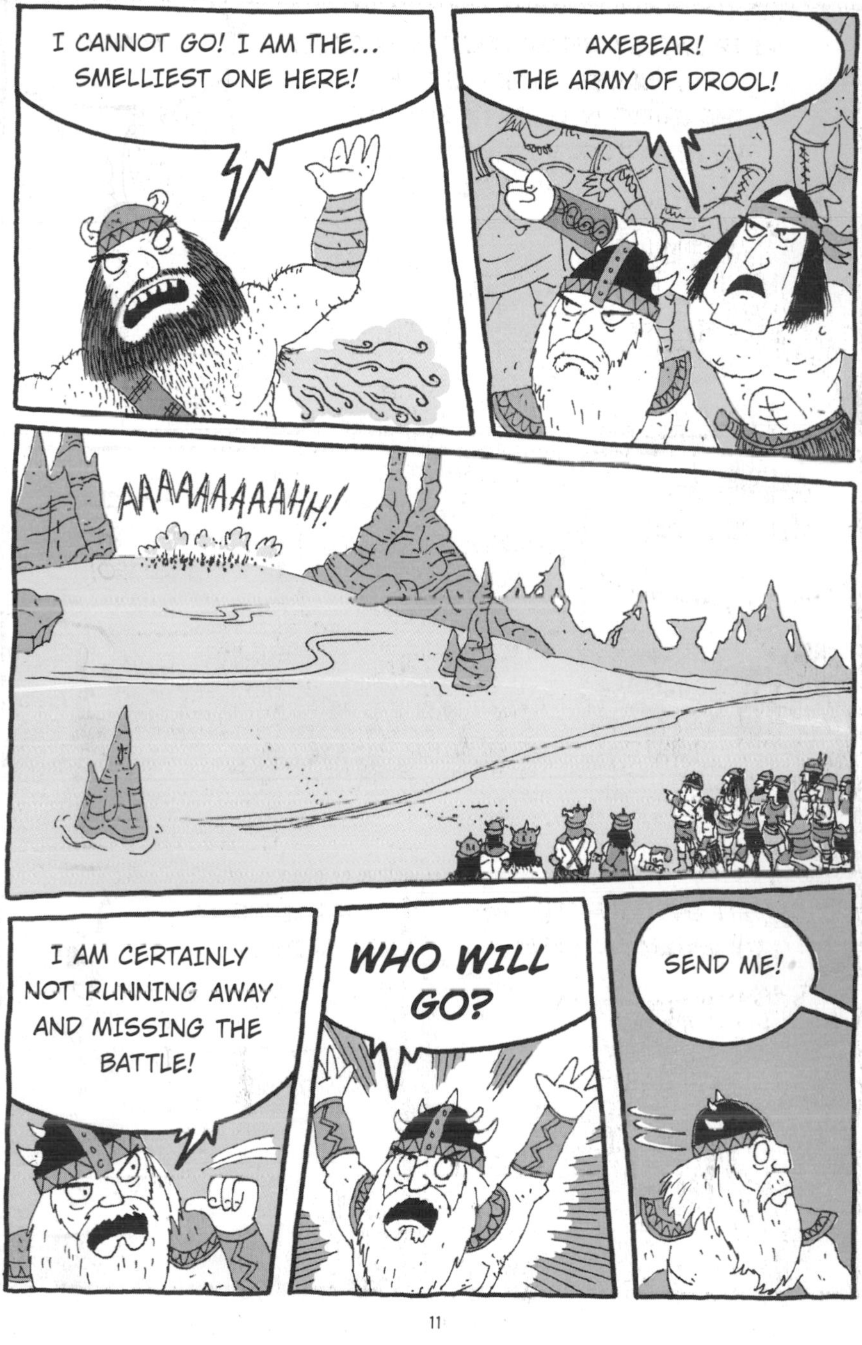
I CANNOT GO! I AM THE... SMELLIEST ONE HERE!
AXEBEAR! THE ARMY OF DROOL!
AAAAAAAAAHH!
I AM CERTAINLY NOT RUNNING AWAY AND MISSING THE BATTLE!
WHO WILL GO?
SEND ME!

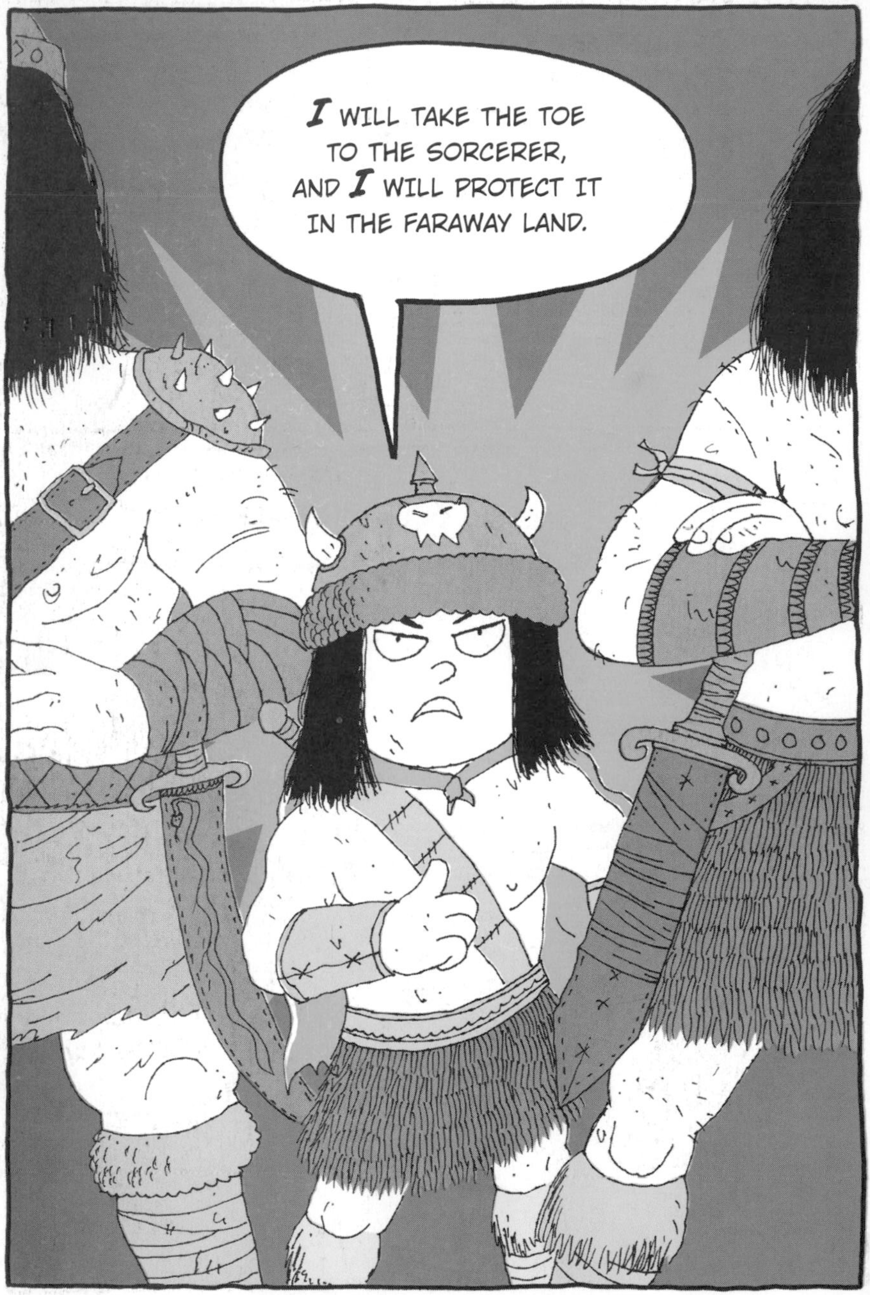
I WILL TAKE THE TOE TO THE SORCERER, AND *I* WILL PROTECT IT IN THE FARAWAY LAND.

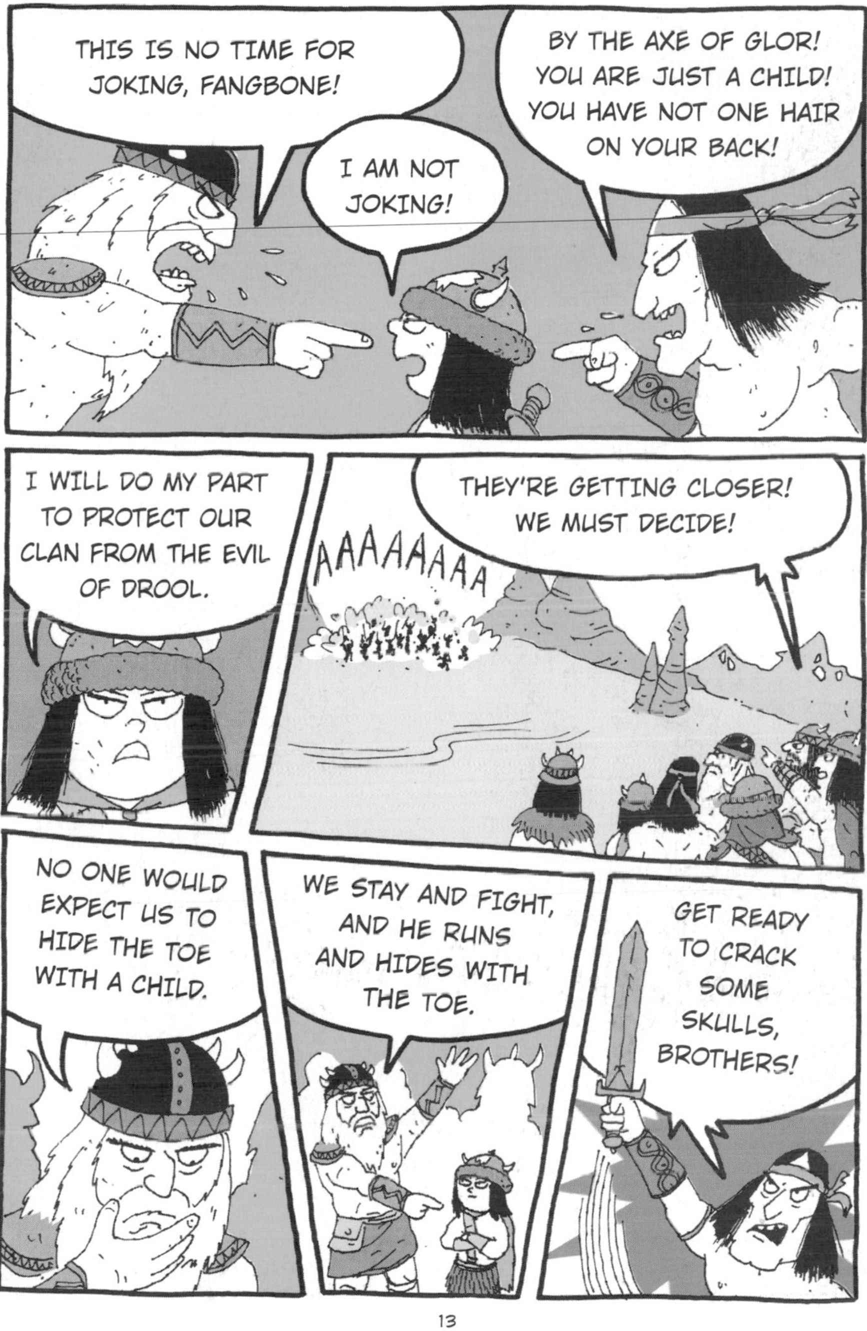
THIS IS NO TIME FOR JOKING, FANGBONE!
I AM NOT JOKING!
BY THE AXE OF GLOR! YOU ARE JUST A CHILD! YOU HAVE NOT ONE HAIR ON YOUR BACK!
I WILL DO MY PART TO PROTECT OUR CLAN FROM THE EVIL OF DROOL.
THEY'RE GETTING CLOSER! WE MUST DECIDE!
AAAAAAAAA
NO ONE WOULD EXPECT US TO HIDE THE TOE WITH A CHILD.
WE STAY AND FIGHT, AND HE RUNS AND HIDES WITH THE TOE.
GET READY TO CRACK SOME SKULLS, BROTHERS!

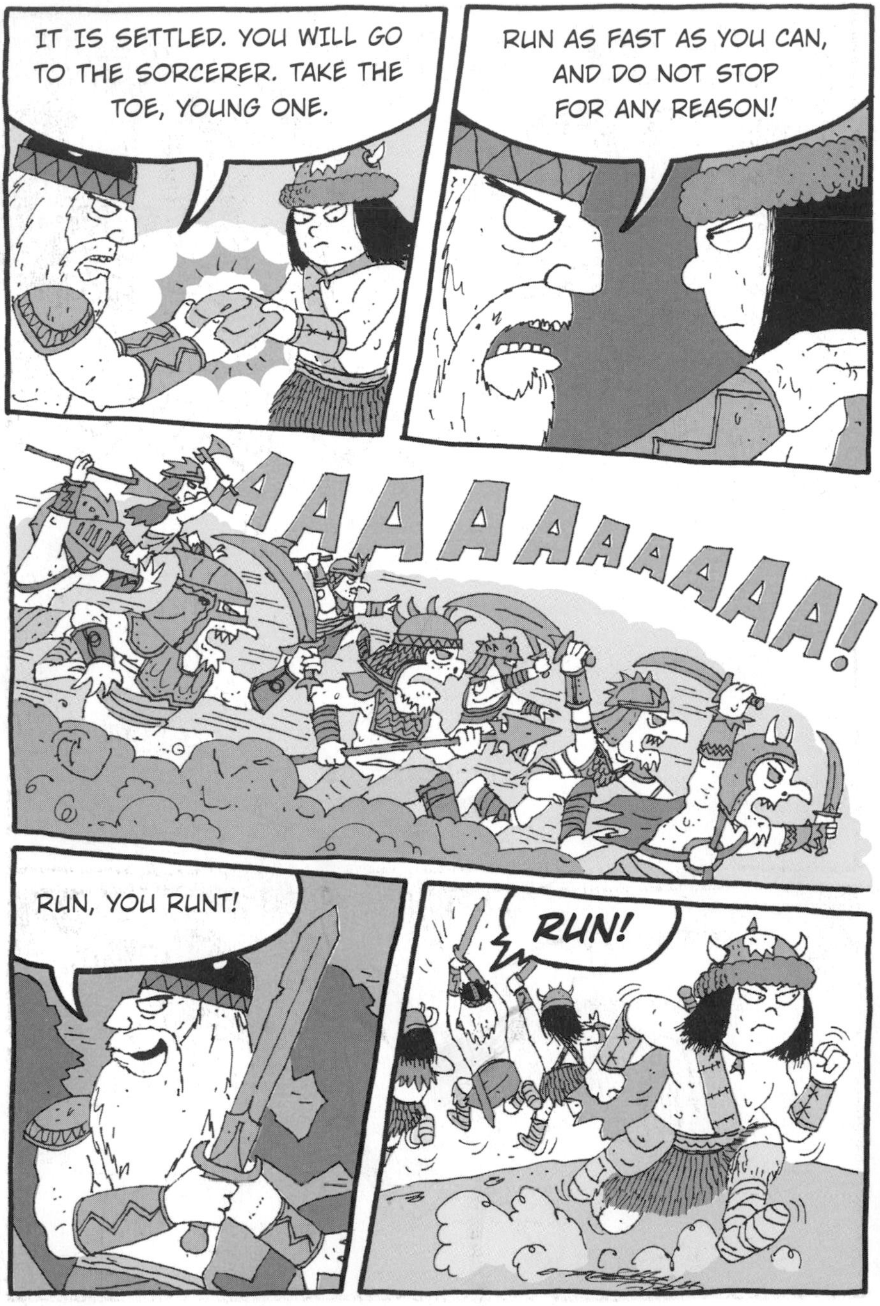
IT IS SETTLED. YOU WILL GO TO THE SORCERER. TAKE THE TOE, YOUNG ONE.
RUN AS FAST AS YOU CAN, AND DO NOT STOP FOR ANY REASON!
AAAAAAAAAAAAA!
RUN, YOU RUNT!
RUN!

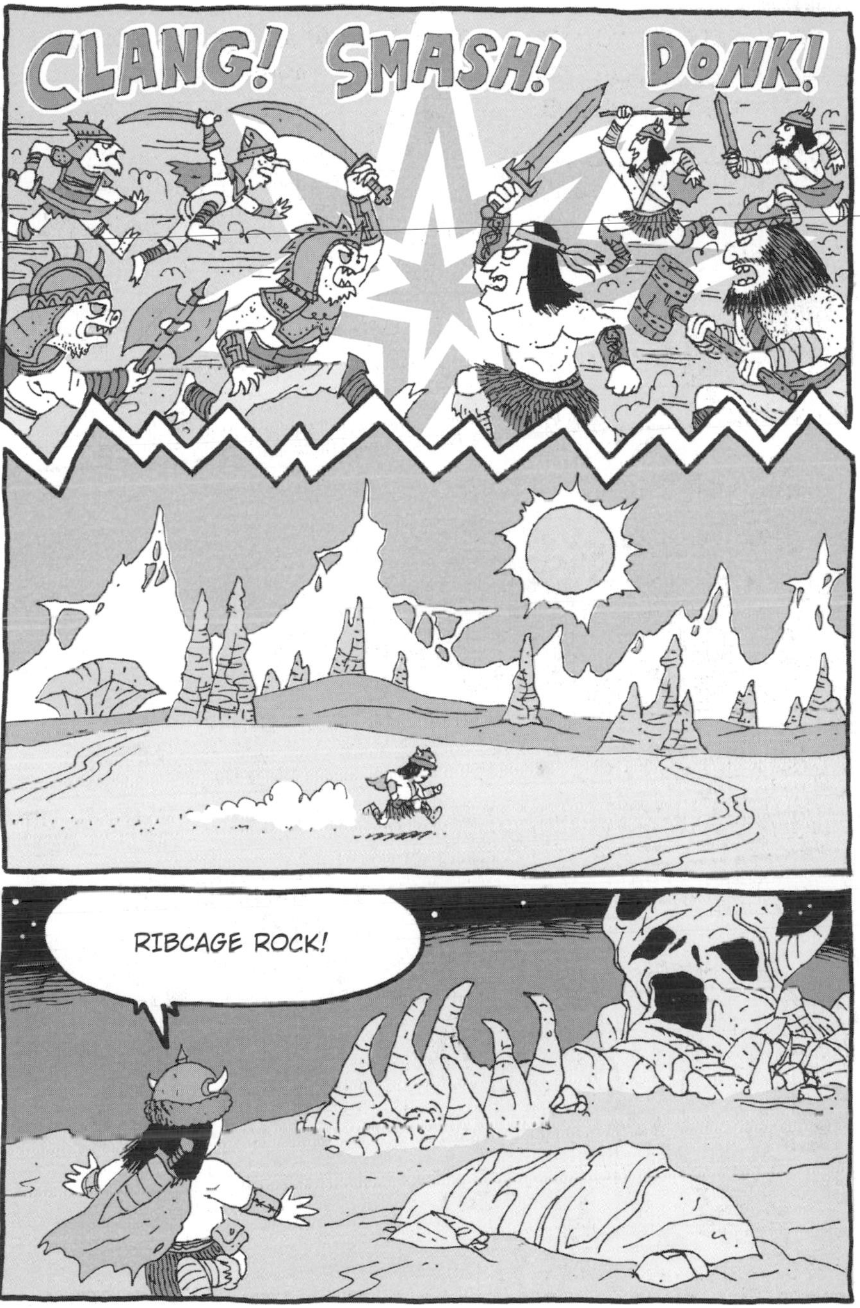
CLANG! SMASH! DONK!
RIBCAGE ROCK!

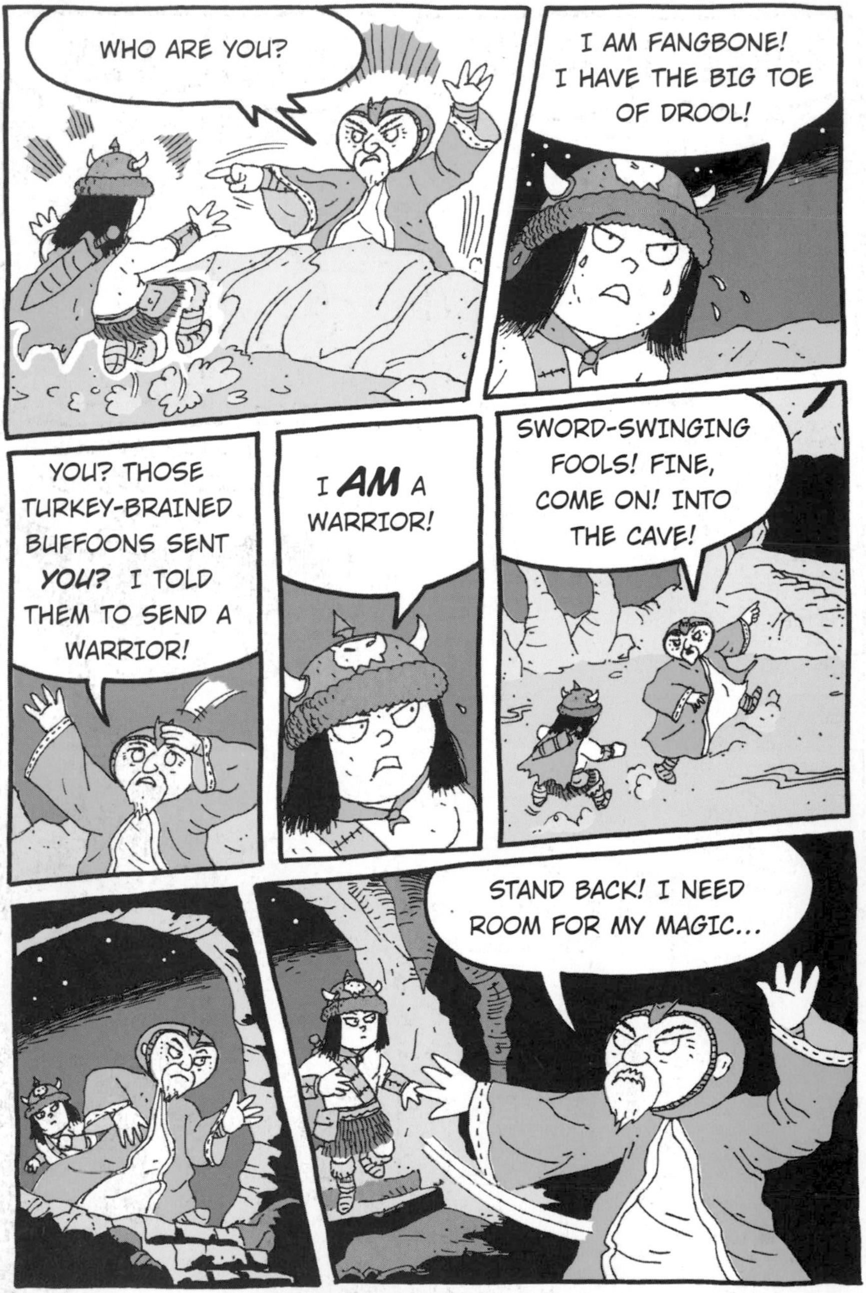
WHO ARE YOU?
I AM FANGBONE! I HAVE THE BIG TOE OF DROOL!
YOU? THOSE TURKEY-BRAINED BUFFOONS SENT *YOU?* I TOLD THEM TO SEND A WARRIOR!
I ***AM*** A WARRIOR!
SWORD-SWINGING FOOLS! FINE, COME ON! INTO THE CAVE!
STAND BACK! I NEED ROOM FOR MY MAGIC...

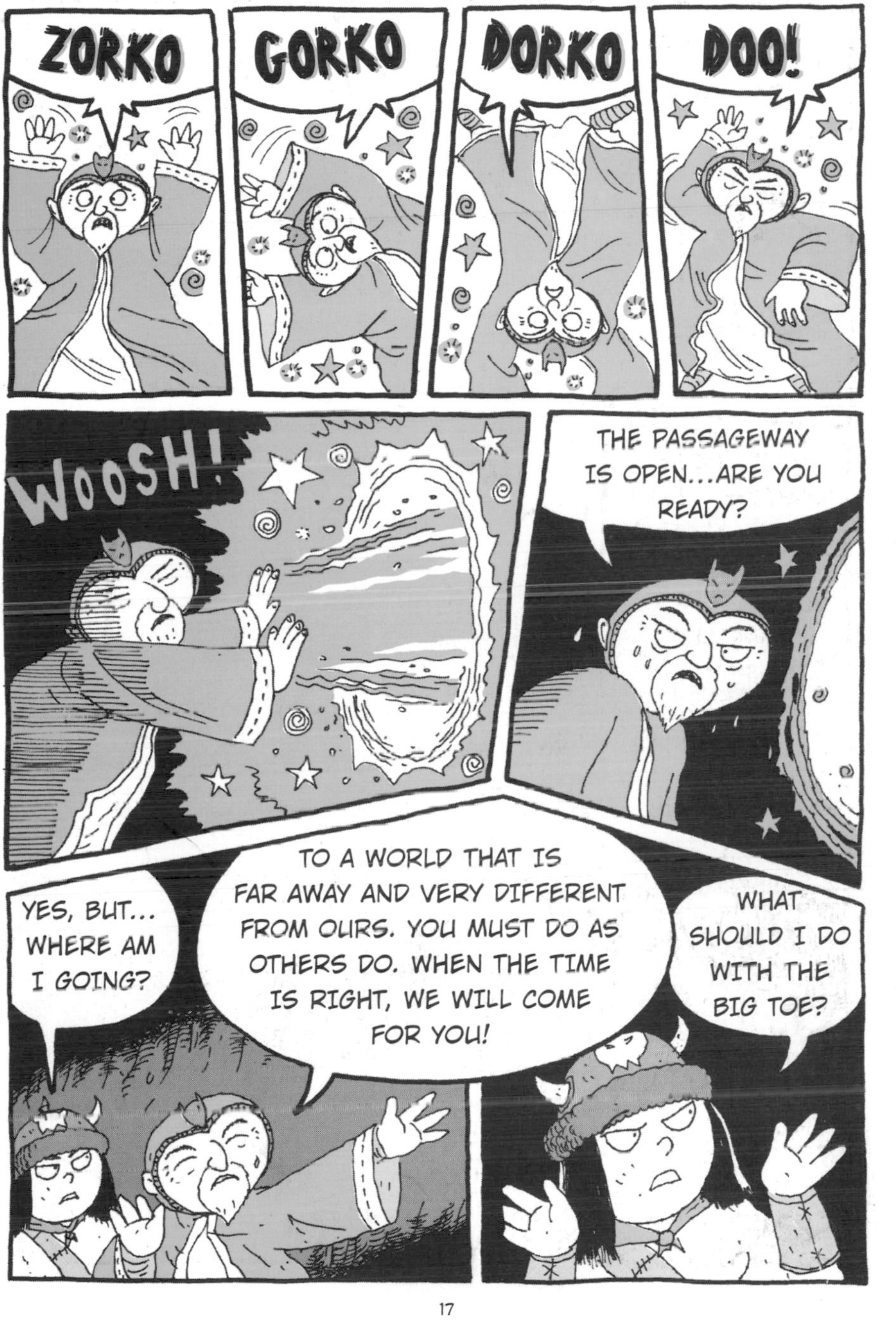
ZORKO
GORKO
DORKO
DOO!
WOOSH!
THE PASSAGEWAY IS OPEN...ARE YOU READY?
YES, BUT... WHERE AM I GOING?
TO A WORLD THAT IS FAR AWAY AND VERY DIFFERENT FROM OURS. YOU MUST DO AS OTHERS DO. WHEN THE TIME IS RIGHT, WE WILL COME FOR YOU!
WHAT SHOULD I DO WITH THE BIG TOE?

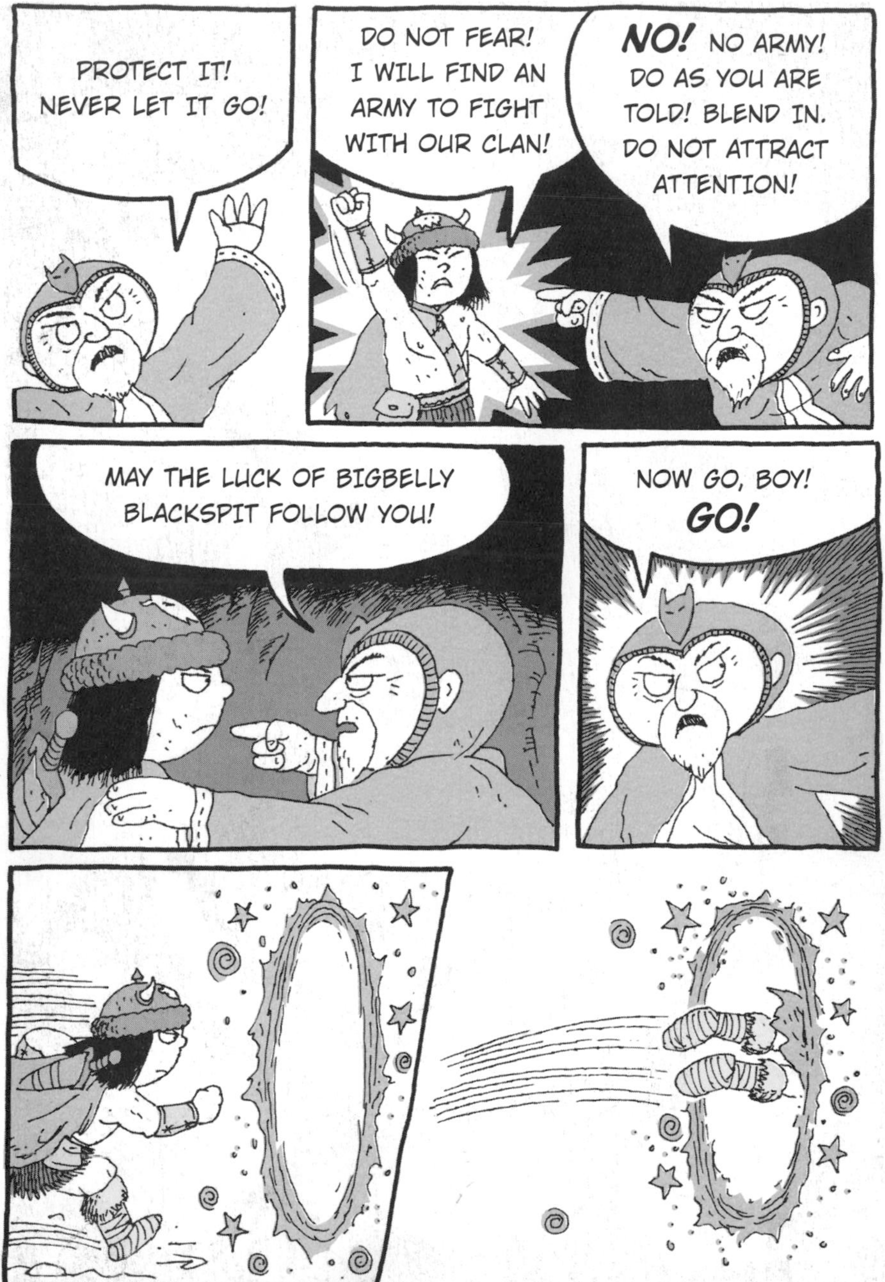
PROTECT IT! NEVER LET IT GO!
DO NOT FEAR! I WILL FIND AN ARMY TO FIGHT WITH OUR CLAN!
NO! NO ARMY! DO AS YOU ARE TOLD! BLEND IN. DO NOT ATTRACT ATTENTION!
MAY THE LUCK OF BIGBELLY BLACKSPIT FOLLOW YOU!
NOW GO, BOY! GO!

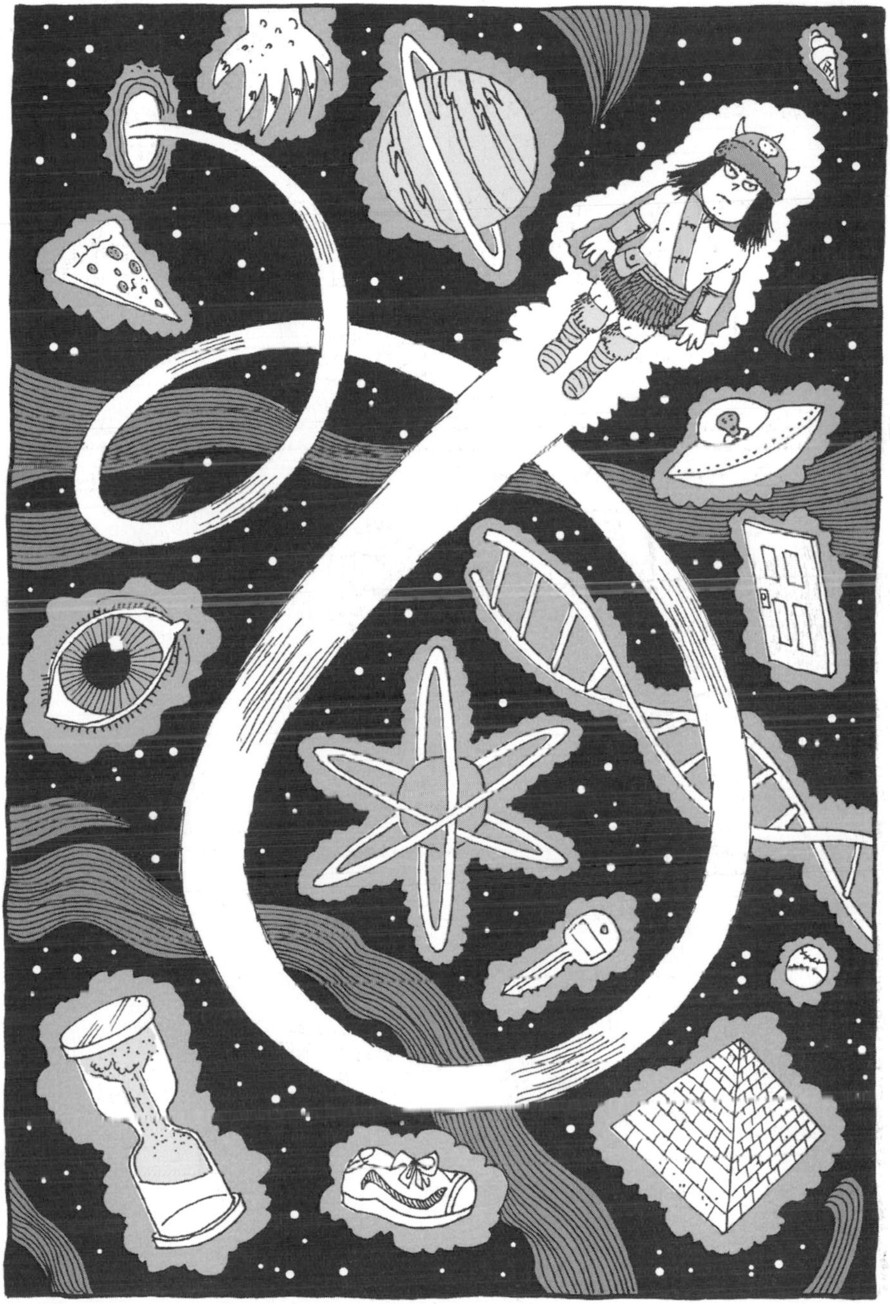

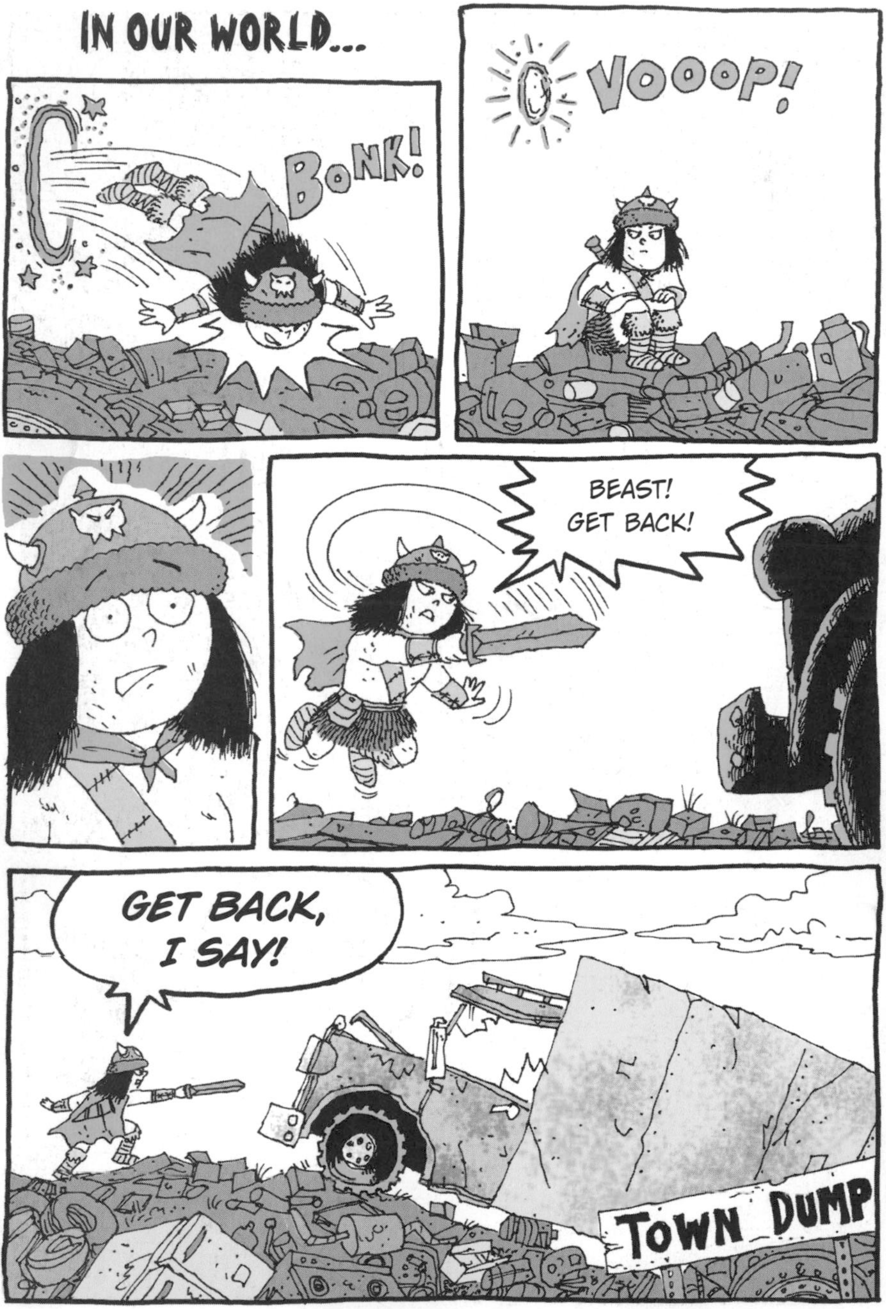
IN OUR WORLD...
BONK!
VOOOP!
BEAST! GET BACK!
GET BACK, I SAY!
TOWN DUMP

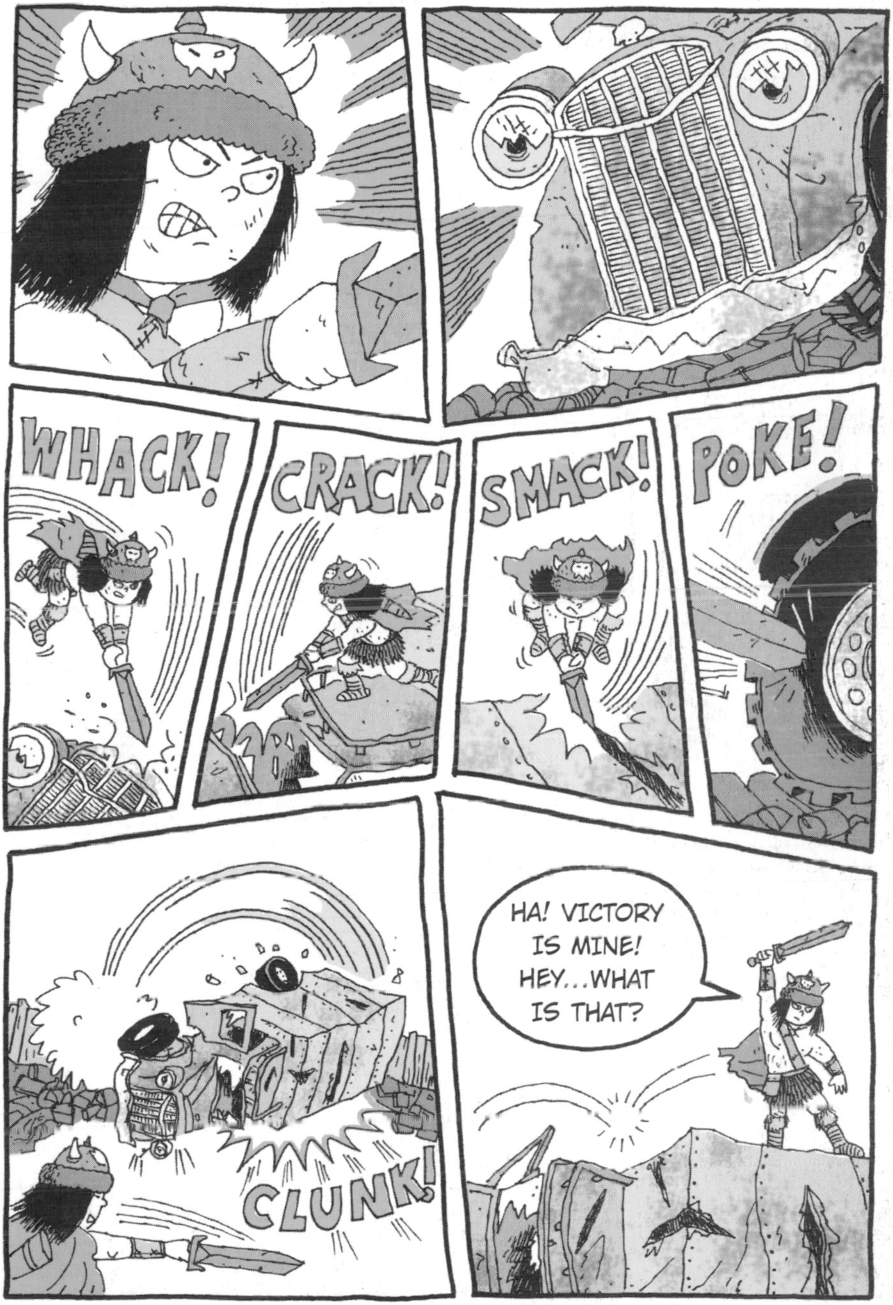
WHACK!
CRACK!
SMACK!
POKE!
CLUNK!
HA! VICTORY IS MINE! HEY...WHAT IS THAT?

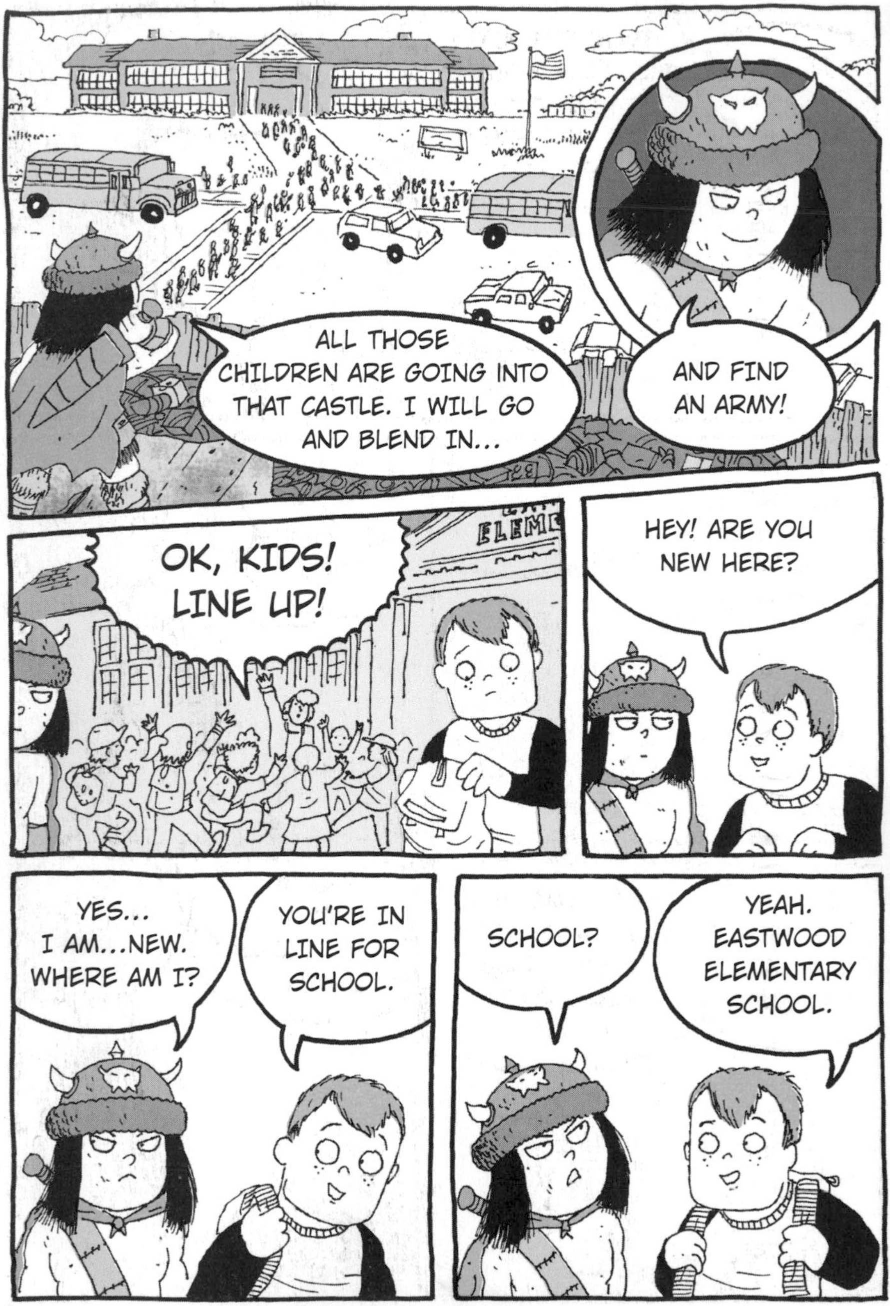
ALL THOSE CHILDREN ARE GOING INTO THAT CASTLE. I WILL GO AND BLEND IN...
AND FIND AN ARMY!
ELEM
OK, KIDS! LINE UP!
HEY! ARE YOU NEW HERE?
YES... I AM...NEW. WHERE AM I?
YOU'RE IN LINE FOR SCHOOL.
SCHOOL?
YEAH. EASTWOOD ELEMENTARY SCHOOL.

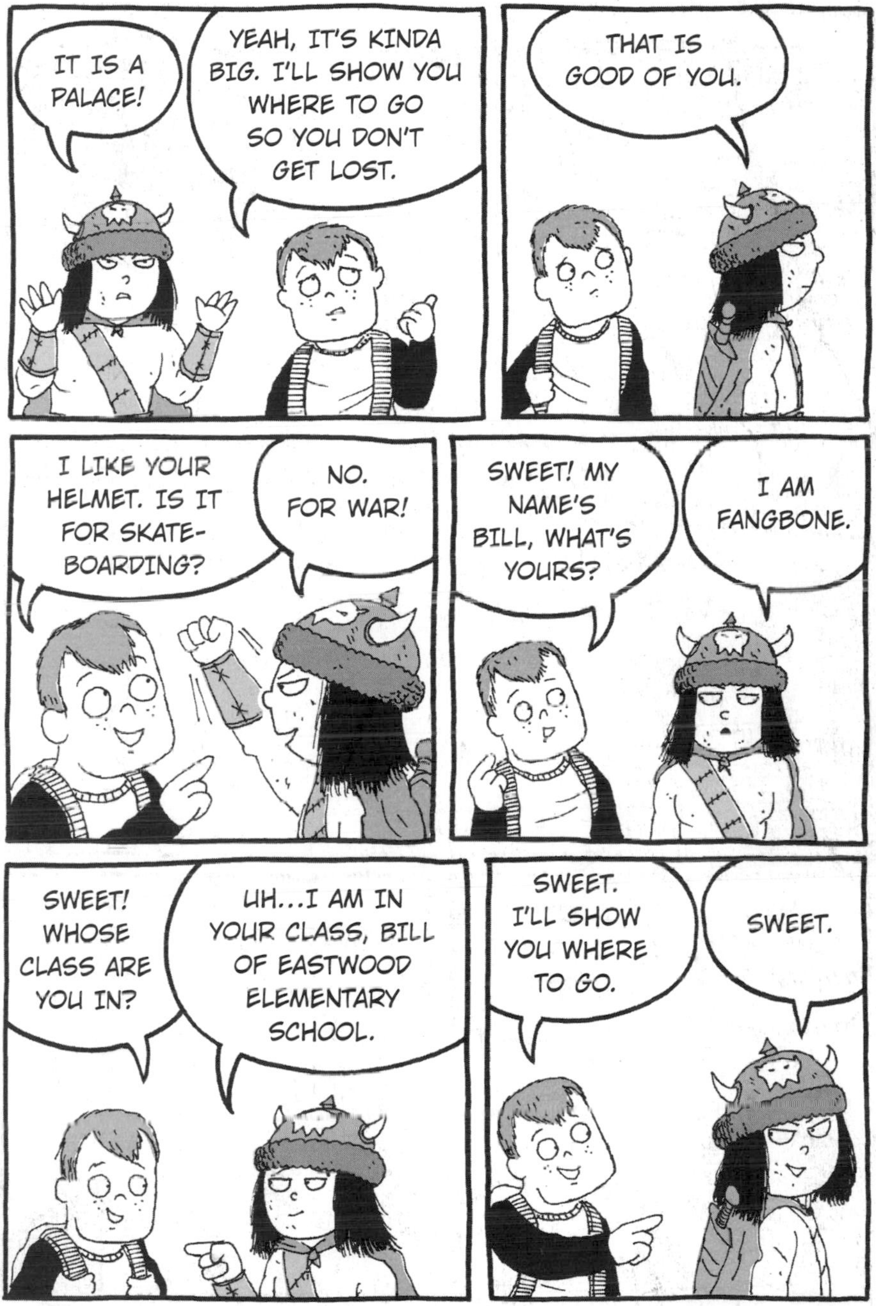
IT IS A PALACE!
YEAH, IT'S KINDA BIG. I'LL SHOW YOU WHERE TO GO SO YOU DON'T GET LOST.
THAT IS GOOD OF YOU.
I LIKE YOUR HELMET. IS IT FOR SKATE-BOARDING?
NO. FOR WAR!
SWEET! MY NAME'S BILL, WHAT'S YOURS?
I AM FANGBONE.
SWEET! WHOSE CLASS ARE YOU IN?
UH...I AM IN YOUR CLASS, BILL OF EASTWOOD ELEMENTARY SCHOOL.
SWEET. I'LL SHOW YOU WHERE TO GO.
SWEET.

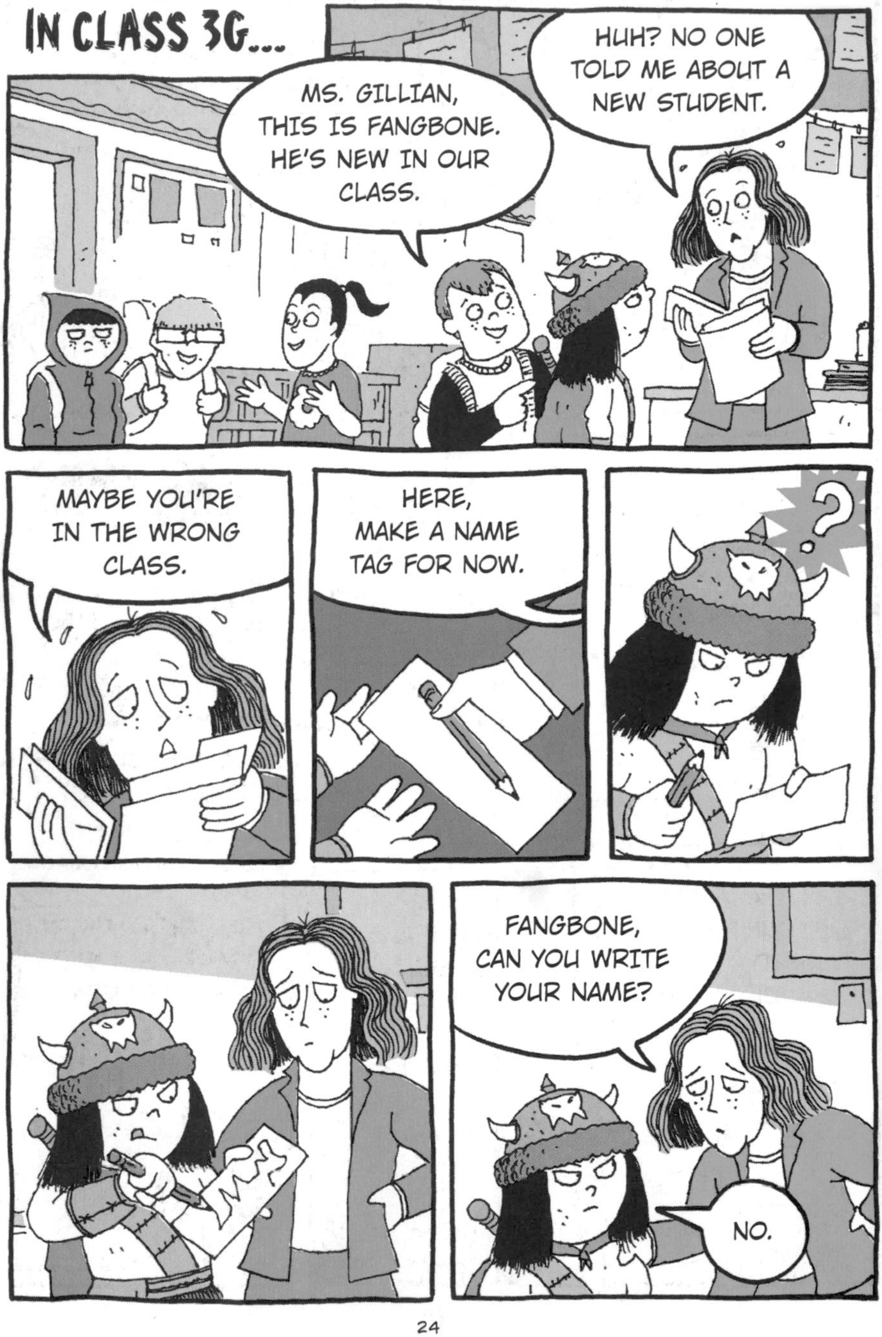
IN CLASS 3G....
MS. GILLIAN, THIS IS FANGBONE. HE'S NEW IN OUR CLASS.
HUH? NO ONE TOLD ME ABOUT A NEW STUDENT.
MAYBE YOU'RE IN THE WRONG CLASS.
HERE, MAKE A NAME TAG FOR NOW.
?
FANGBONE, CAN YOU WRITE YOUR NAME?
NO.

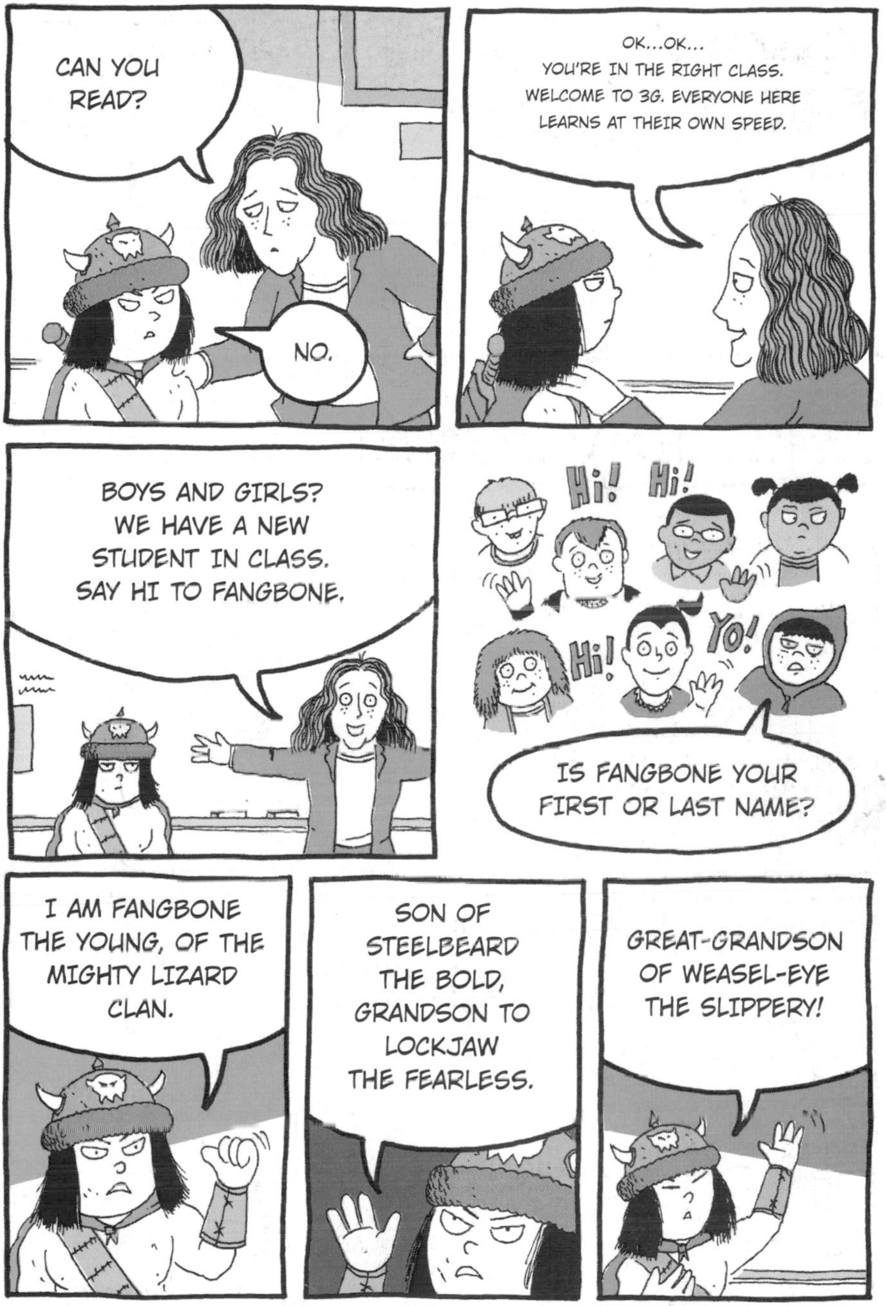
CAN YOU READ?
NO.
OK...OK...
YOU'RE IN THE RIGHT CLASS. WELCOME TO 3G. EVERYONE HERE LEARNS AT THEIR OWN SPEED.
BOYS AND GIRLS? WE HAVE A NEW STUDENT IN CLASS. SAY HI TO FANGBONE.
HI!
HI!
HI!
YO!
IS FANGBONE YOUR FIRST OR LAST NAME?
I AM FANGBONE THE YOUNG, OF THE MIGHTY LIZARD CLAN.
SON OF STEELBEARD THE BOLD, GRANDSON TO LOCKJAW THE FEARLESS.
GREAT-GRANDSON OF WEASEL-EYE THE SLIPPERY!

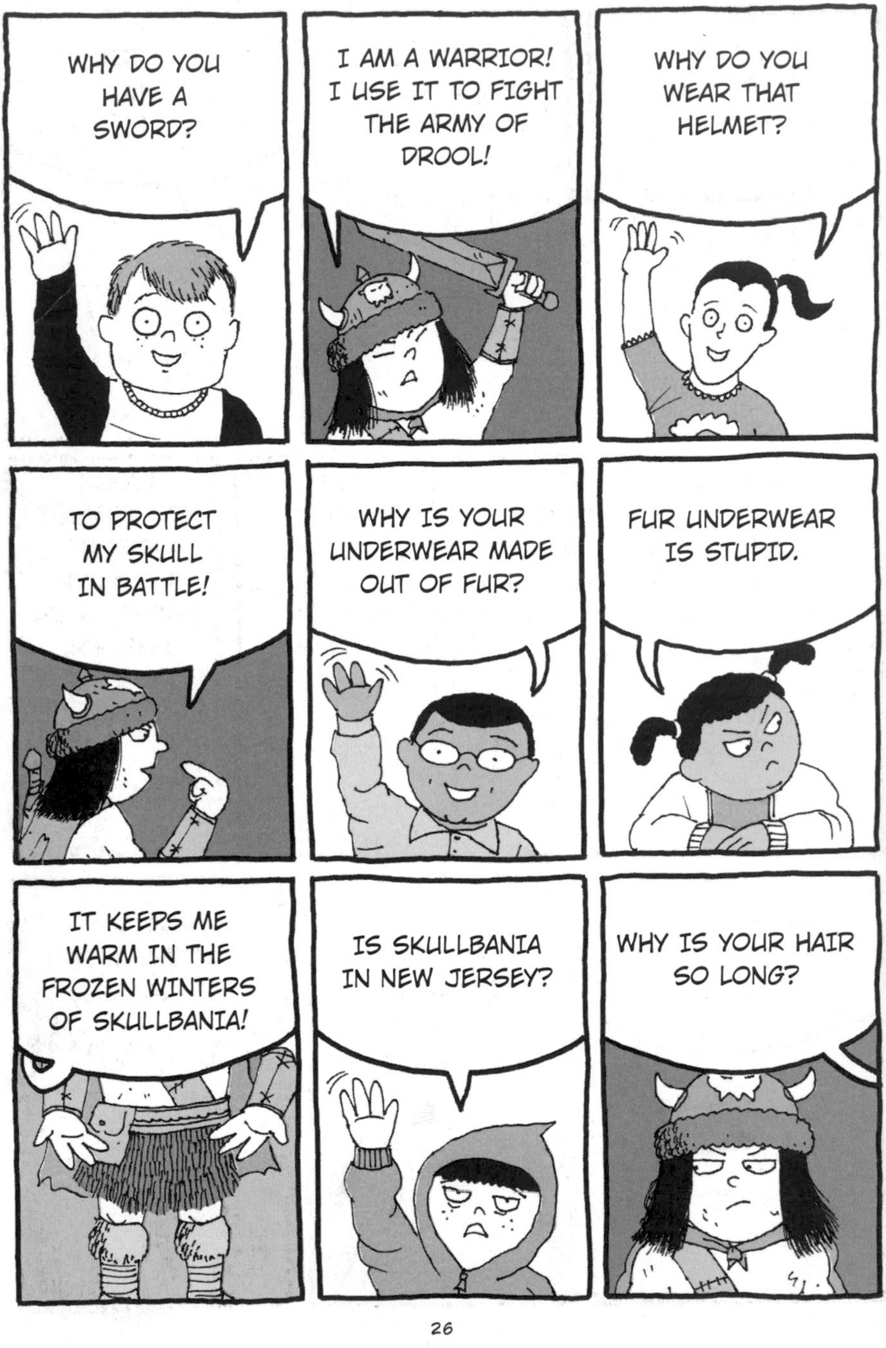
WHY DO YOU HAVE A SWORD?
I AM A WARRIOR! I USE IT TO FIGHT THE ARMY OF DROOL!
WHY DO YOU WEAR THAT HELMET?
TO PROTECT MY SKULL IN BATTLE!
WHY IS YOUR UNDERWEAR MADE OUT OF FUR?
FUR UNDERWEAR IS STUPID.
IT KEEPS ME WARM IN THE FROZEN WINTERS OF SKULLBANIA!
IS SKULLBANIA IN NEW JERSEY?
WHY IS YOUR HAIR SO LONG?

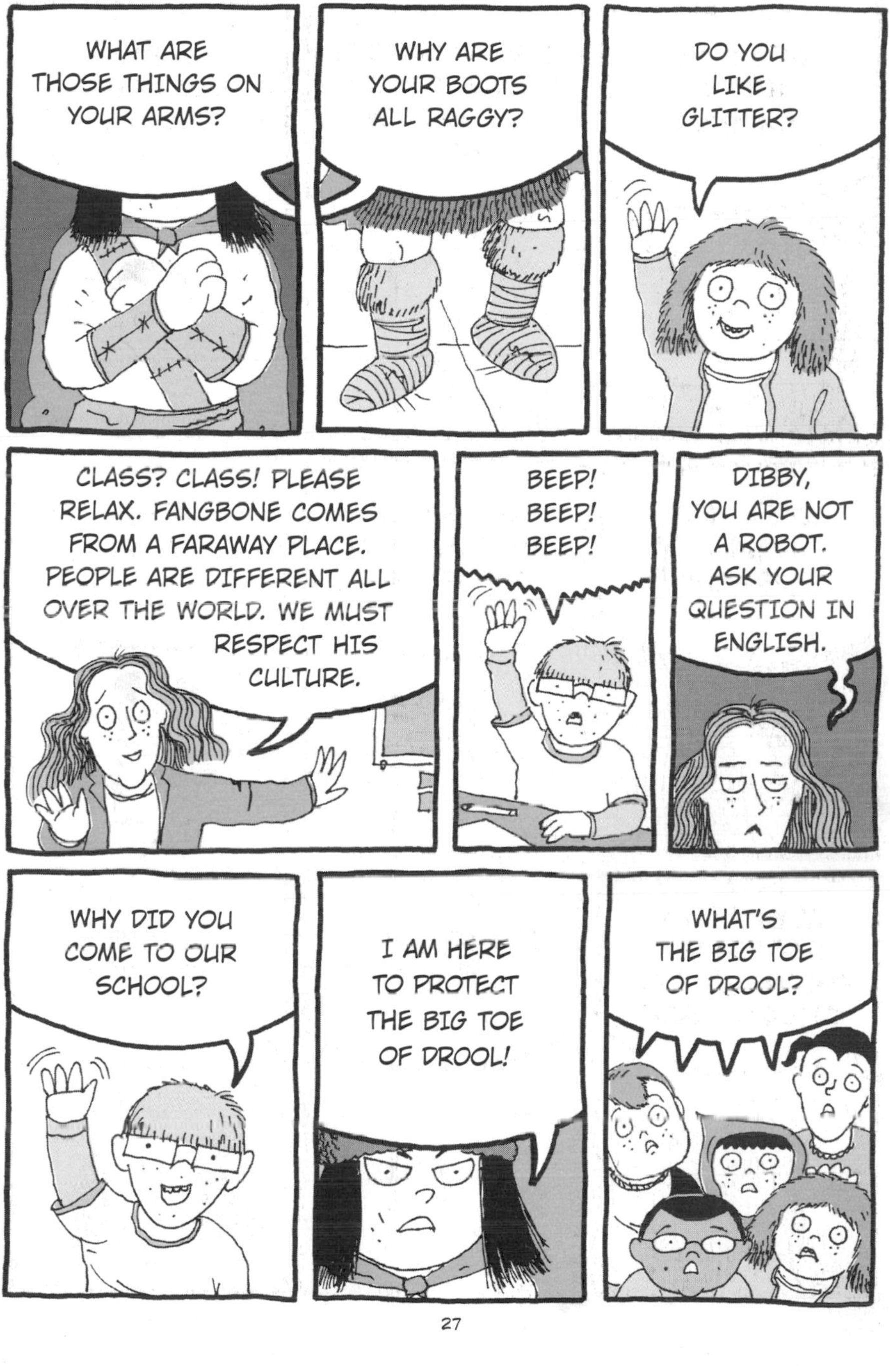
WHAT ARE THOSE THINGS ON YOUR ARMS?
WHY ARE YOUR BOOTS ALL RAGGY?
DO YOU LIKE GLITTER?
CLASS? CLASS! PLEASE RELAX. FANGBONE COMES FROM A FARAWAY PLACE. PEOPLE ARE DIFFERENT ALL OVER THE WORLD. WE MUST RESPECT HIS CULTURE.
BEEP! BEEP! BEEP!
DIBBY, YOU ARE NOT A ROBOT. ASK YOUR QUESTION IN ENGLISH.
WHY DID YOU COME TO OUR SCHOOL?
I AM HERE TO PROTECT THE BIG TOE OF DROOL!
WHAT'S THE BIG TOE OF DROOL?

FIVE HUNDRED WINTERS AGO,
THE GREATEST EVIL THAT EVER LIVED RULED OVER SKULLBANIA. VENOMOUS DROOL WAS HIS NAME.
HE BUILT AN ARMY THAT SWEPT THROUGH THE LANDS AND ALMOST WIPED OUT THE CLANS.

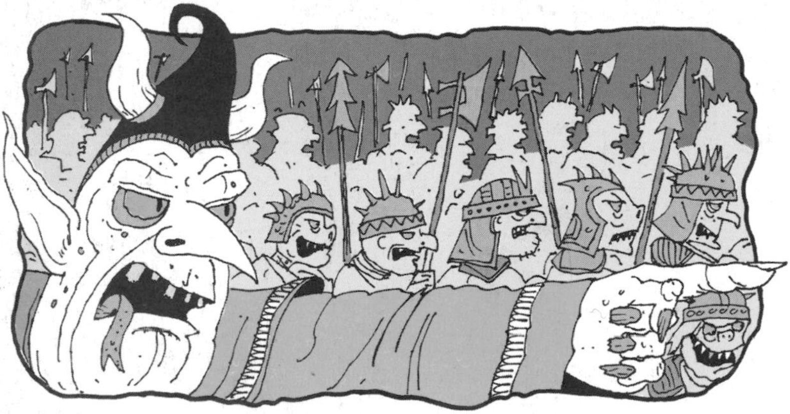

MANY BATTLES WERE FOUGHT, AND MANY GREAT WARRIORS DIED TO KEEP HIS EVIL FROM SPREADING.

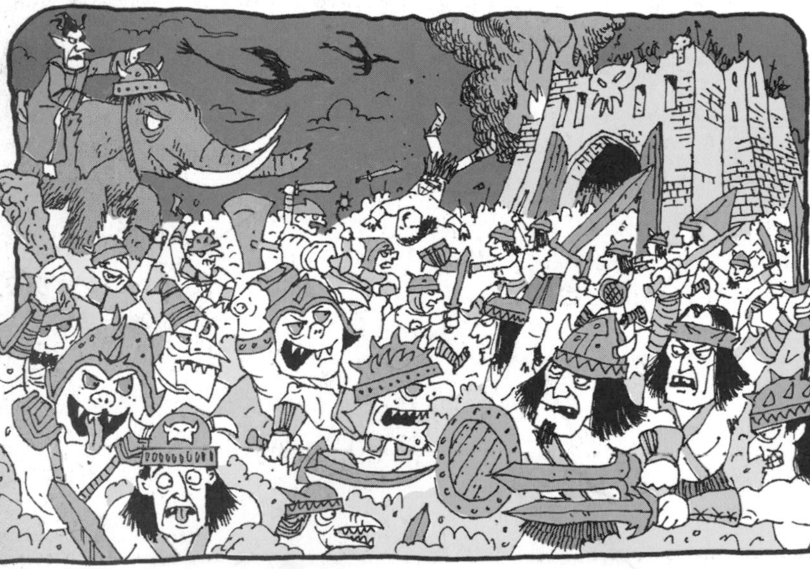

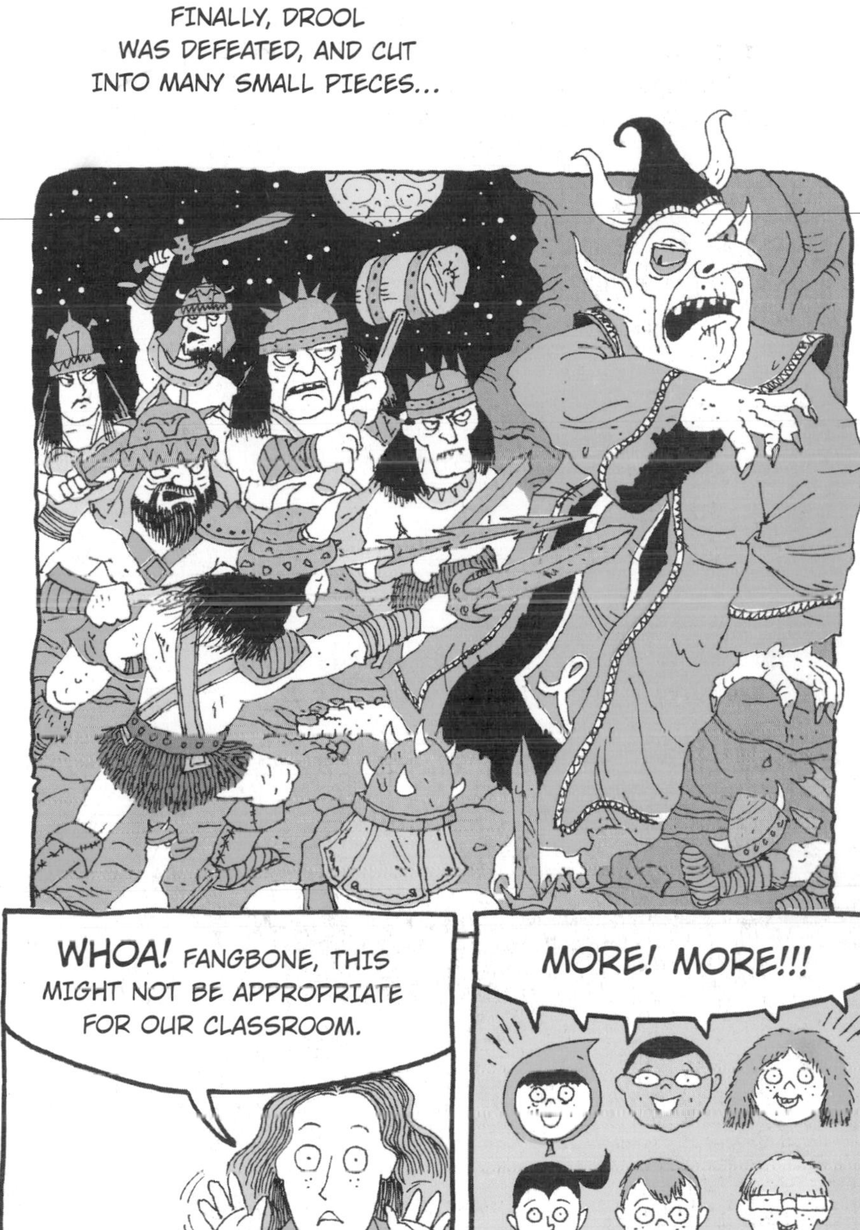
FINALLY, DROOL WAS DEFEATED, AND CUT INTO MANY SMALL PIECES...
WHOA! FANGBONE, THIS MIGHT NOT BE APPROPRIATE FOR OUR CLASSROOM.
MORE! MORE!!!

THE PIECES WERE SEPARATED AND TAKEN TO DIFFERENT LANDS SO THAT VENOMOUS DROOL COULD NEVER RULE AGAIN.

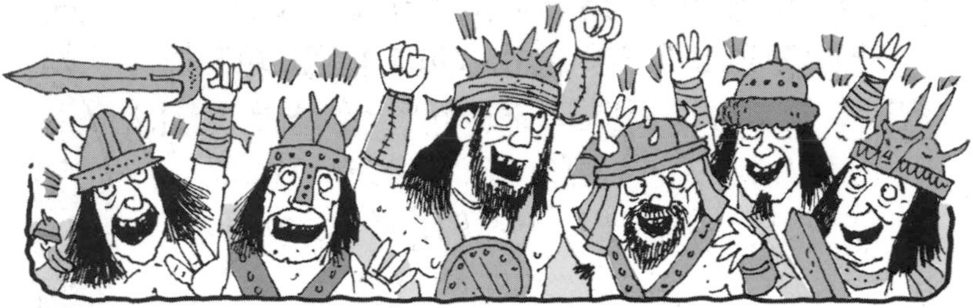

BUT SINCE MY BIRTH, A NEW ARMY OF DROOL WORSHIPERS HAS BEEN MOVING THROUGH SKULLBANIA, COLLECTING THE PIECES ONE BY ONE, AND REBUILDING DROOL.

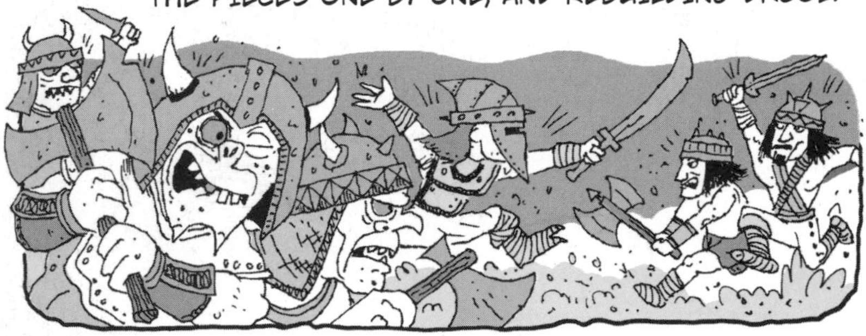

THE ONLY PIECE THAT THEY DO NOT HAVE IS HIS BIG TOE! MY CLAN WAS PUT IN CHARGE OF PROTECTING THE BIG TOE BECAUSE IT IS THE MOST EVIL, CURSED, WRETCHED PART OF HIS BODY.

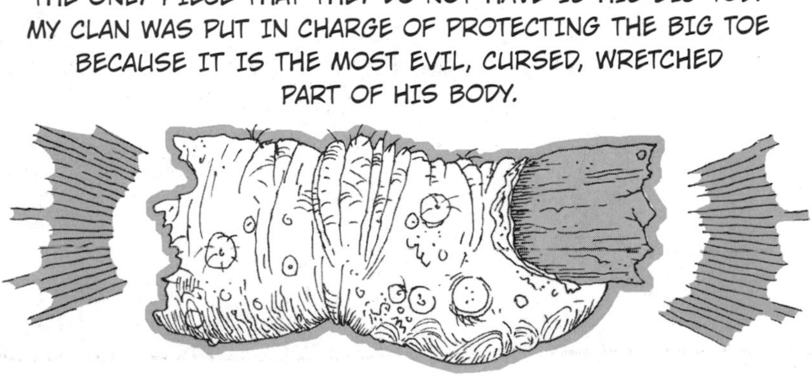

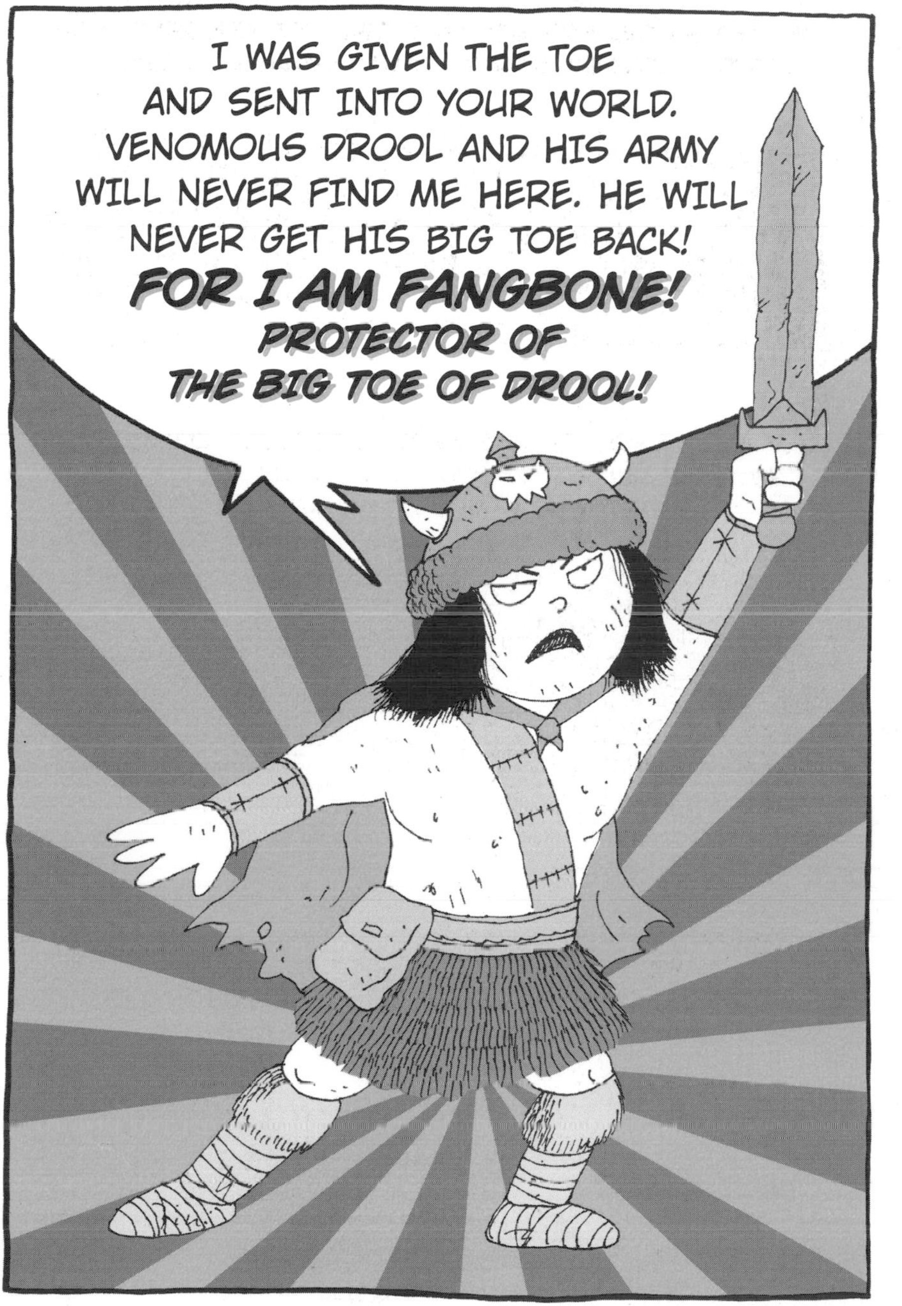
I WAS GIVEN THE TOE AND SENT INTO YOUR WORLD. VENOMOUS DROOL AND HIS ARMY WILL NEVER FIND ME HERE. HE WILL NEVER GET HIS BIG TOE BACK!
FOR I AM FANGBONE!
PROTECTOR OF THE BIG TOE OF DROOL!

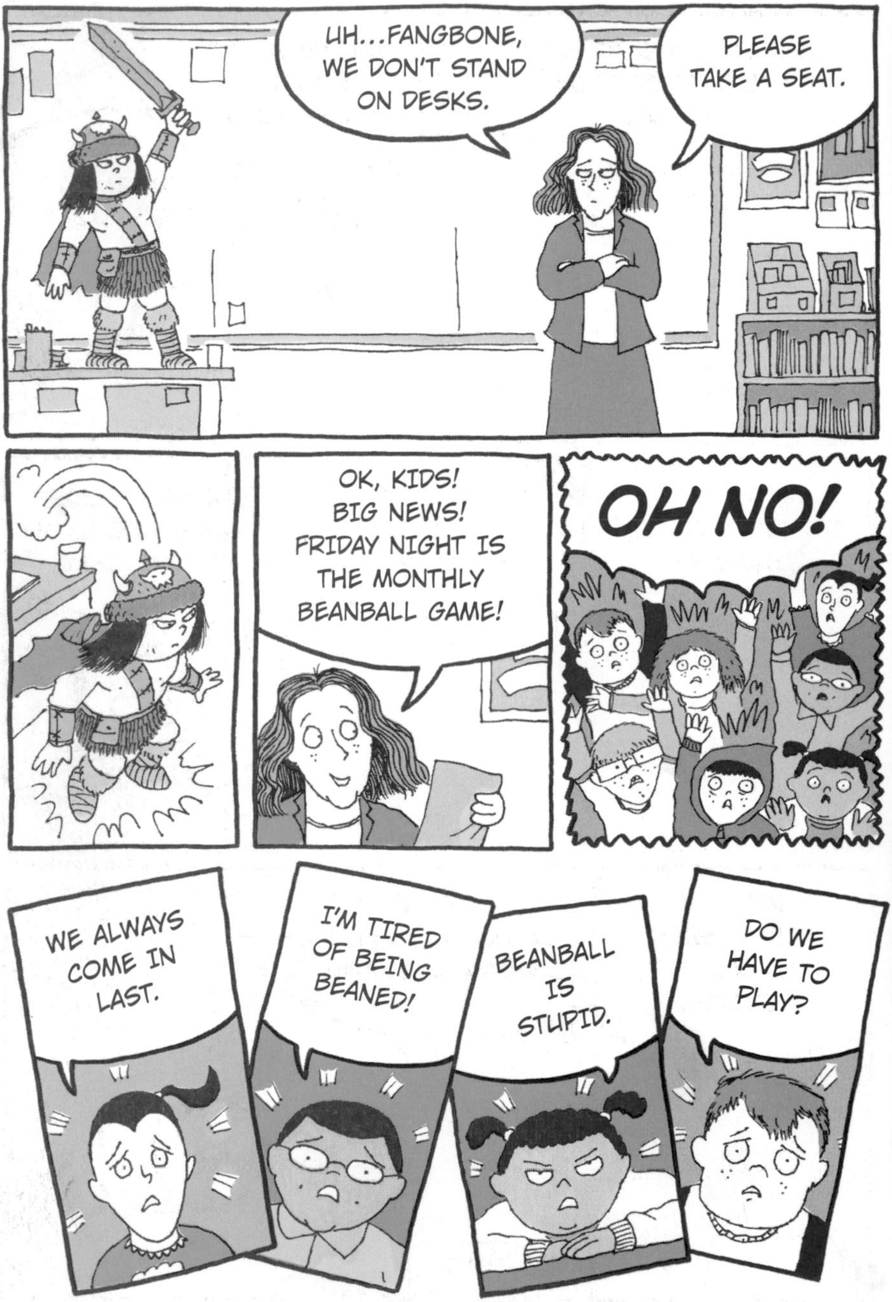
UH...FANGBONE, WE DON'T STAND ON DESKS.
PLEASE TAKE A SEAT.
OK, KIDS! BIG NEWS! FRIDAY NIGHT IS THE MONTHLY BEANBALL GAME!
OH NO!
WE ALWAYS COME IN LAST.
I'M TIRED OF BEING BEANED!
BEANBALL IS STUPID.
DO WE HAVE TO PLAY?

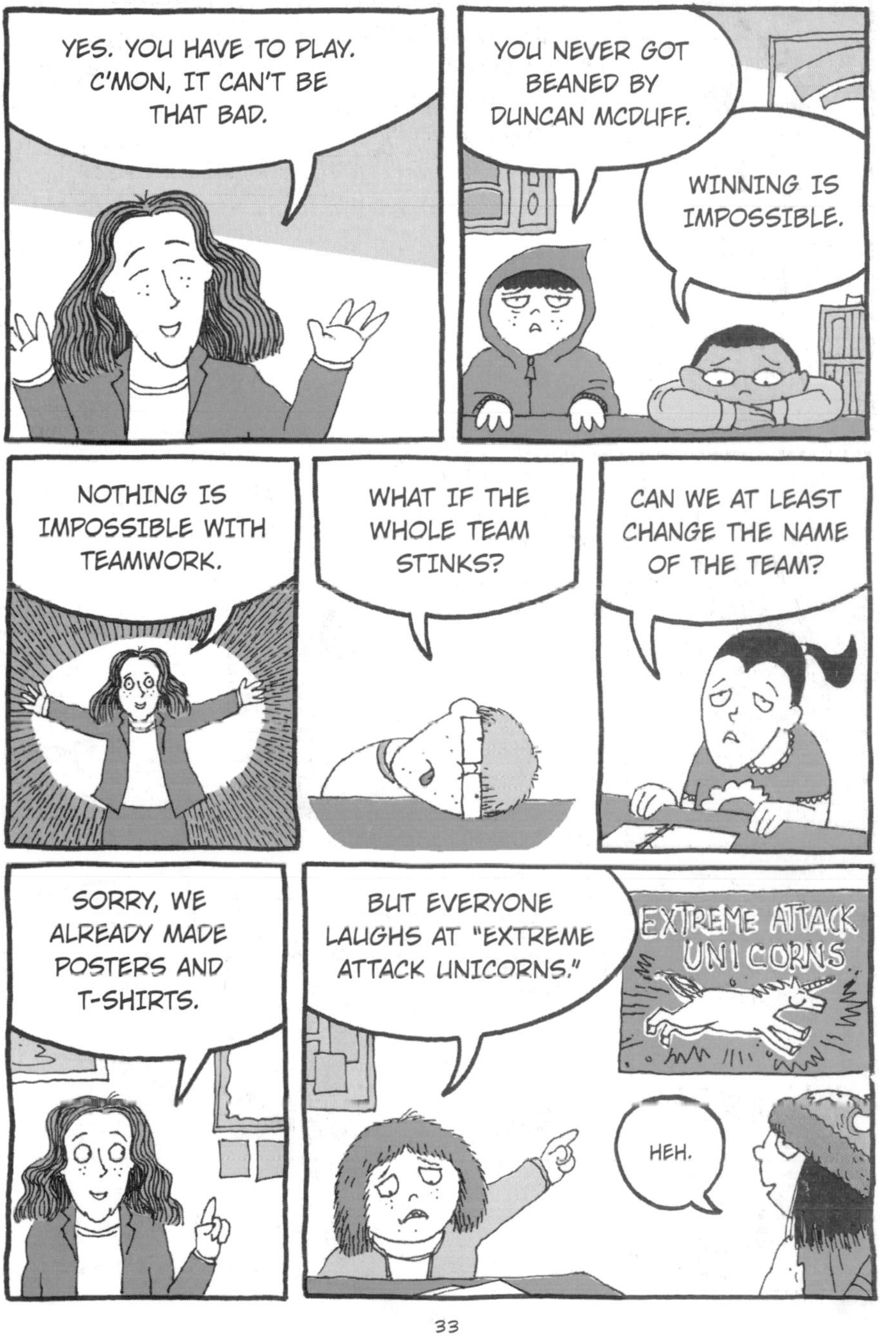
YES. YOU HAVE TO PLAY. C'MON, IT CAN'T BE THAT BAD.
YOU NEVER GOT BEANED BY DUNCAN MCDUFF.
WINNING IS IMPOSSIBLE.
NOTHING IS IMPOSSIBLE WITH TEAMWORK.
WHAT IF THE WHOLE TEAM STINKS?
CAN WE AT LEAST CHANGE THE NAME OF THE TEAM?
SORRY, WE ALREADY MADE POSTERS AND T-SHIRTS.
BUT EVERYONE LAUGHS AT "EXTREME ATTACK UNICORNS."
EXTREME ATTACK UNICORNS
HEH.

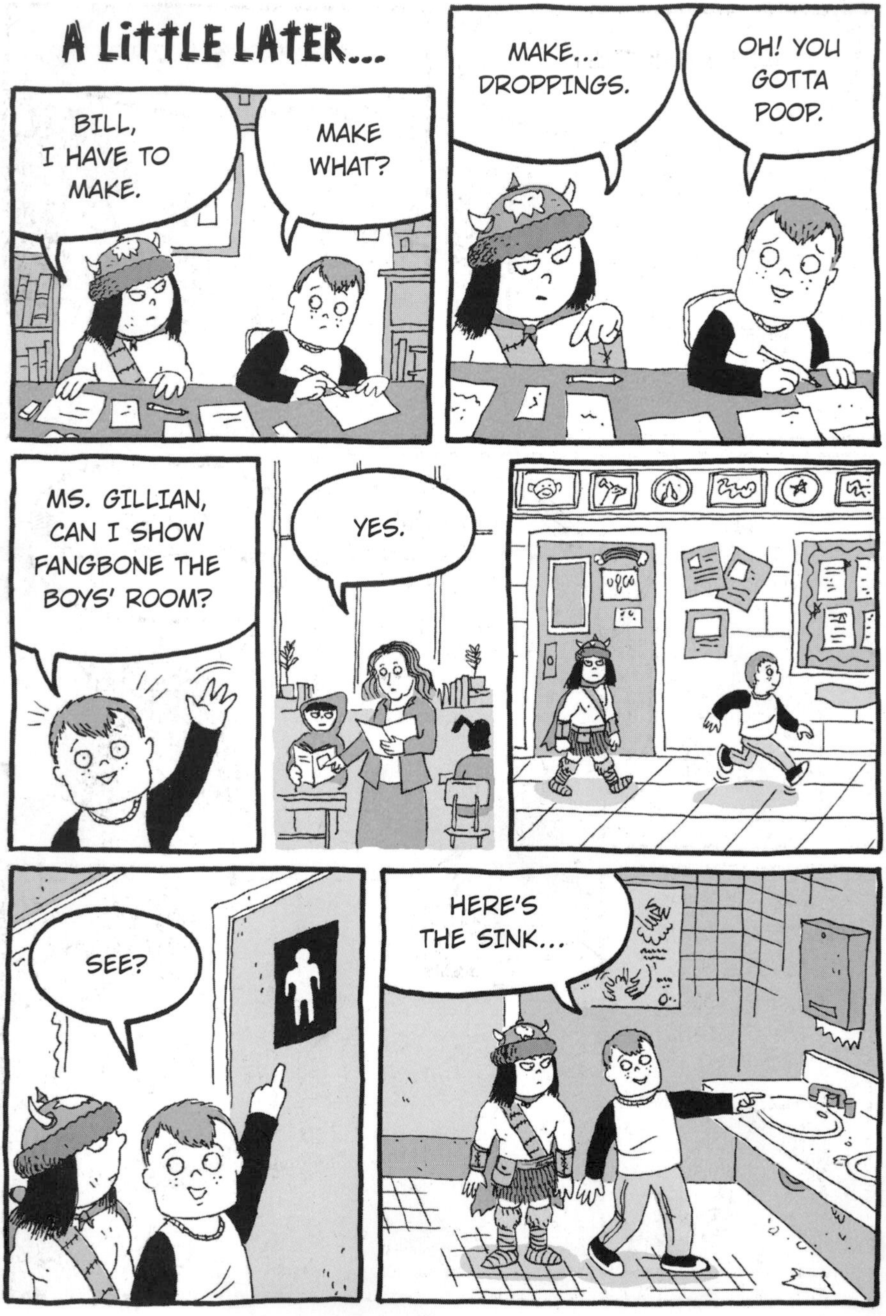
A LITTLE LATER...
BILL, I HAVE TO MAKE.
MAKE WHAT?
MAKE... DROPPINGS.
OH! YOU GOTTA POOP.
MS. GILLIAN, CAN I SHOW FANGBONE THE BOYS' ROOM?
YES.
SEE?
HERE'S THE SINK...

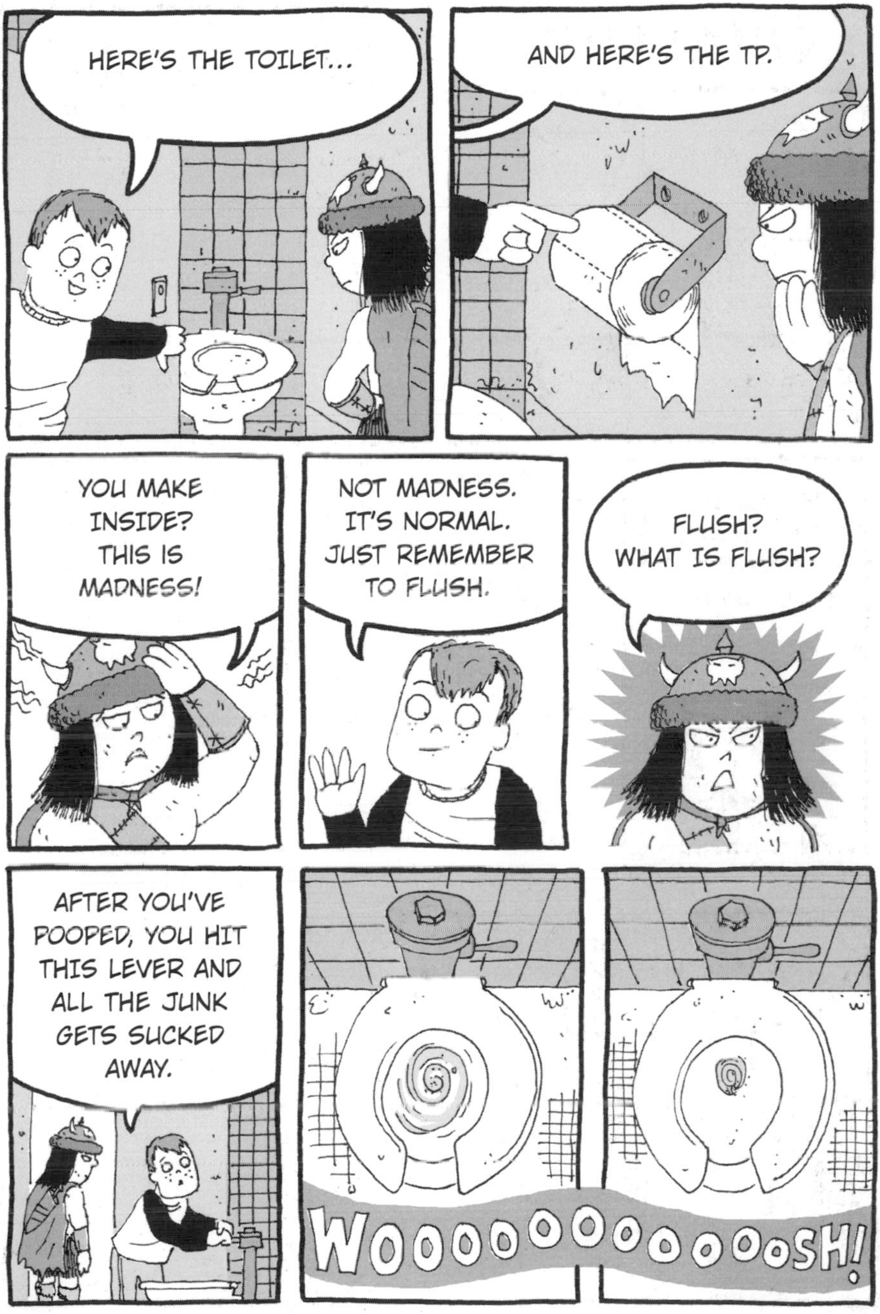
HERE'S THE TOILET...
AND HERE'S THE TP.
YOU MAKE INSIDE? THIS IS MADNESS!
NOT MADNESS. IT'S NORMAL. JUST REMEMBER TO FLUSH.
FLUSH? WHAT IS FLUSH?
AFTER YOU'VE POOPED, YOU HIT THIS LEVER AND ALL THE JUNK GETS SUCKED AWAY.
WOOOOOOOOOOOOSH!

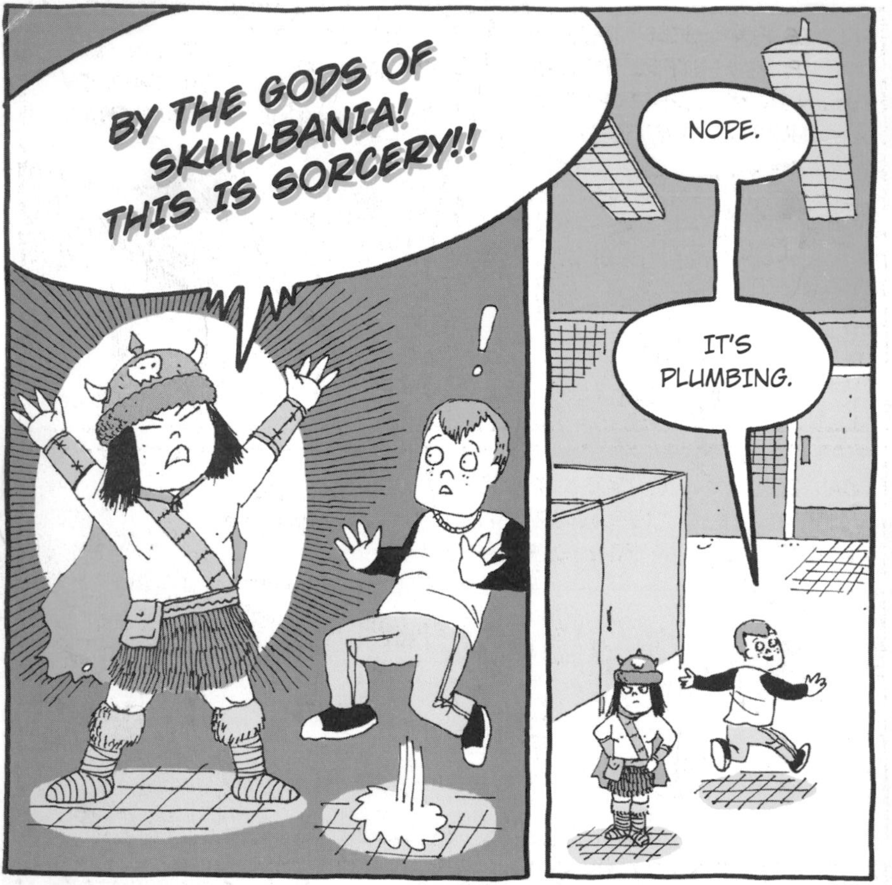
BY THE GODS OF SKULLBANIA! THIS IS SORCERY!!
!
NOPE.
IT'S PLUMBING.
!

AFTER LUNCH...

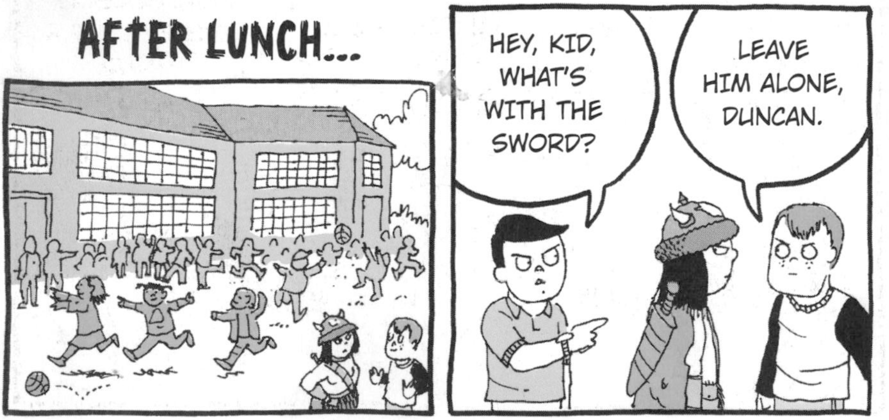
HEY, KID, WHAT'S WITH THE SWORD?
LEAVE HIM ALONE, DUNCAN.

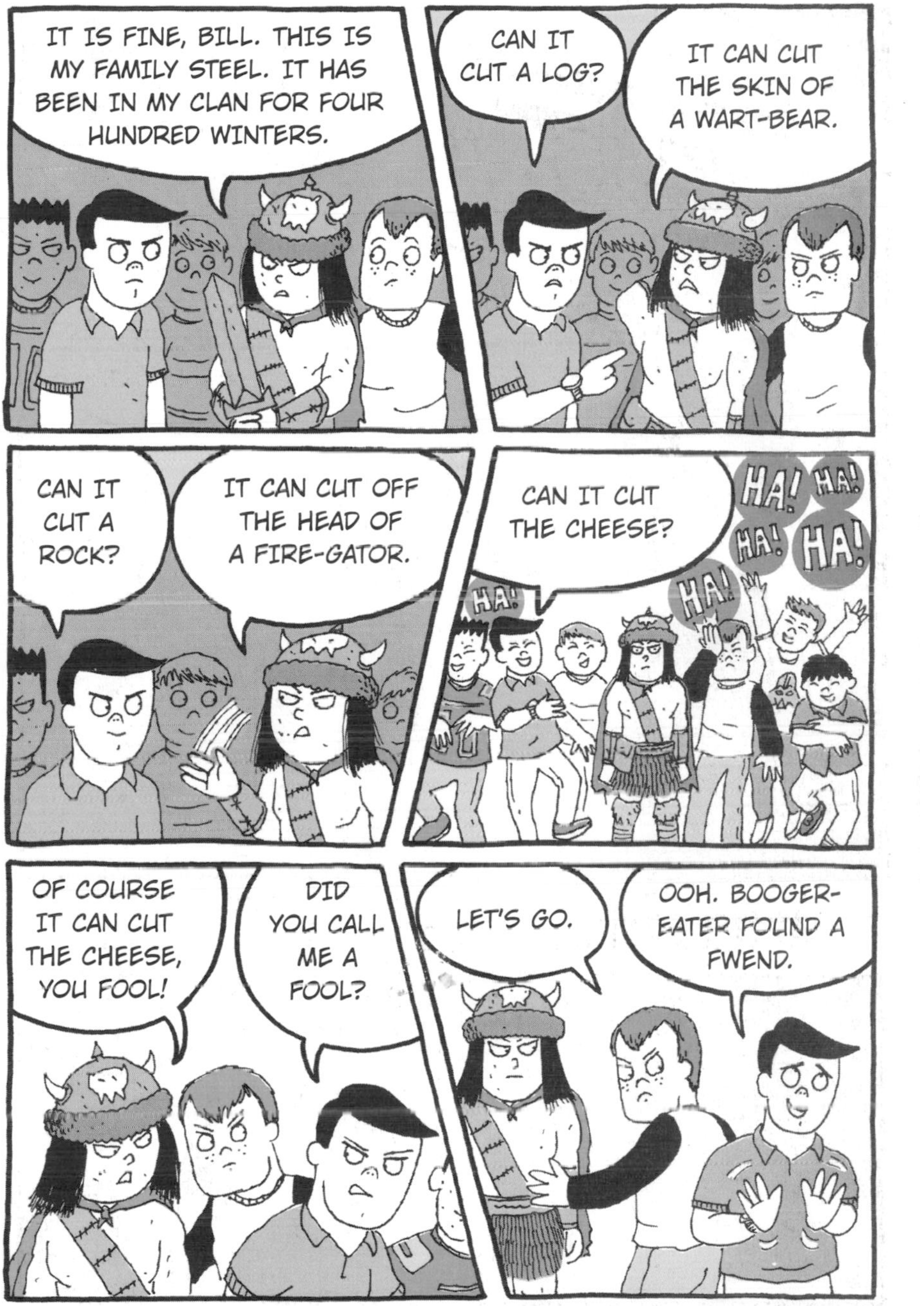
IT IS FINE, BILL. THIS IS MY FAMILY STEEL. IT HAS BEEN IN MY CLAN FOR FOUR HUNDRED WINTERS.
CAN IT CUT A LOG?
IT CAN CUT THE SKIN OF A WART-BEAR.
CAN IT CUT A ROCK?
IT CAN CUT OFF THE HEAD OF A FIRE-GATOR.
CAN IT CUT THE CHEESE?
HA! HA! HA! HA! HA! HA!
OF COURSE IT CAN CUT THE CHEESE, YOU FOOL!
DID YOU CALL ME A FOOL?
LET'S GO.
OOH. BOOGER-EATER FOUND A FWEND.

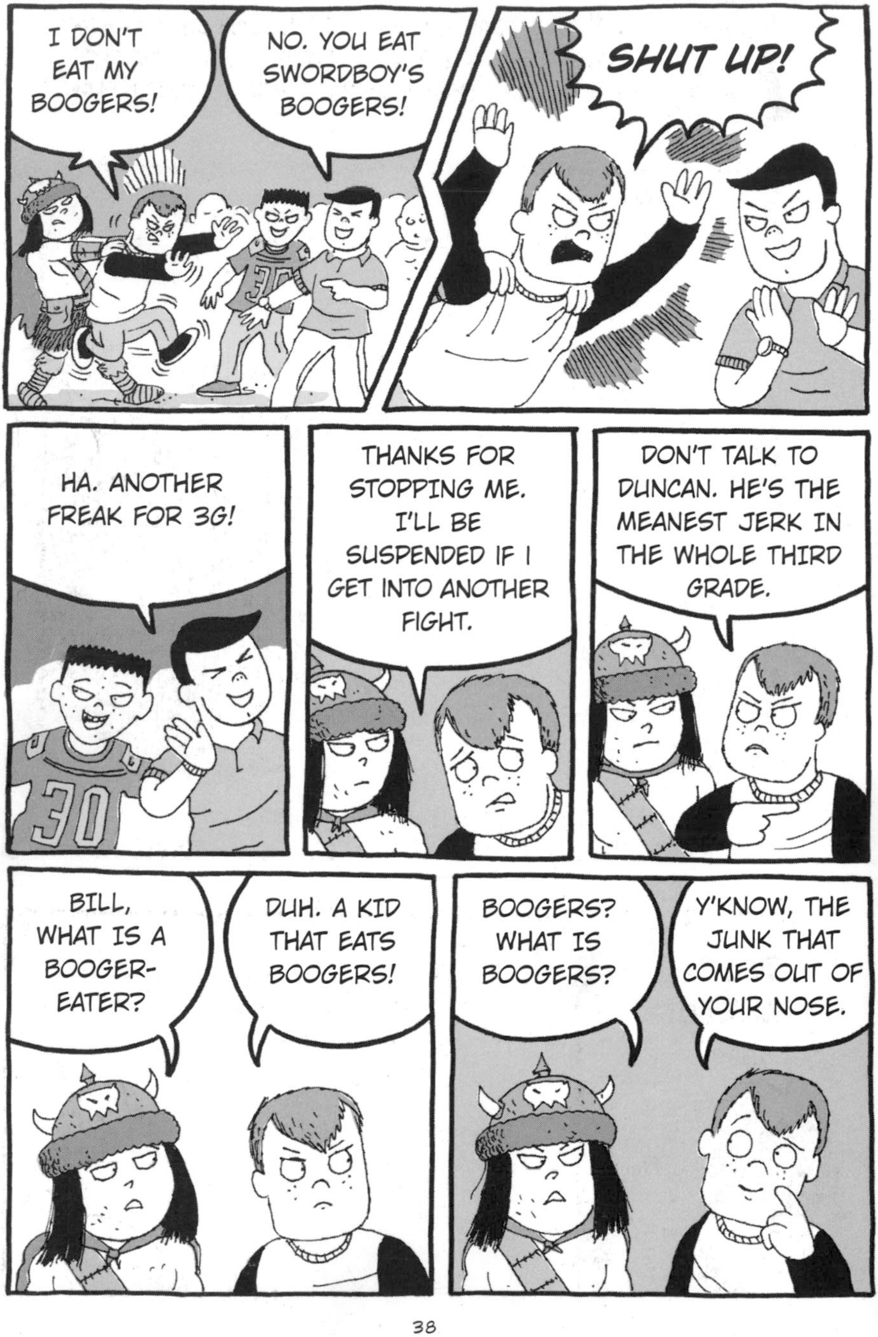

I DON'T EAT MY BOOGERS!
NO. YOU EAT SWORDBOY'S BOOGERS!
SHUT UP!
HA. ANOTHER FREAK FOR 3G!
THANKS FOR STOPPING ME. I'LL BE SUSPENDED IF I GET INTO ANOTHER FIGHT.
DON'T TALK TO DUNCAN. HE'S THE MEANEST JERK IN THE WHOLE THIRD GRADE.
BILL, WHAT IS A BOOGER-EATER?
DUH. A KID THAT EATS BOOGERS!
BOOGERS? WHAT IS BOOGERS?
Y'KNOW, THE JUNK THAT COMES OUT OF YOUR NOSE.

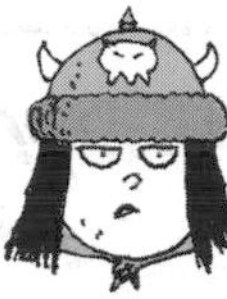

AH...MY CLAN CALLS THAT "GLOOBUS." THERE WAS ONCE A GREAT WARRIOR LOST IN THE DESERT OF HORRIBLE PAIN FOR TWO WINTERS.

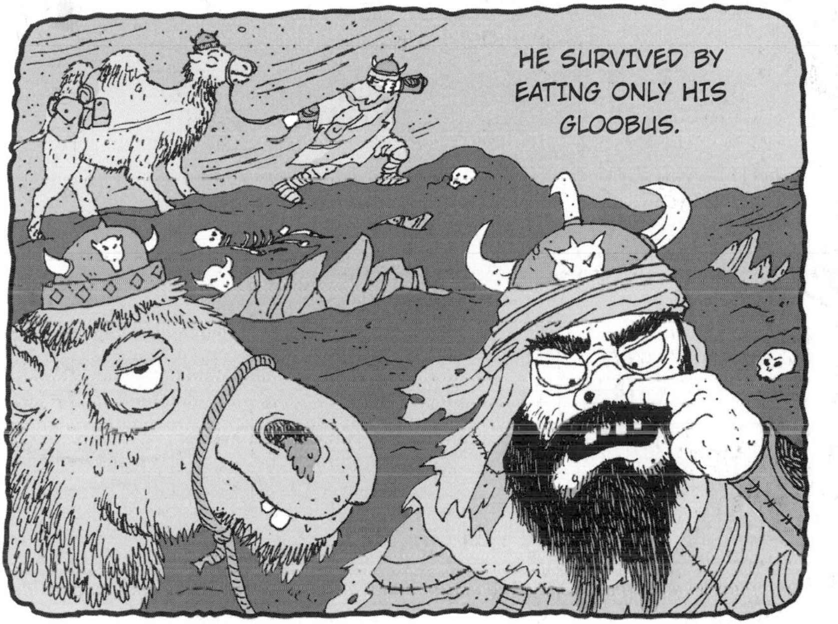
HE SURVIVED BY EATING ONLY HIS GLOOBUS.

AND THE GLOOBUS OF HIS CAMEL.
HE WAS FOREVER AFTER CALLED "GLOOBUS THE GREAT."

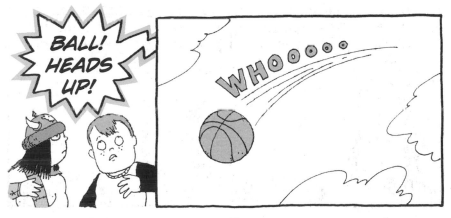

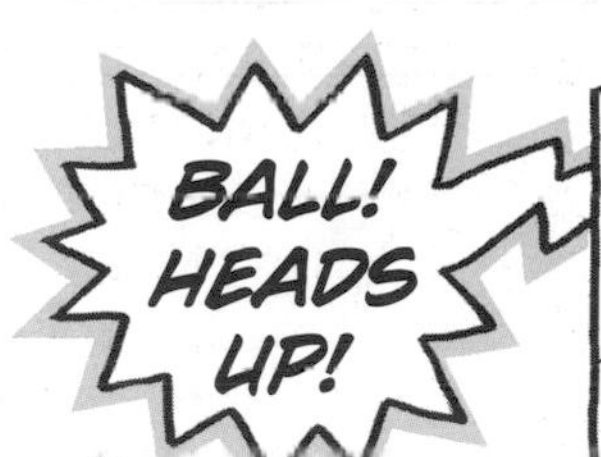
BALL! HEADS UP!

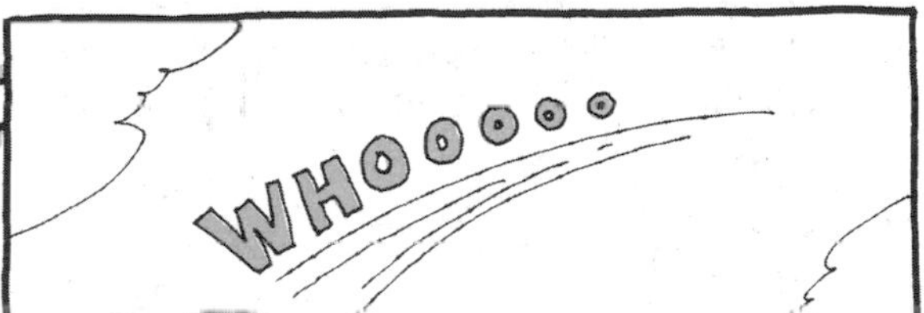
WHOOOOOO

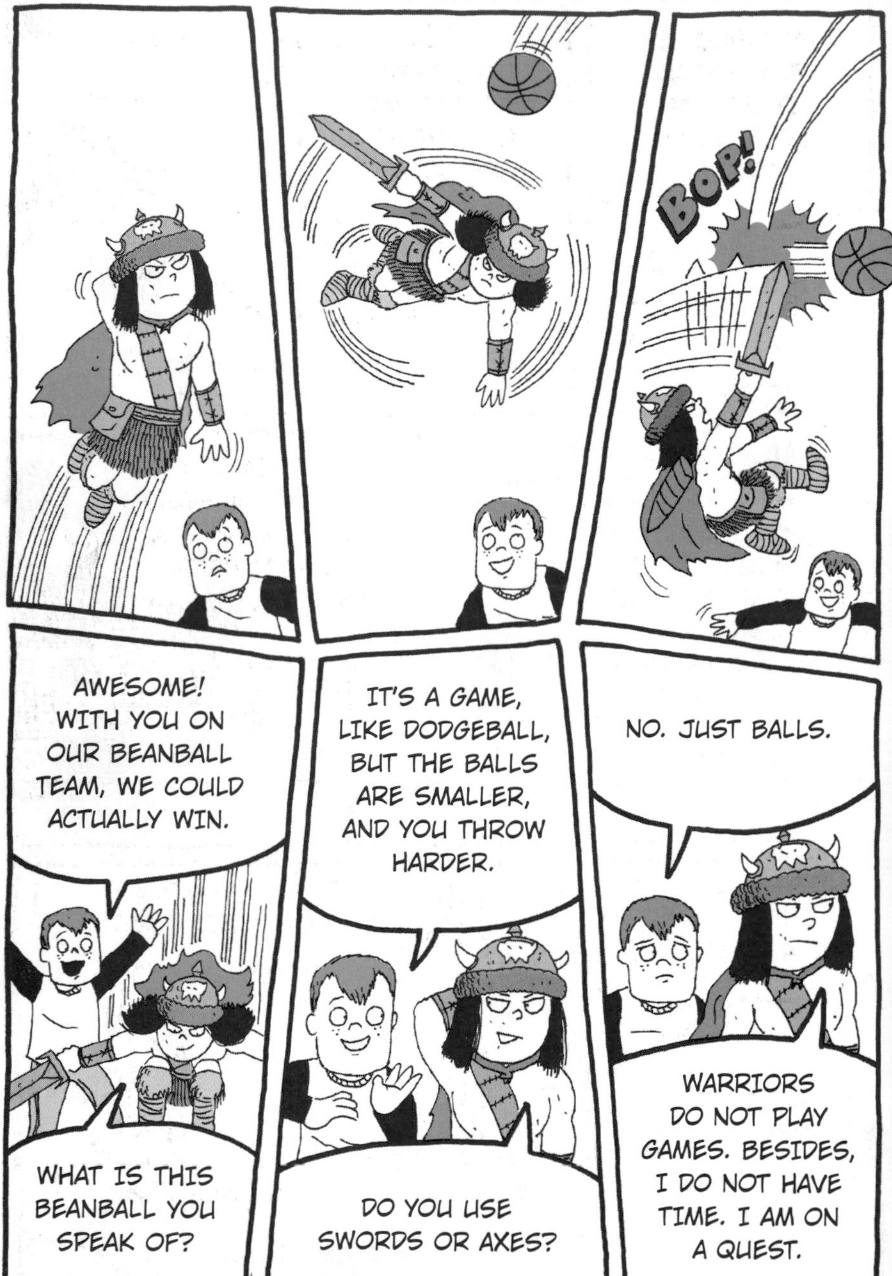
BOP!
AWESOME! WITH YOU ON OUR BEANBALL TEAM, WE COULD ACTUALLY WIN.
WHAT IS THIS BEANBALL YOU SPEAK OF?
IT'S A GAME, LIKE DODGEBALL, BUT THE BALLS ARE SMALLER, AND YOU THROW HARDER.
DO YOU USE SWORDS OR AXES?
NO. JUST BALLS.
WARRIORS DO NOT PLAY GAMES. BESIDES, I DO NOT HAVE TIME. I AM ON A QUEST.

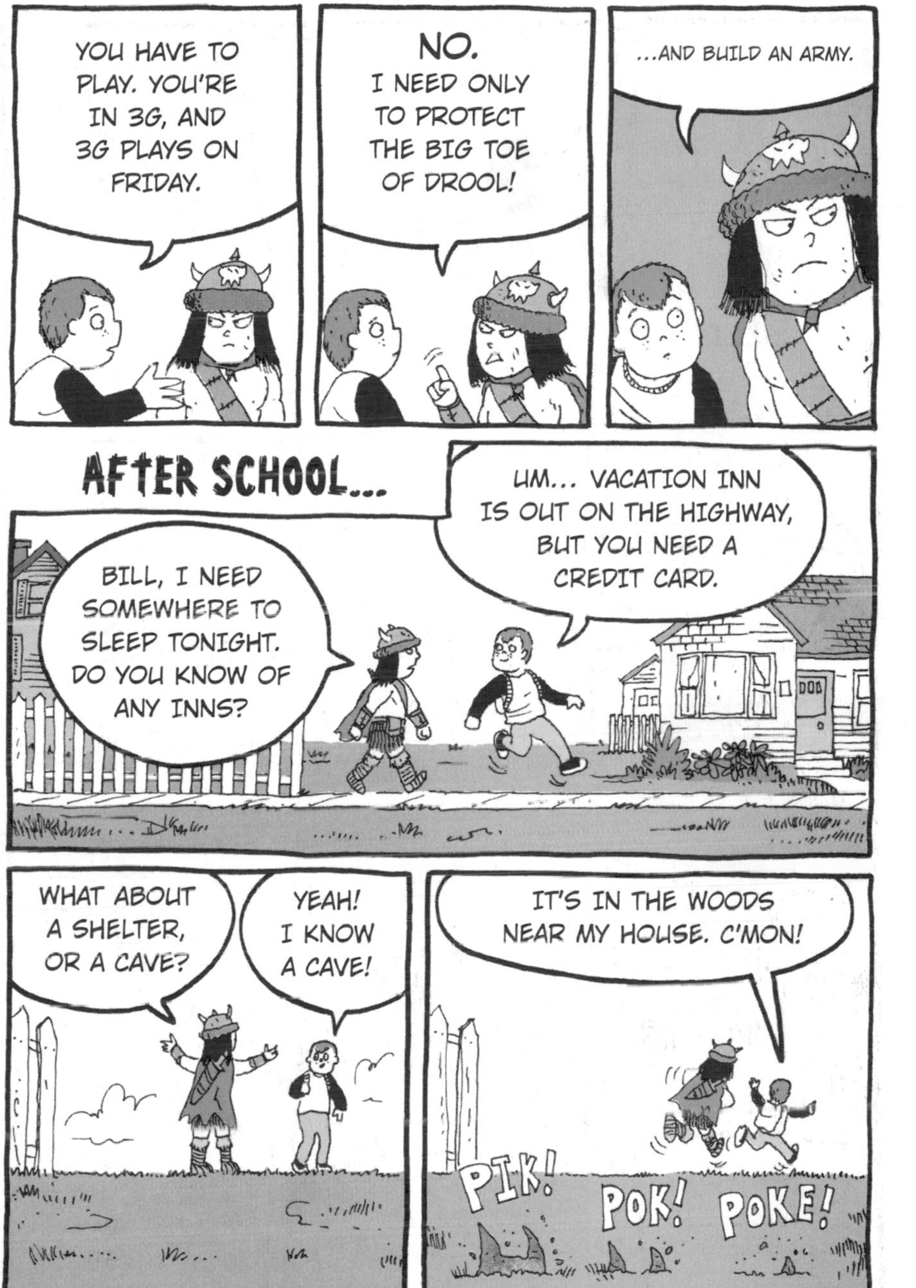
YOU HAVE TO PLAY. YOU'RE IN 3G, AND 3G PLAYS ON FRIDAY.
NO. I NEED ONLY TO PROTECT THE BIG TOE OF DROOL!
...AND BUILD AN ARMY.
AFTER SCHOOL...
BILL, I NEED SOMEWHERE TO SLEEP TONIGHT. DO YOU KNOW OF ANY INNS?
UM... VACATION INN IS OUT ON THE HIGHWAY, BUT YOU NEED A CREDIT CARD.
WHAT ABOUT A SHELTER, OR A CAVE?
YEAH! I KNOW A CAVE!
IT'S IN THE WOODS NEAR MY HOUSE. C'MON!
PIK!
POK!
POKE!

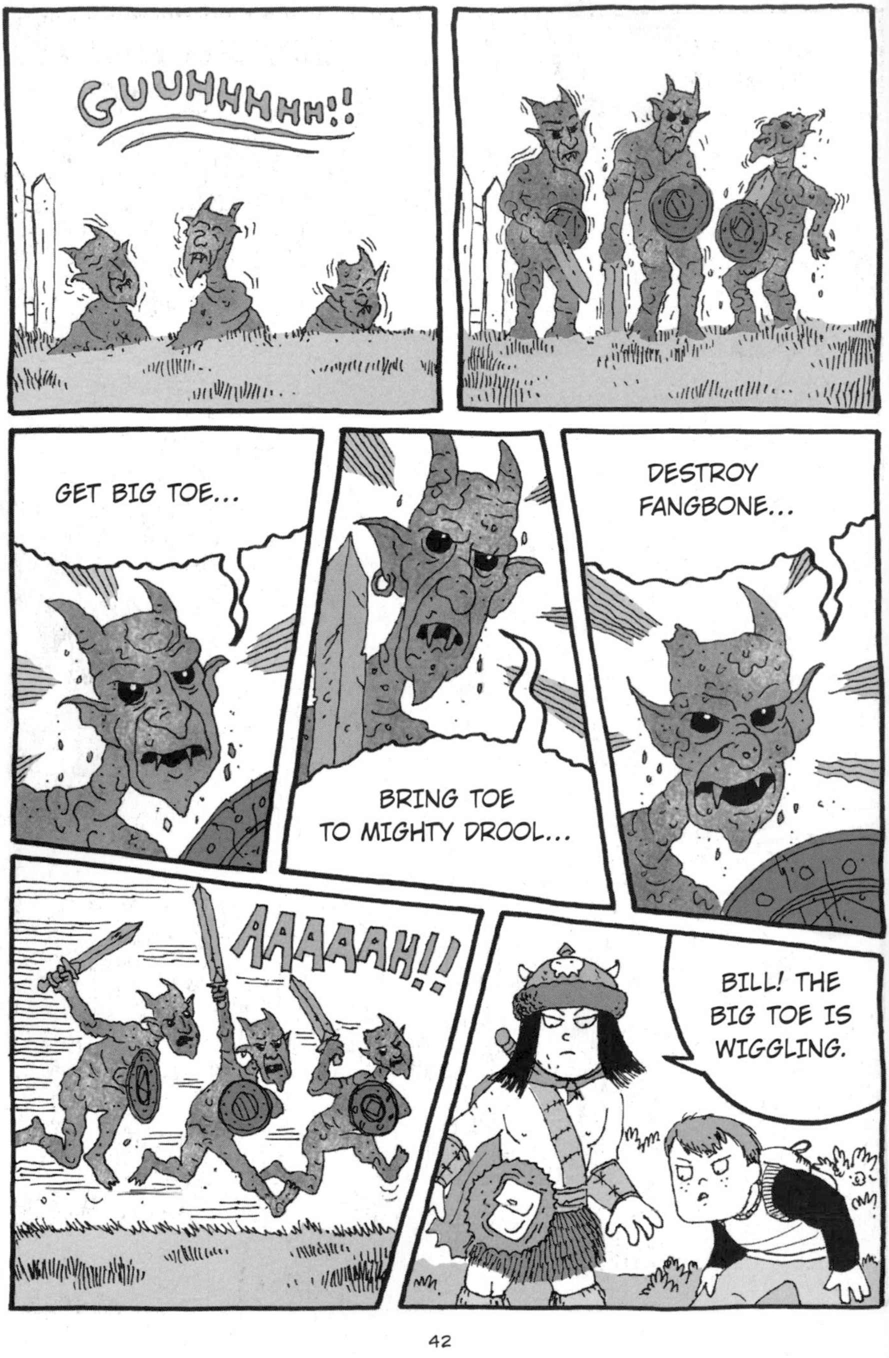
GUUHHHHH!!
GET BIG TOE...
BRING TOE TO MIGHTY DROOL...
DESTROY FANGBONE...
AAAAAH!!
BILL! THE BIG TOE IS WIGGLING.

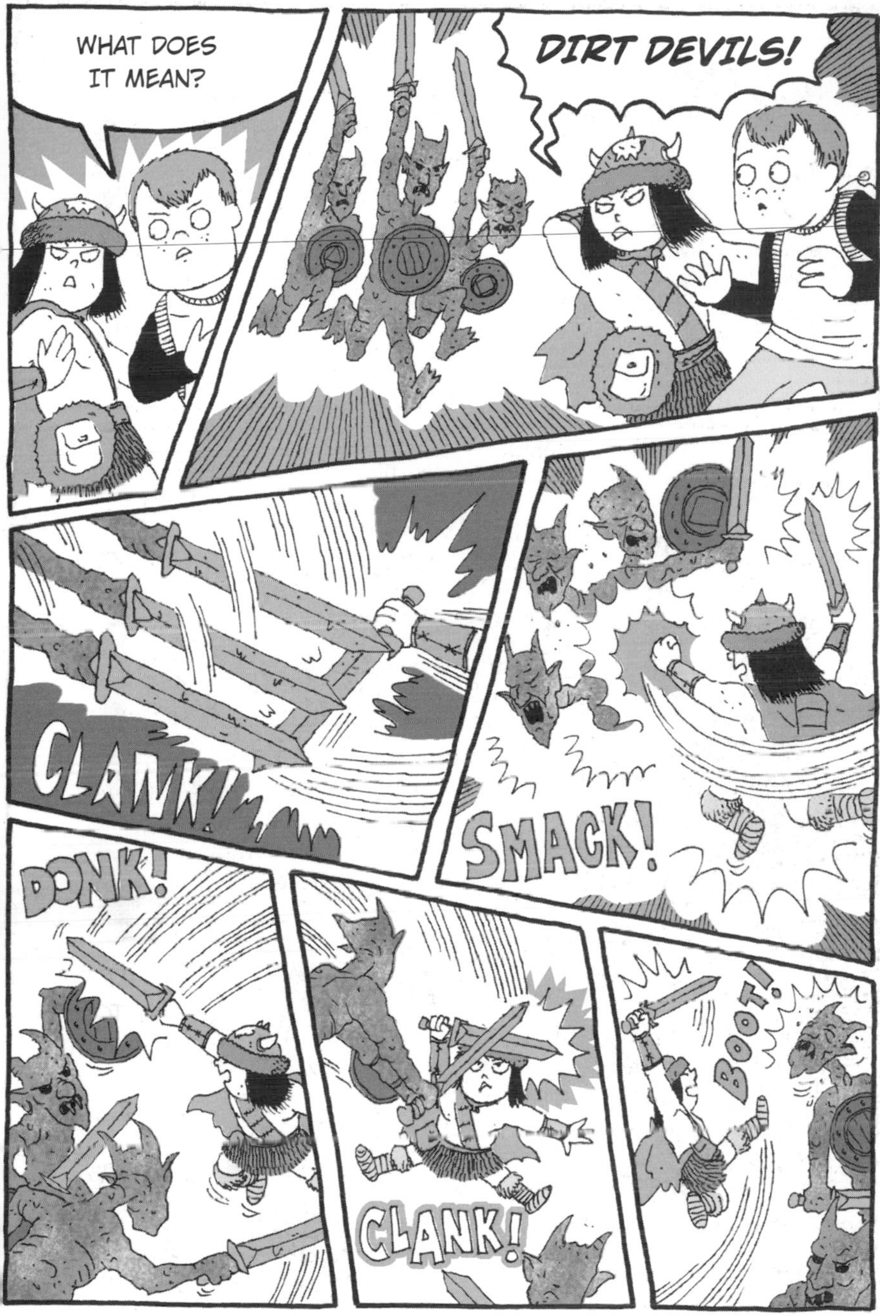
WHAT DOES IT MEAN?
DIRT DEVILS!
CLANK!
SMACK!
DONK!
CLANK!
BOOOT!

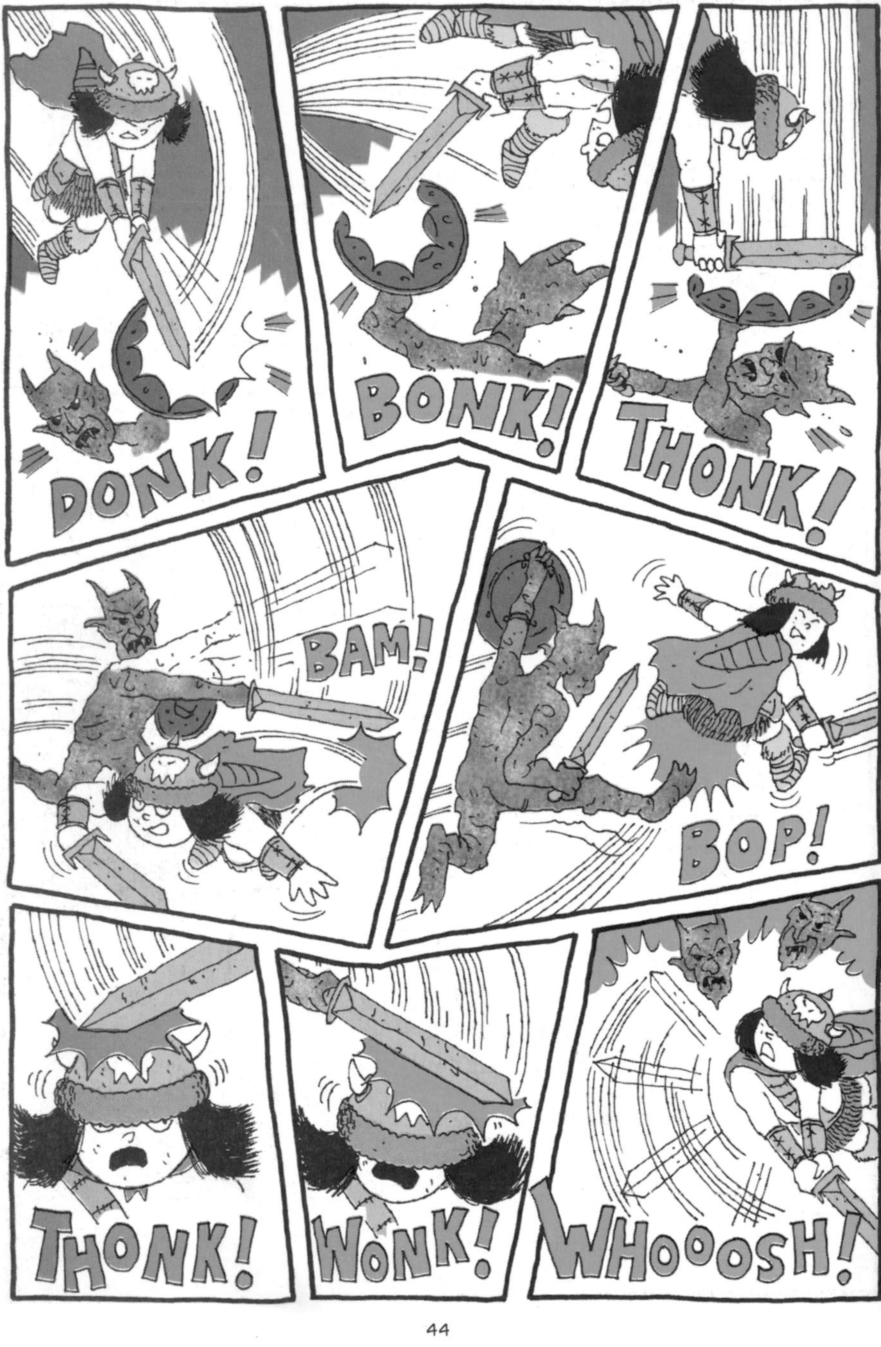
DONK!
BONK!
THONK!
BAM!
BOP!
THONK!
WONK!
WHOOOSH!

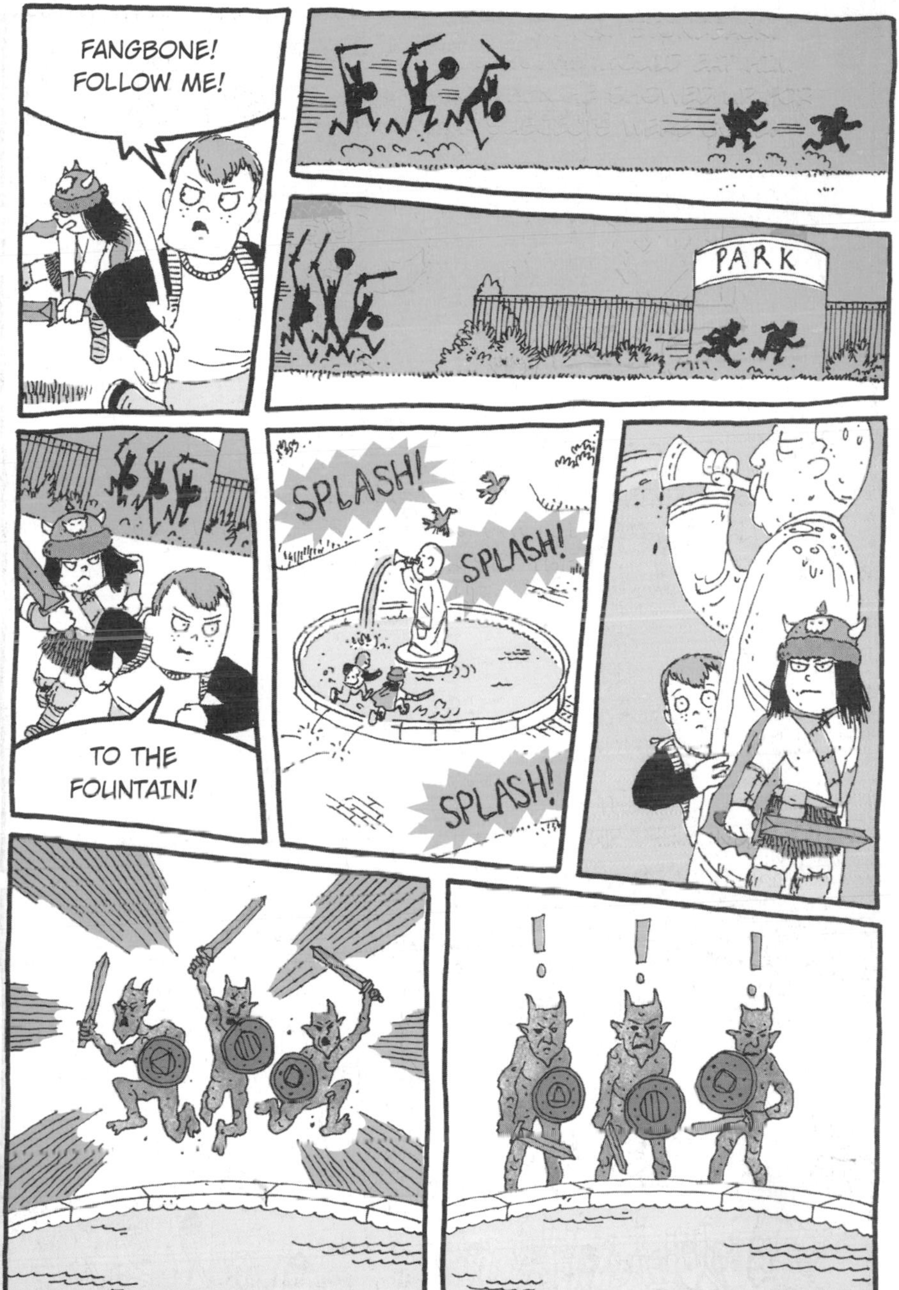
FANGBONE! FOLLOW ME!
PARK
TO THE FOUNTAIN!
SPLASH!
SPLASH!
SPLASH!

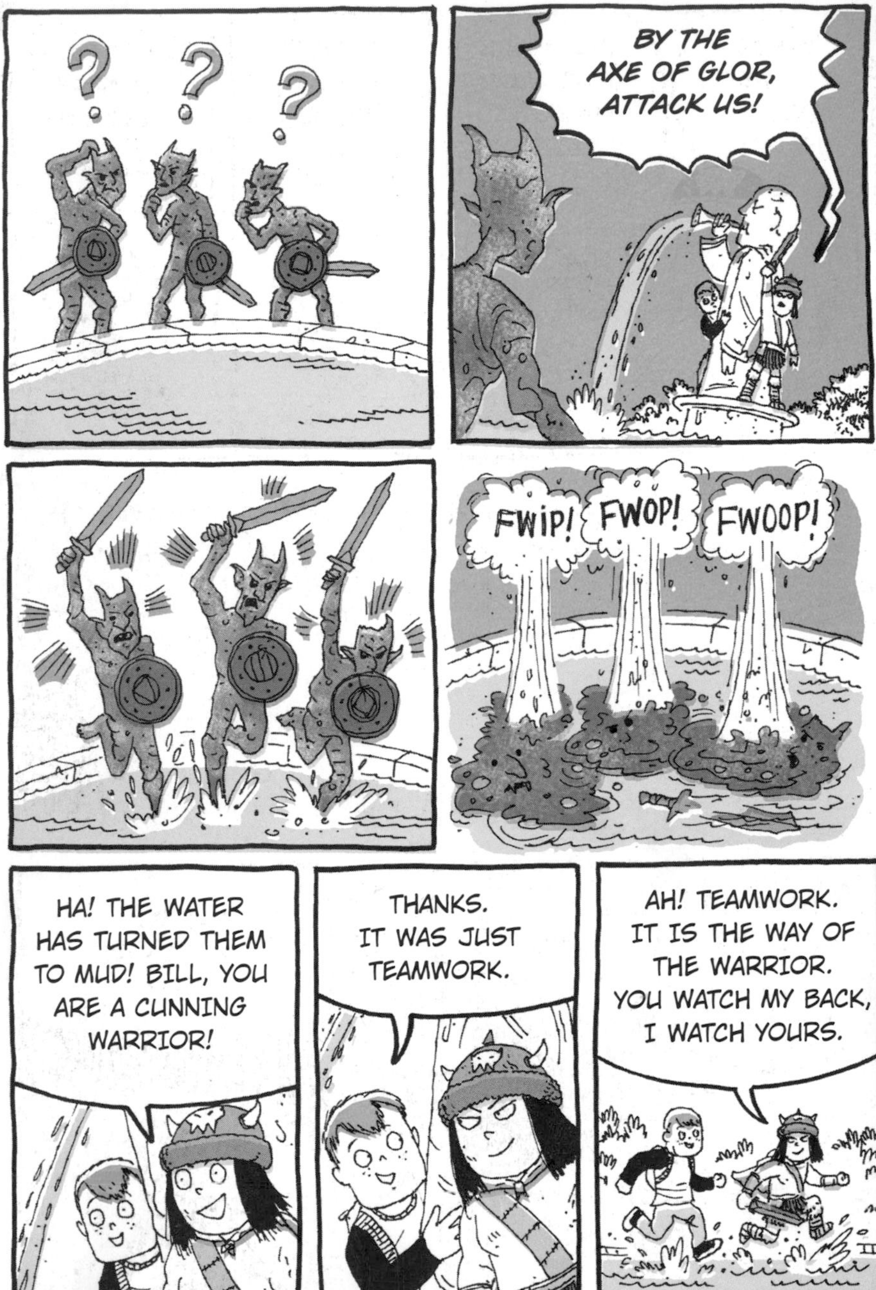
BY THE AXE OF GLOR, ATTACK US!
FWIP!
FWOP!
FWOOP!
HA! THE WATER HAS TURNED THEM TO MUD! BILL, YOU ARE A CUNNING WARRIOR!
THANKS. IT WAS JUST TEAMWORK.
AH! TEAMWORK. IT IS THE WAY OF THE WARRIOR. YOU WATCH MY BACK, I WATCH YOURS.

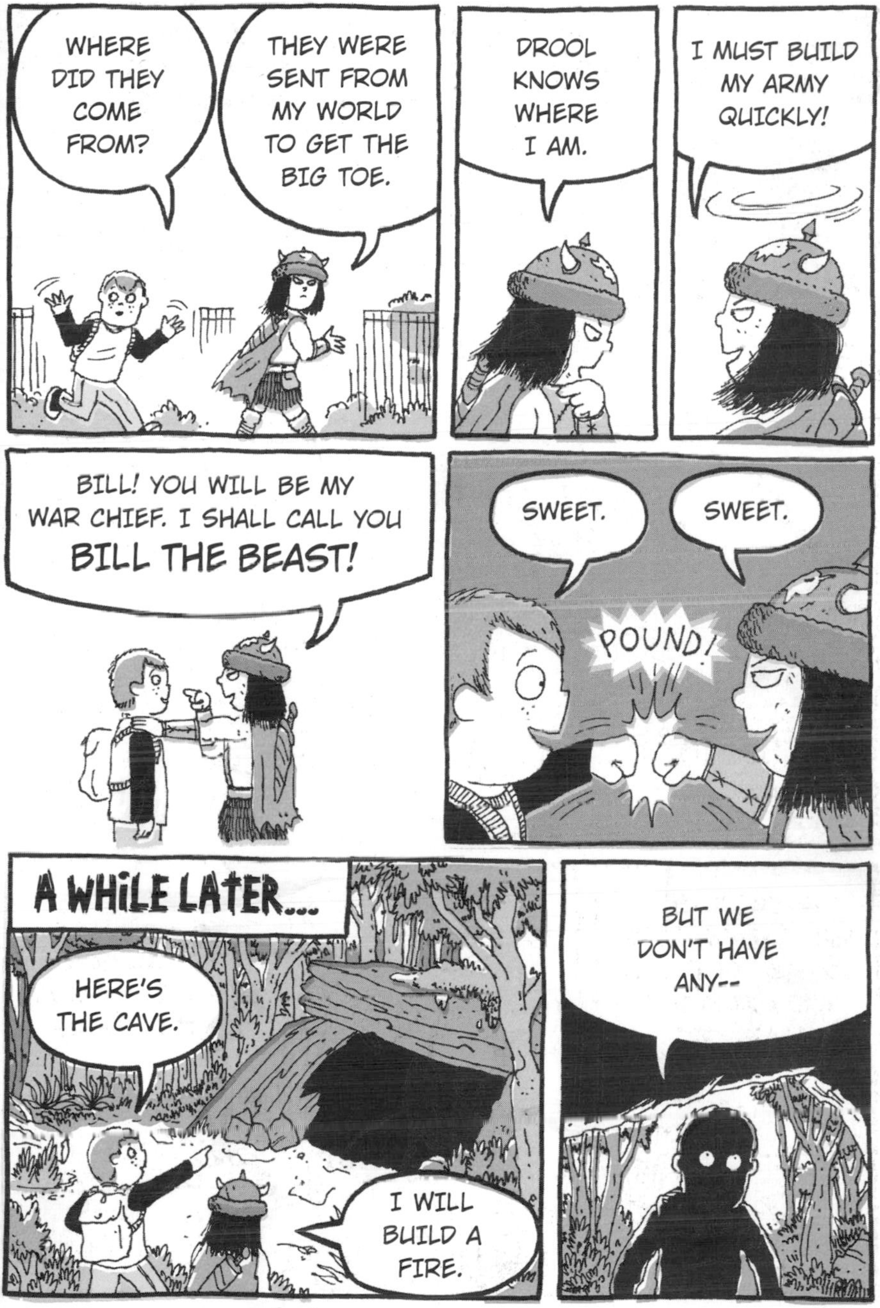
WHERE DID THEY COME FROM?
THEY WERE SENT FROM MY WORLD TO GET THE BIG TOE.
DROOL KNOWS WHERE I AM.
I MUST BUILD MY ARMY QUICKLY!
BILL! YOU WILL BE MY WAR CHIEF. I SHALL CALL YOU BILL THE BEAST!
SWEET.
SWEET.
POUND!
A WHILE LATER...
HERE'S THE CAVE.
I WILL BUILD A FIRE.
BUT WE DON'T HAVE ANY--

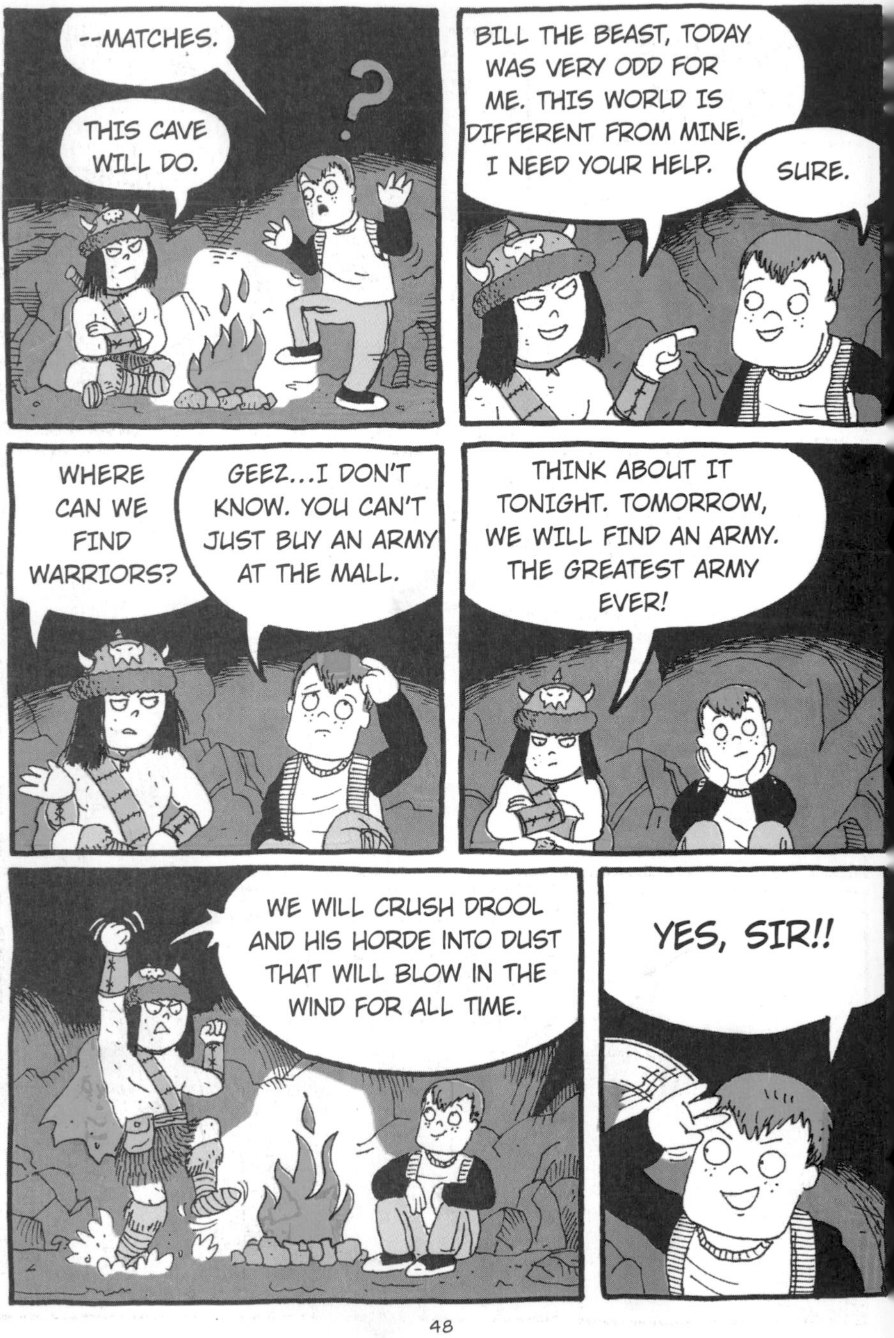
--MATCHES.
THIS CAVE WILL DO.
?
BILL THE BEAST, TODAY WAS VERY ODD FOR ME. THIS WORLD IS DIFFERENT FROM MINE. I NEED YOUR HELP.
SURE.
WHERE CAN WE FIND WARRIORS?
GEEZ...I DON'T KNOW. YOU CAN'T JUST BUY AN ARMY AT THE MALL.
THINK ABOUT IT TONIGHT. TOMORROW, WE WILL FIND AN ARMY. THE GREATEST ARMY EVER!
WE WILL CRUSH DROOL AND HIS HORDE INTO DUST THAT WILL BLOW IN THE WIND FOR ALL TIME.
YES, SIR!!

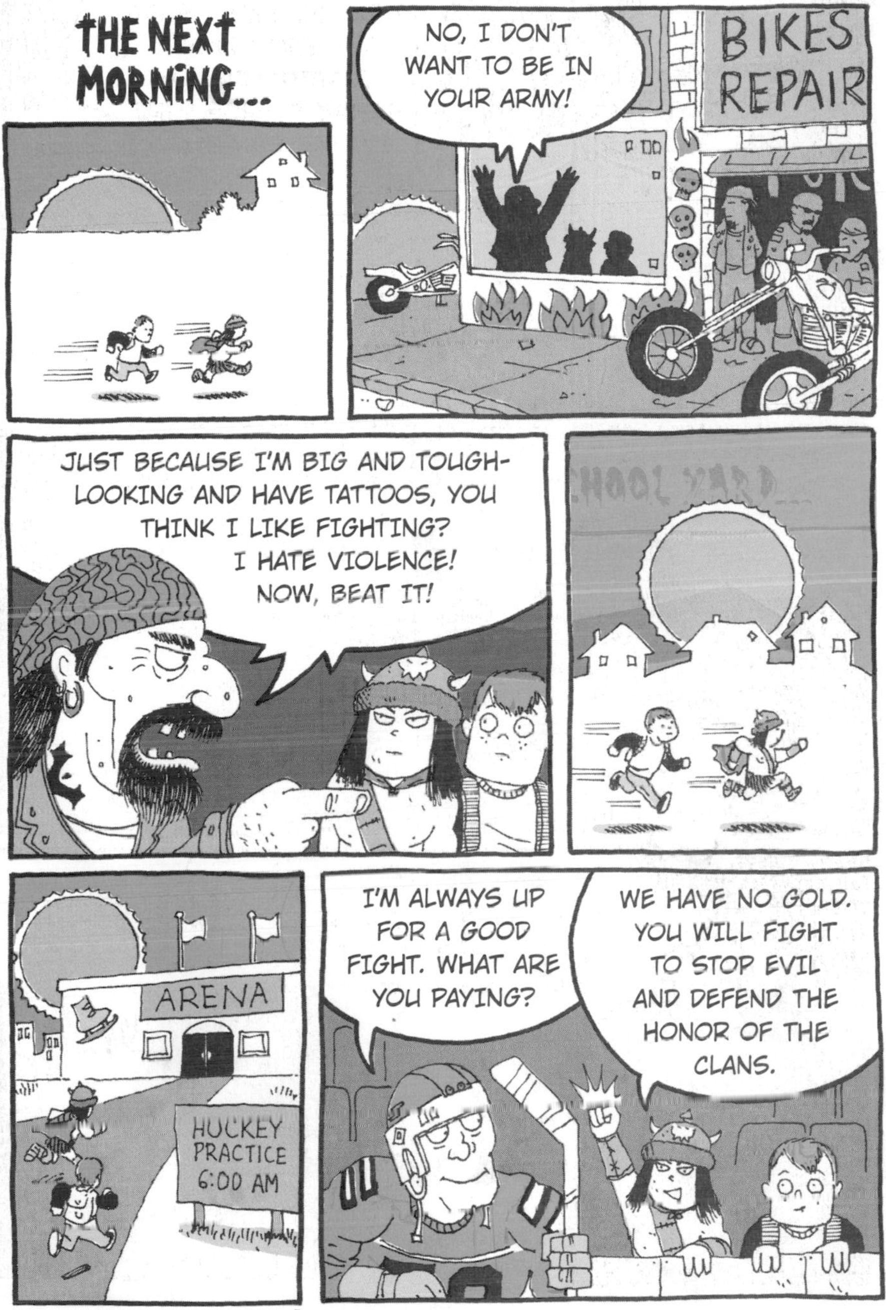
THE NEXT MORNING...
NO, I DON'T WANT TO BE IN YOUR ARMY!
BIKES REPAIR
JUST BECAUSE I'M BIG AND TOUGH-LOOKING AND HAVE TATTOOS, YOU THINK I LIKE FIGHTING? I HATE VIOLENCE! NOW, BEAT IT!
ARENA
HOCKEY PRACTICE 6:00 AM
I'M ALWAYS UP FOR A GOOD FIGHT. WHAT ARE YOU PAYING?
WE HAVE NO GOLD. YOU WILL FIGHT TO STOP EVIL AND DEFEND THE HONOR OF THE CLANS.

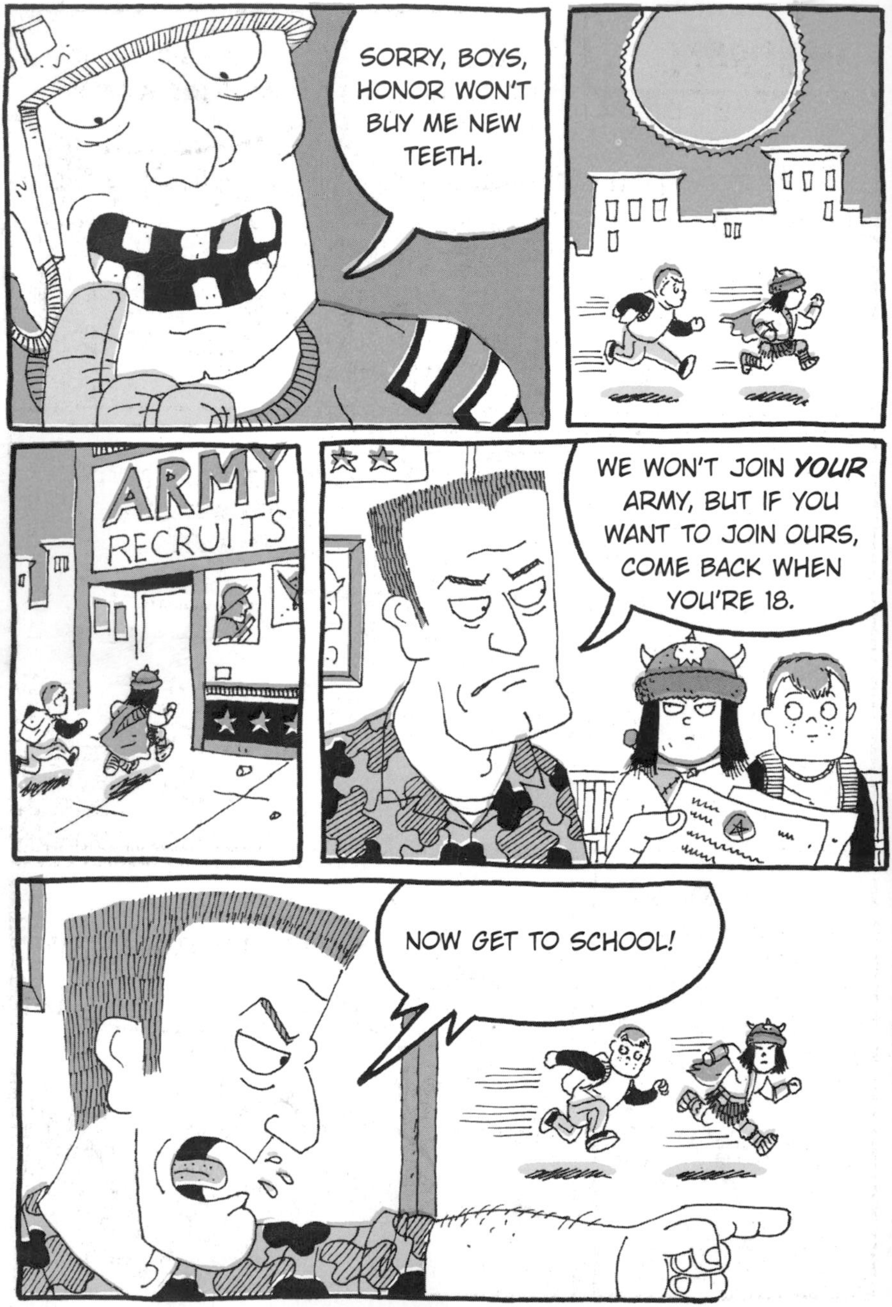
SORRY, BOYS, HONOR WON'T BUY ME NEW TEETH.
ARMY
RECRUITS
WE WON'T JOIN *YOUR* ARMY, BUT IF YOU WANT TO JOIN OURS, COME BACK WHEN YOU'RE 18.
NOW GET TO SCHOOL!

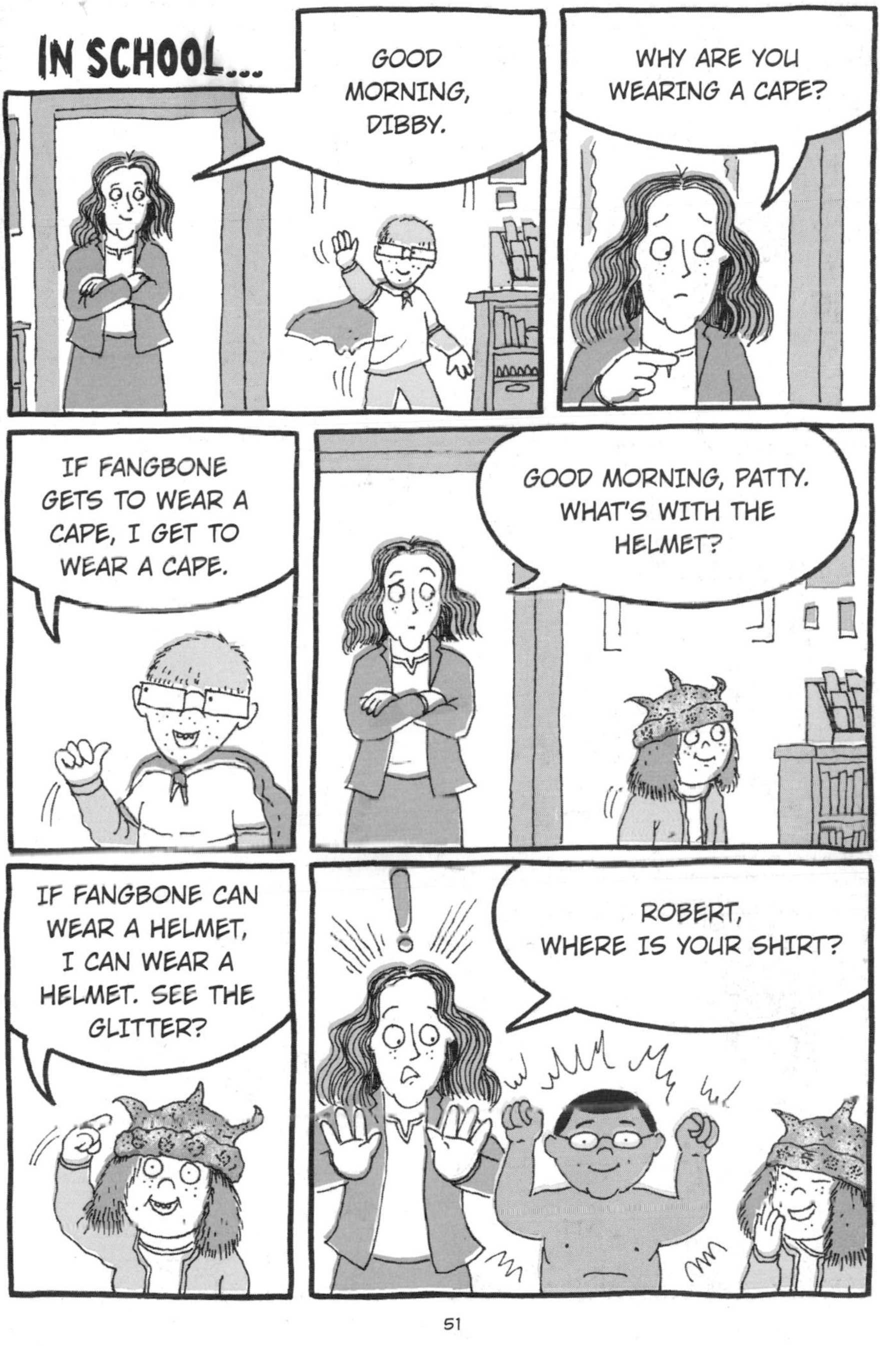
IN SCHOOL...
GOOD MORNING, DIBBY.
WHY ARE YOU WEARING A CAPE?
IF FANGBONE GETS TO WEAR A CAPE, I GET TO WEAR A CAPE.
GOOD MORNING, PATTY. WHAT'S WITH THE HELMET?
IF FANGBONE CAN WEAR A HELMET, I CAN WEAR A HELMET. SEE THE GLITTER?
!
ROBERT, WHERE IS YOUR SHIRT?

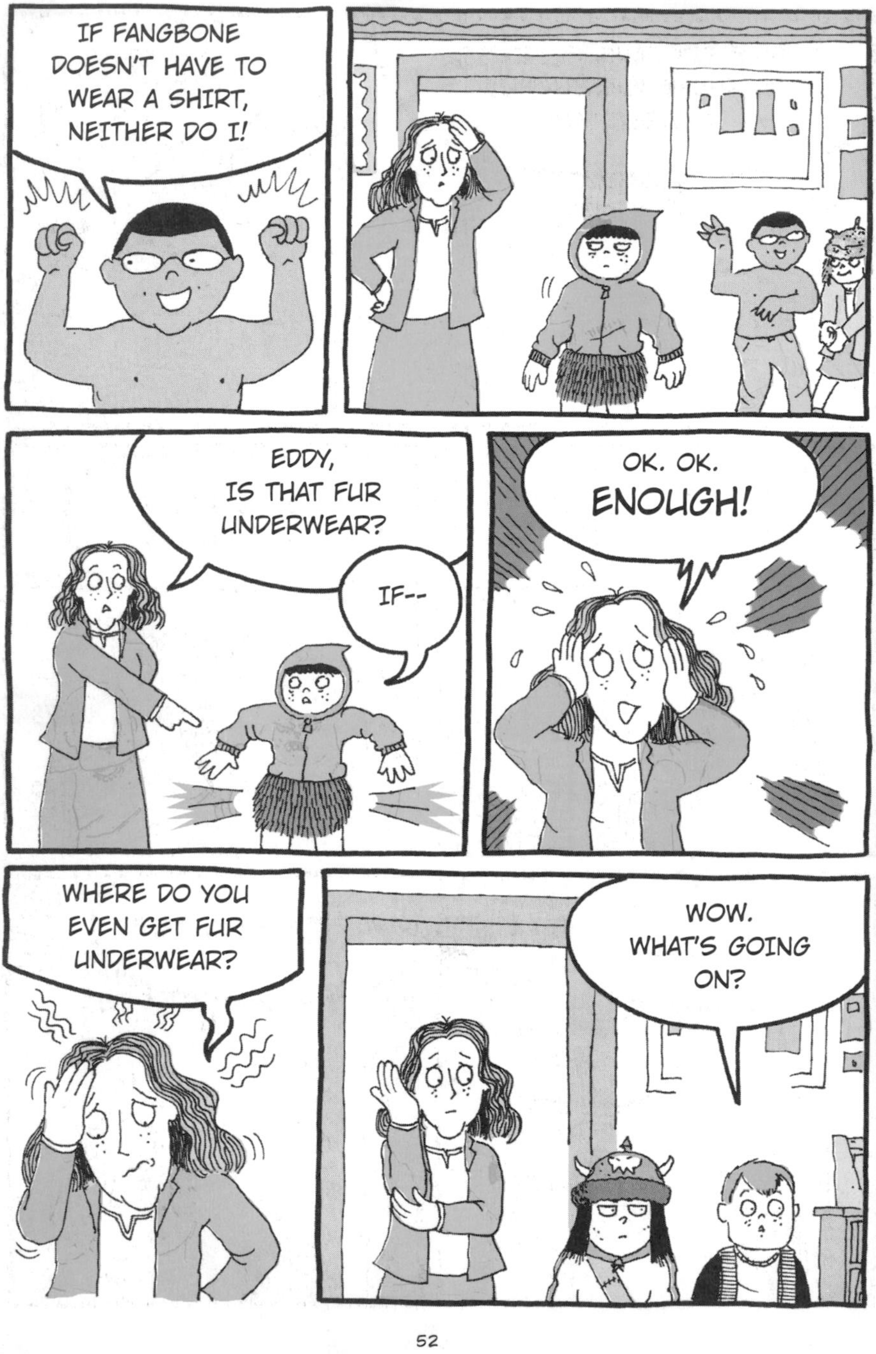
IF FANGBONE DOESN'T HAVE TO WEAR A SHIRT, NEITHER DO I!
EDDY, IS THAT FUR UNDERWEAR?
IF--
OK. OK. ENOUGH!
WHERE DO YOU EVEN GET FUR UNDERWEAR?
WOW. WHAT'S GOING ON?

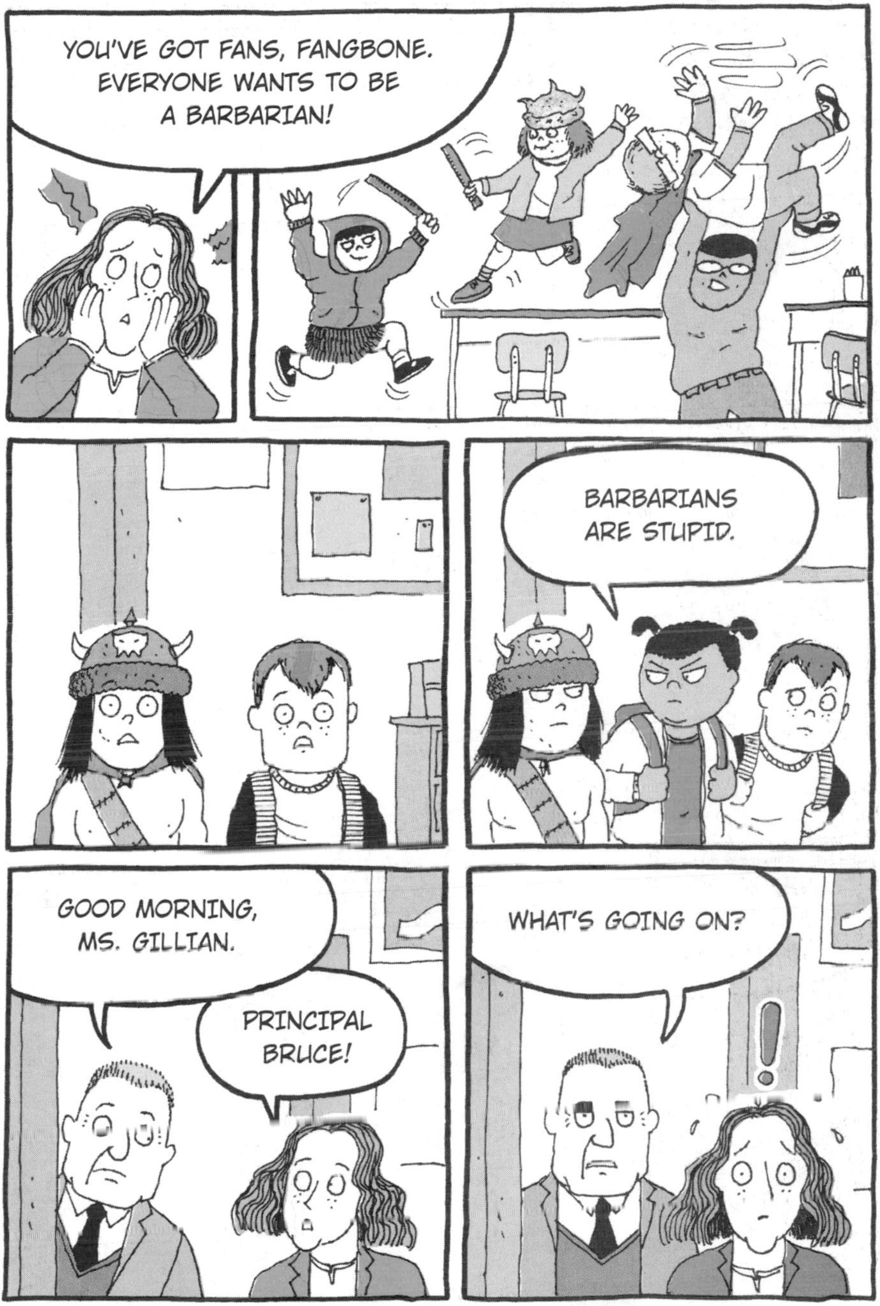
YOU'VE GOT FANS, FANGBONE. EVERYONE WANTS TO BE A BARBARIAN!
BARBARIANS ARE STUPID.
GOOD MORNING, MS. GILLIAN.
PRINCIPAL BRUCE!
WHAT'S GOING ON?
!

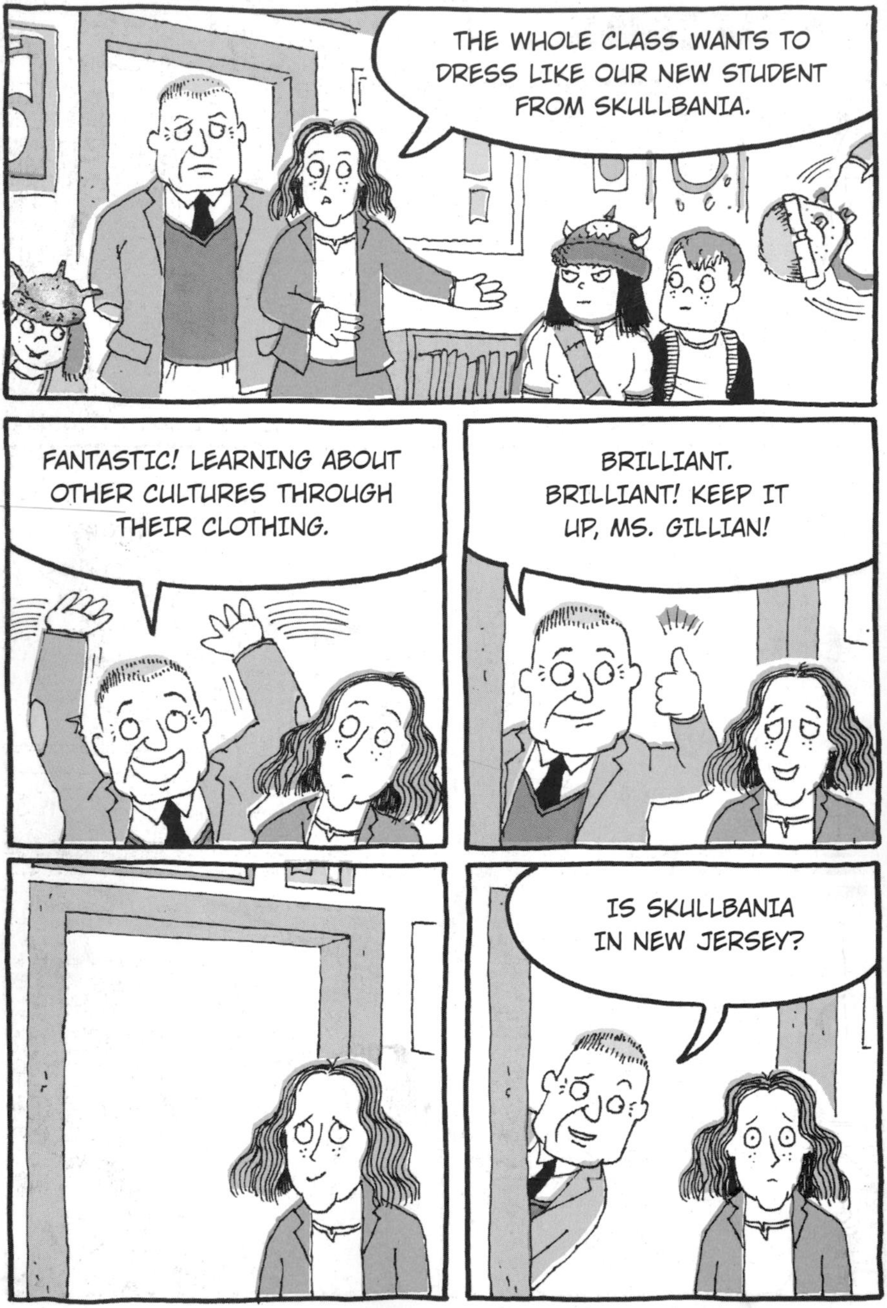
THE WHOLE CLASS WANTS TO DRESS LIKE OUR NEW STUDENT FROM SKULLBANIA.
FANTASTIC! LEARNING ABOUT OTHER CULTURES THROUGH THEIR CLOTHING.
BRILLIANT. BRILLIANT! KEEP IT UP, MS. GILLIAN!
IS SKULLBANIA IN NEW JERSEY?

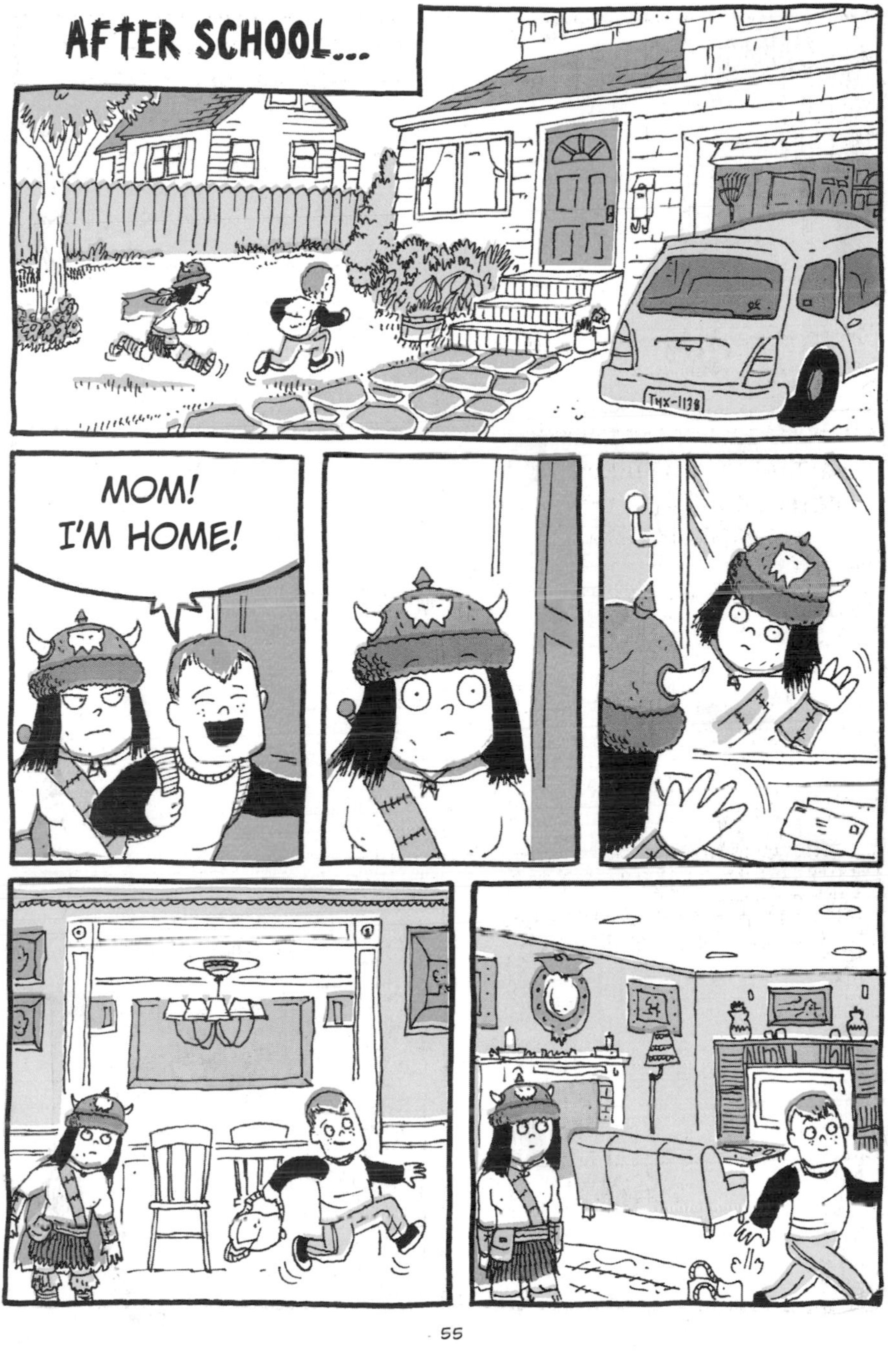

AFTER SCHOOL...
THX-1138
MOM! I'M HOME!

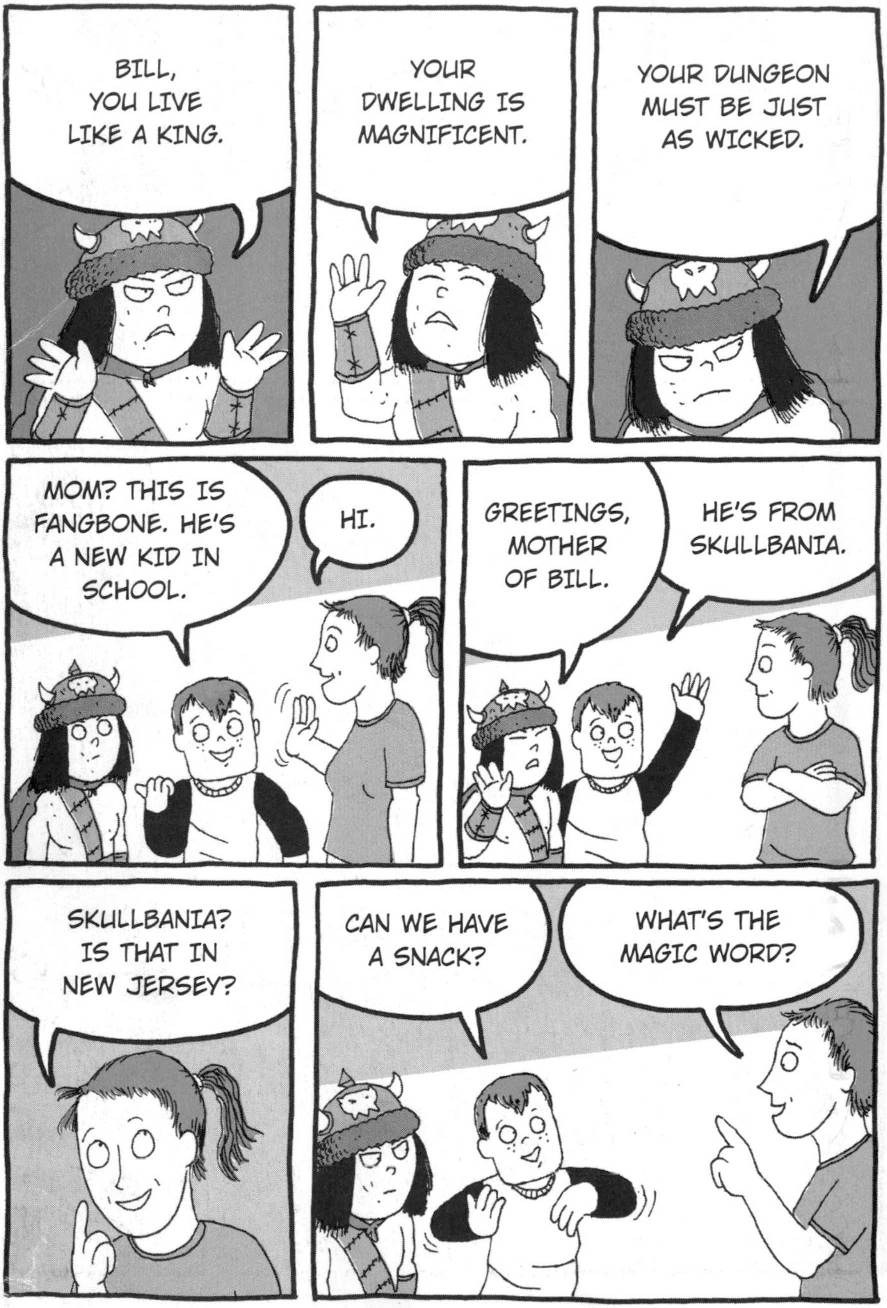
BILL, YOU LIVE LIKE A KING.
YOUR DWELLING IS MAGNIFICENT.
YOUR DUNGEON MUST BE JUST AS WICKED.
MOM? THIS IS FANGBONE. HE'S A NEW KID IN SCHOOL.
HI.
GREETINGS, MOTHER OF BILL.
HE'S FROM SKULLBANIA.
SKULLBANIA? IS THAT IN NEW JERSEY?
CAN WE HAVE A SNACK?
WHAT'S THE MAGIC WORD?

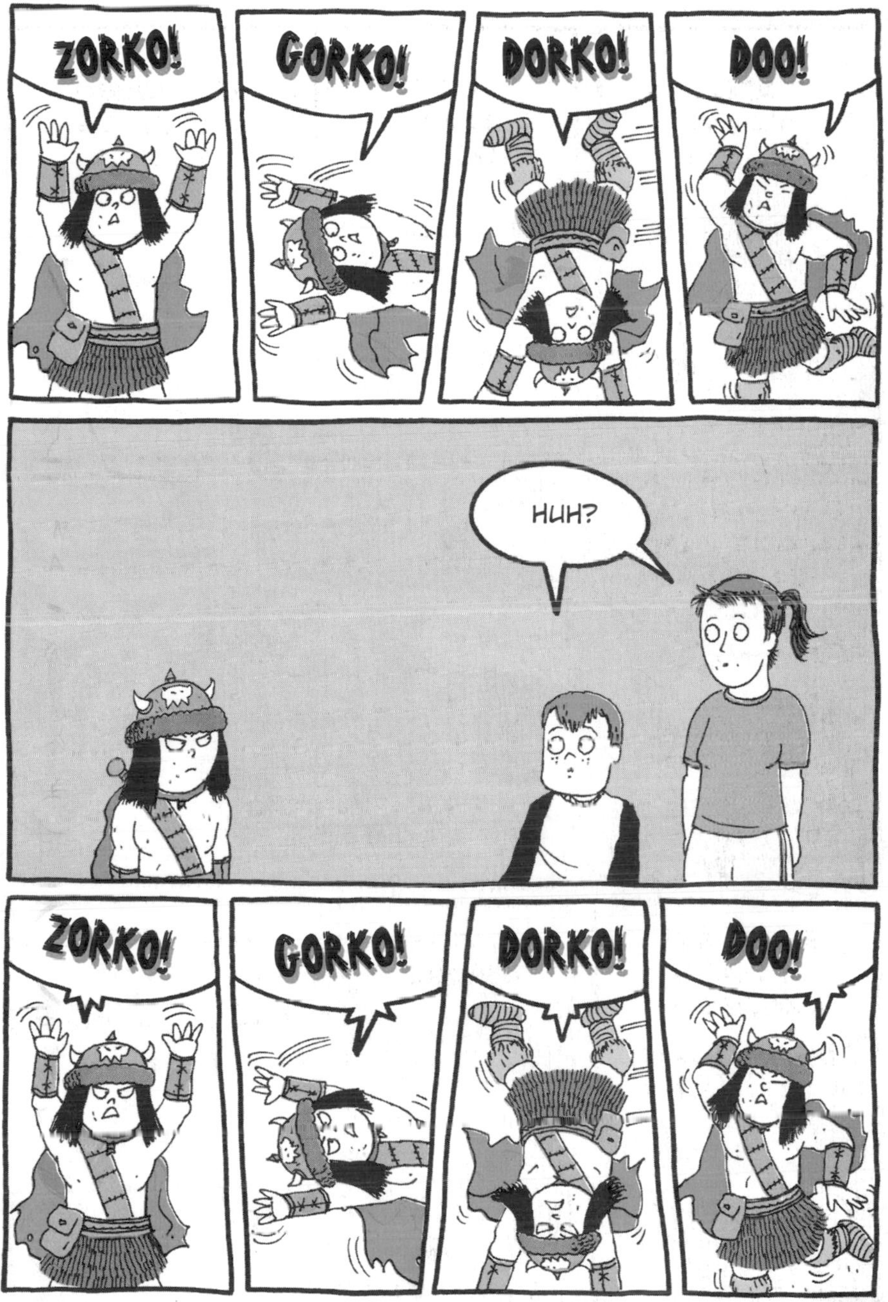
ZORKO!
GORKO!
DORKO!
DOO!
HUH?
ZORKO!
GORKO!
DORKO!
DOO!

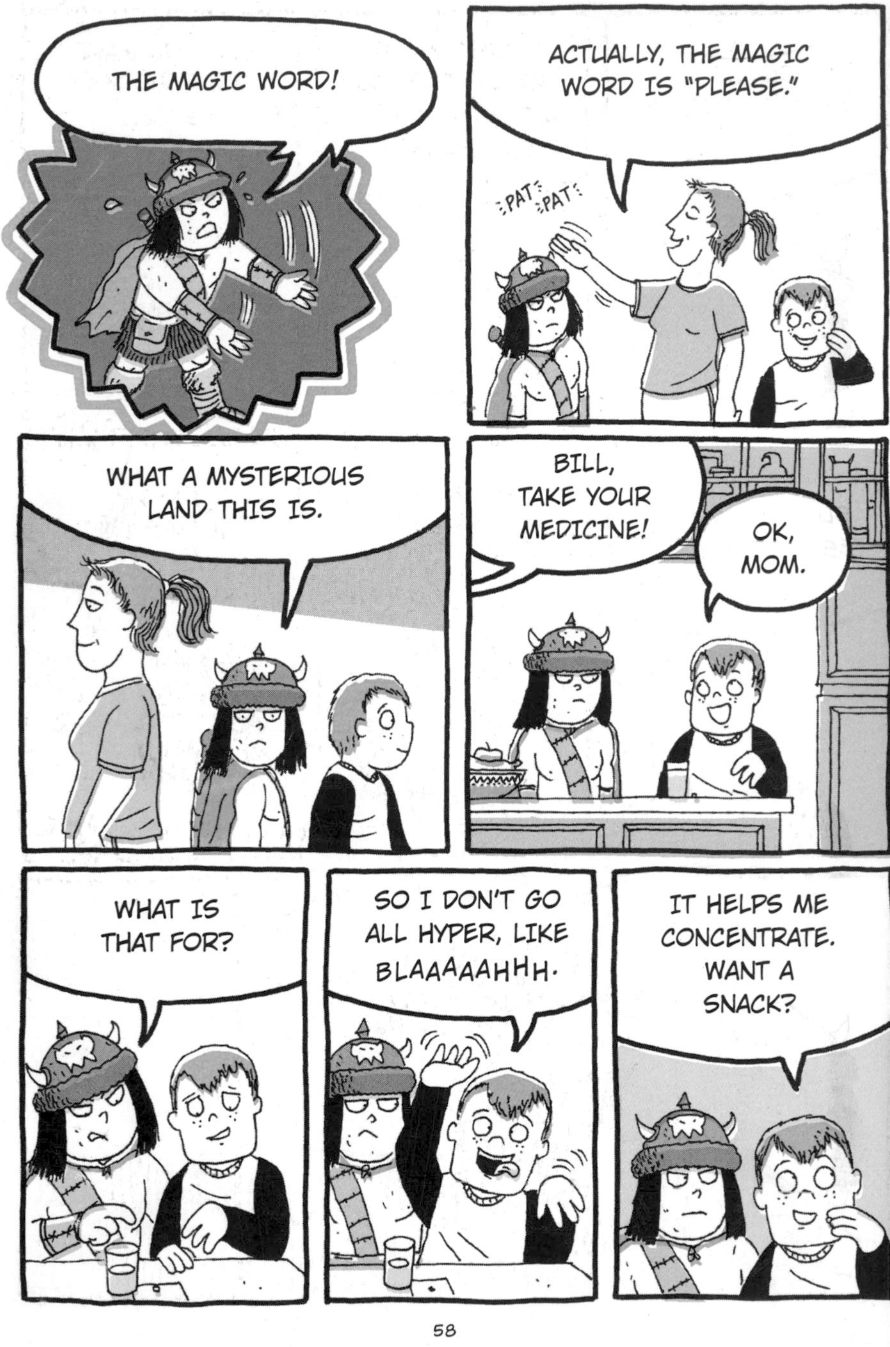
THE MAGIC WORD!
ACTUALLY, THE MAGIC WORD IS "PLEASE."
PAT PAT
WHAT A MYSTERIOUS LAND THIS IS.
BILL, TAKE YOUR MEDICINE!
OK, MOM.
WHAT IS THAT FOR?
SO I DON'T GO ALL HYPER, LIKE BLAAAAAHHH.
IT HELPS ME CONCENTRATE. WANT A SNACK?

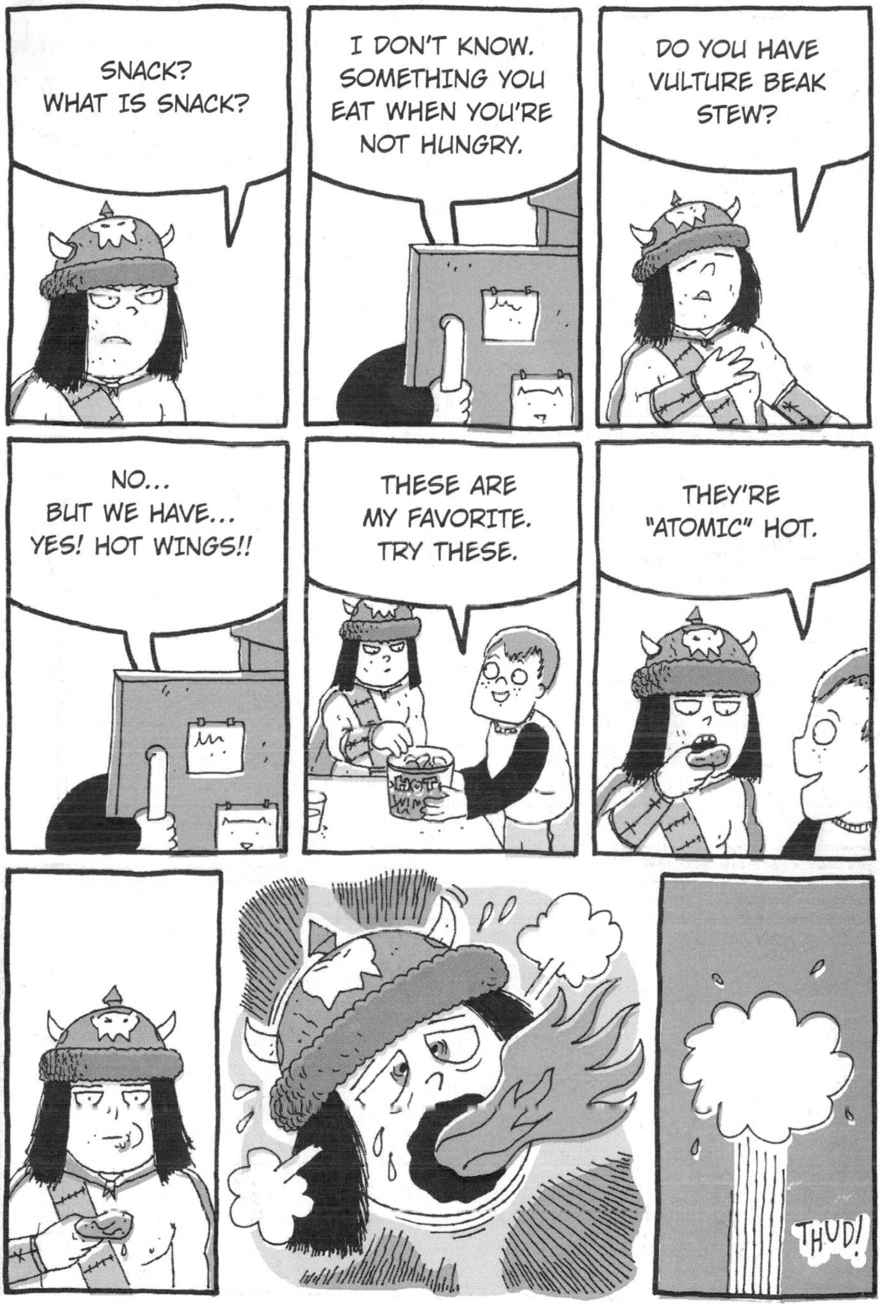
SNACK? WHAT IS SNACK?
I DON'T KNOW. SOMETHING YOU EAT WHEN YOU'RE NOT HUNGRY.
DO YOU HAVE VULTURE BEAK STEW?
NO... BUT WE HAVE... YES! HOT WINGS!!
THESE ARE MY FAVORITE. TRY THESE.
HOT WINGS
THEY'RE "ATOMIC" HOT.
THUD!

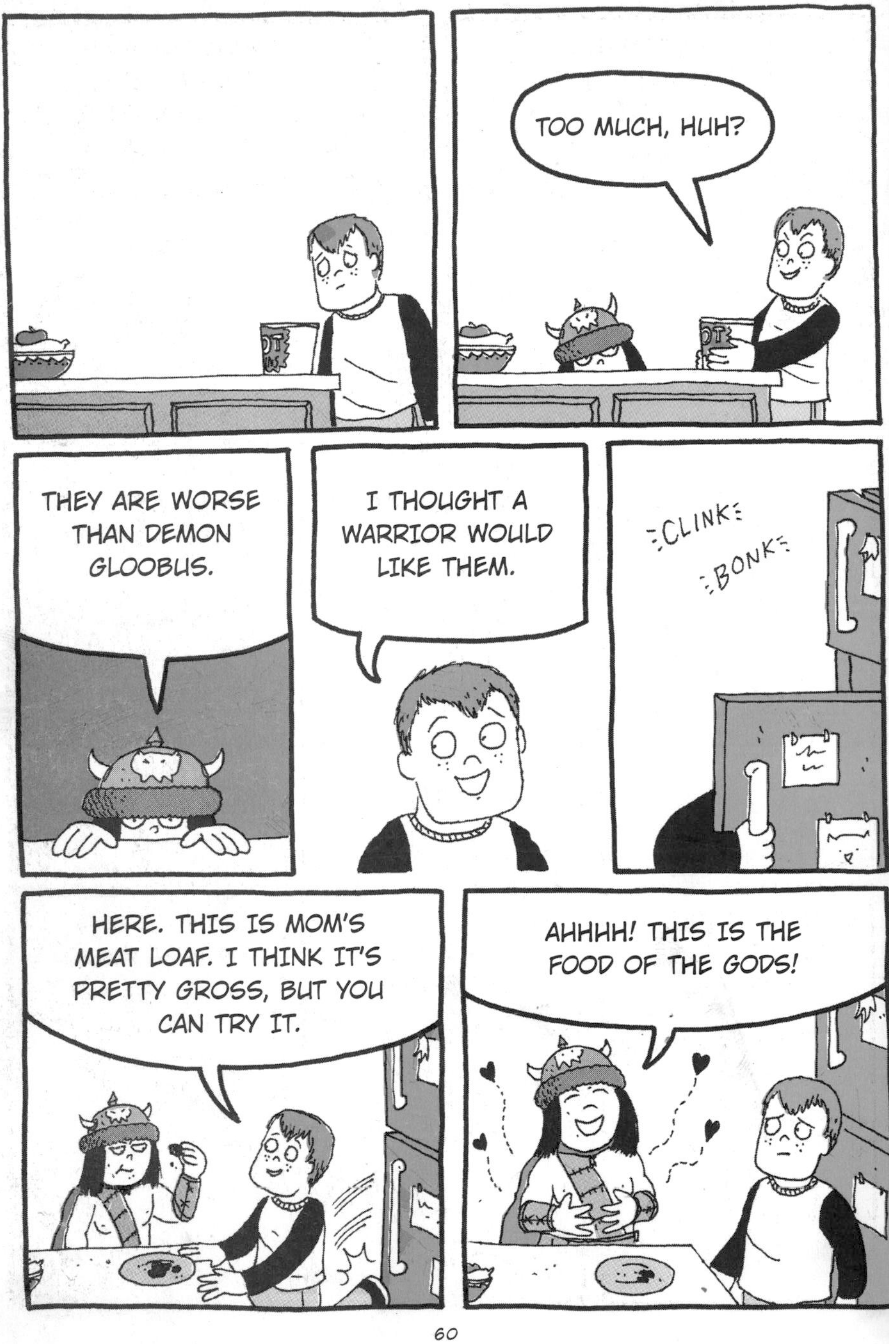
TOO MUCH, HUH?
THEY ARE WORSE THAN DEMON GLOOBUS.
I THOUGHT A WARRIOR WOULD LIKE THEM.
CLINK
BONK
HERE. THIS IS MOM'S MEAT LOAF. I THINK IT'S PRETTY GROSS, BUT YOU CAN TRY IT.
AHHHH! THIS IS THE FOOD OF THE GODS!

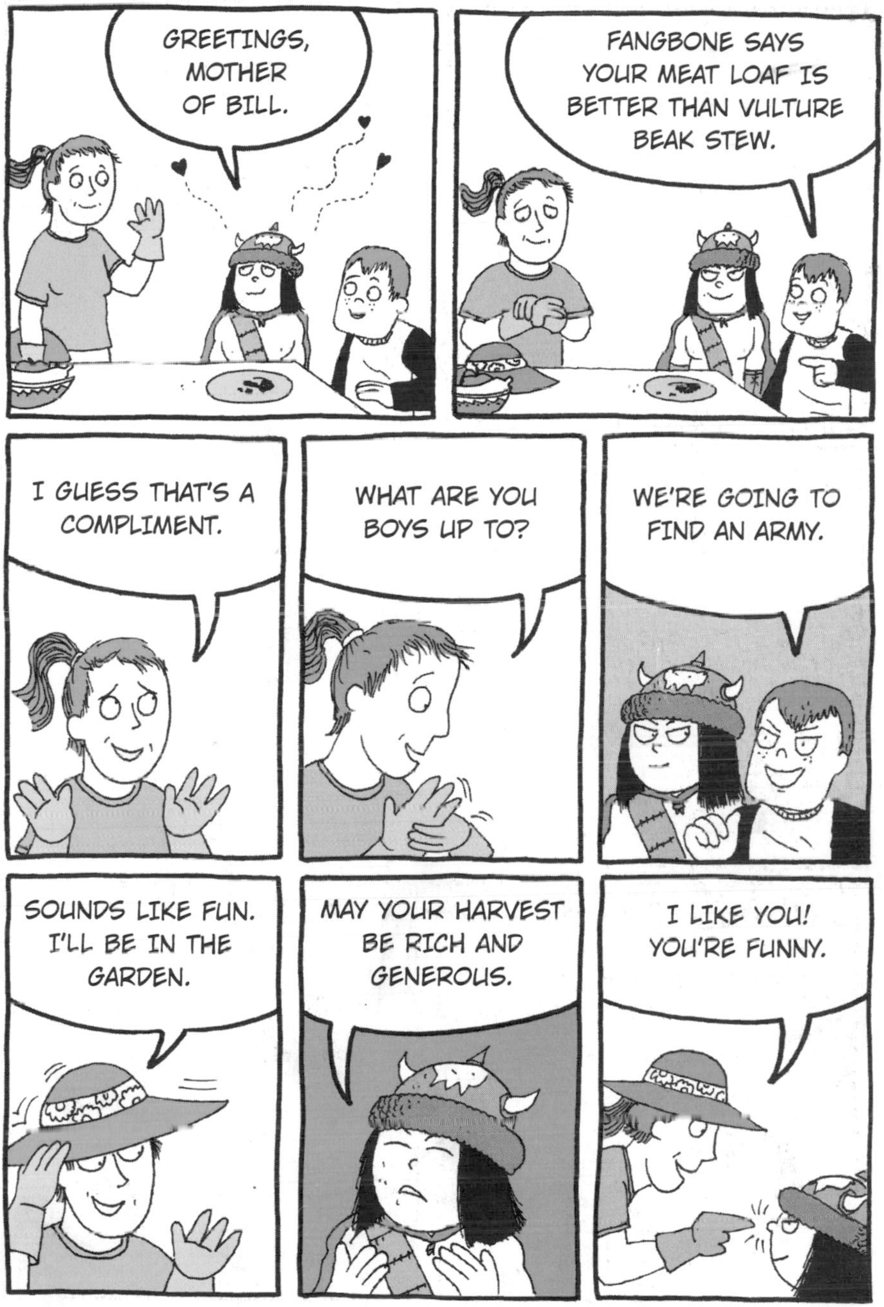
GREETINGS, MOTHER OF BILL.
FANGBONE SAYS YOUR MEAT LOAF IS BETTER THAN VULTURE BEAK STEW.
I GUESS THAT'S A COMPLIMENT.
WHAT ARE YOU BOYS UP TO?
WE'RE GOING TO FIND AN ARMY.
SOUNDS LIKE FUN. I'LL BE IN THE GARDEN.
MAY YOUR HARVEST BE RICH AND GENEROUS.
I LIKE YOU! YOU'RE FUNNY.

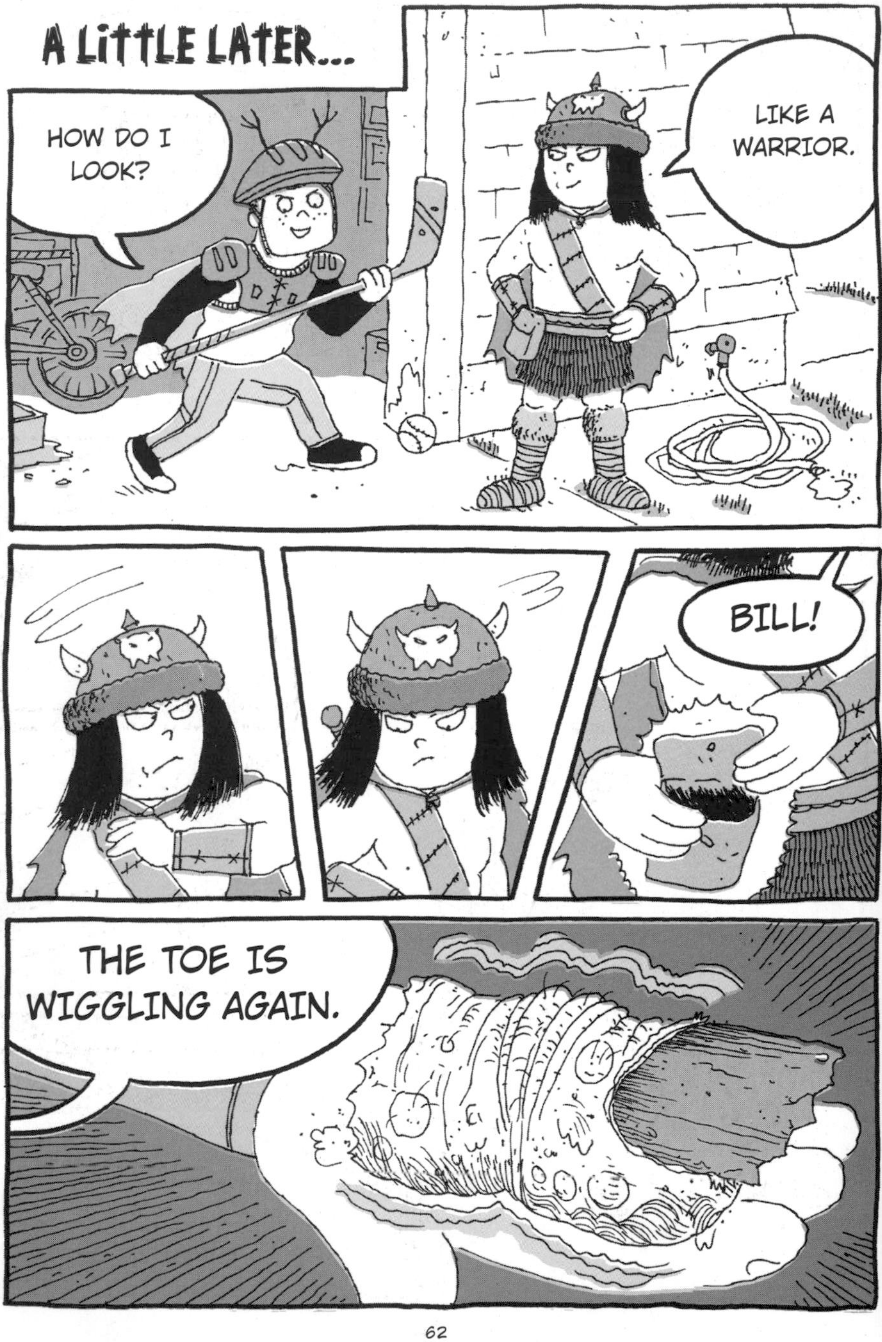
A LITTLE LATER...
HOW DO I LOOK?
LIKE A WARRIOR.
BILL!
THE TOE IS WIGGLING AGAIN.

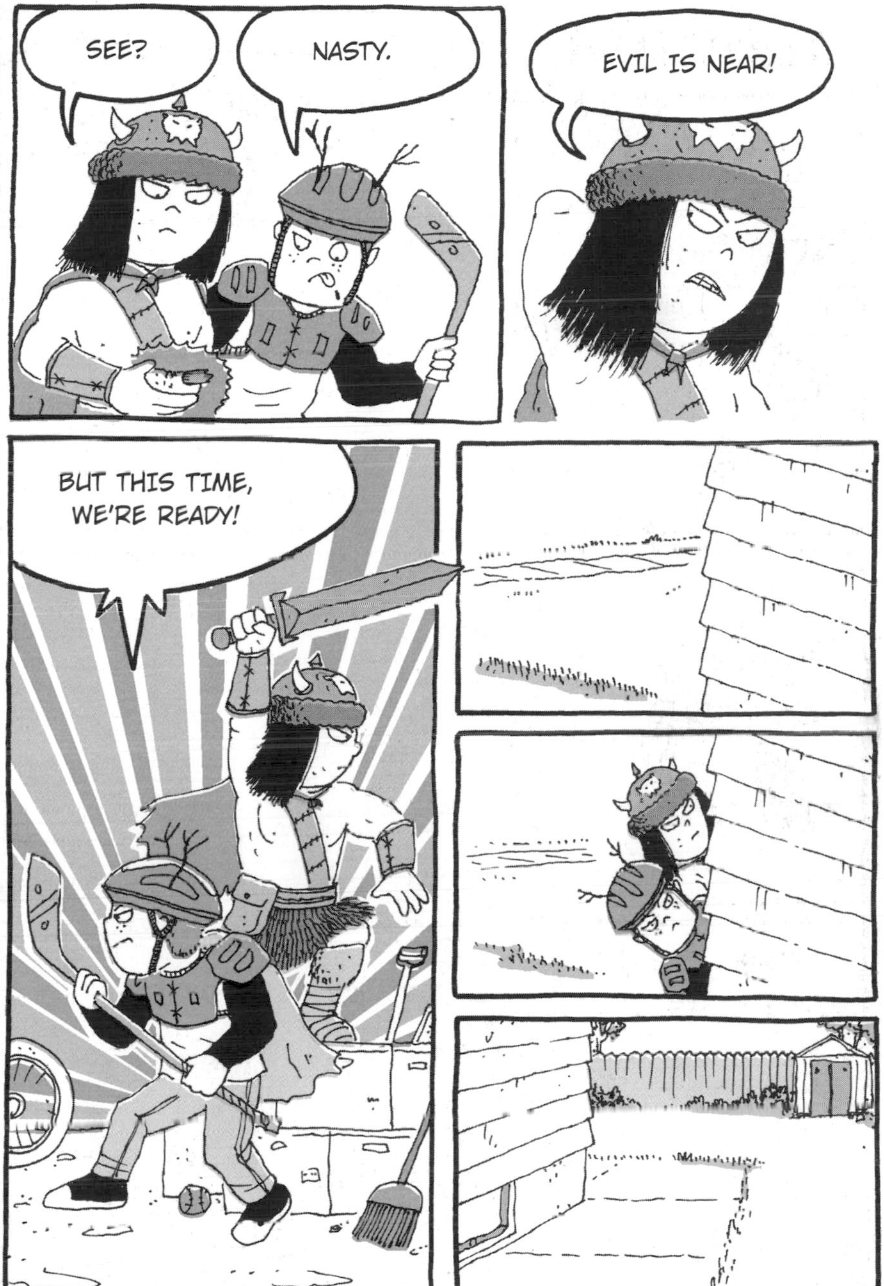
SEE?
NASTY.
EVIL IS NEAR!
BUT THIS TIME, WE'RE READY!

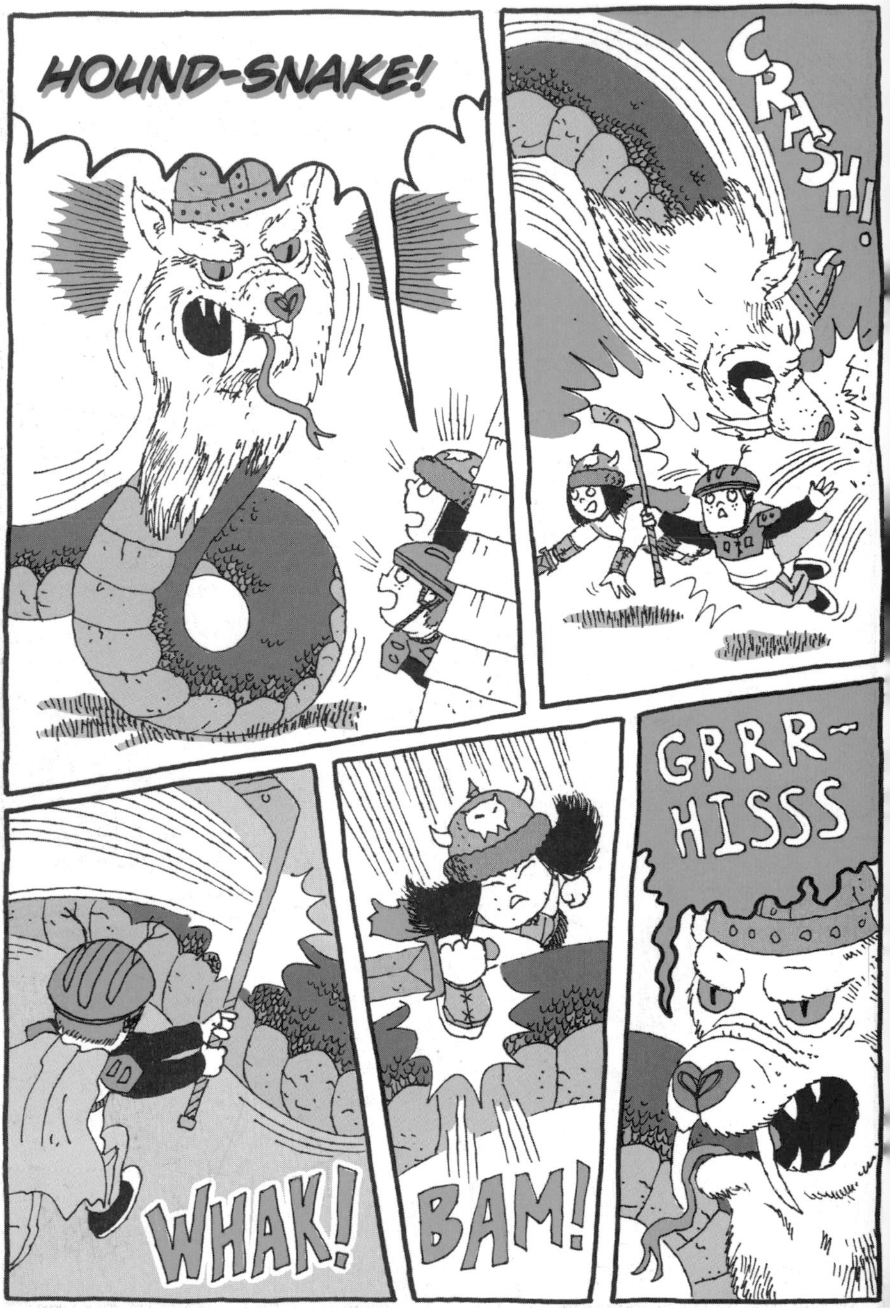
HOUND-SNAKE!
CRASH!
GRRR-HISSS
WHAK!
BAM!

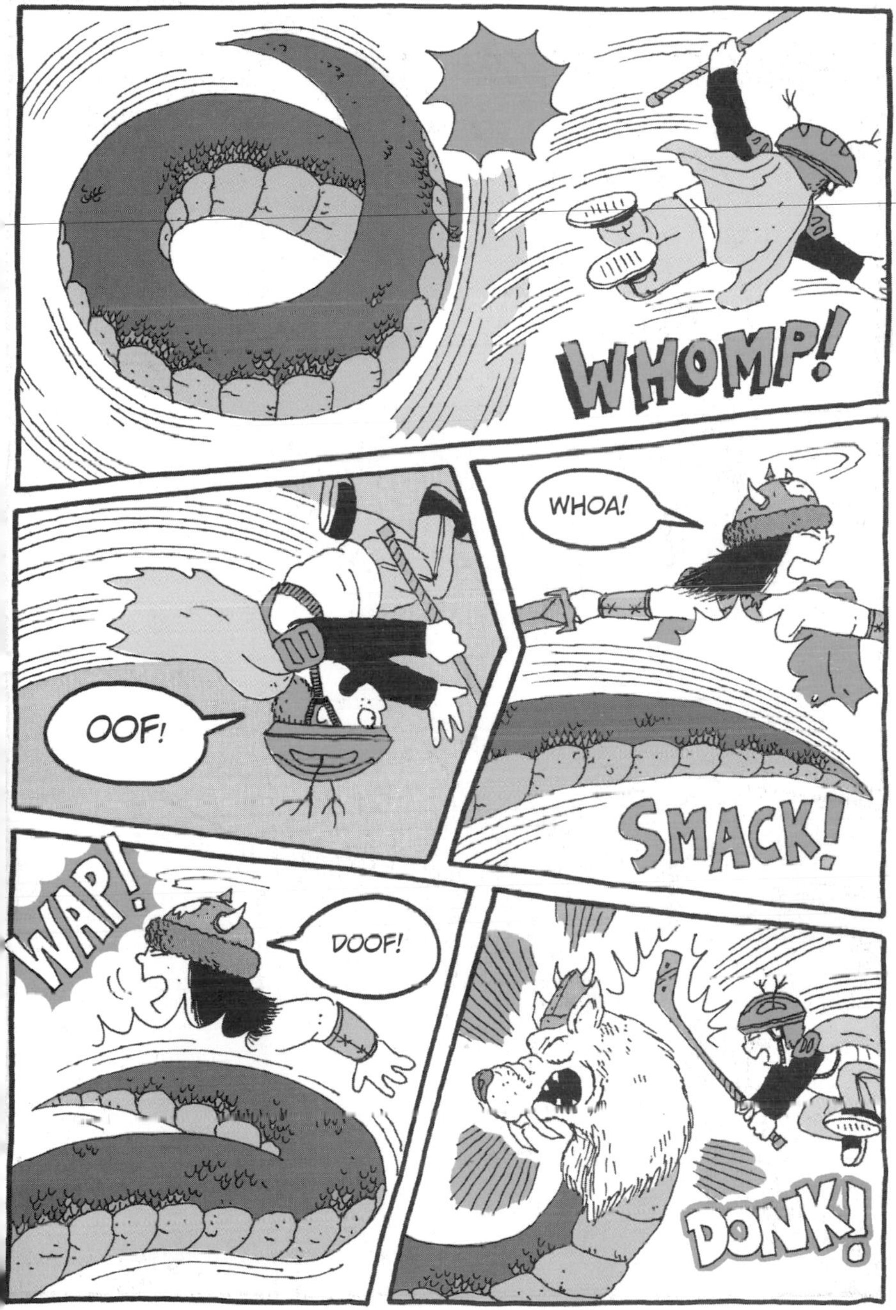
WHOMP!
OOF!
WHOA!
SMACK!
WAP!
DOOF!
DONK!

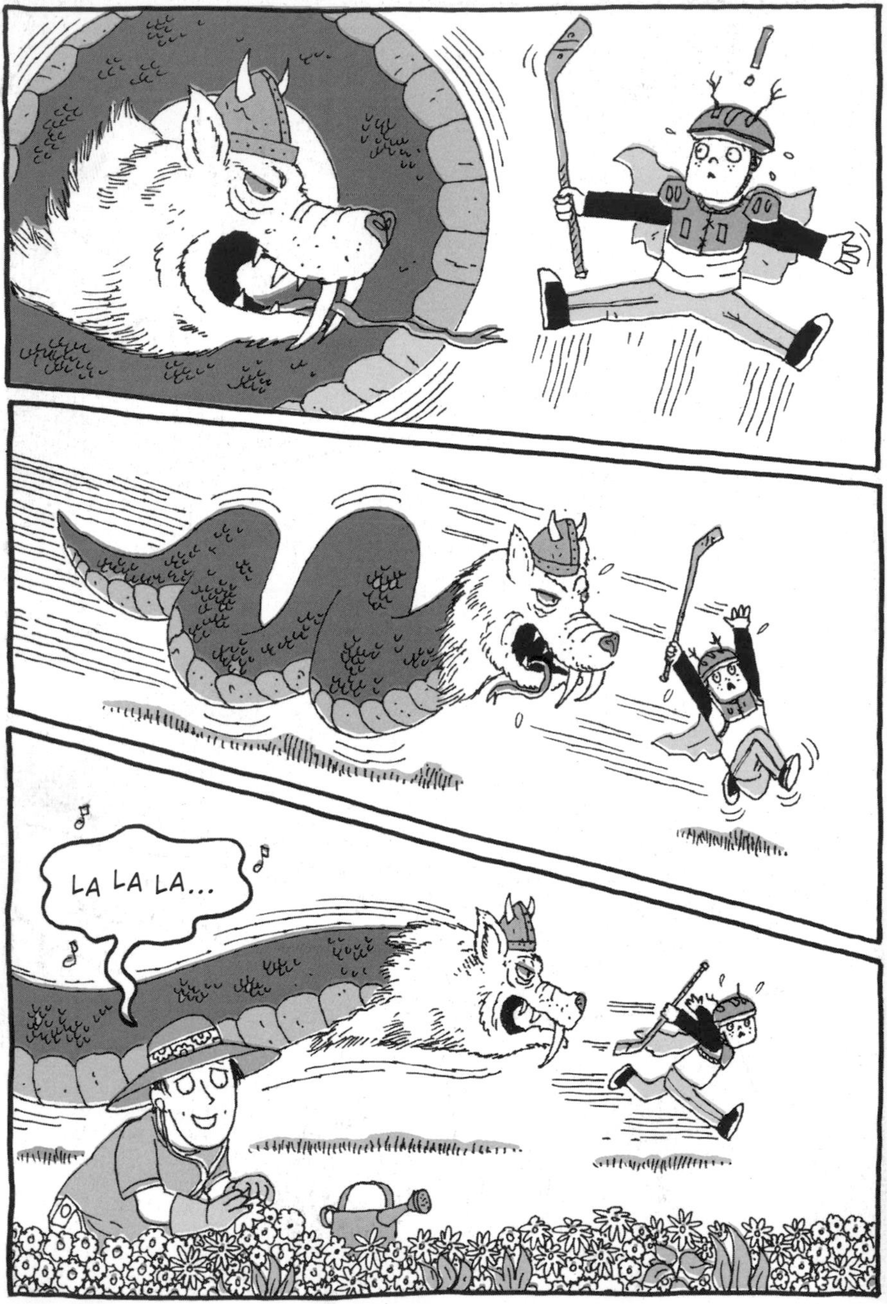
LA LA LA...

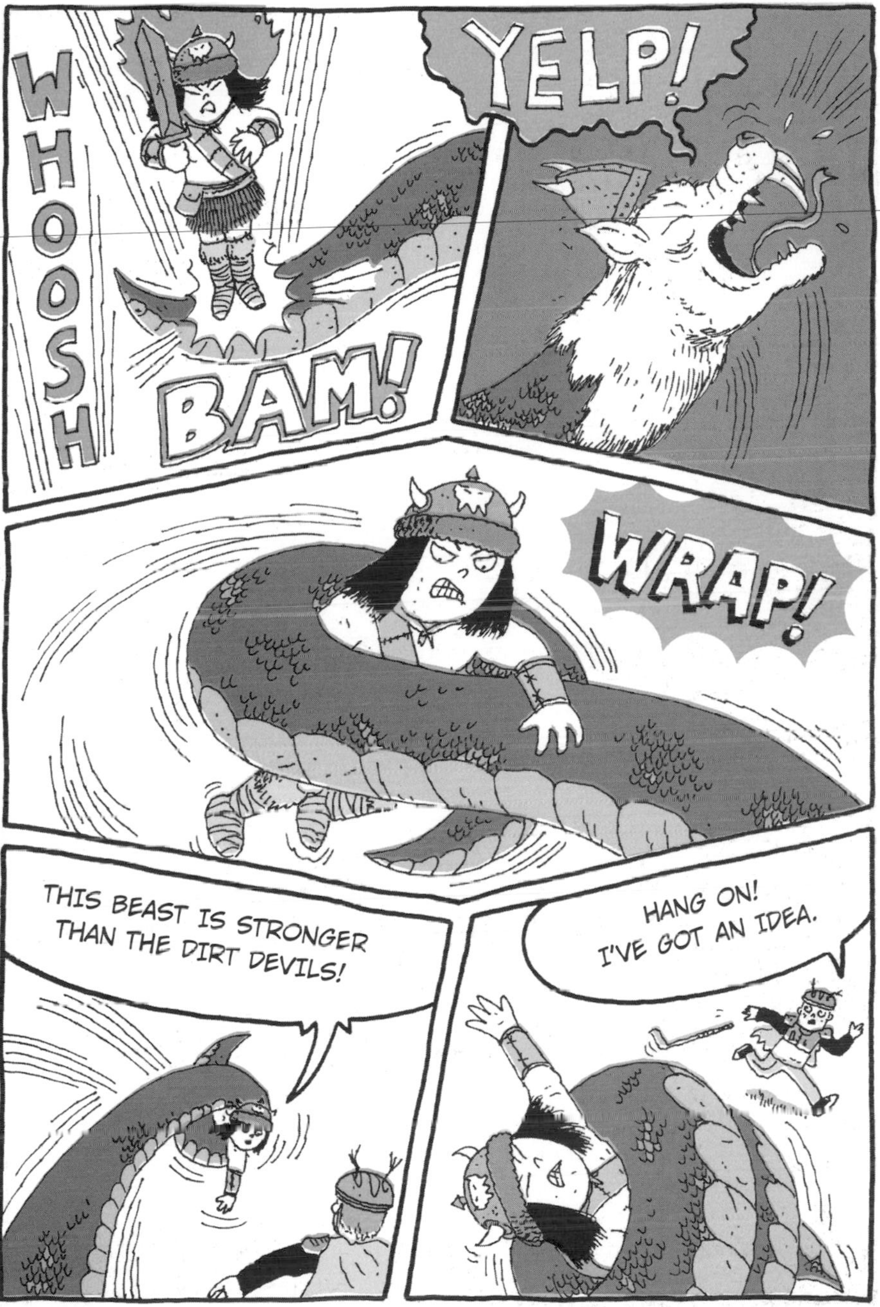
WHOOSH
BAM!
YELP!
WRAP!
THIS BEAST IS STRONGER THAN THE DIRT DEVILS!
HANG ON! I'VE GOT AN IDEA.

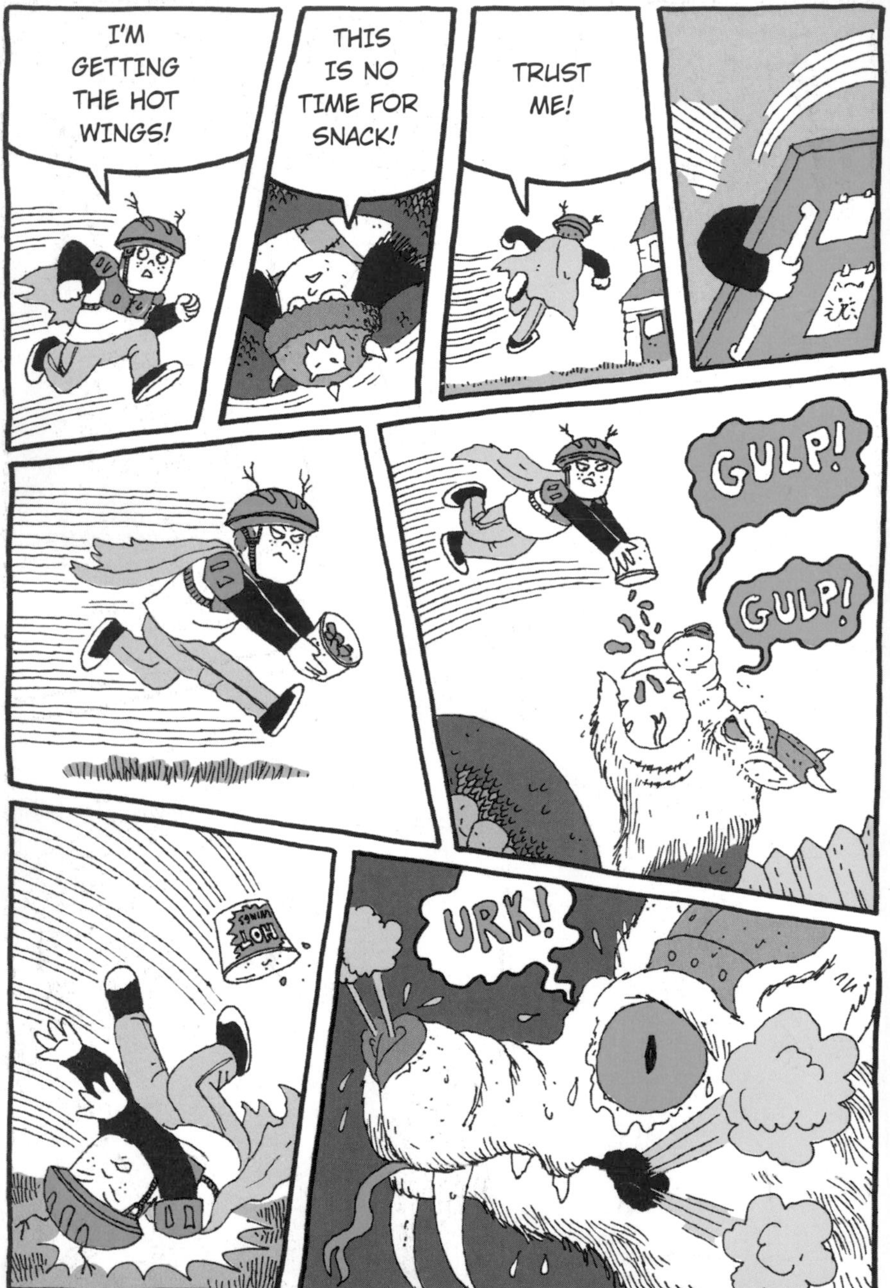
I'M GETTING THE HOT WINGS!
THIS IS NO TIME FOR SNACK!
TRUST ME!
GULP!
GULP!
URK!

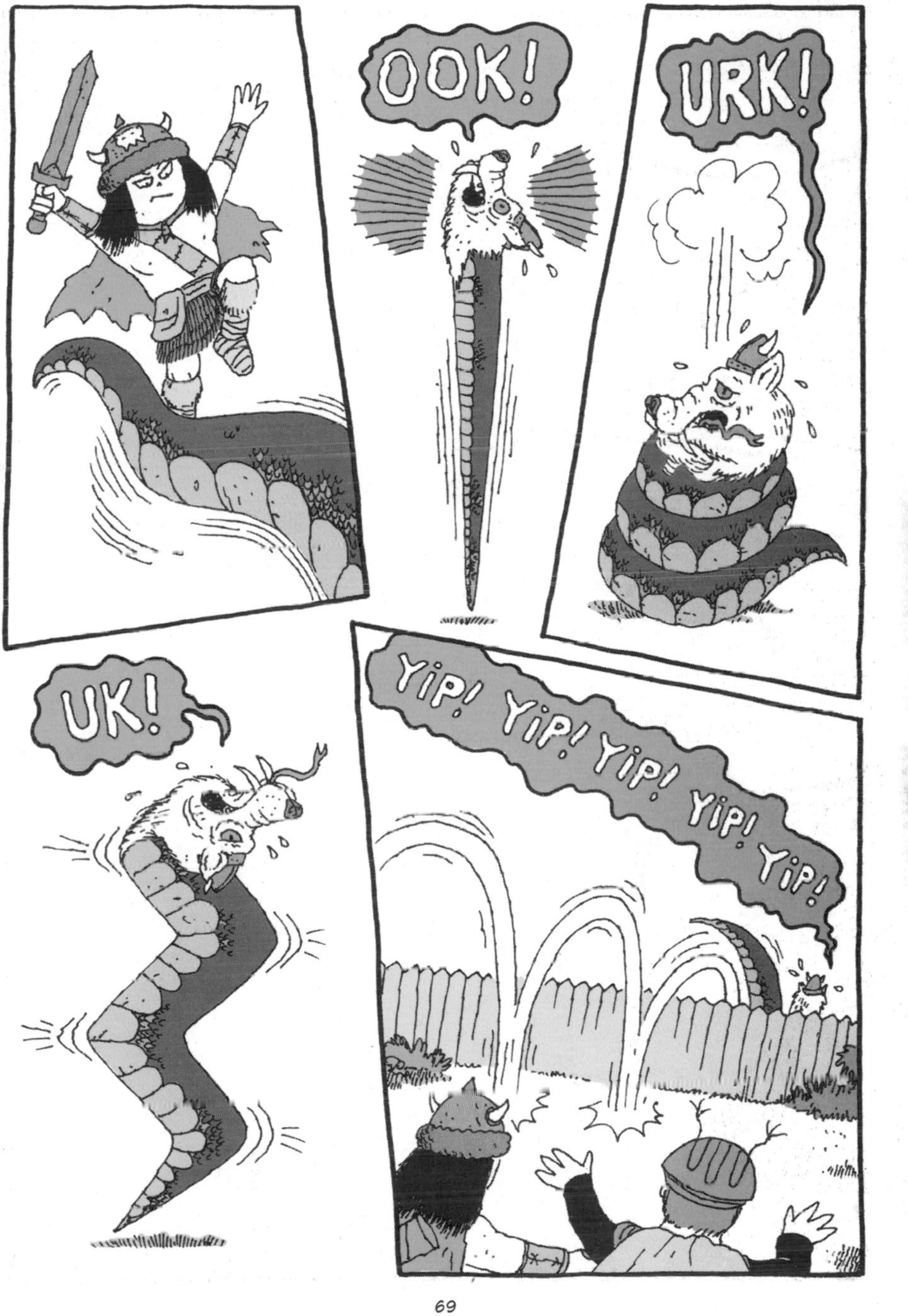
OOK!
URK!
UK!
YIP! YIP! YIP! YIP! YIP!

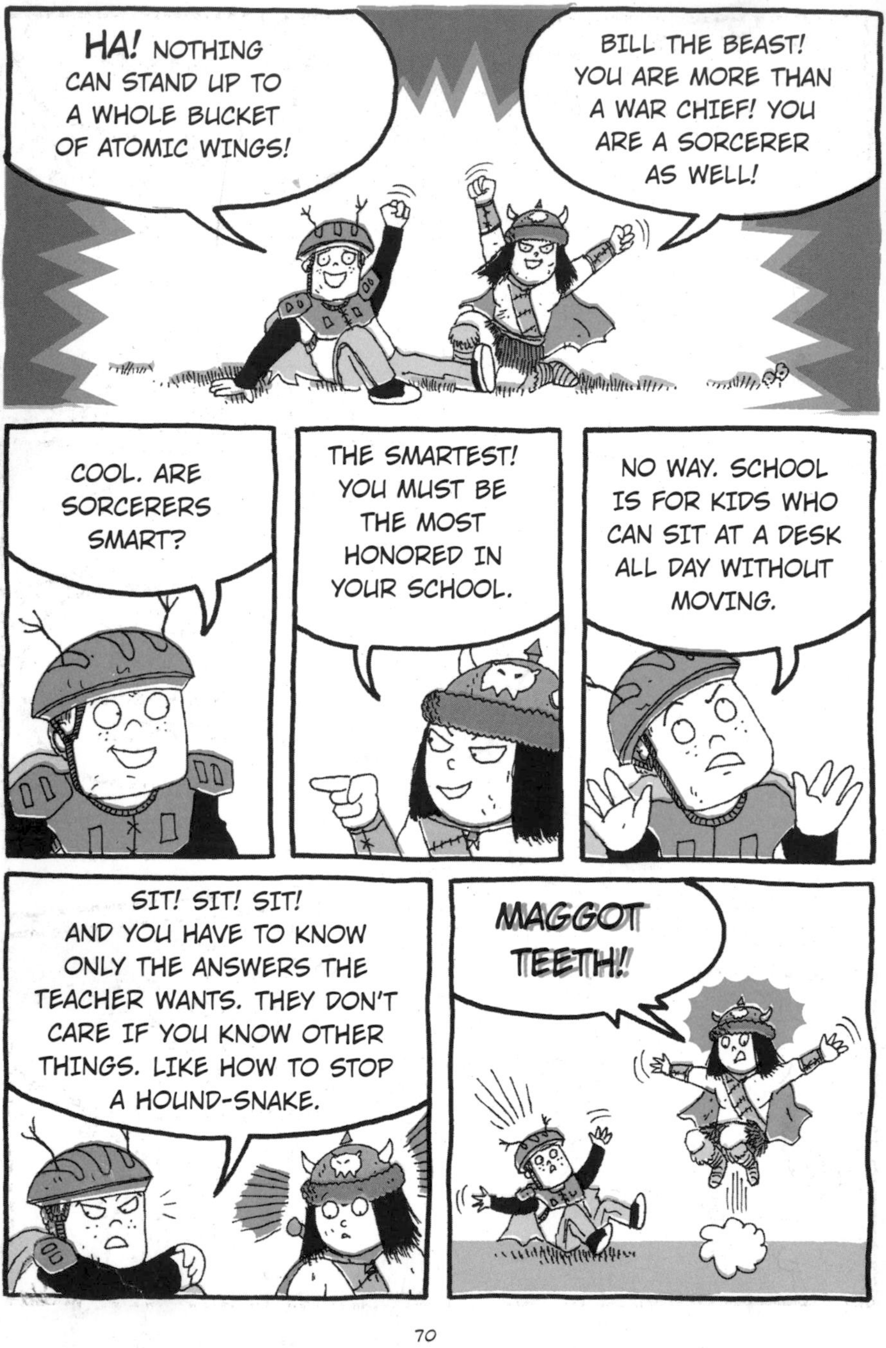
HA! NOTHING CAN STAND UP TO A WHOLE BUCKET OF ATOMIC WINGS!
BILL THE BEAST! YOU ARE MORE THAN A WAR CHIEF! YOU ARE A SORCERER AS WELL!
COOL. ARE SORCERERS SMART?
THE SMARTEST! YOU MUST BE THE MOST HONORED IN YOUR SCHOOL.
NO WAY. SCHOOL IS FOR KIDS WHO CAN SIT AT A DESK ALL DAY WITHOUT MOVING.
SIT! SIT! SIT! AND YOU HAVE TO KNOW ONLY THE ANSWERS THE TEACHER WANTS. THEY DON'T CARE IF YOU KNOW OTHER THINGS. LIKE HOW TO STOP A HOUND-SNAKE.
MAGGOT TEETH!

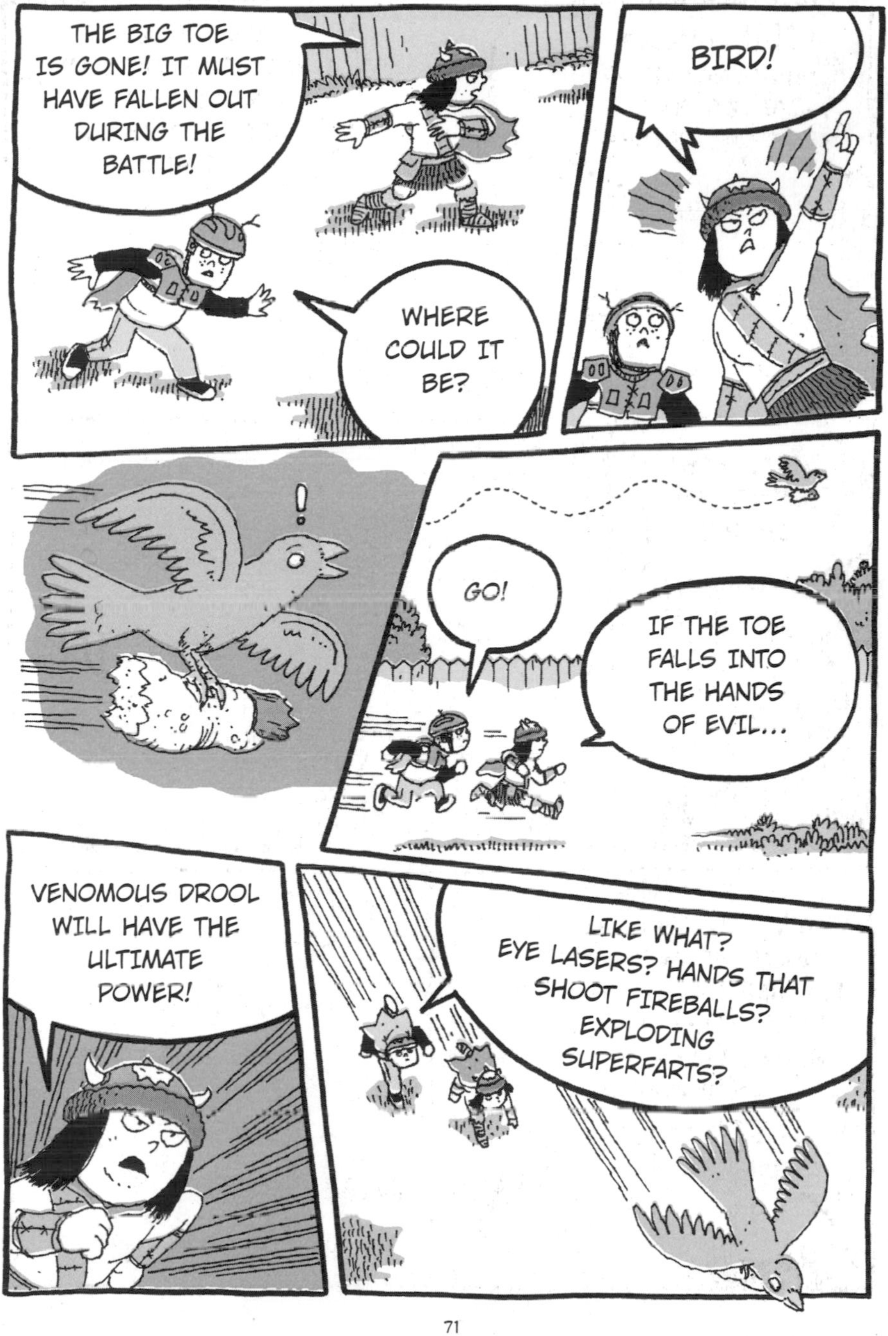
THE BIG TOE IS GONE! IT MUST HAVE FALLEN OUT DURING THE BATTLE!
WHERE COULD IT BE?
BIRD!
!
GO!
IF THE TOE FALLS INTO THE HANDS OF EVIL...
VENOMOUS DROOL WILL HAVE THE ULTIMATE POWER!
LIKE WHAT? EYE LASERS? HANDS THAT SHOOT FIREBALLS? EXPLODING SUPERFARTS?

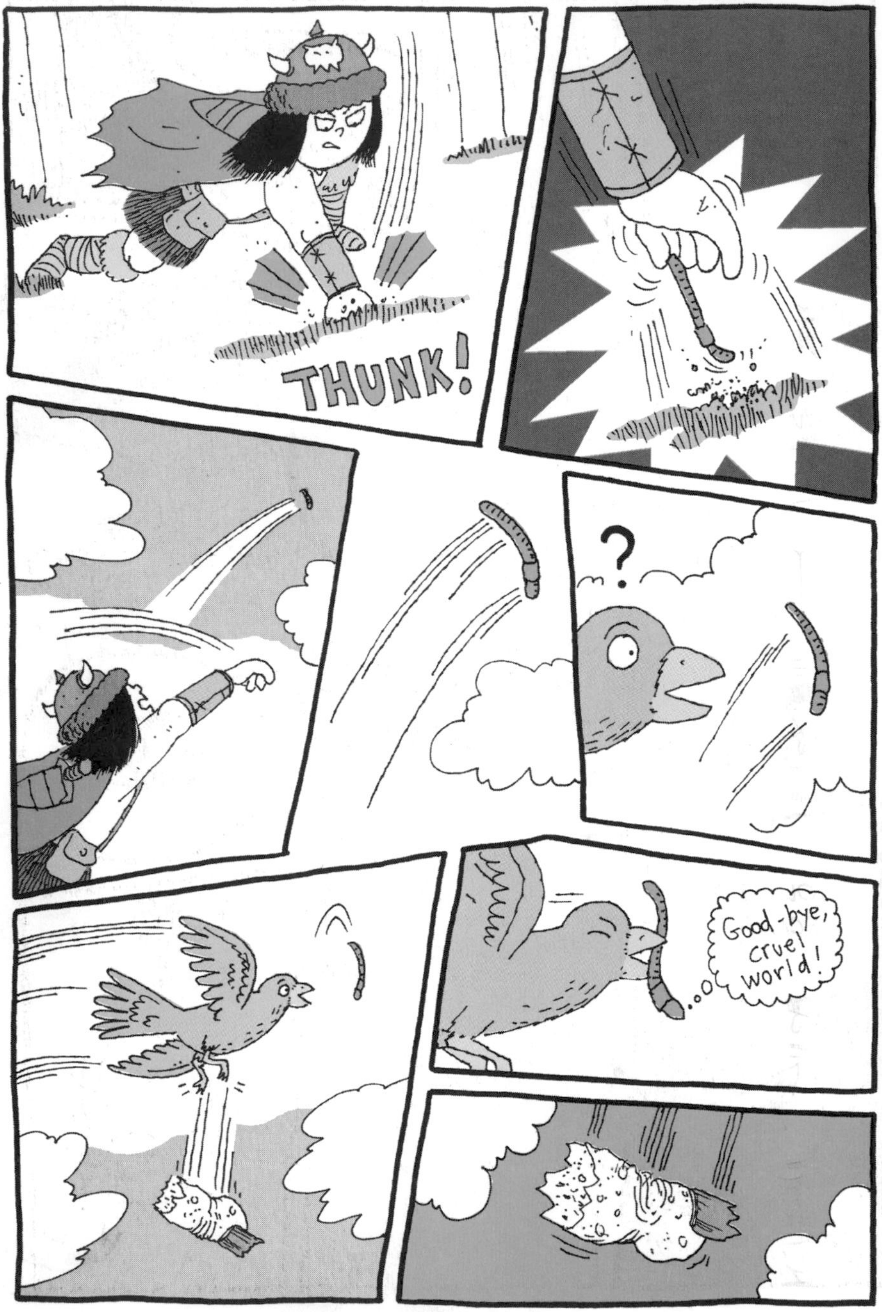
THUNK!
?
Good-bye, cruel world!

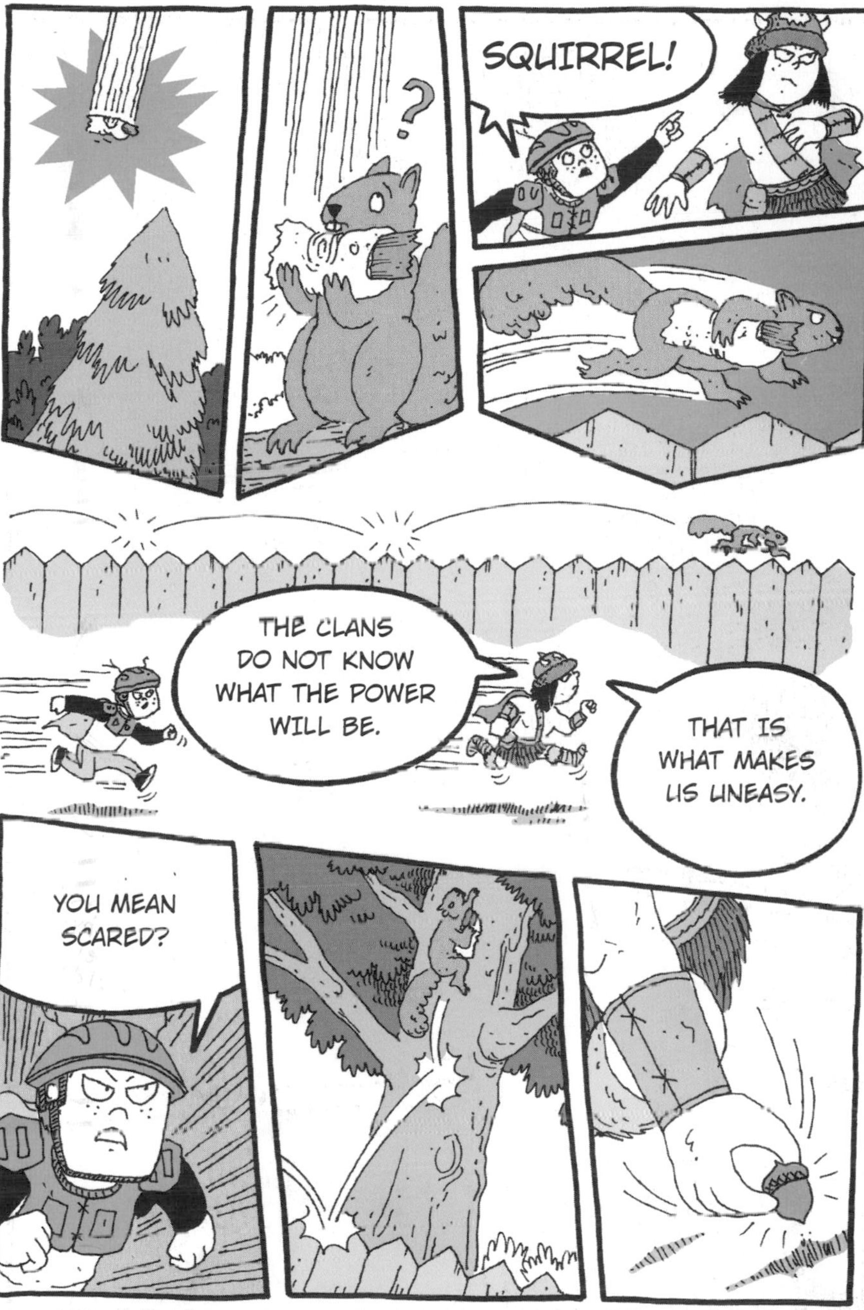
?
SQUIRREL!
THE CLANS DO NOT KNOW WHAT THE POWER WILL BE.
THAT IS WHAT MAKES US UNEASY.
YOU MEAN SCARED?

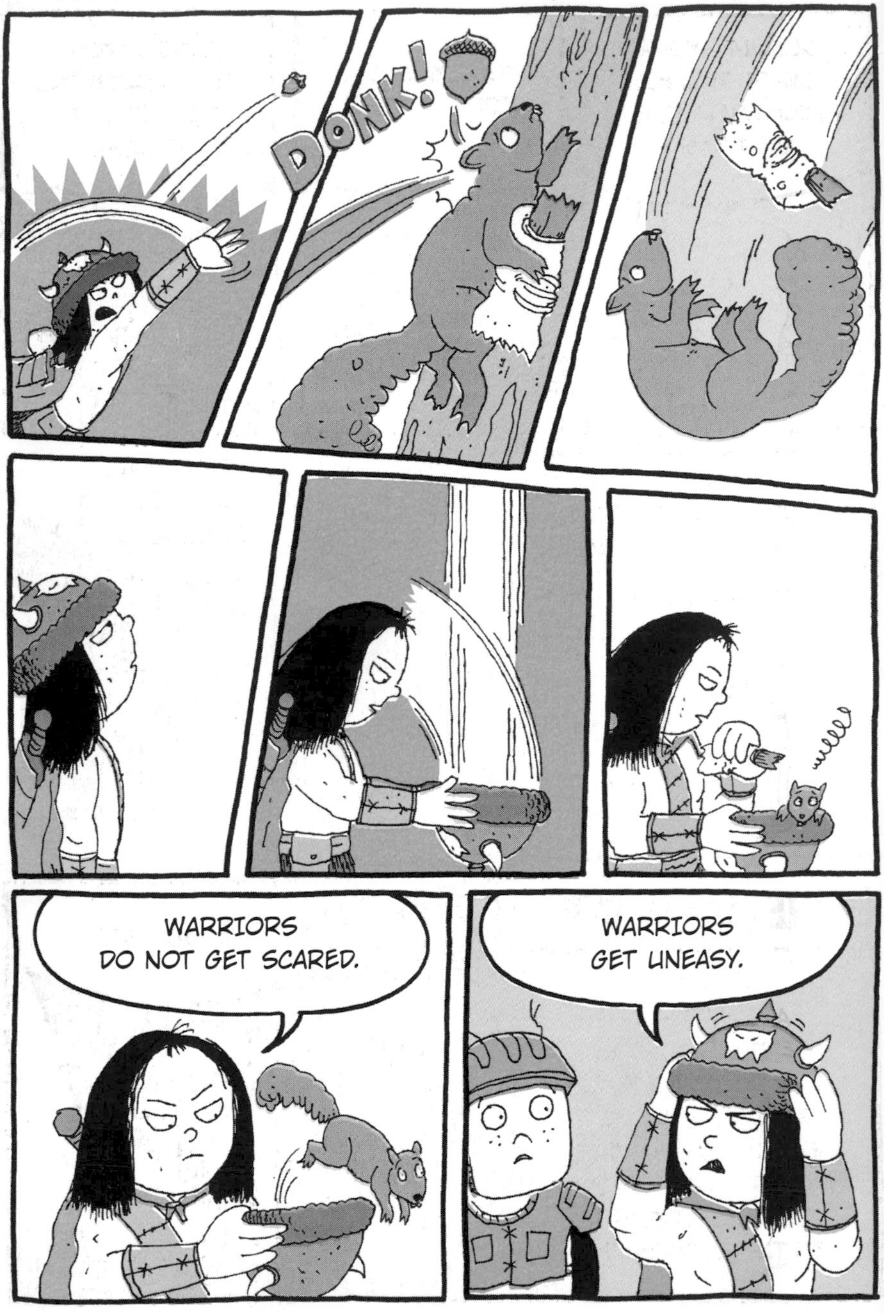
DONK!
WARRIORS DO NOT GET SCARED.
WARRIORS GET UNEASY.

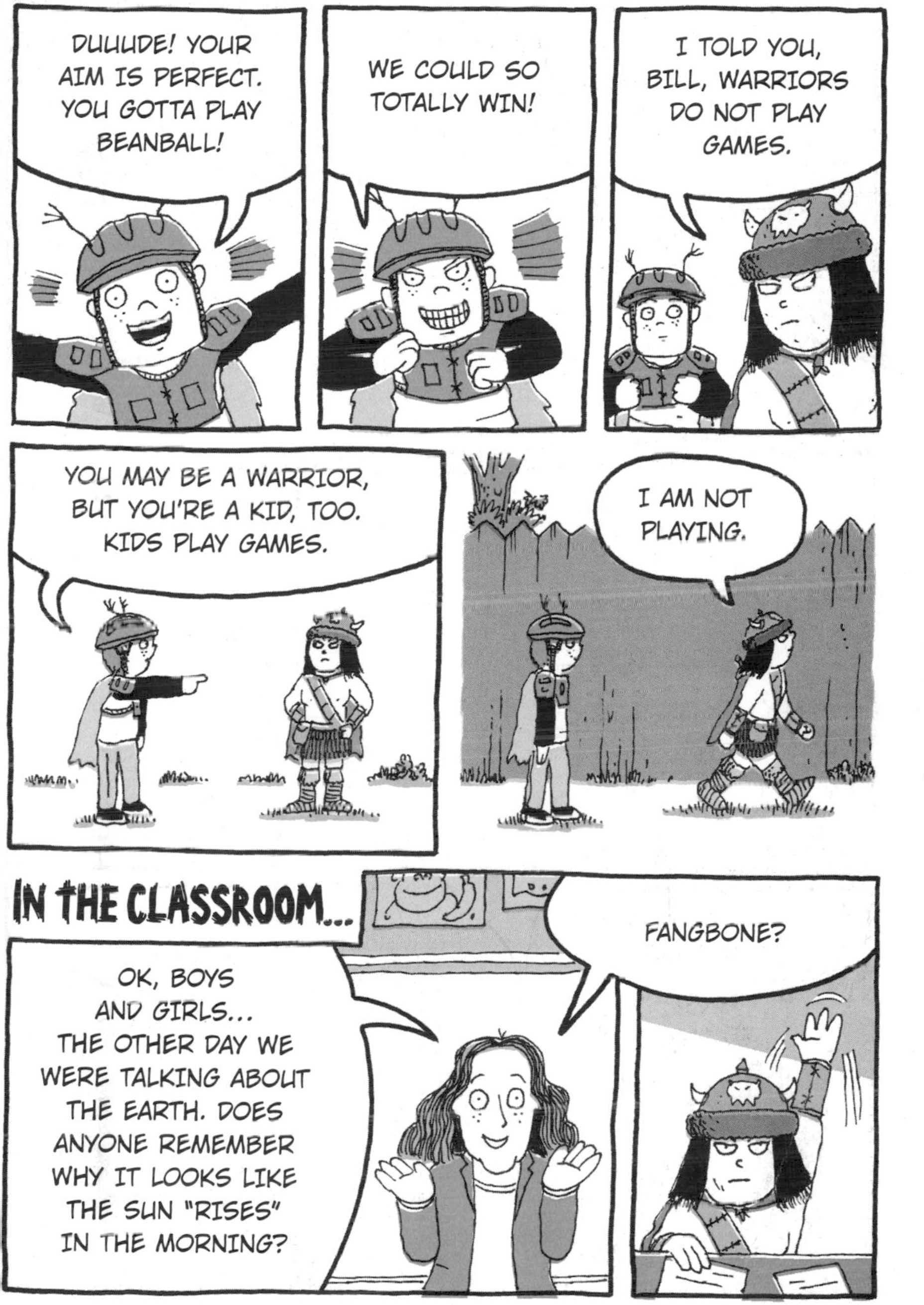
DUUUDE! YOUR AIM IS PERFECT. YOU GOTTA PLAY BEANBALL!
WE COULD SO TOTALLY WIN!
I TOLD YOU, BILL, WARRIORS DO NOT PLAY GAMES.
YOU MAY BE A WARRIOR, BUT YOU'RE A KID, TOO. KIDS PLAY GAMES.
I AM NOT PLAYING.
IN THE CLASSROOM...
OK, BOYS AND GIRLS... THE OTHER DAY WE WERE TALKING ABOUT THE EARTH. DOES ANYONE REMEMBER WHY IT LOOKS LIKE THE SUN "RISES" IN THE MORNING?
FANGBONE?

MANY THOUSANDS OF WINTERS AGO, THE WORLD WAS TOTALLY DARK. A BEAUTIFUL BUT EVIL PRINCESS NAMED ZIZZELLA RULED OVER THE ENTIRE LAND.

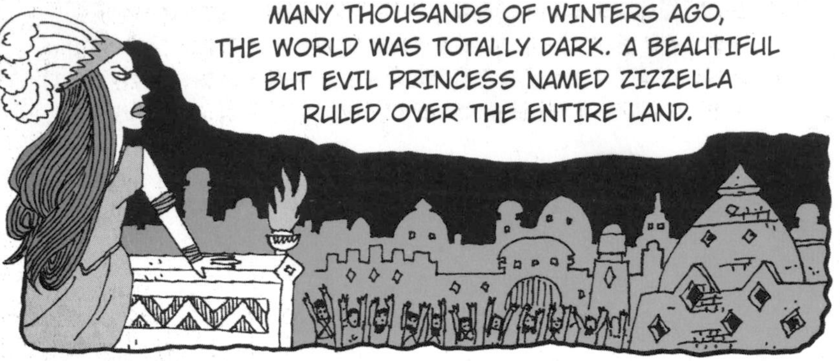

A GREAT WARRIOR NAMED STONEBACK THE SOLID ASKED ZIZZELLA TO MARRY HIM. SHE AGREED, BUT ONLY IF HE COULD BRING HER THE EYE OF THE CYCLOPTOPUS.

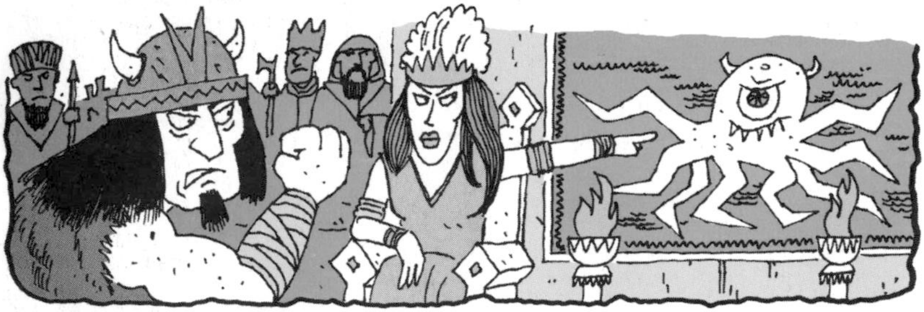

FOR YEARS, STONEBACK SEARCHED FOR THE FEARSOME CYCLOPTOPUS, WHICH WAS HARD TO FIND IN A WORLD THAT WAS TOTALLY DARK. FINALLY HE FOUND IT, SLAYED IT, AND RETURNED WITH THE EYE.

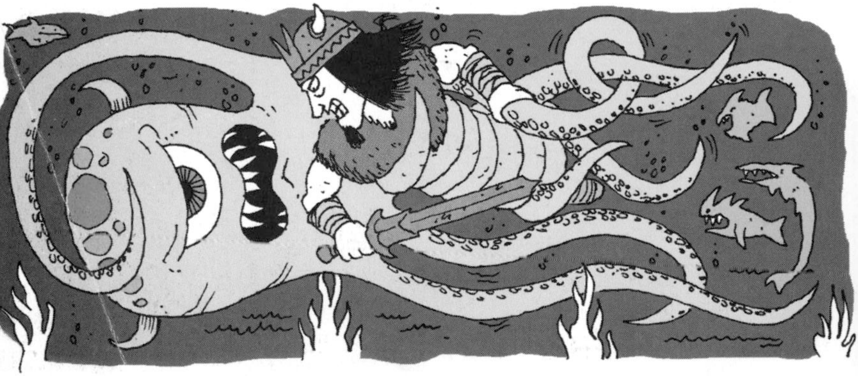

BUT ZIZZELLA NEVER WANTED TO MARRY STONEBACK. SHE THOUGHT THAT THE CYCLOPTOPUS WOULD EAT HIM AND HE WOULD NEVER RETURN. WHEN HE SHOWED UP FOR THE WEDDING, SHE AND HER SUBJECTS WERE GONE.

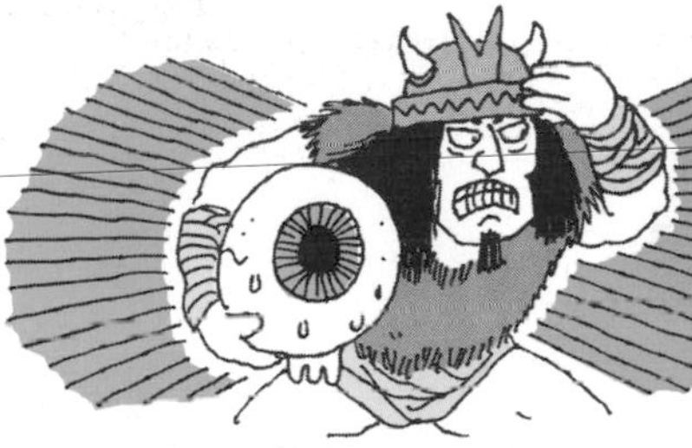

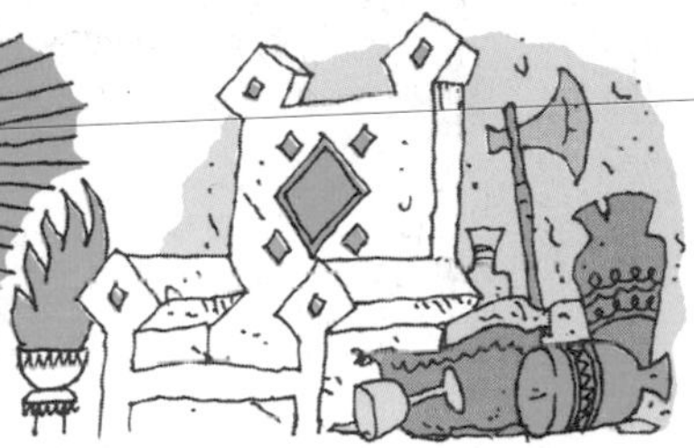

STONEBACK WAS FURIOUS! HE VOWED TO FIND HER. BUT IT WAS EASY TO HIDE IN A WORLD THAT WAS ALWAYS DARK. IN A RAGE, STONEBACK SET THE CYCLOPTOPUS EYE ON FIRE AND KICKED IT INTO THE SKY.

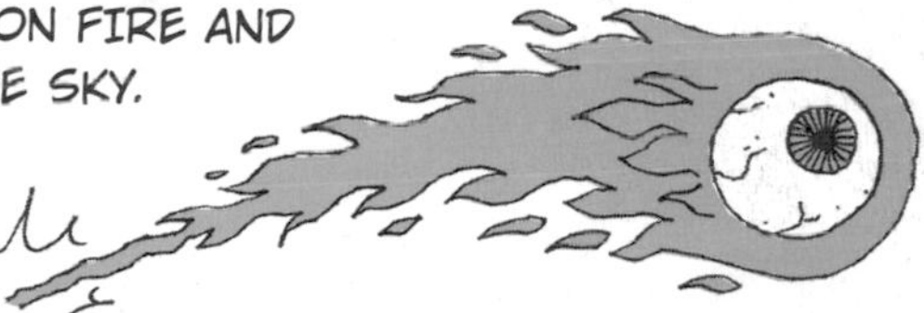

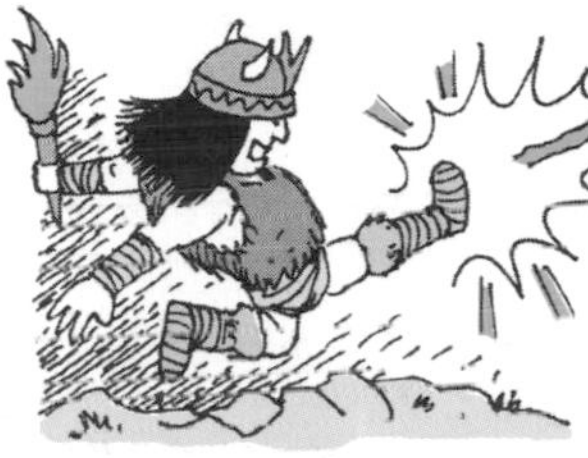

THE EYE LIT UP THE LAND, AND DAY WAS CREATED.

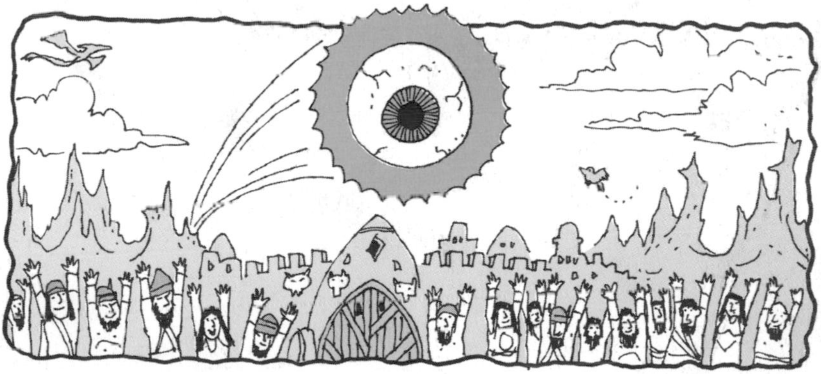

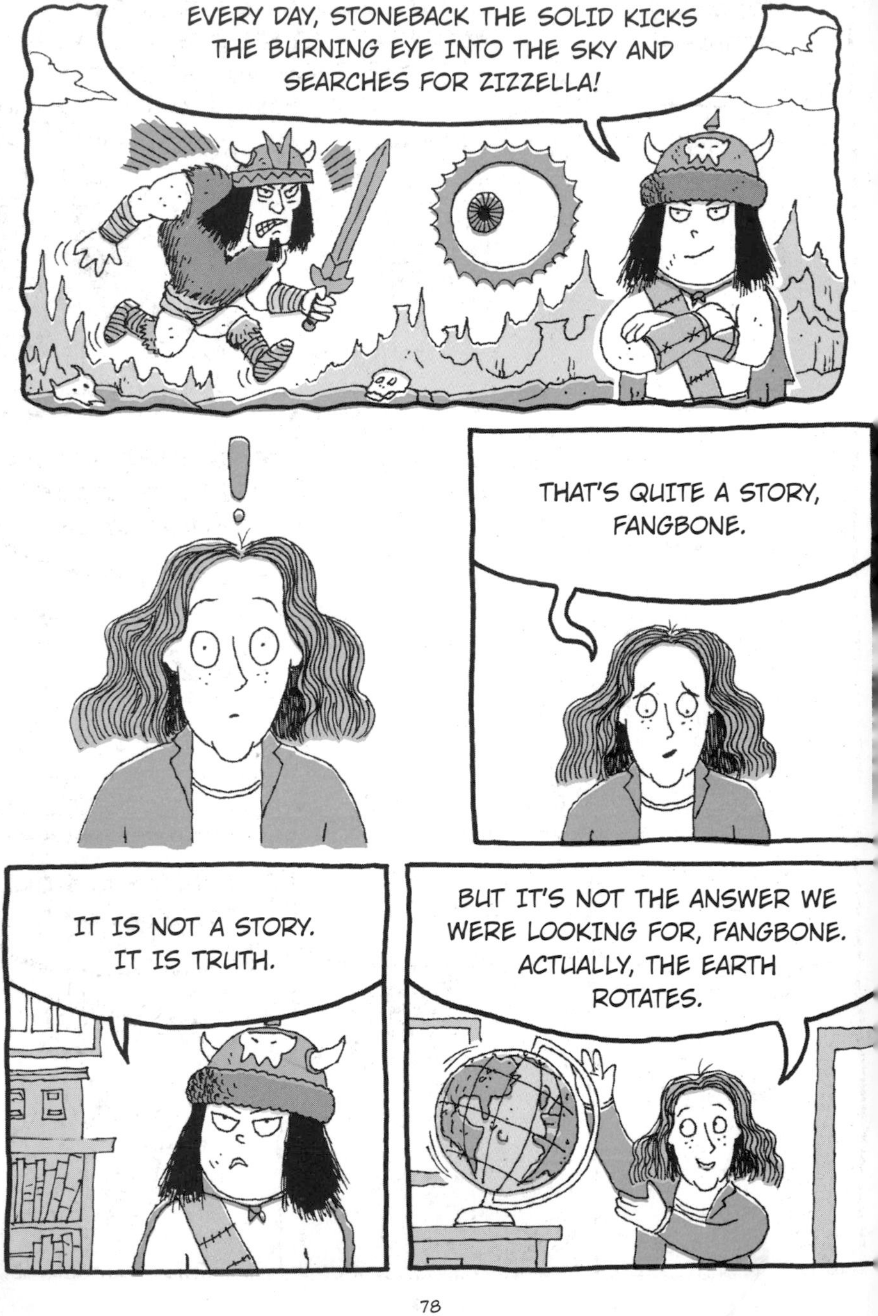
EVERY DAY, STONEBACK THE SOLID KICKS THE BURNING EYE INTO THE SKY AND SEARCHES FOR ZIZZELLA!
!
THAT'S QUITE A STORY, FANGBONE.
IT IS NOT A STORY. IT IS TRUTH.
BUT IT'S NOT THE ANSWER WE WERE LOOKING FOR, FANGBONE. ACTUALLY, THE EARTH ROTATES.

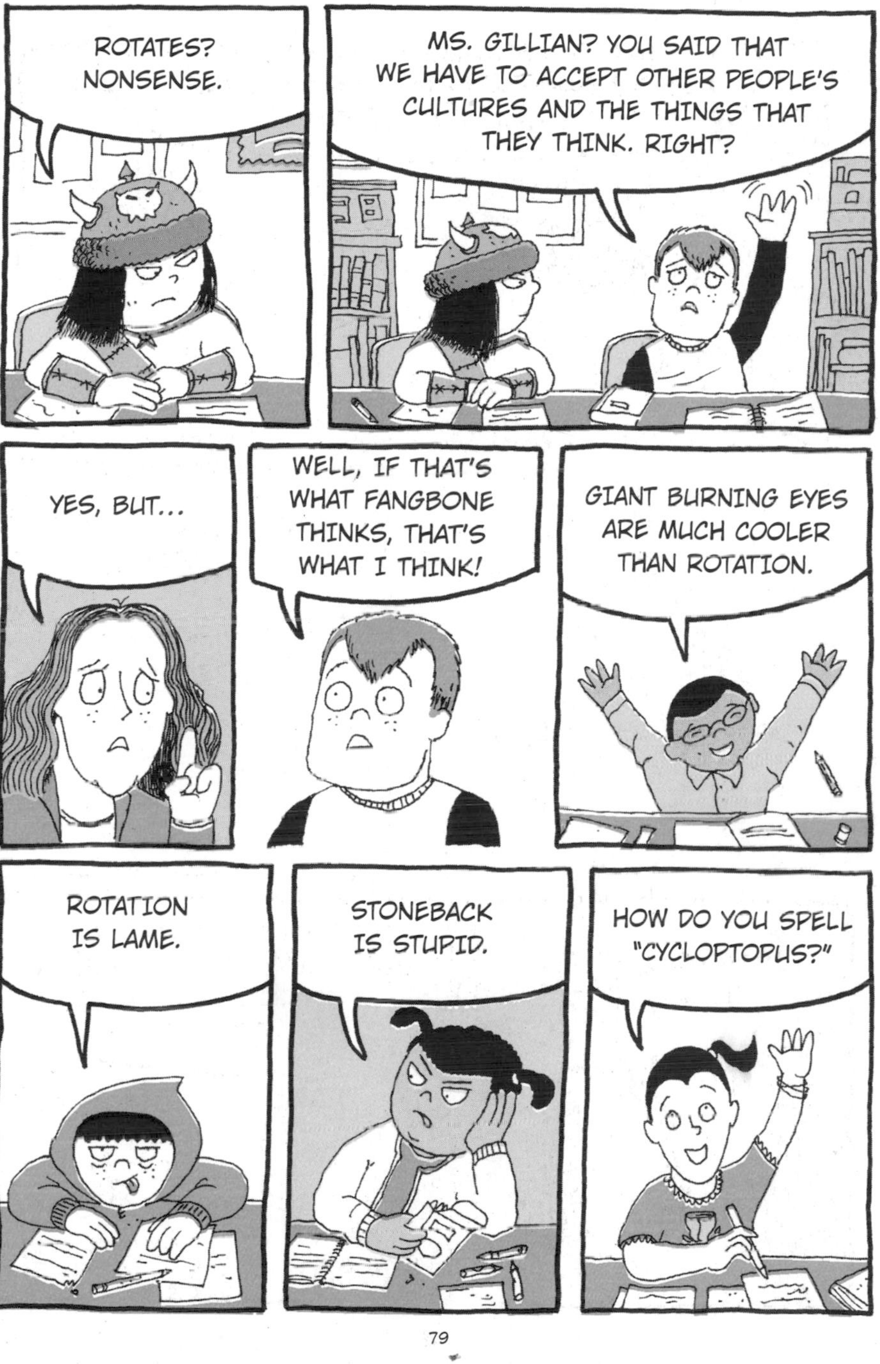
ROTATES? NONSENSE.
MS. GILLIAN? YOU SAID THAT WE HAVE TO ACCEPT OTHER PEOPLE'S CULTURES AND THE THINGS THAT THEY THINK. RIGHT?
YES, BUT...
WELL, IF THAT'S WHAT FANGBONE THINKS, THAT'S WHAT I THINK!
GIANT BURNING EYES ARE MUCH COOLER THAN ROTATION.
ROTATION IS LAME.
STONEBACK IS STUPID.
HOW DO YOU SPELL "CYCLOPTOPUS?"

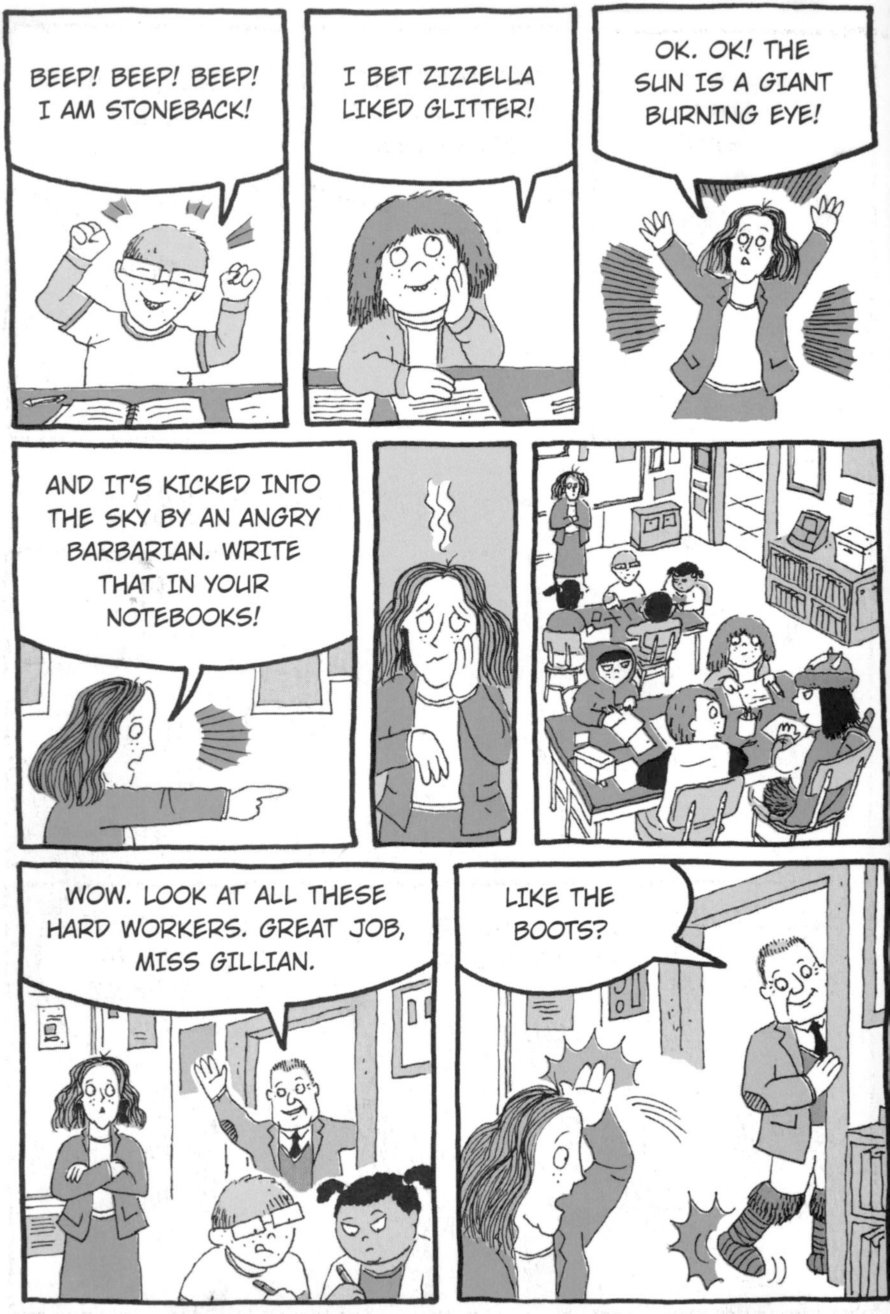
BEEP! BEEP! BEEP! I AM STONEBACK!
I BET ZIZZELLA LIKED GLITTER!
OK. OK! THE SUN IS A GIANT BURNING EYE!
AND IT'S KICKED INTO THE SKY BY AN ANGRY BARBARIAN. WRITE THAT IN YOUR NOTEBOOKS!
WOW. LOOK AT ALL THESE HARD WORKERS. GREAT JOB, MISS GILLIAN.
LIKE THE BOOTS?

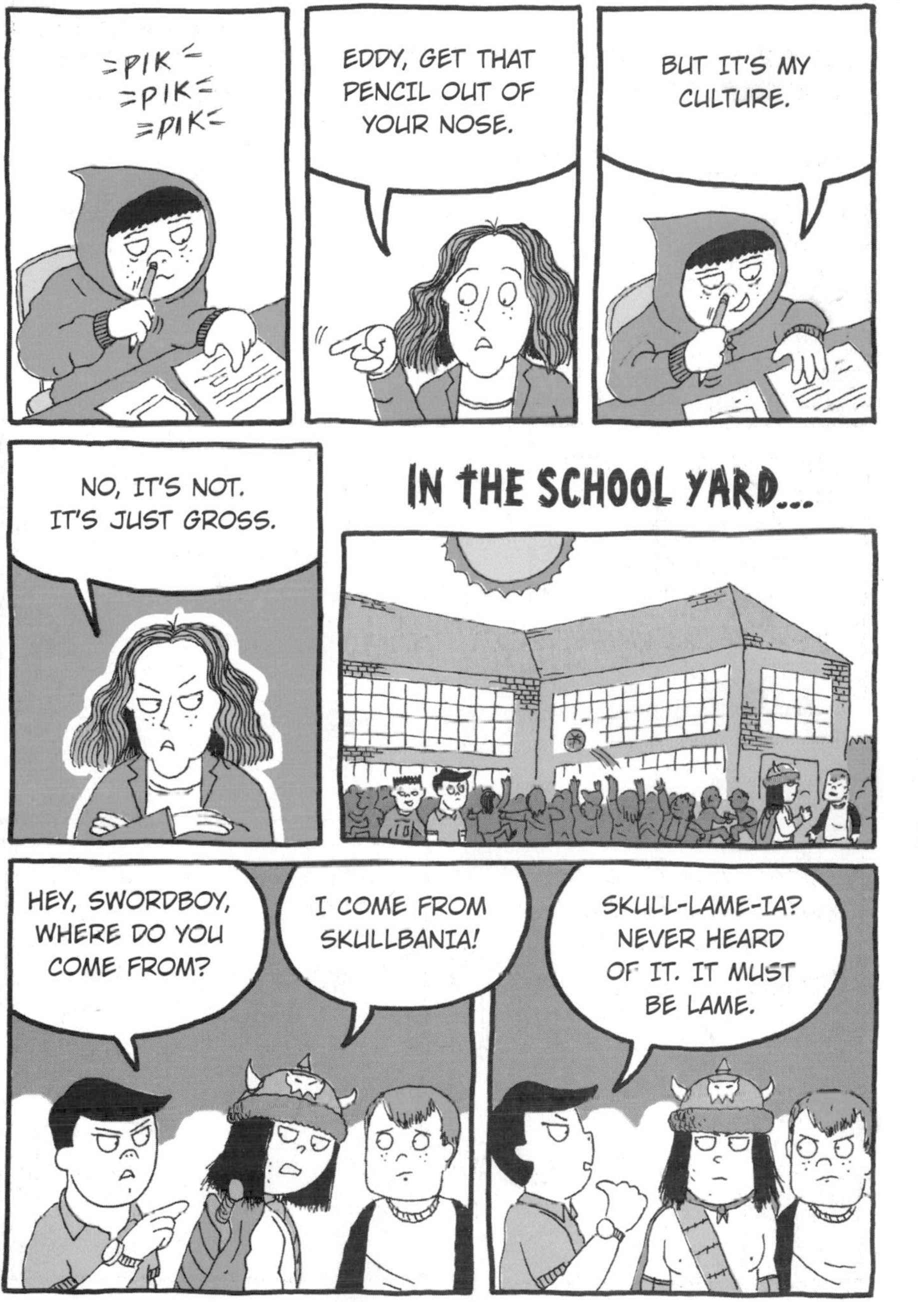
PIK
PIK
PIK
EDDY, GET THAT PENCIL OUT OF YOUR NOSE.
BUT IT'S MY CULTURE.
NO, IT'S NOT. IT'S JUST GROSS.
IN THE SCHOOL YARD...
HEY, SWORDBOY, WHERE DO YOU COME FROM?
I COME FROM SKULLBANIA!
SKULL-LAME-IA? NEVER HEARD OF IT. IT MUST BE LAME.

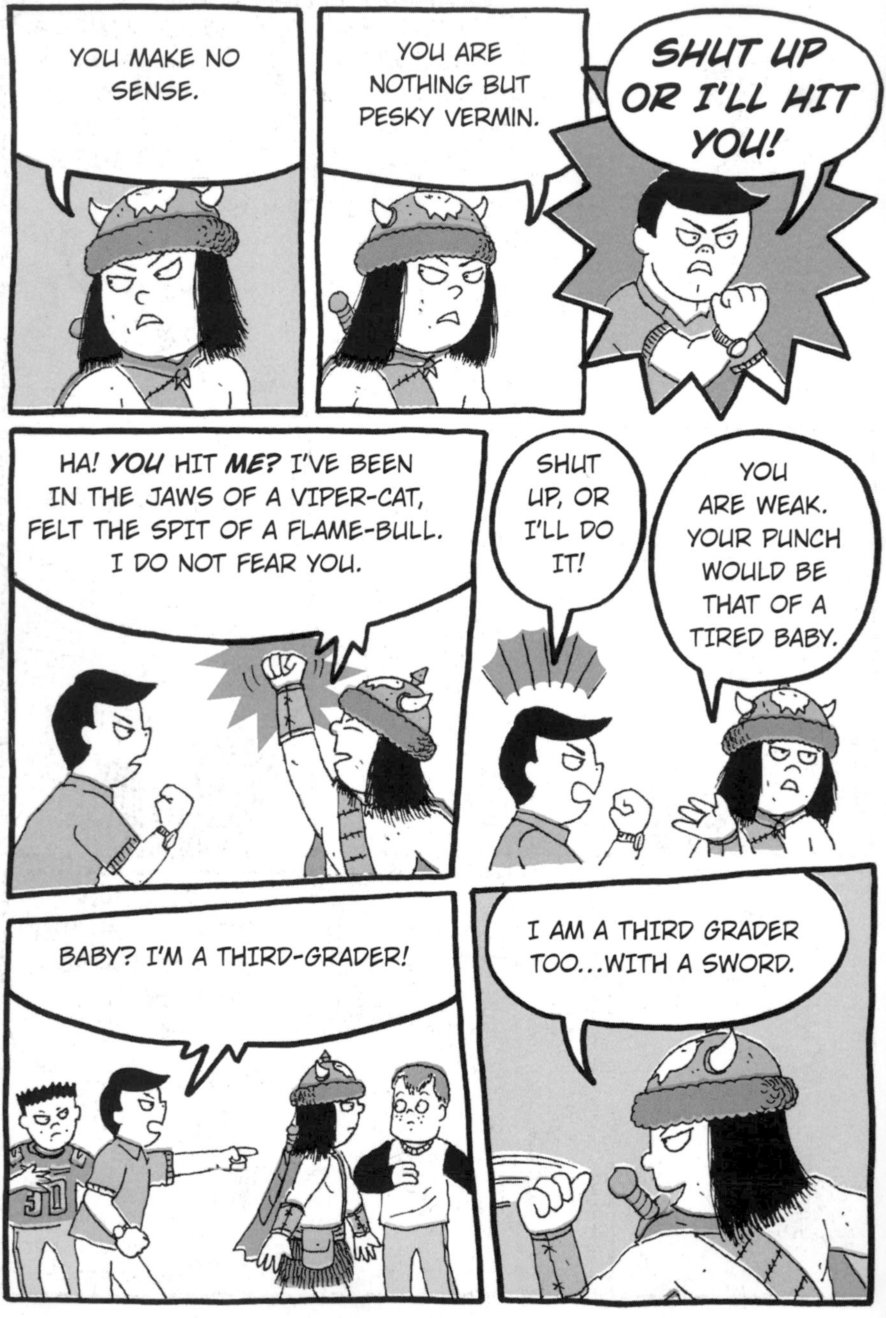
YOU MAKE NO SENSE.
YOU ARE NOTHING BUT PESKY VERMIN.
SHUT UP OR I'LL HIT YOU!
HA! YOU HIT ME? I'VE BEEN IN THE JAWS OF A VIPER-CAT, FELT THE SPIT OF A FLAME-BULL. I DO NOT FEAR YOU.
SHUT UP, OR I'LL DO IT!
YOU ARE WEAK. YOUR PUNCH WOULD BE THAT OF A TIRED BABY.
BABY? I'M A THIRD-GRADER!
I AM A THIRD GRADER TOO...WITH A SWORD.

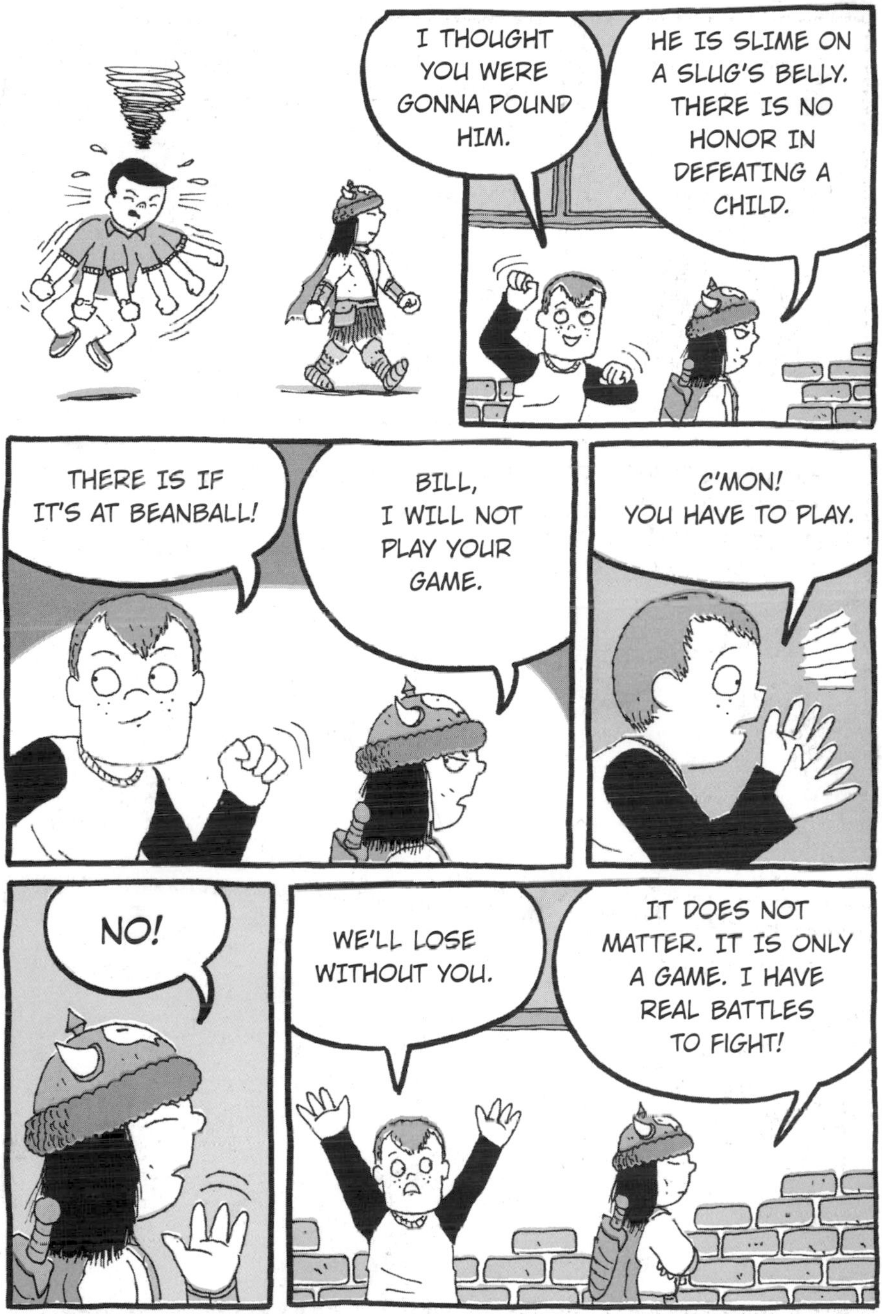
I THOUGHT YOU WERE GONNA POUND HIM.
HE IS SLIME ON A SLUG'S BELLY. THERE IS NO HONOR IN DEFEATING A CHILD.
THERE IS IF IT'S AT BEANBALL!
BILL, I WILL NOT PLAY YOUR GAME.
C'MON! YOU HAVE TO PLAY.
NO!
WE'LL LOSE WITHOUT YOU.
IT DOES NOT MATTER. IT IS ONLY A GAME. I HAVE REAL BATTLES TO FIGHT!

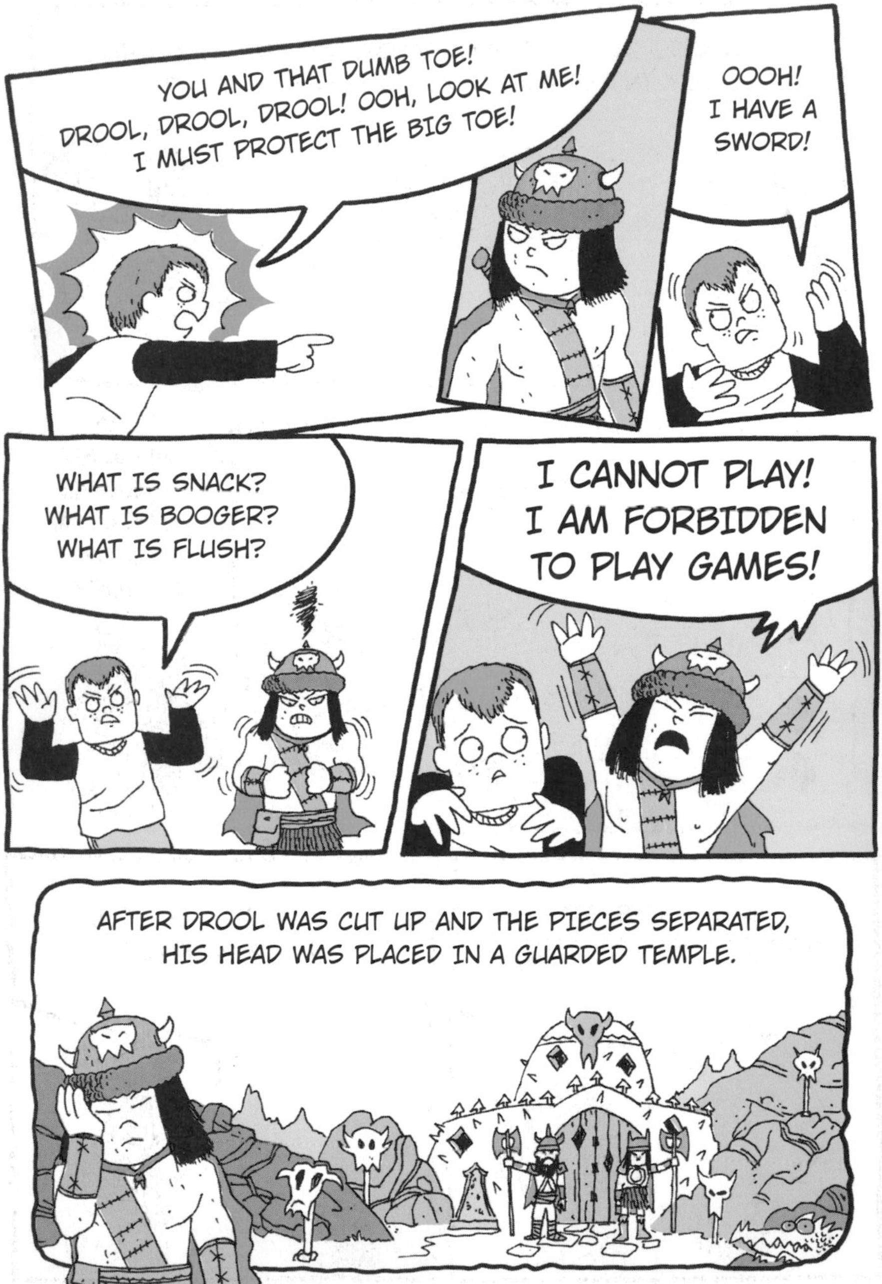
YOU AND THAT DUMB TOE! DROOL, DROOL, DROOL! OOH, LOOK AT ME! I MUST PROTECT THE BIG TOE!
OOOH! I HAVE A SWORD!
WHAT IS SNACK? WHAT IS BOOGER? WHAT IS FLUSH?
I CANNOT PLAY! I AM FORBIDDEN TO PLAY GAMES!
AFTER DROOL WAS CUT UP AND THE PIECES SEPARATED, HIS HEAD WAS PLACED IN A GUARDED TEMPLE.

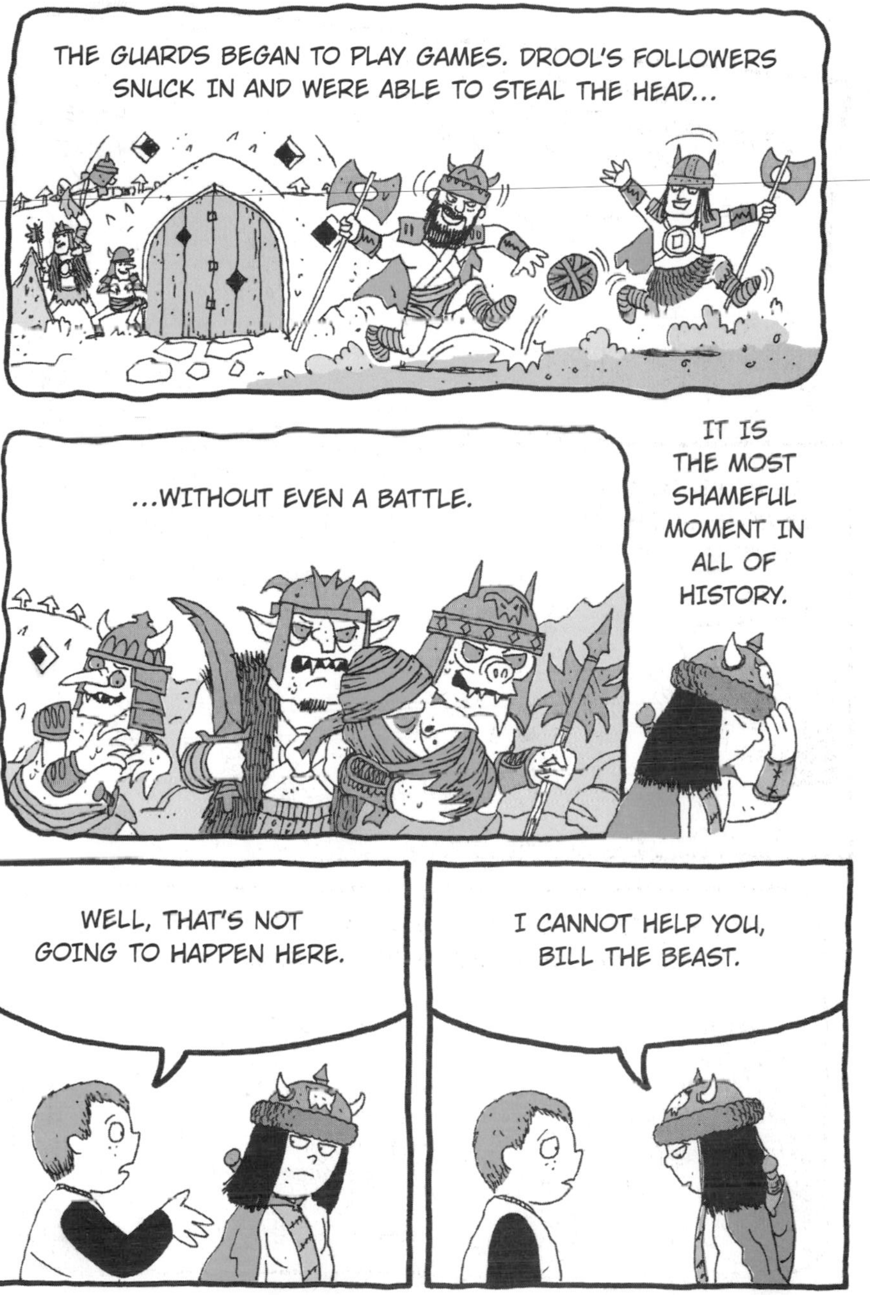
THE GUARDS BEGAN TO PLAY GAMES. DROOL'S FOLLOWERS SNUCK IN AND WERE ABLE TO STEAL THE HEAD...
...WITHOUT EVEN A BATTLE.
IT IS THE MOST SHAMEFUL MOMENT IN ALL OF HISTORY.
WELL, THAT'S NOT GOING TO HAPPEN HERE.
I CANNOT HELP YOU, BILL THE BEAST.

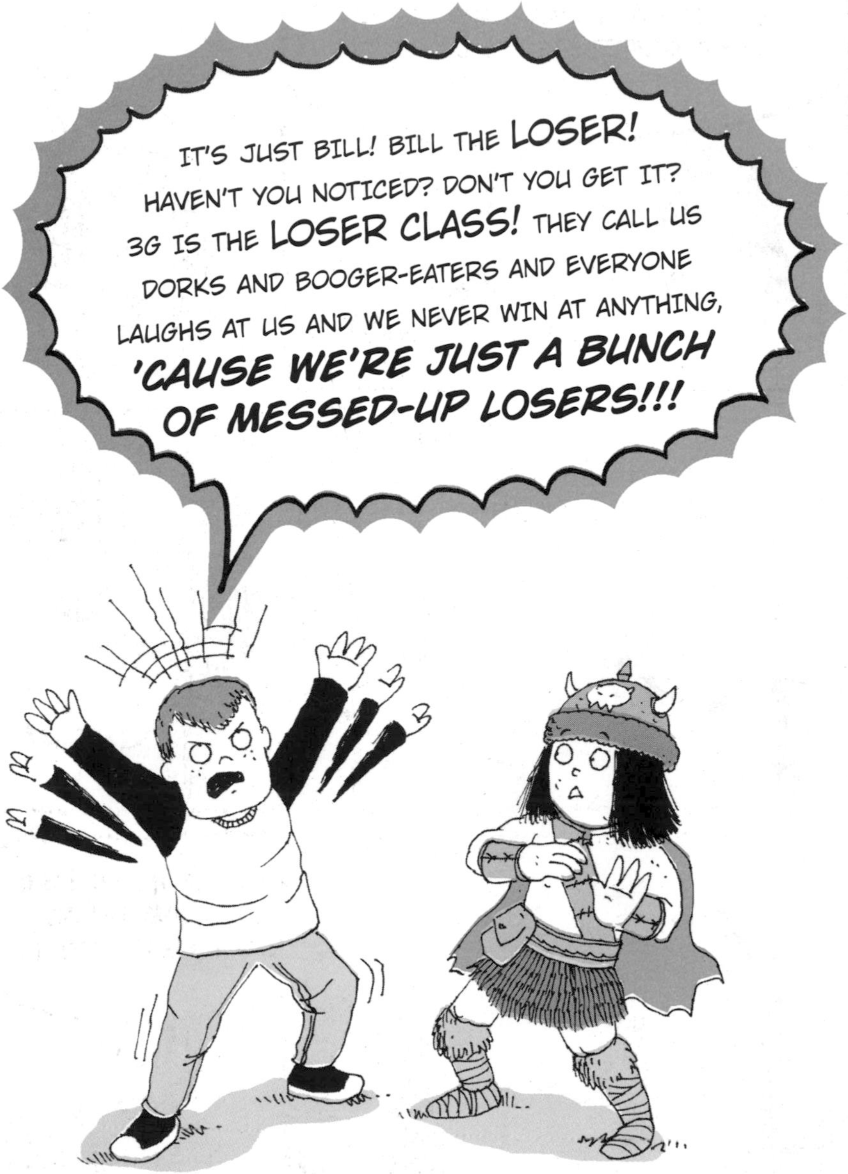
IT'S JUST BILL! BILL THE LOSER! HAVEN'T YOU NOTICED? DON'T YOU GET IT? 3G IS THE LOSER CLASS! THEY CALL US DORKS AND BOOGER-EATERS AND EVERYONE LAUGHS AT US AND WE NEVER WIN AT ANYTHING, 'CAUSE WE'RE JUST A BUNCH OF MESSED-UP LOSERS!!!

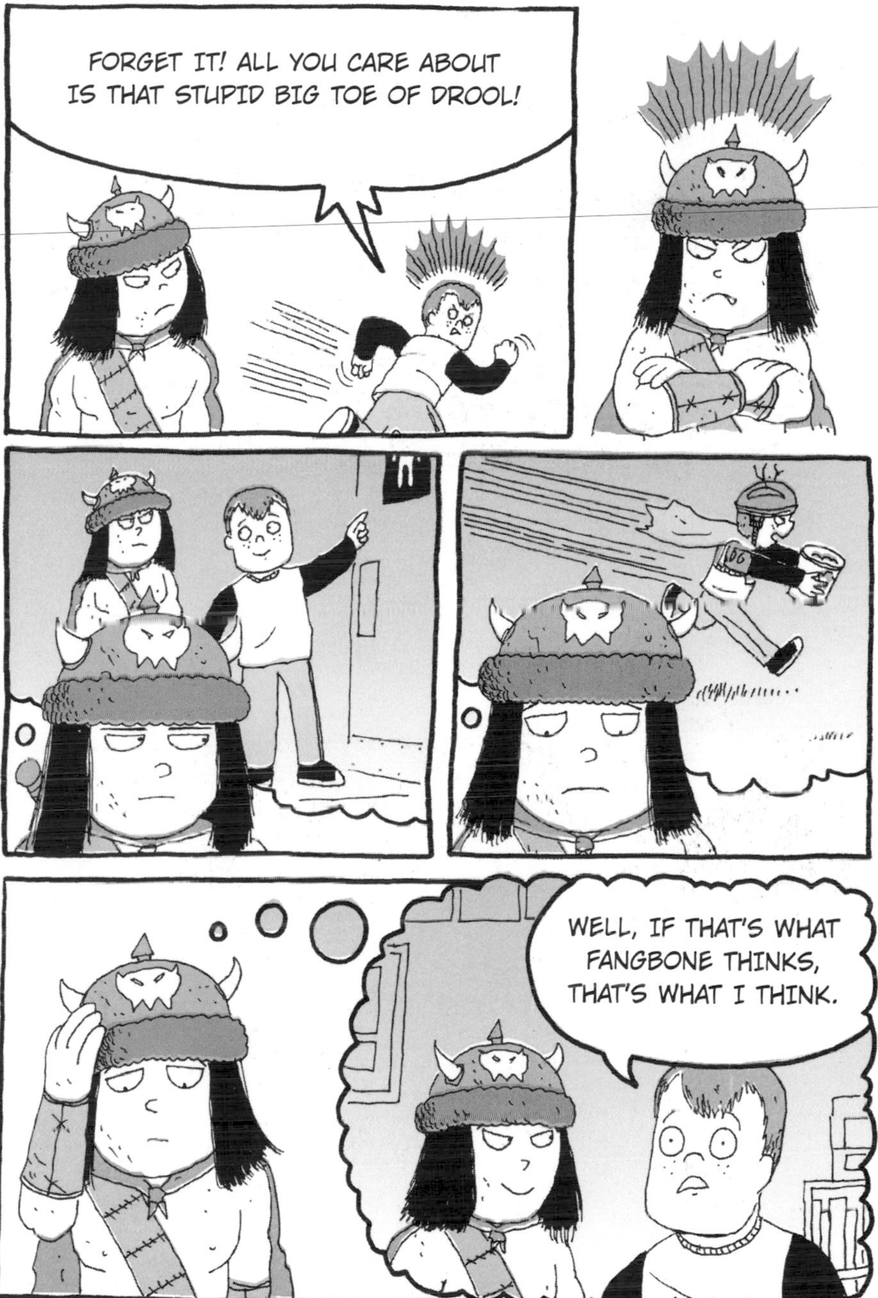
FORGET IT! ALL YOU CARE ABOUT IS THAT STUPID BIG TOE OF DROOL!
WELL, IF THAT'S WHAT FANGBONE THINKS, THAT'S WHAT I THINK.

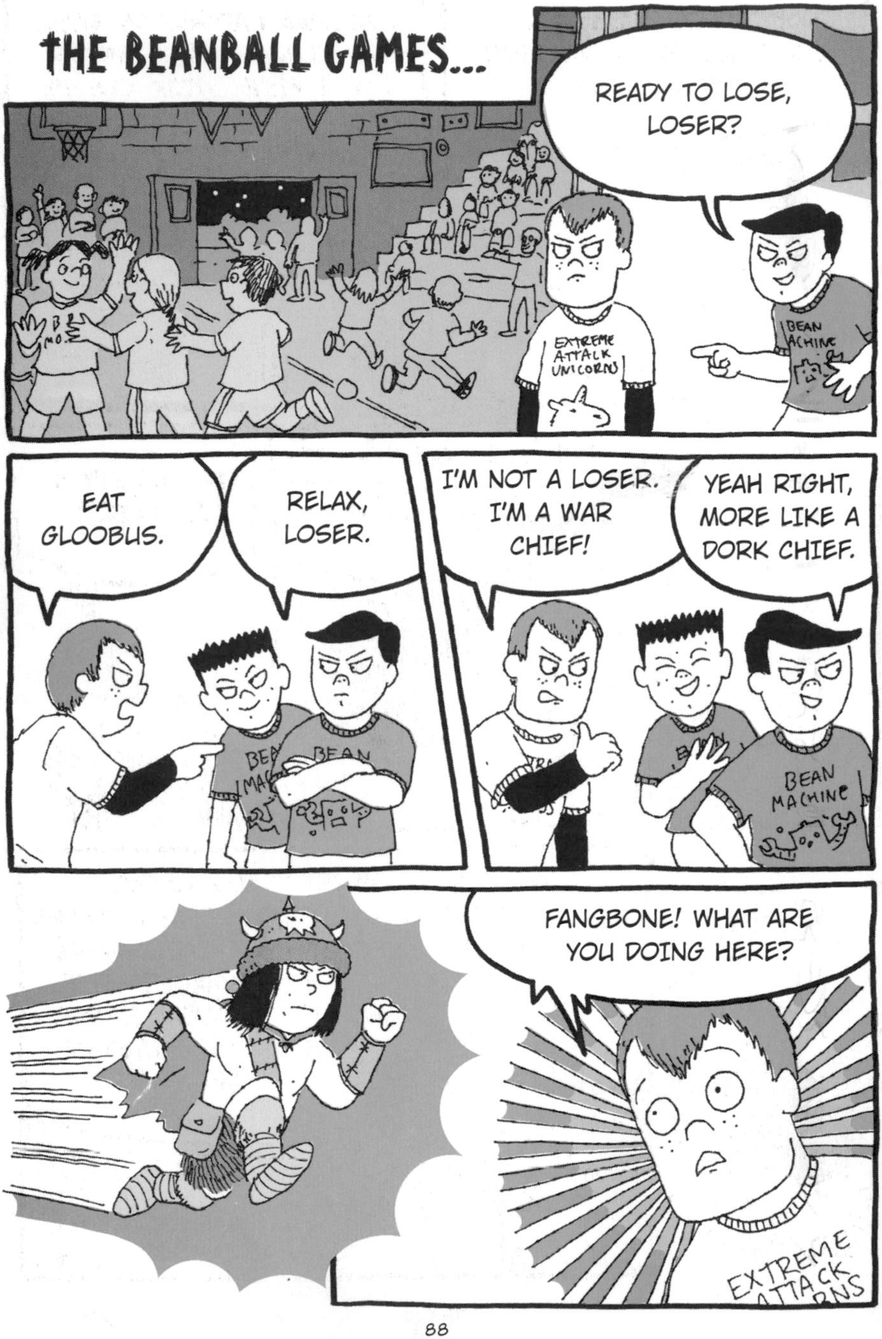
THE BEANBALL GAMES...
READY TO LOSE, LOSER?
EAT GLOOBUS.
RELAX, LOSER.
I'M NOT A LOSER. I'M A WAR CHIEF!
YEAH RIGHT, MORE LIKE A DORK CHIEF.
FANGBONE! WHAT ARE YOU DOING HERE?

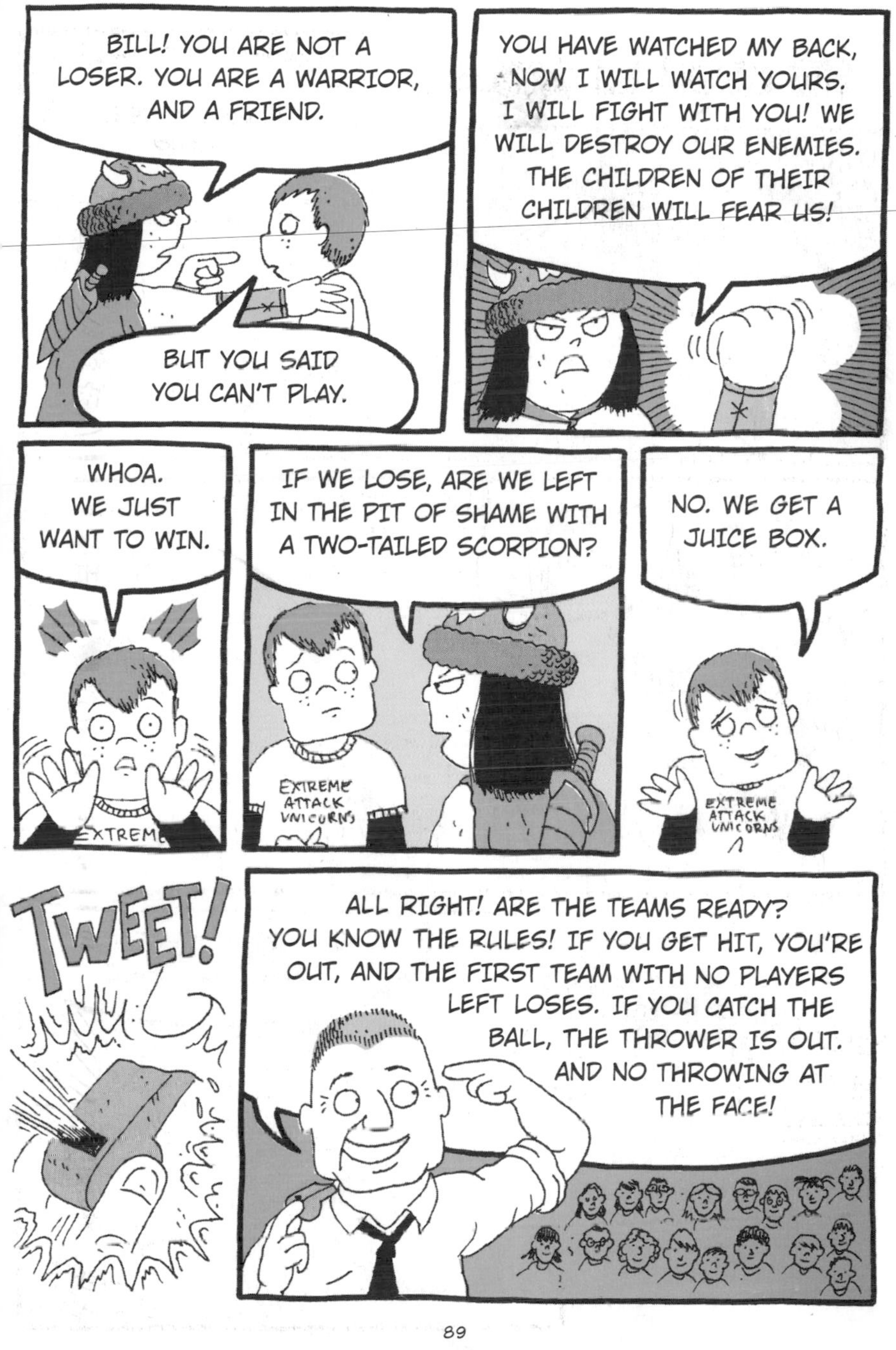
BILL! YOU ARE NOT A LOSER. YOU ARE A WARRIOR, AND A FRIEND.
BUT YOU SAID YOU CAN'T PLAY.
YOU HAVE WATCHED MY BACK, NOW I WILL WATCH YOURS. I WILL FIGHT WITH YOU! WE WILL DESTROY OUR ENEMIES. THE CHILDREN OF THEIR CHILDREN WILL FEAR US!
WHOA. WE JUST WANT TO WIN.
EXTREME
IF WE LOSE, ARE WE LEFT IN THE PIT OF SHAME WITH A TWO-TAILED SCORPION?
EXTREME ATTACK UNICORNS
NO. WE GET A JUICE BOX.
EXTREME ATTACK UNICORNS
TWEET!
ALL RIGHT! ARE THE TEAMS READY? YOU KNOW THE RULES! IF YOU GET HIT, YOU'RE OUT, AND THE FIRST TEAM WITH NO PLAYERS LEFT LOSES. IF YOU CATCH THE BALL, THE THROWER IS OUT. AND NO THROWING AT THE FACE!

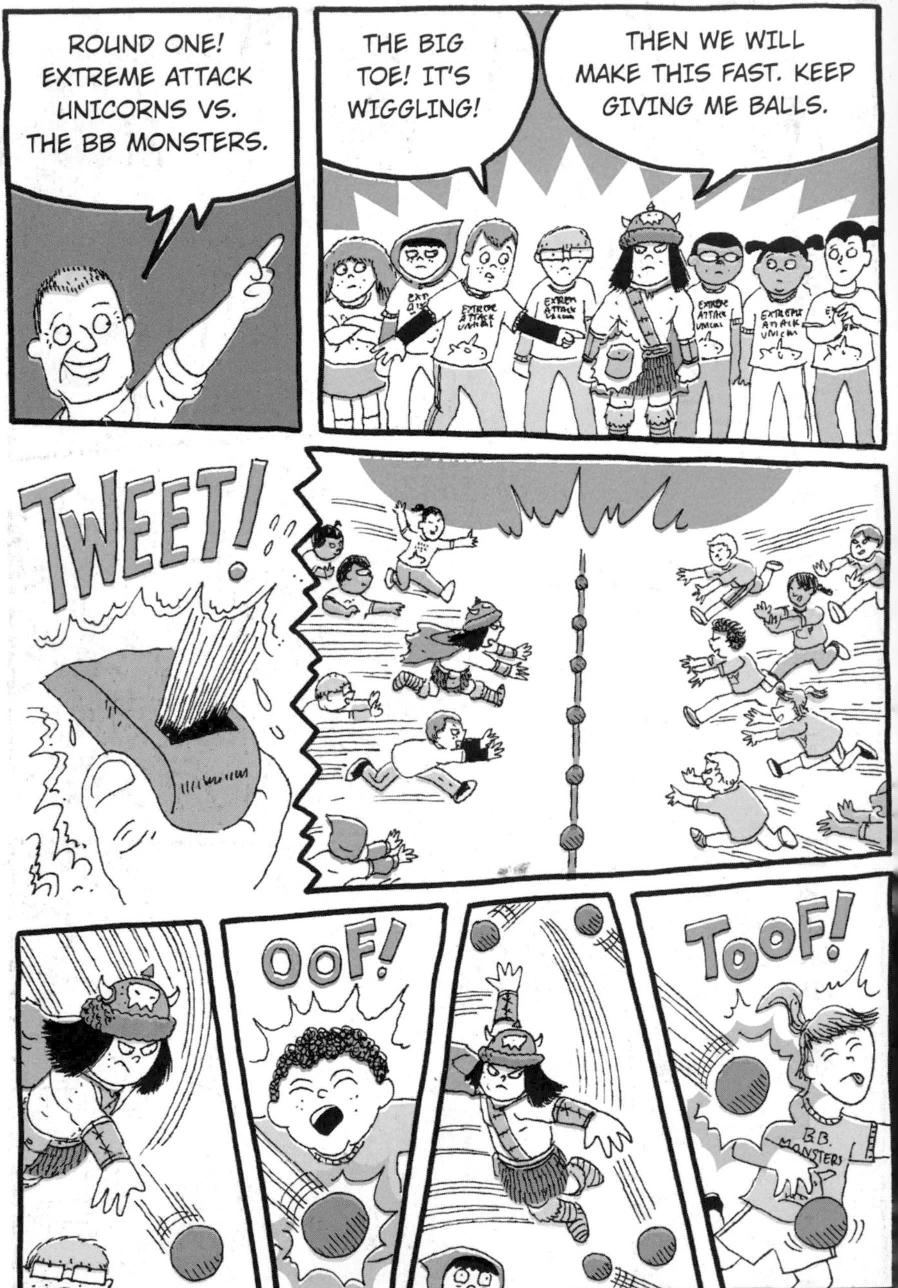
ROUND ONE! EXTREME ATTACK UNICORNS VS. THE BB MONSTERS.
THE BIG TOE! IT'S WIGGLING!
THEN WE WILL MAKE THIS FAST. KEEP GIVING ME BALLS.
TWEET!
OOF!
TOOF!
B.B. MONSTERS

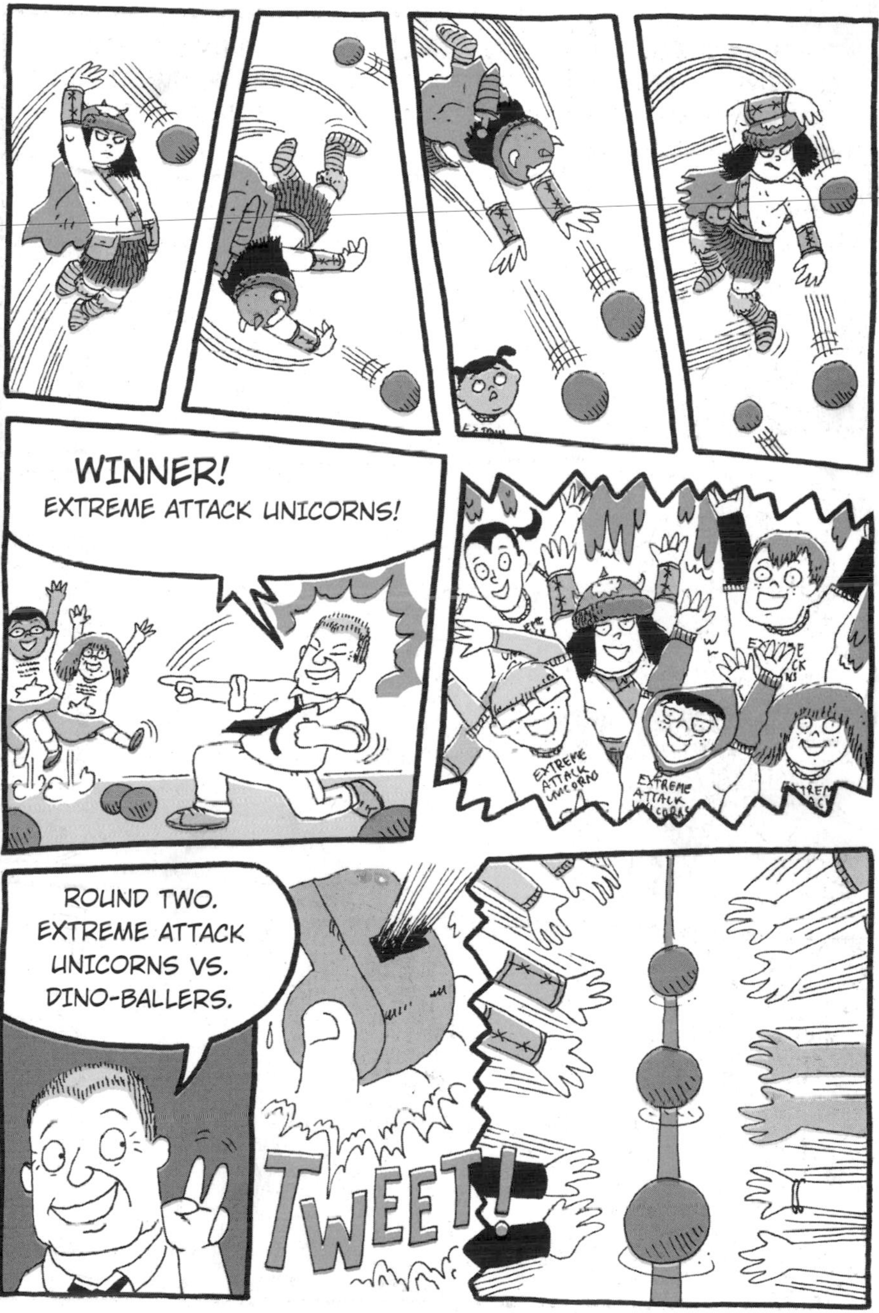
WINNER!
EXTREME ATTACK UNICORNS!
EXTREME ATTACK UNICORNS
ROUND TWO. EXTREME ATTACK UNICORNS VS. DINO-BALLERS.
TWEET!

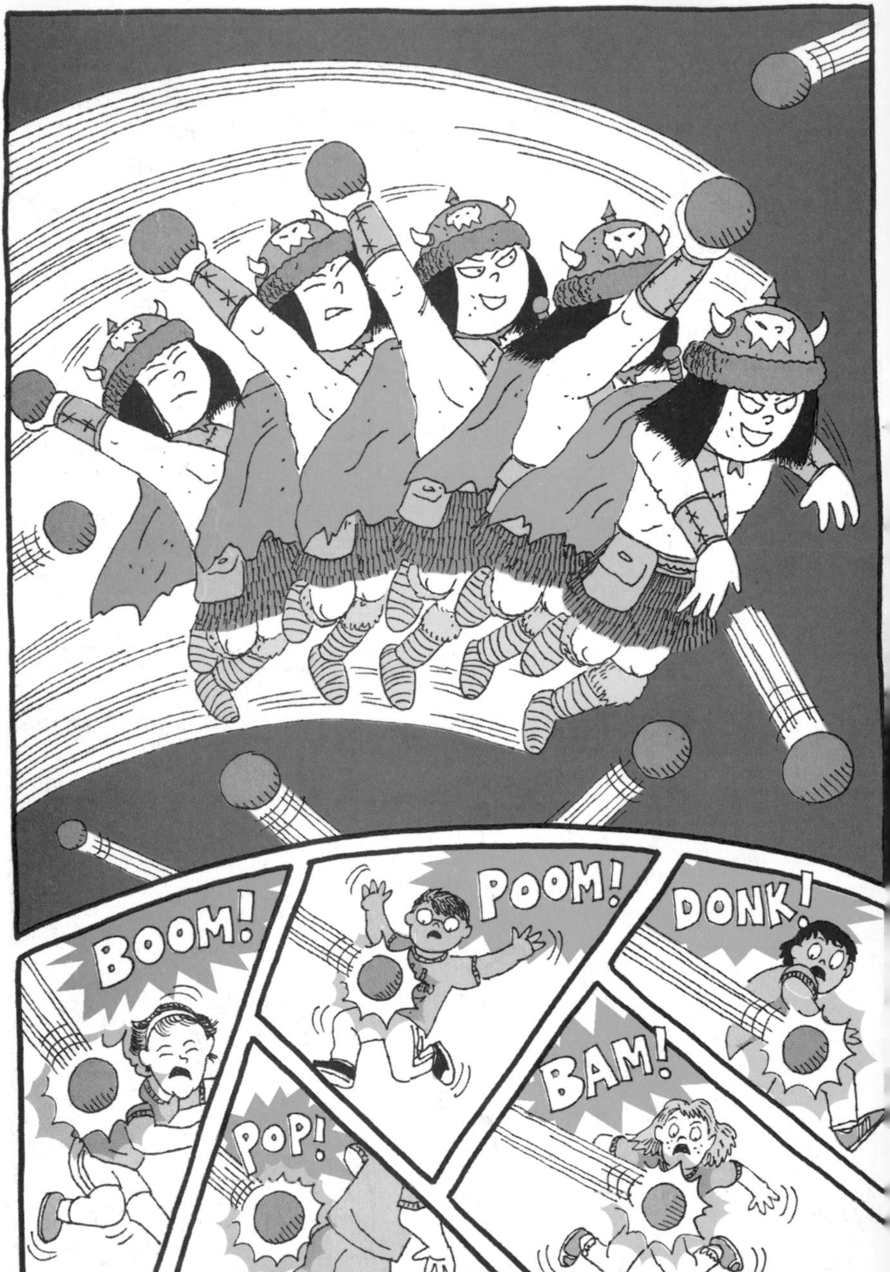
BOOM!
POOM!
DONK!
POP!
BAM!

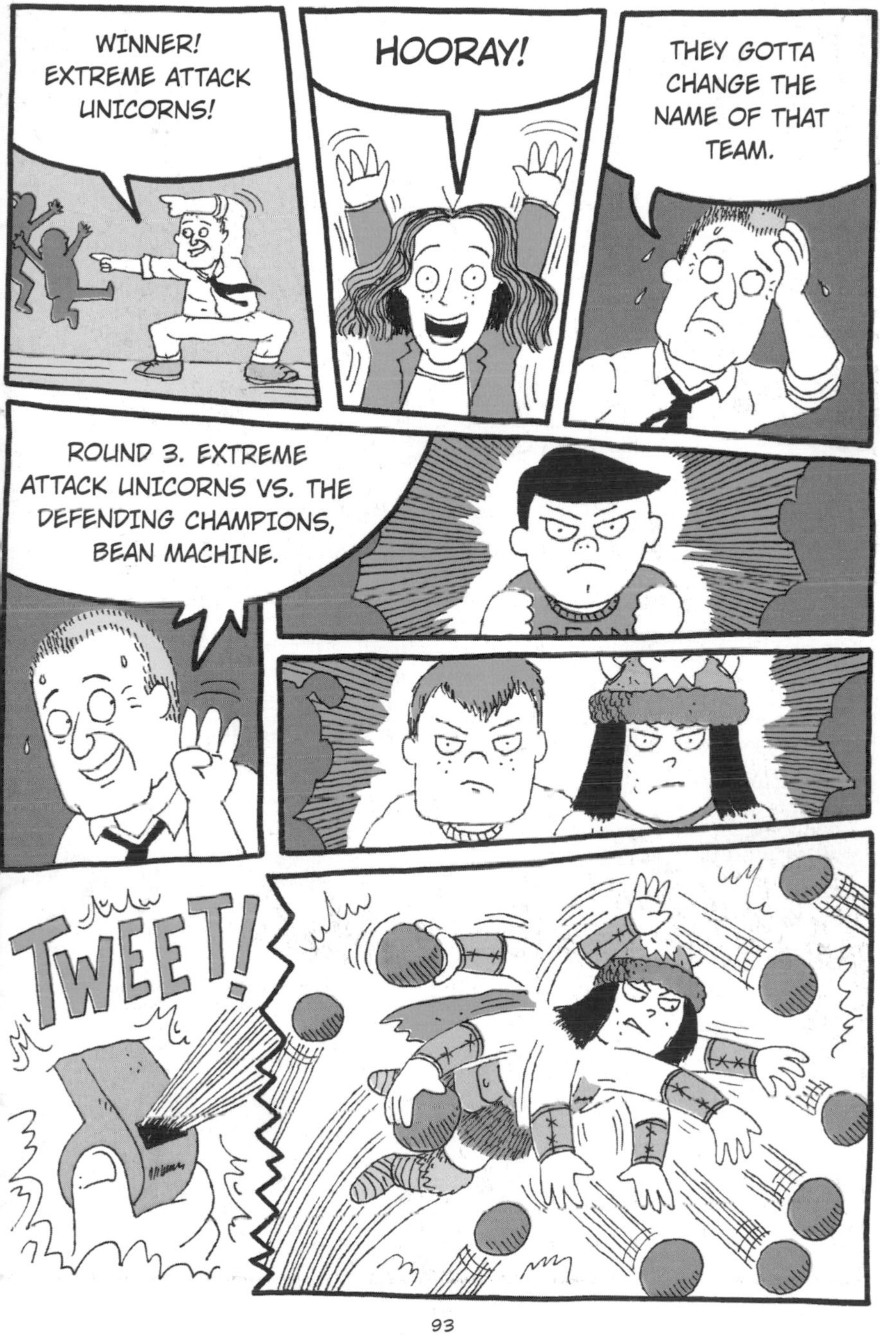
WINNER! EXTREME ATTACK UNICORNS!
HOORAY!
THEY GOTTA CHANGE THE NAME OF THAT TEAM.
ROUND 3. EXTREME ATTACK UNICORNS VS. THE DEFENDING CHAMPIONS, BEAN MACHINE.
TWEET!

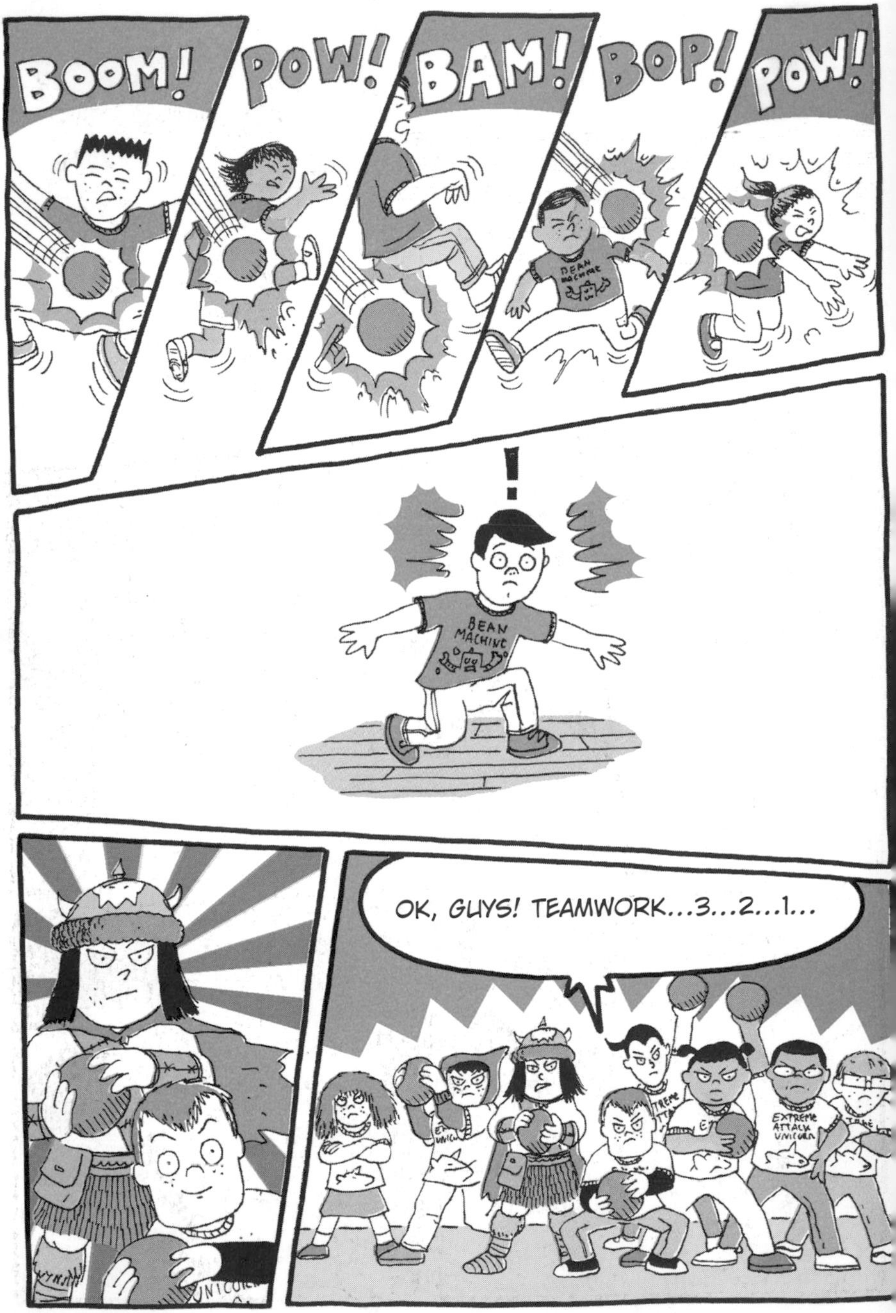
BOOM!
POW!
BAM!
BOP!
POW!
!
OK, GUYS! TEAMWORK...3...2...1...

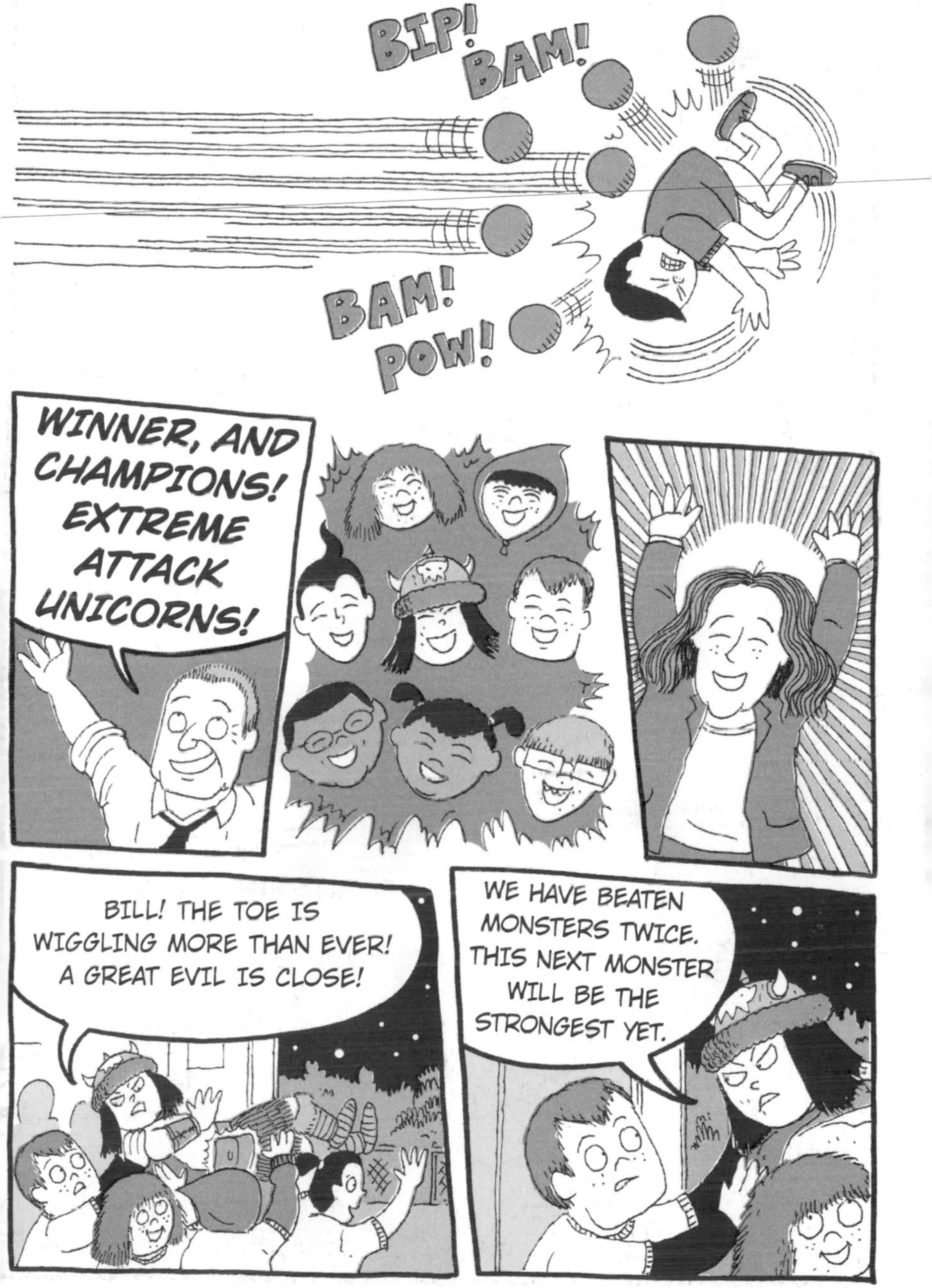
BIP!
BAM!
BAM!
POW!
WINNER, AND CHAMPIONS! EXTREME ATTACK UNICORNS!
BILL! THE TOE IS WIGGLING MORE THAN EVER! A GREAT EVIL IS CLOSE!
WE HAVE BEATEN MONSTERS TWICE. THIS NEXT MONSTER WILL BE THE STRONGEST YET.

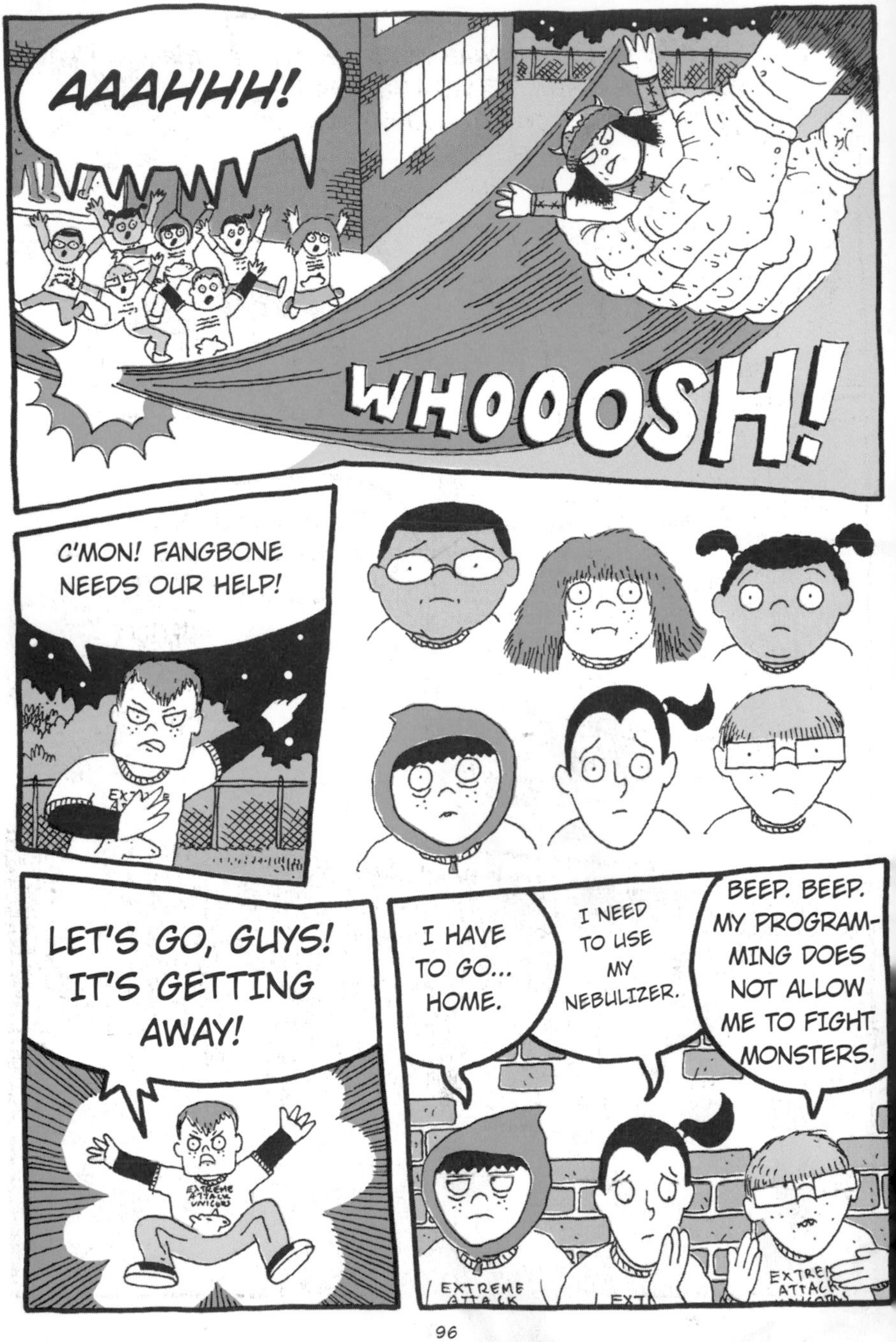
AAAHHH!
WHOOOSH!
C'MON! FANGBONE NEEDS OUR HELP!
LET'S GO, GUYS! IT'S GETTING AWAY!
EXTREME ATTACK UNICORNS
I HAVE TO GO... HOME.
I NEED TO USE MY NEBULIZER.
BEEP. BEEP. MY PROGRAMMING DOES NOT ALLOW ME TO FIGHT MONSTERS.

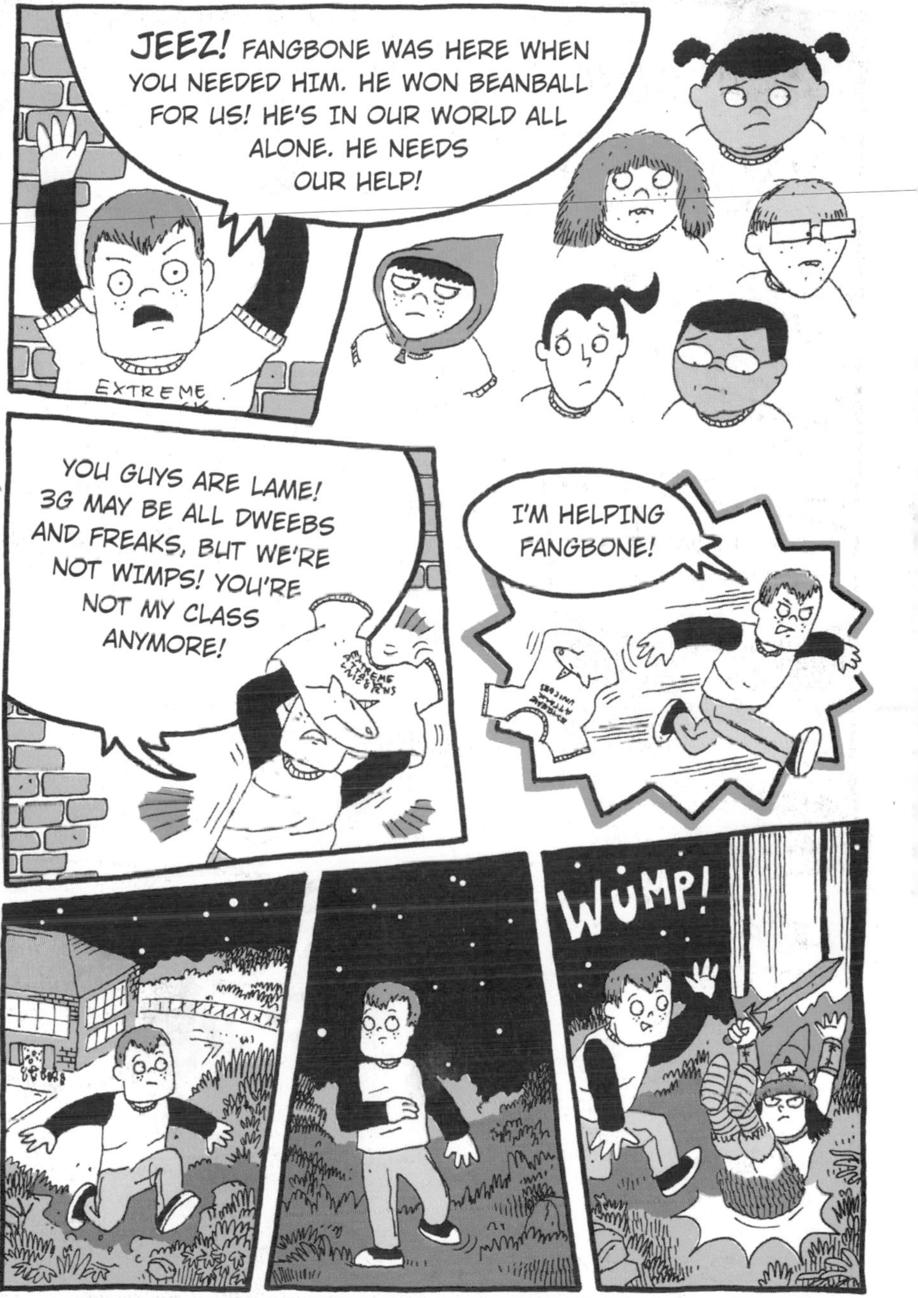
JEEZ! FANGBONE WAS HERE WHEN YOU NEEDED HIM. HE WON BEANBALL FOR US! HE'S IN OUR WORLD ALL ALONE. HE NEEDS OUR HELP!
EXTREME
YOU GUYS ARE LAME! 3G MAY BE ALL DWEEBS AND FREAKS, BUT WE'RE NOT WIMPS! YOU'RE NOT MY CLASS ANYMORE!
I'M HELPING FANGBONE!
WUMP!

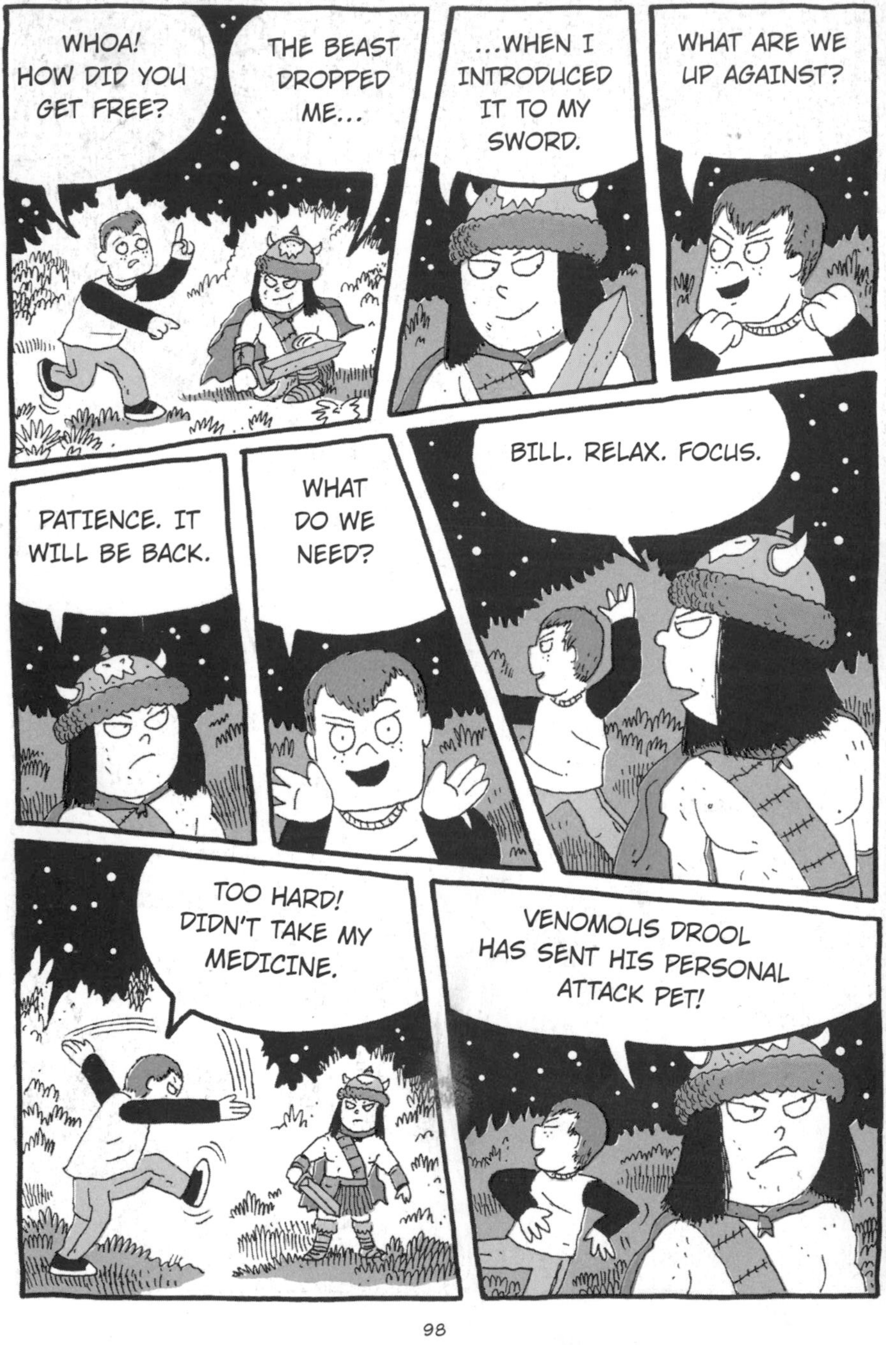
WHOA! HOW DID YOU GET FREE?
THE BEAST DROPPED ME...
...WHEN I INTRODUCED IT TO MY SWORD.
WHAT ARE WE UP AGAINST?
PATIENCE. IT WILL BE BACK.
WHAT DO WE NEED?
BILL. RELAX. FOCUS.
TOO HARD! DIDN'T TAKE MY MEDICINE.
VENOMOUS DROOL HAS SENT HIS PERSONAL ATTACK PET!

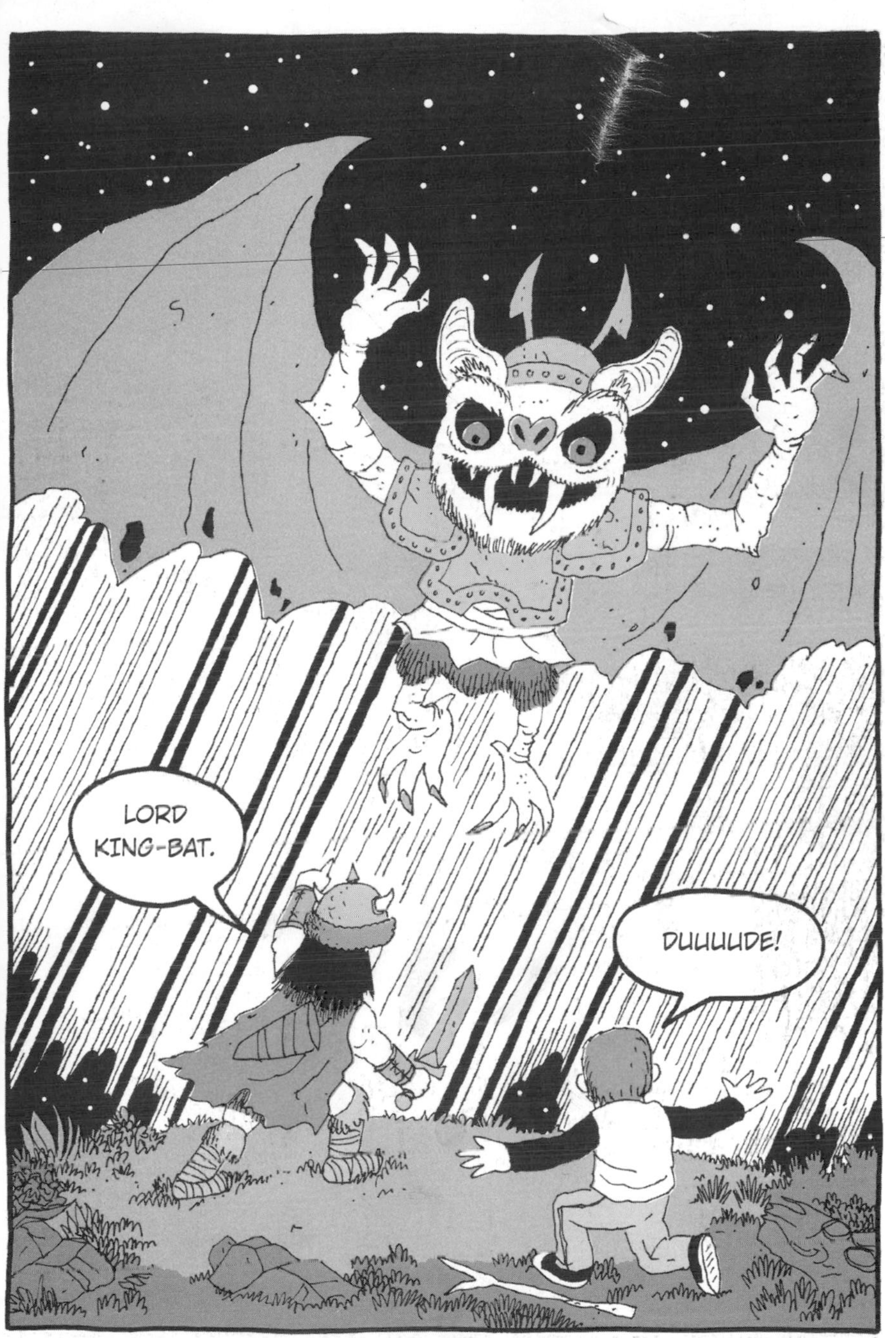
LORD KING-BAT.
DUUUUDE!

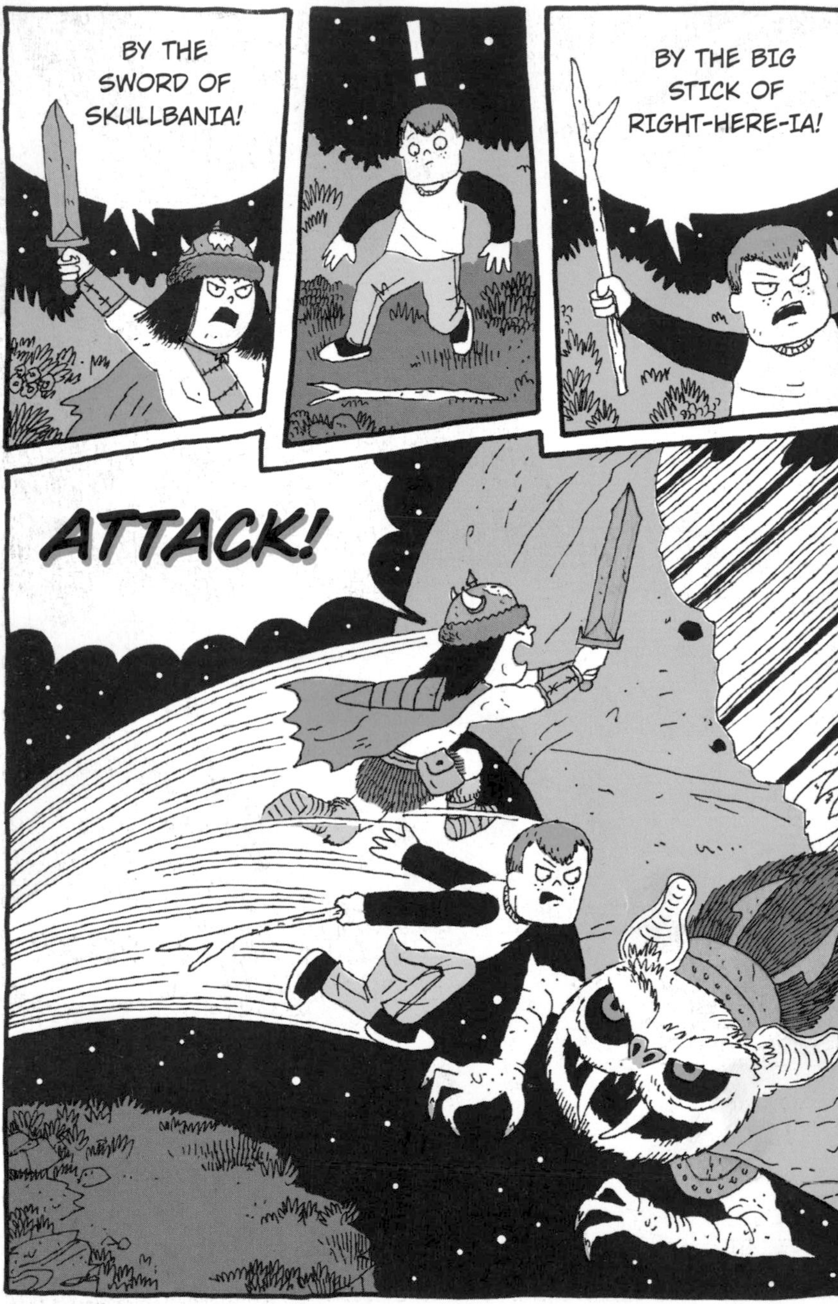

BY THE SWORD OF SKULLBANIA!
!
BY THE BIG STICK OF RIGHT-HERE-IA!
ATTACK!

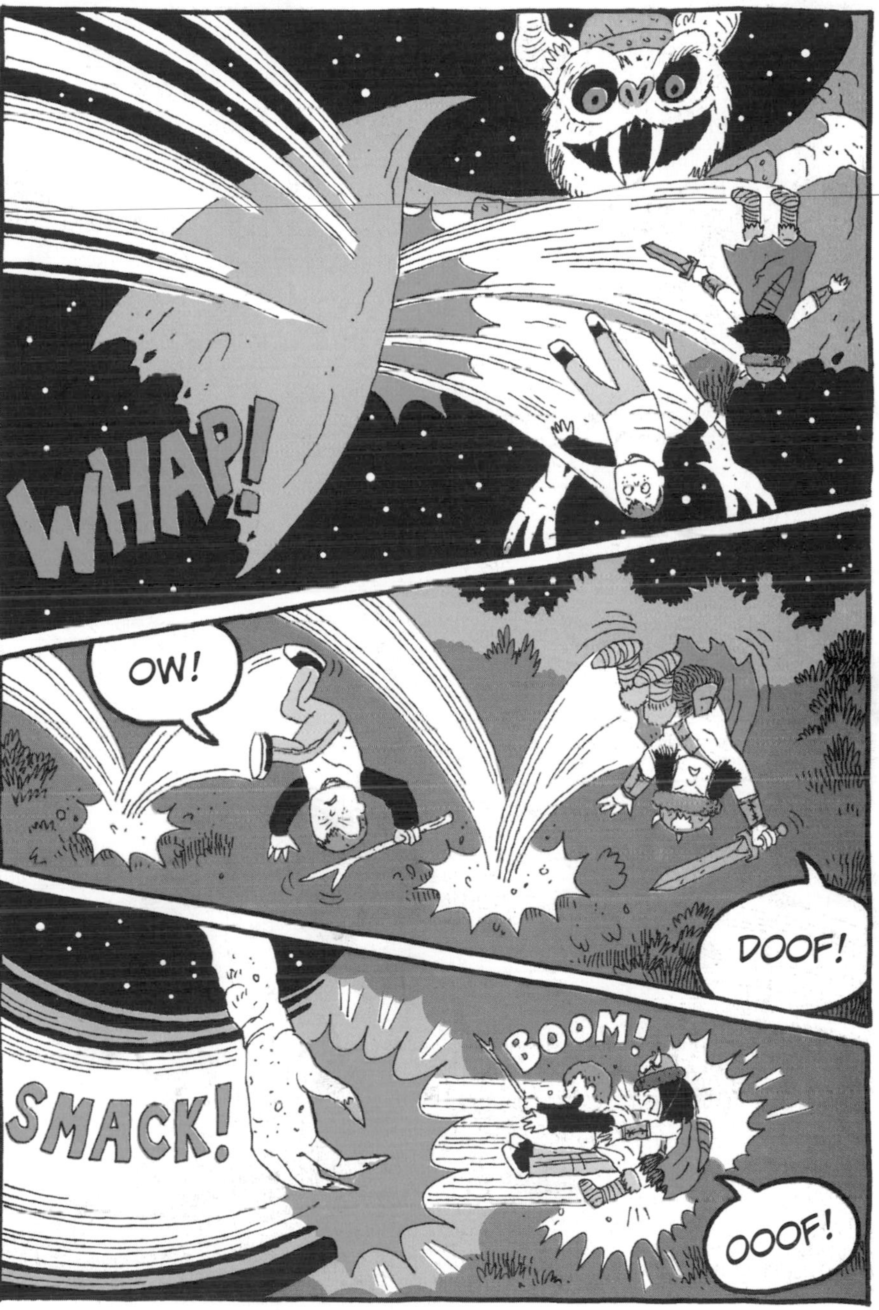
WHAP!
OW!
DOOF!
SMACK!
BOOM!
OOOF!

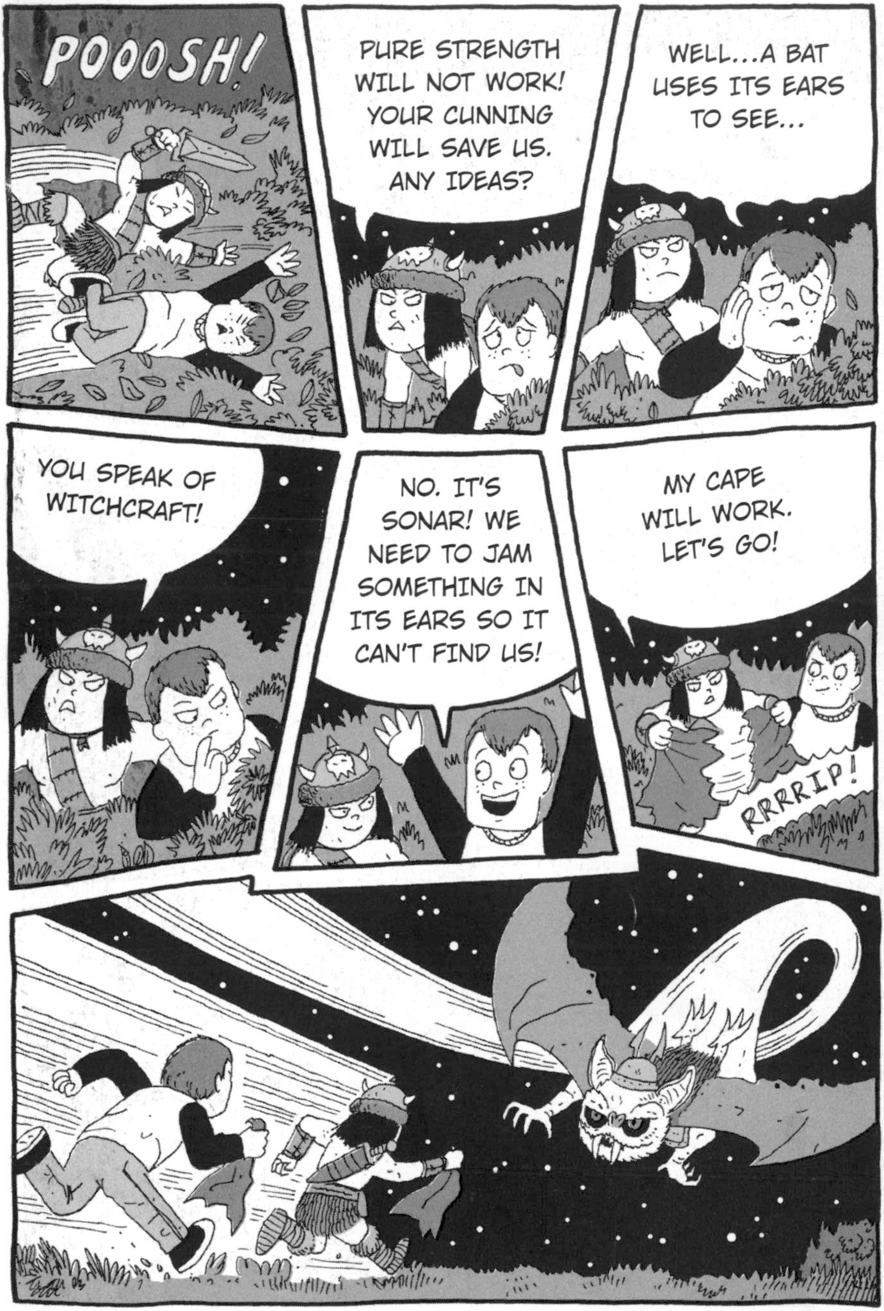
POOOSH!
PURE STRENGTH WILL NOT WORK! YOUR CUNNING WILL SAVE US. ANY IDEAS?
WELL...A BAT USES ITS EARS TO SEE...
YOU SPEAK OF WITCHCRAFT!
NO. IT'S SONAR! WE NEED TO JAM SOMETHING IN ITS EARS SO IT CAN'T FIND US!
MY CAPE WILL WORK. LET'S GO!
RRRRIP!

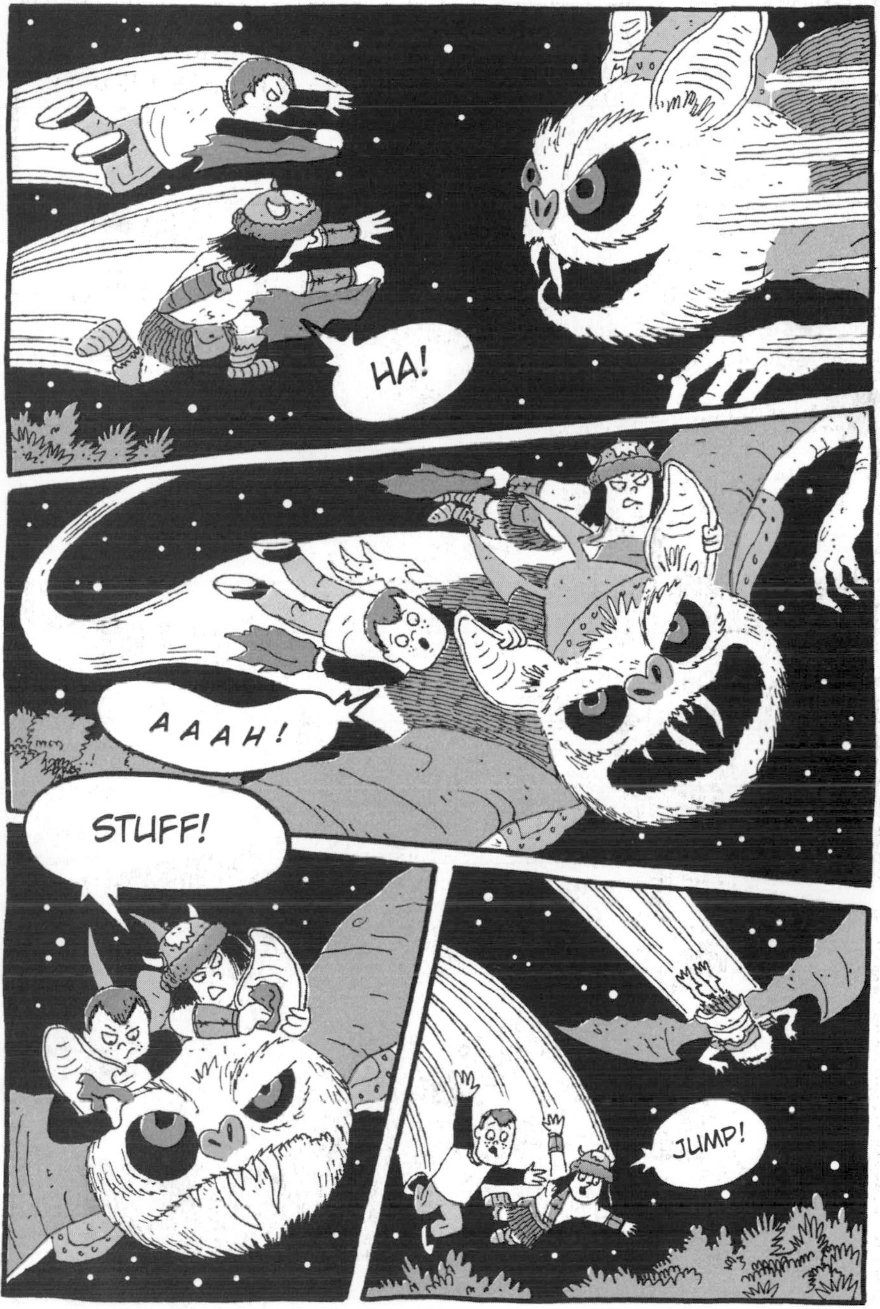
HA!
A A A H!
STUFF!
JUMP!

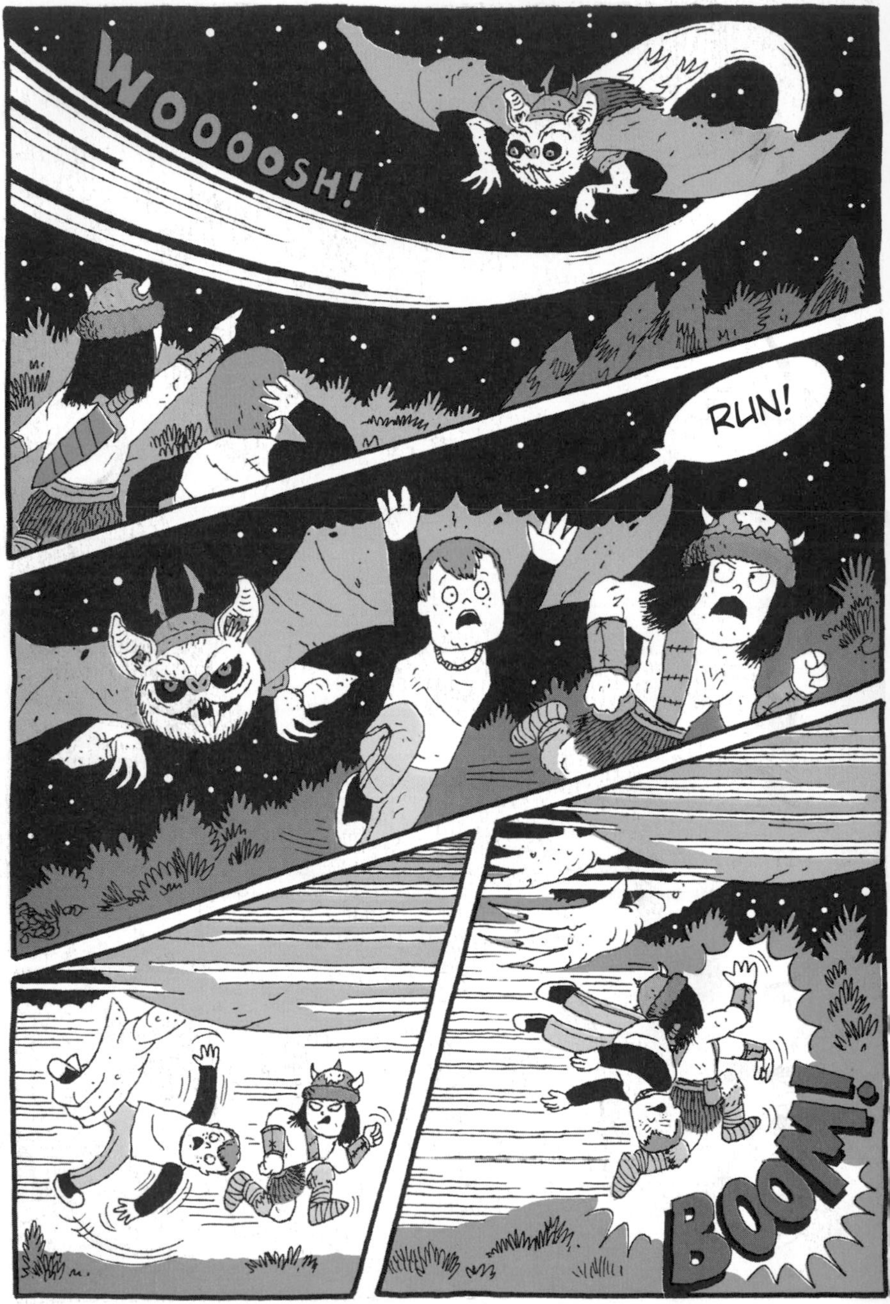
WOOOOSH!
RUN!
BOOM!

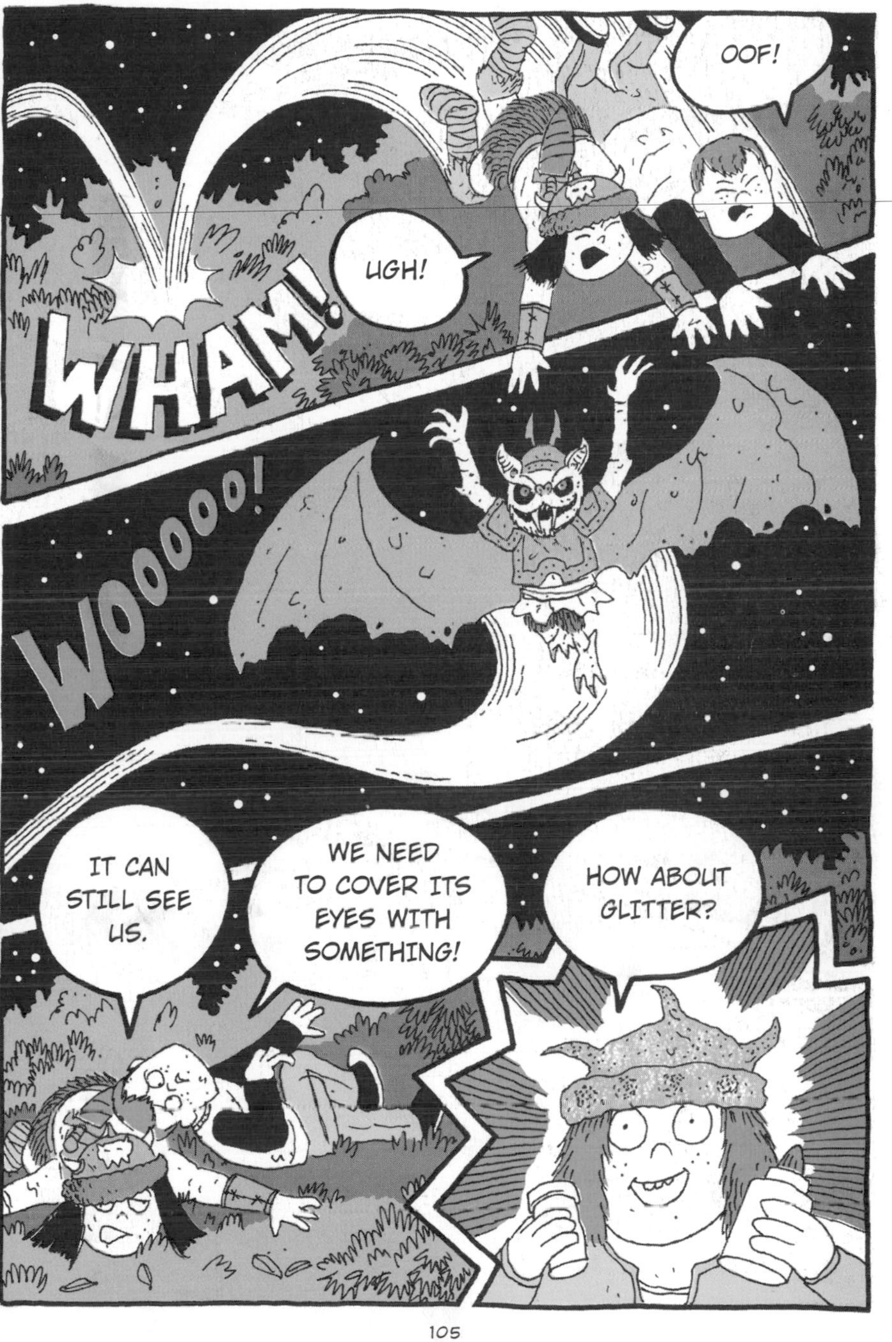
OOF!
UGH!
WHAM!
WOOOOO!
IT CAN STILL SEE US.
WE NEED TO COVER ITS EYES WITH SOMETHING!
HOW ABOUT GLITTER?

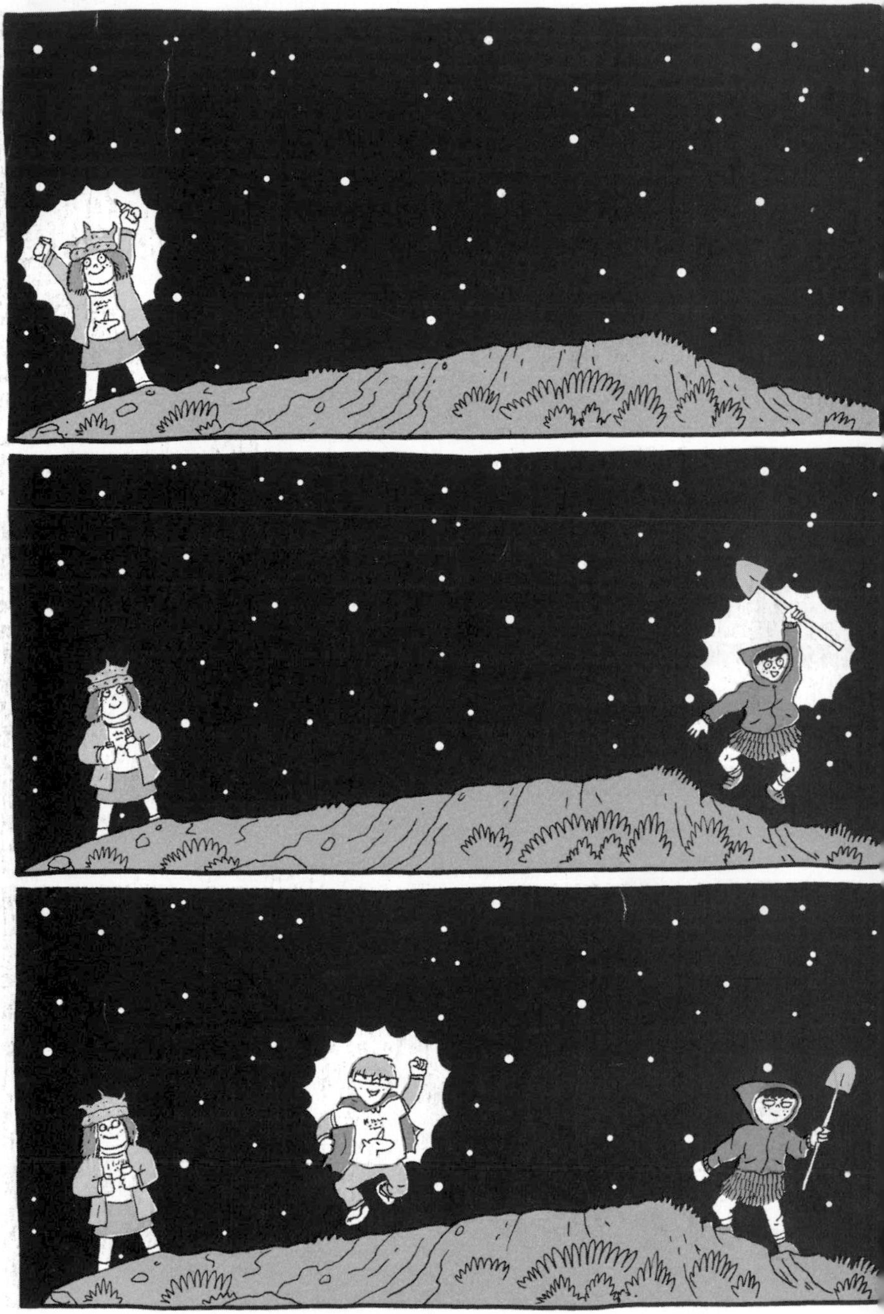

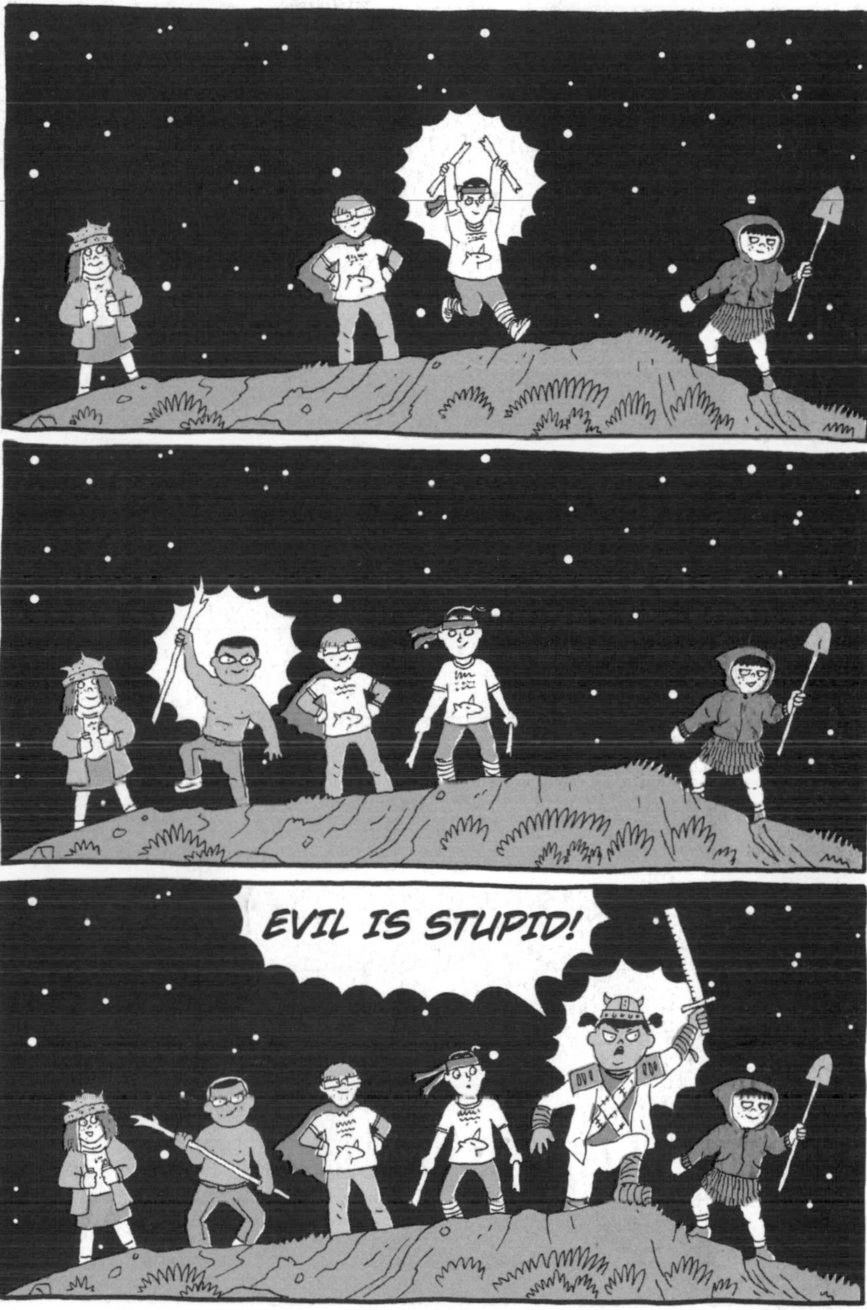
EVIL IS STUPID!

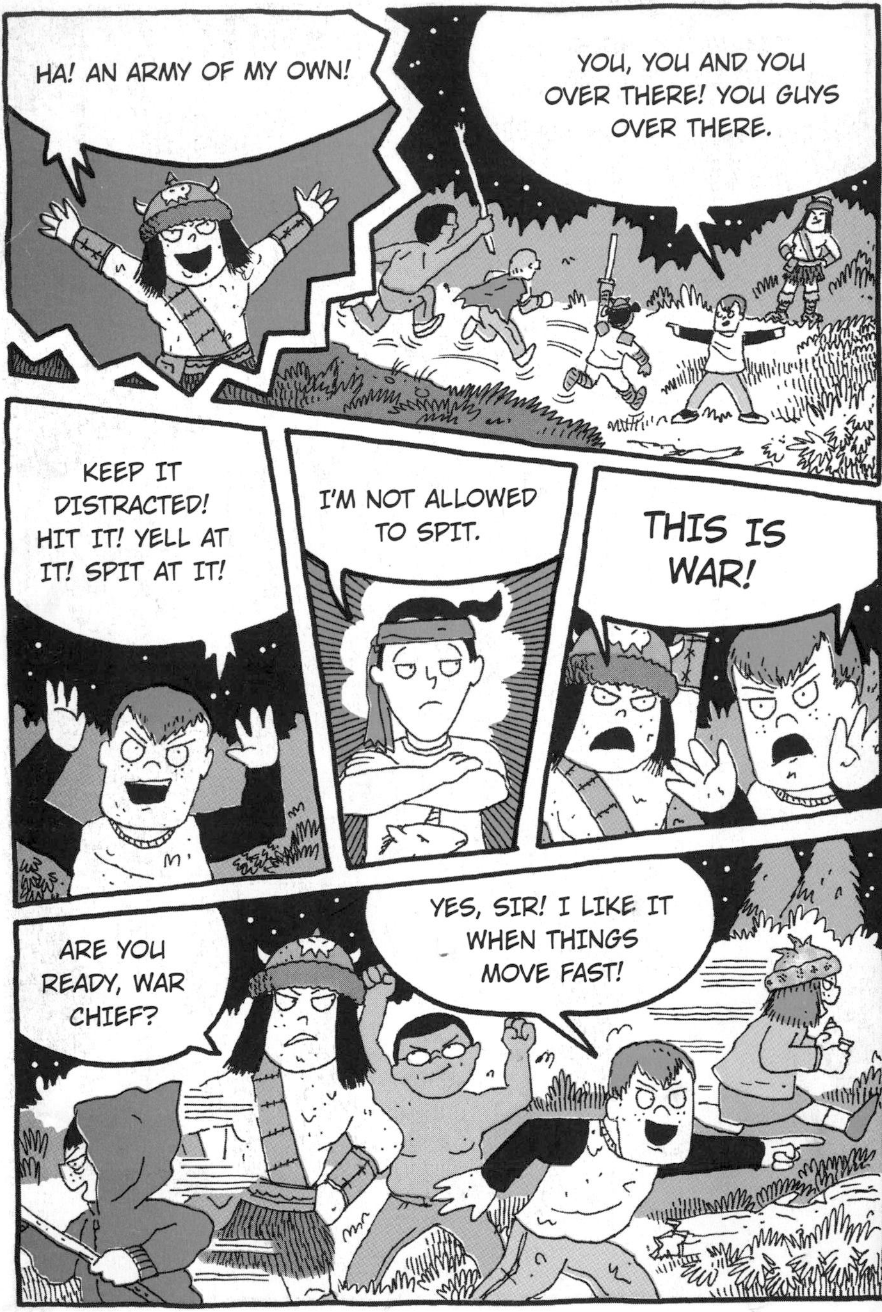

HA! AN ARMY OF MY OWN!
YOU, YOU AND YOU OVER THERE! YOU GUYS OVER THERE.
KEEP IT DISTRACTED! HIT IT! YELL AT IT! SPIT AT IT!
I'M NOT ALLOWED TO SPIT.
THIS IS WAR!
ARE YOU READY, WAR CHIEF?
YES, SIR! I LIKE IT WHEN THINGS MOVE FAST!

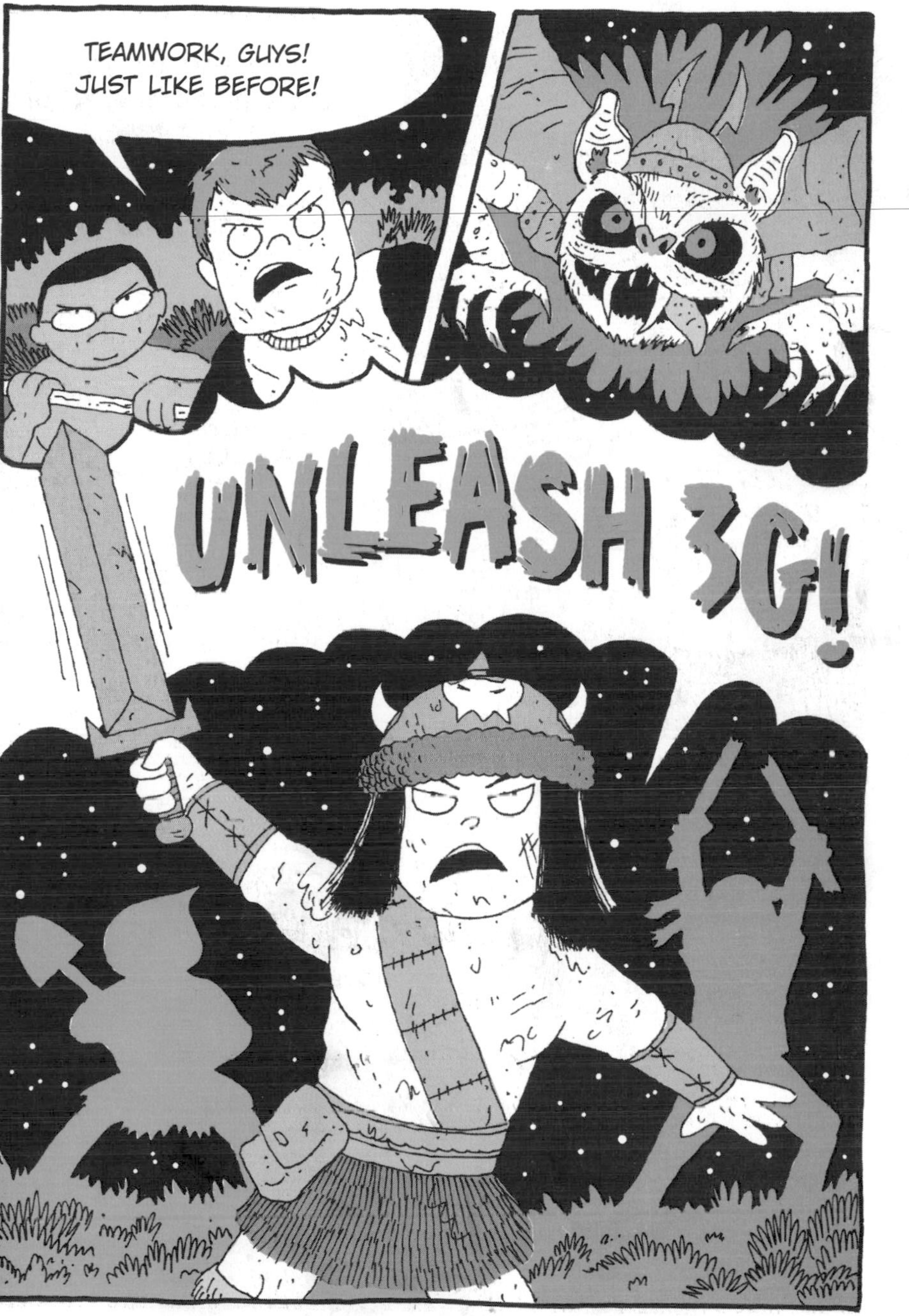
TEAMWORK, GUYS! JUST LIKE BEFORE!
UNLEASH 3G!

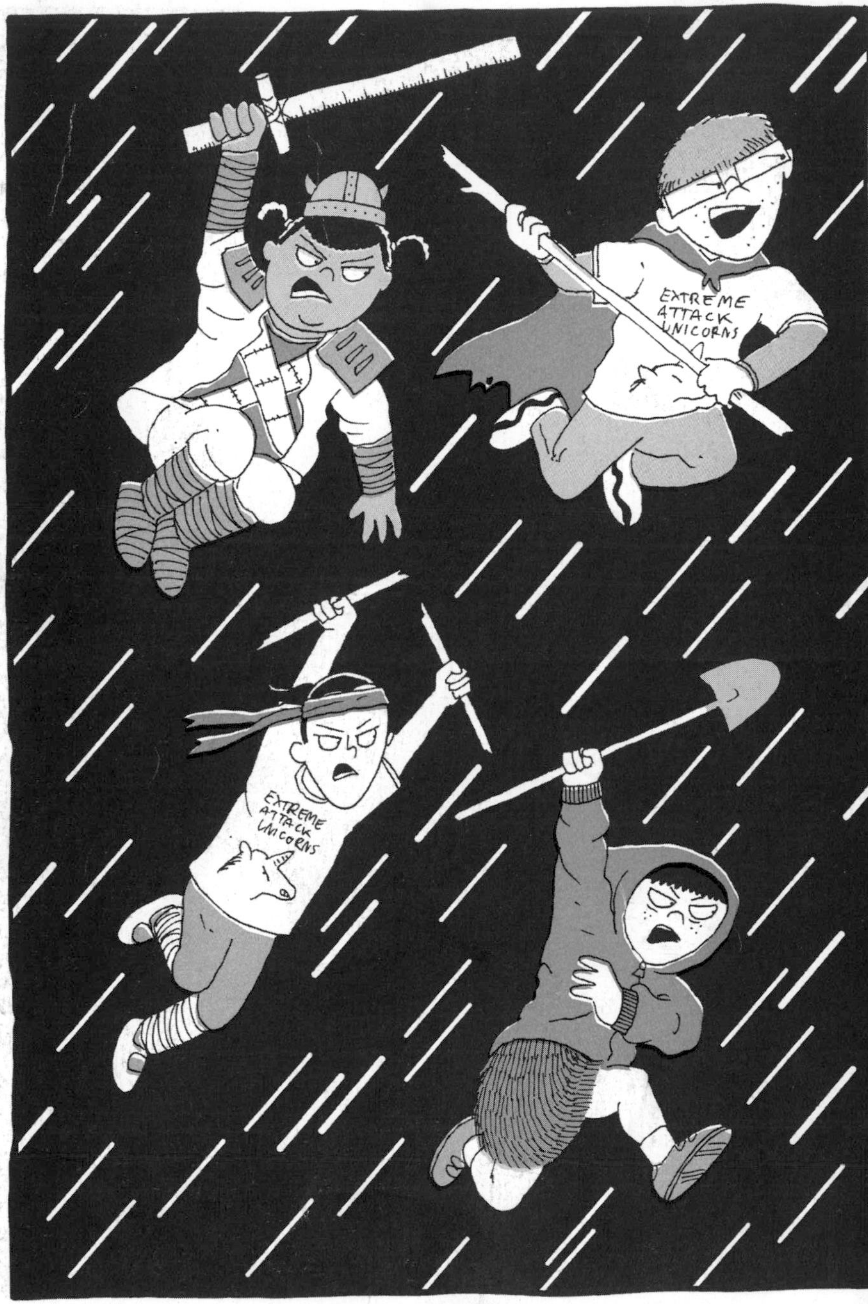
EXTREME
ATTACK
UNICORNS
EXTREME
ATTACK
UNICORNS

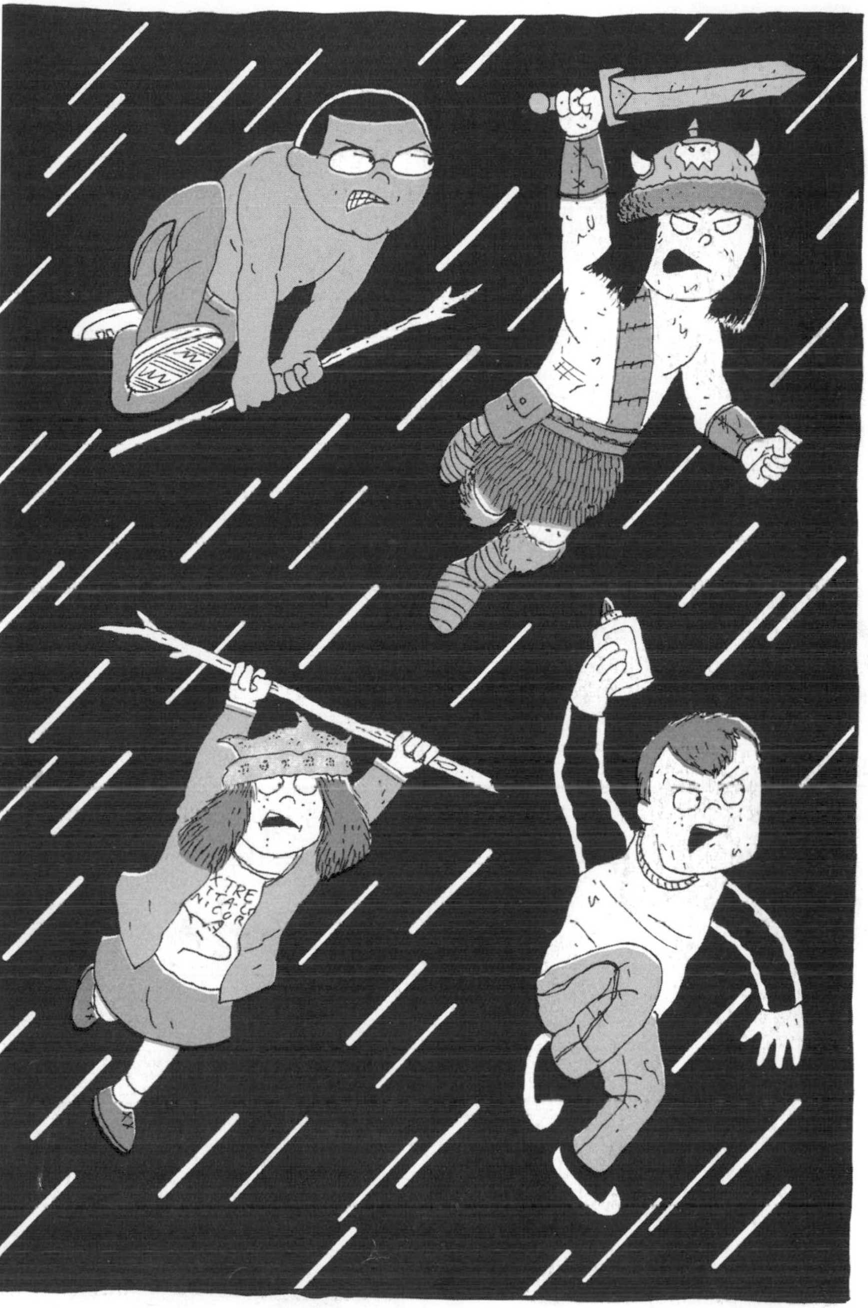

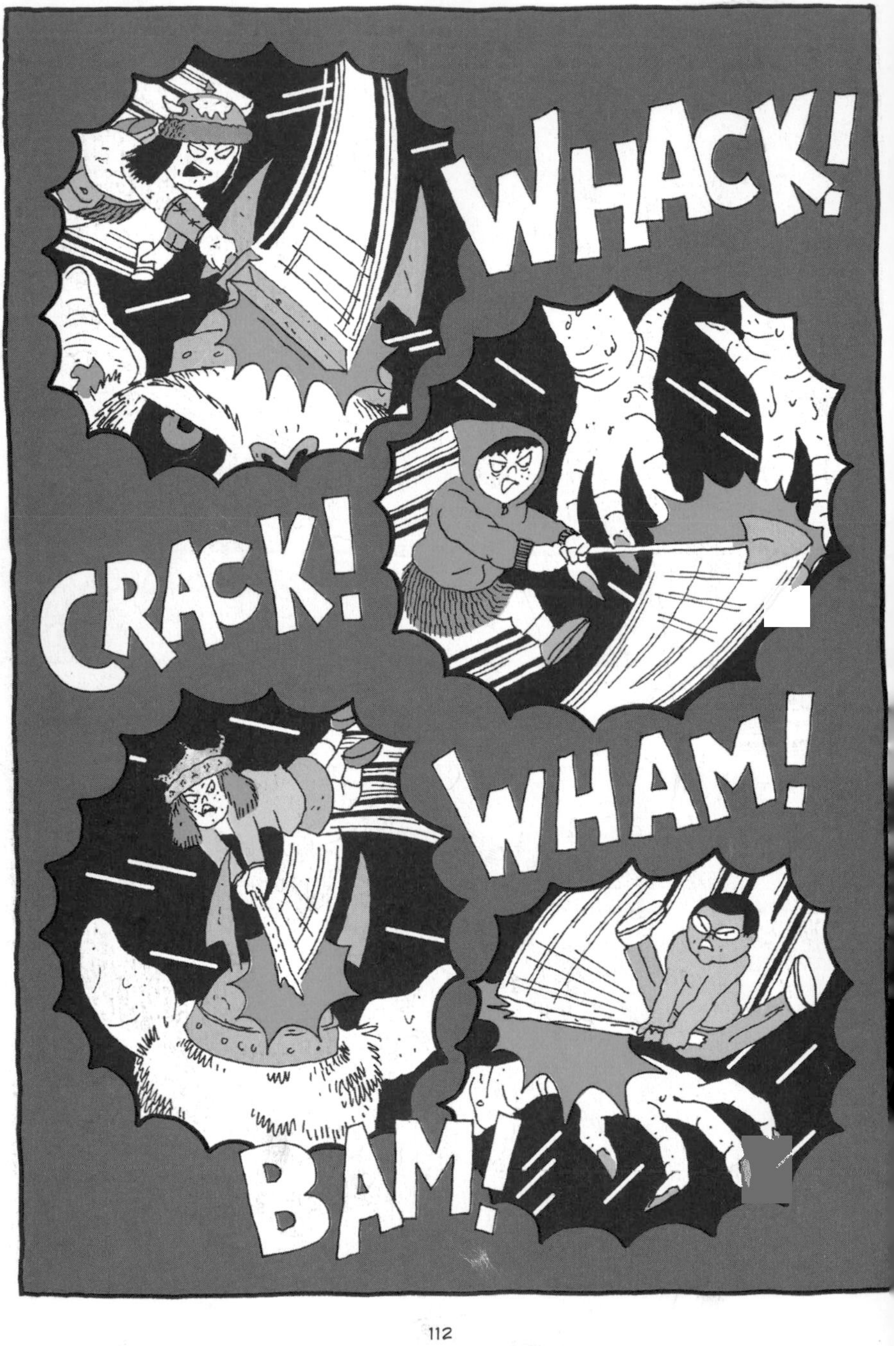
WHACK!
CRACK!
WHAM!
BAM!

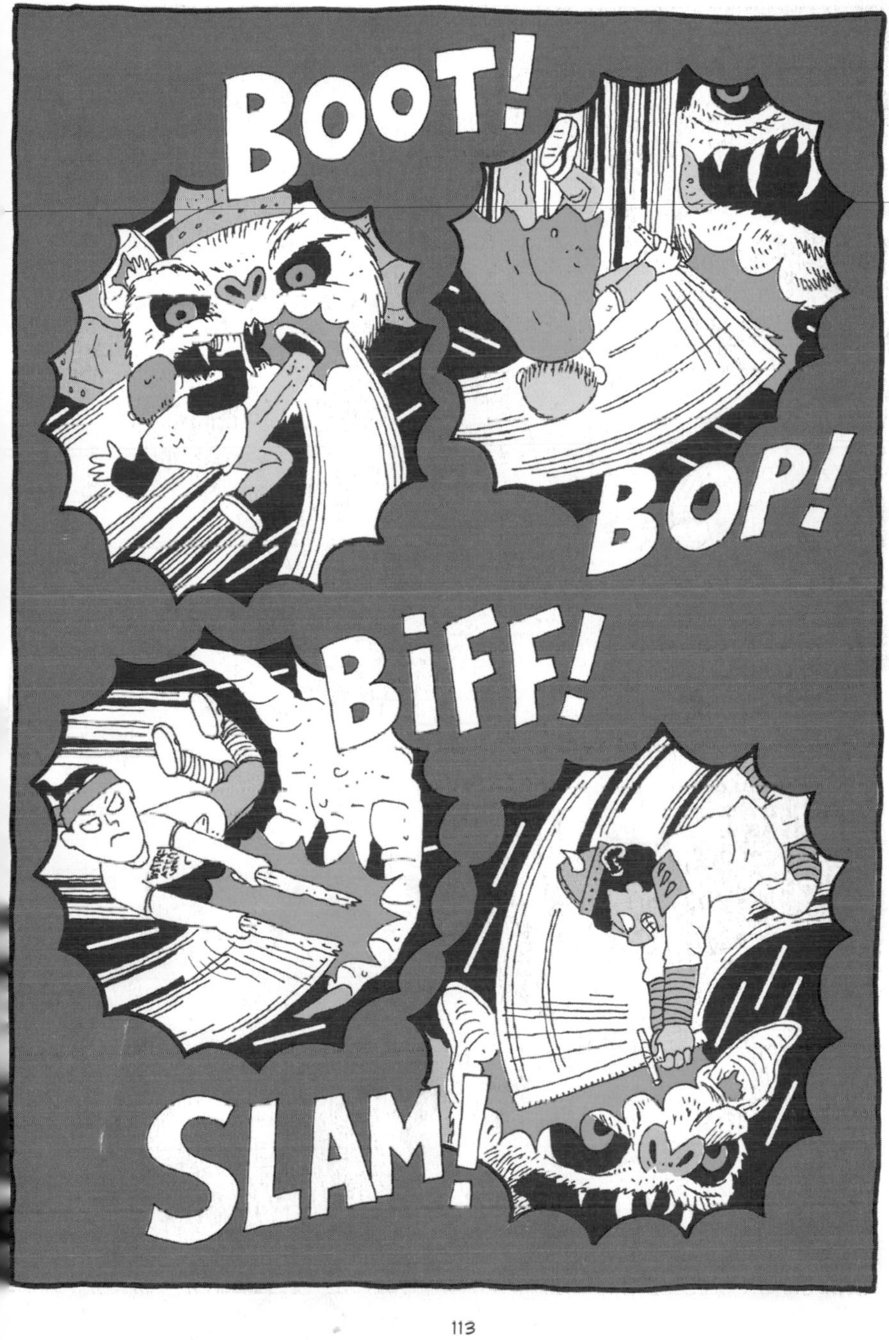
BOOT!
BOP!
BiFF!
SLAM!

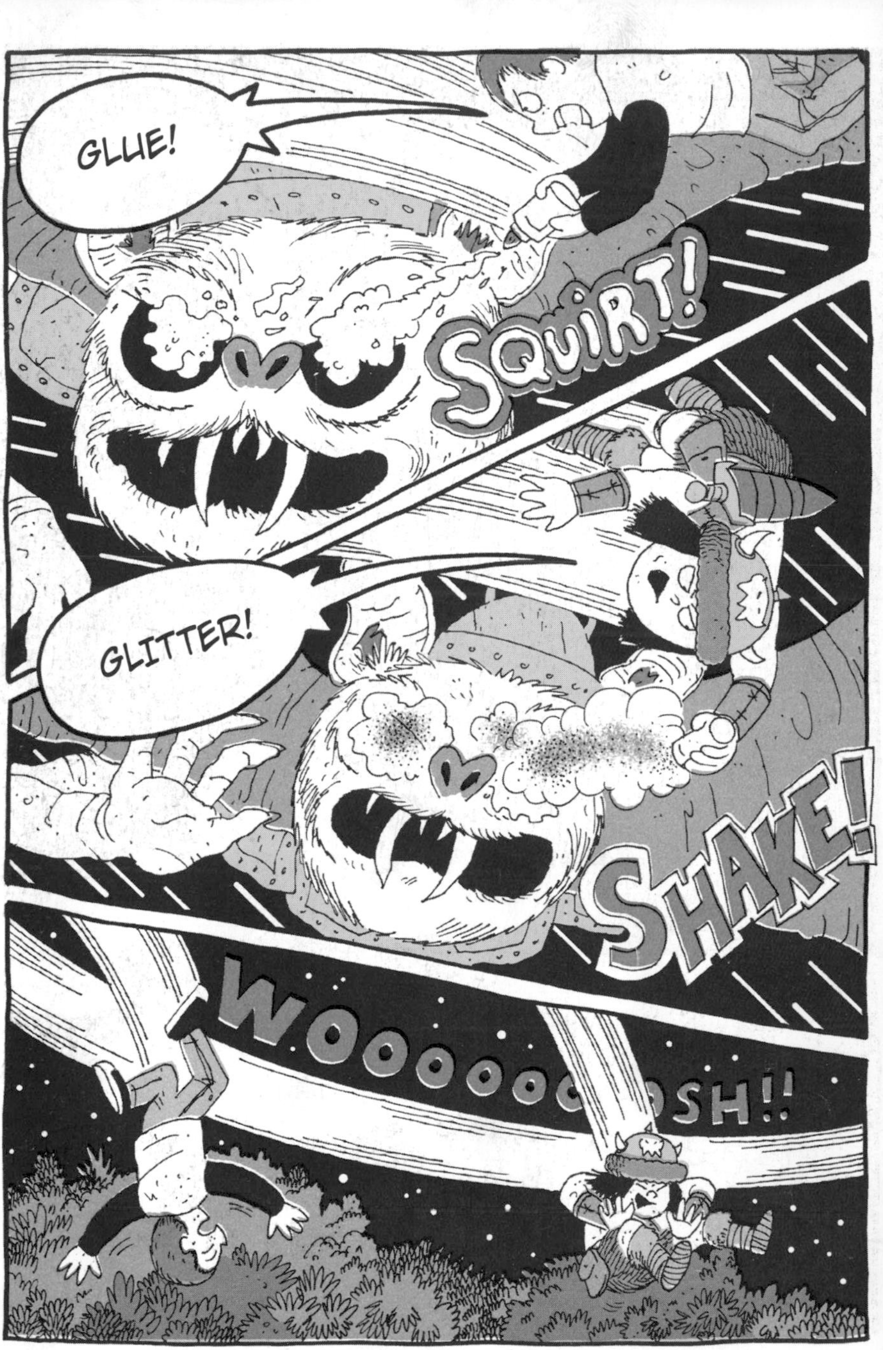
GLUE!
SQUIRT!
GLITTER!
SHAKE!
WOOOOOOOOSH!!

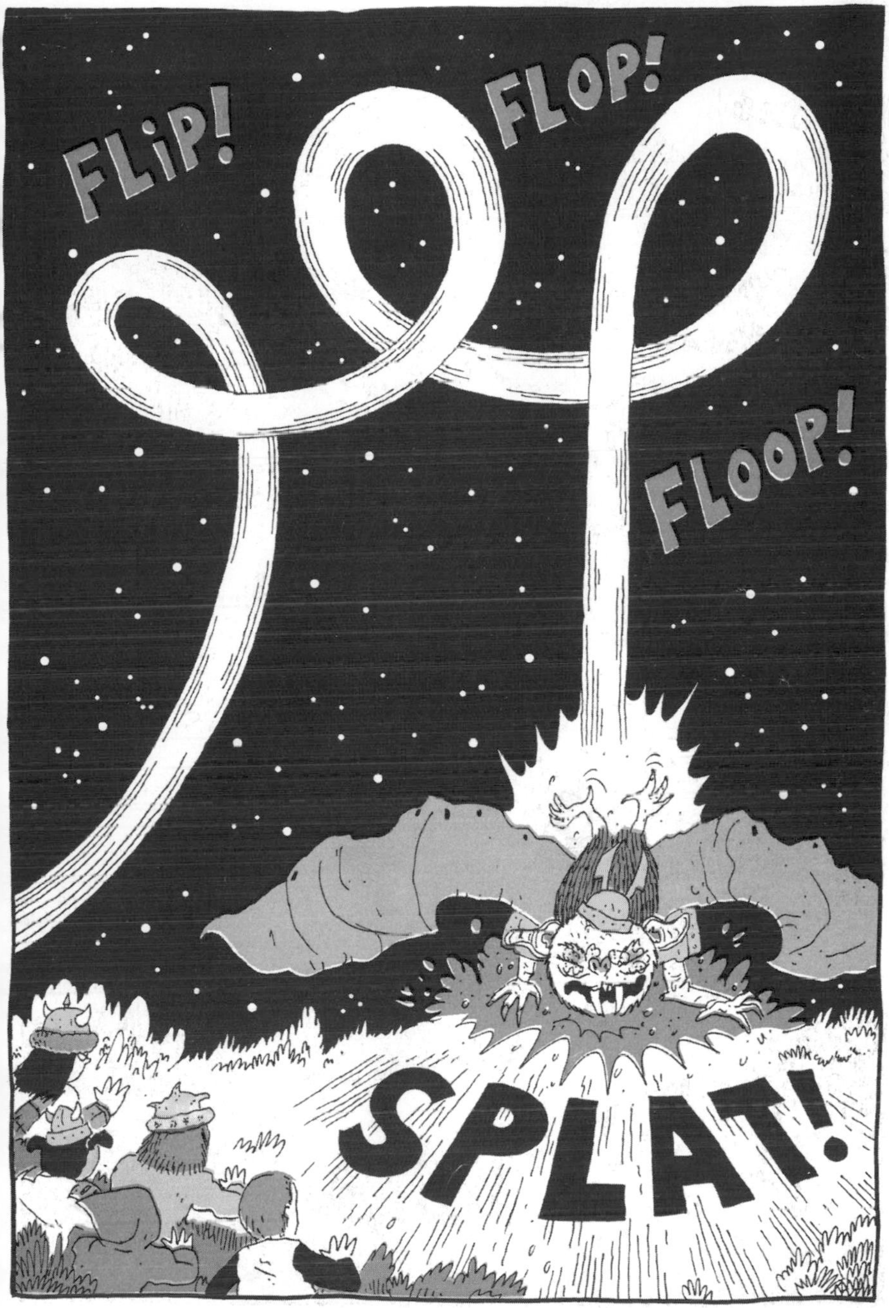
FLIP!
FLOP!
FLOOP!
SPLAT!

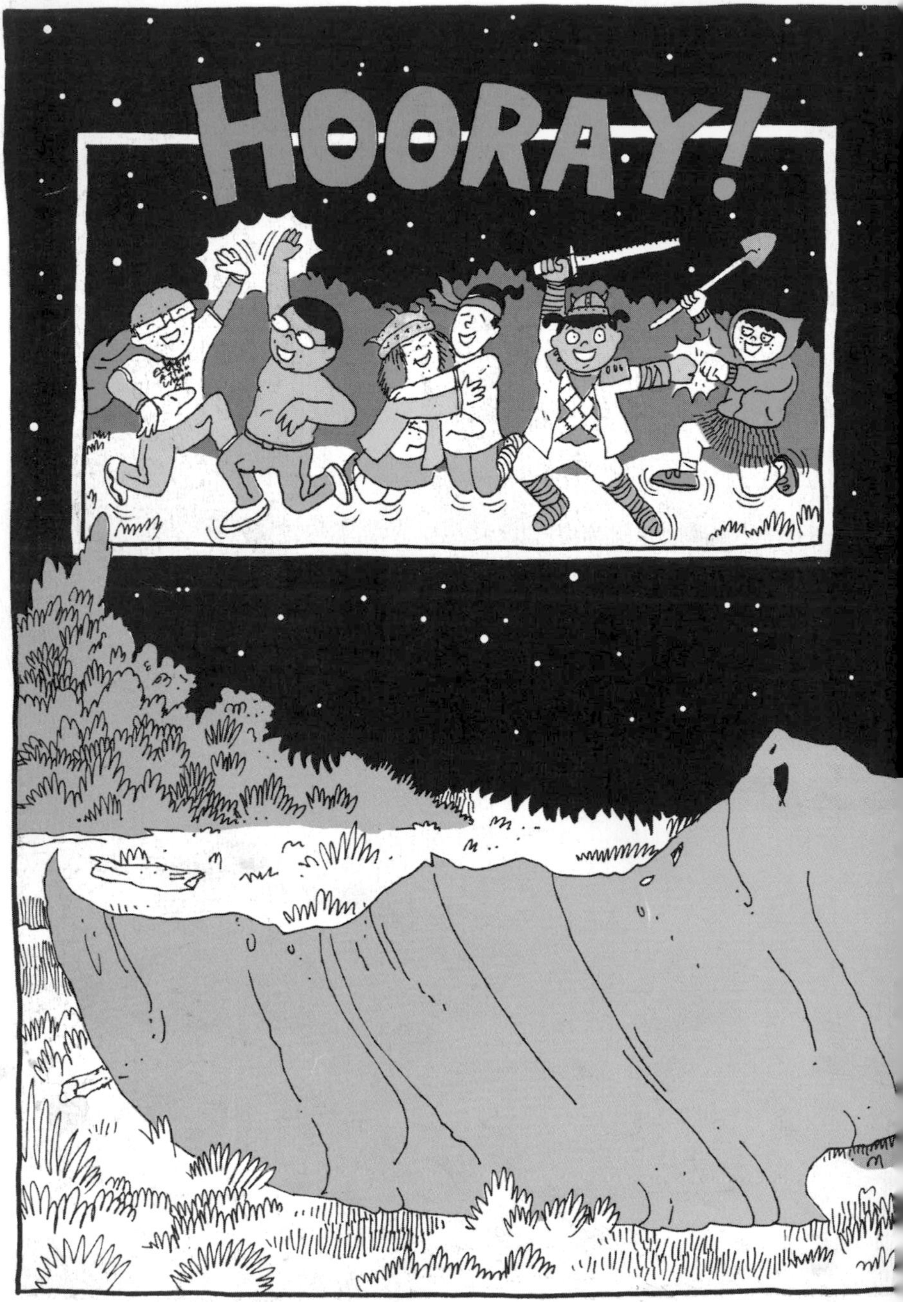
HOORAY!

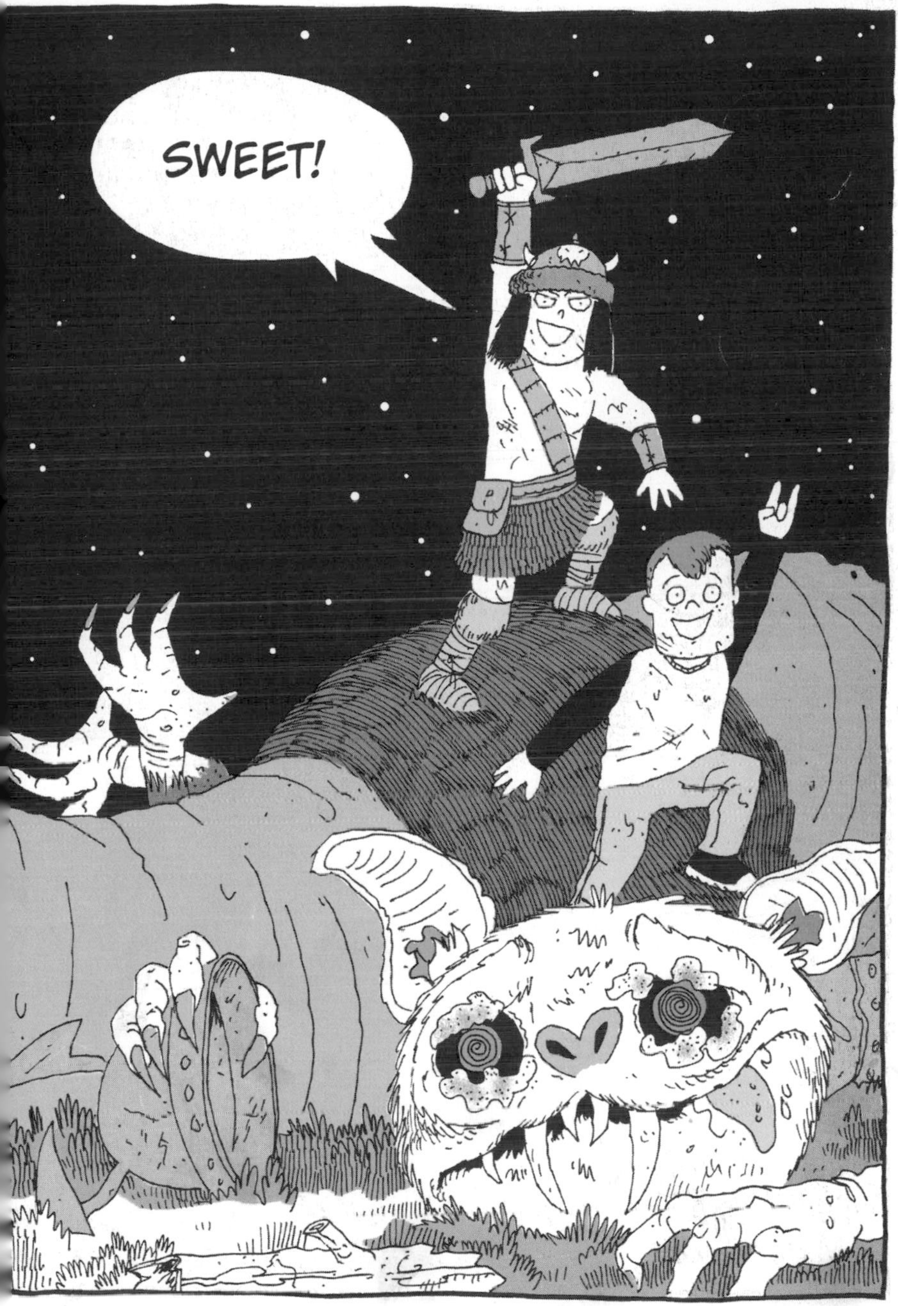
SWEET!

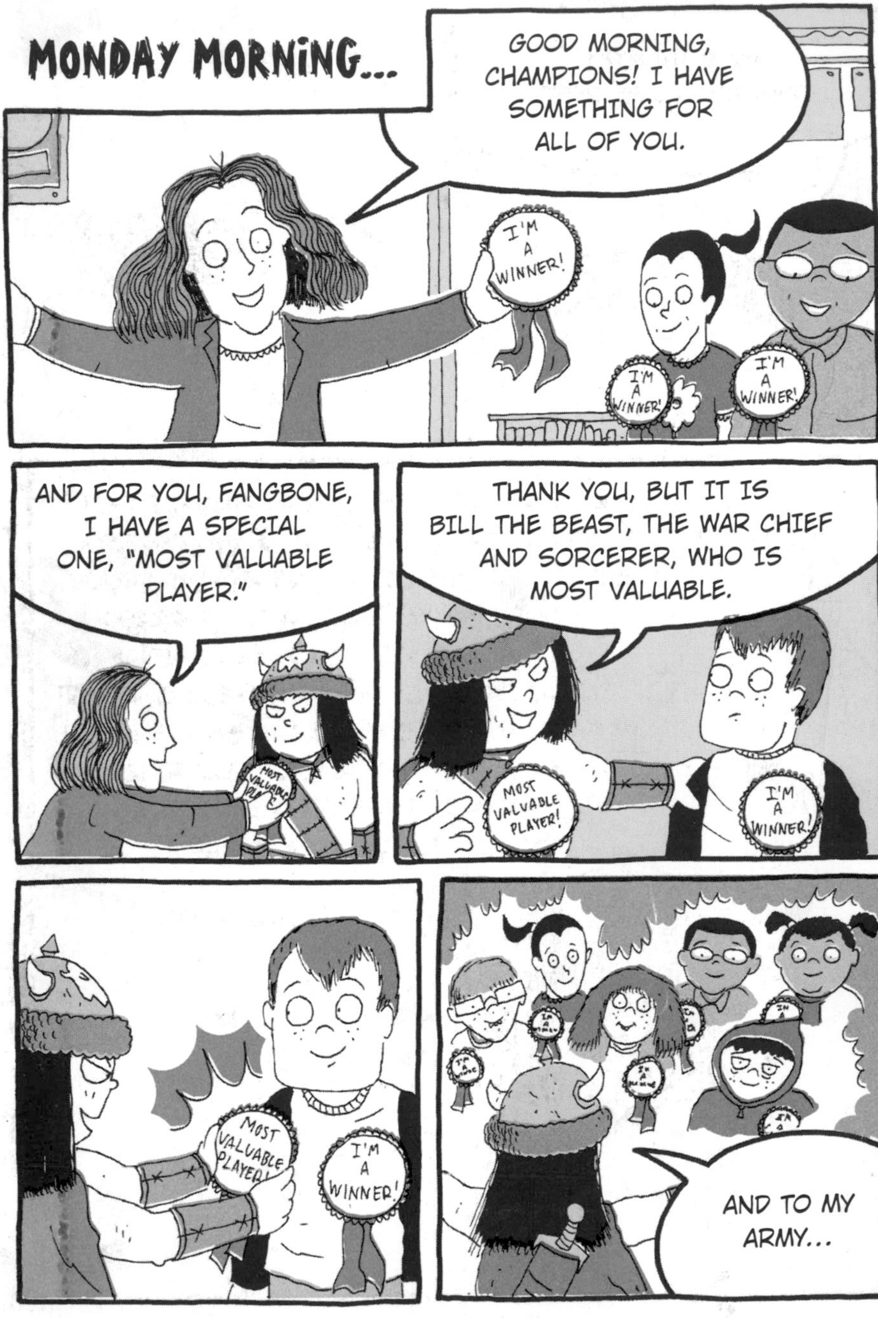
MONDAY MORNING...
GOOD MORNING, CHAMPIONS! I HAVE SOMETHING FOR ALL OF YOU.
I'M A WINNER!
I'M A WINNER!
I'M A WINNER!
AND FOR YOU, FANGBONE, I HAVE A SPECIAL ONE, "MOST VALUABLE PLAYER."
THANK YOU, BUT IT IS BILL THE BEAST, THE WAR CHIEF AND SORCERER, WHO IS MOST VALUABLE.
MOST VALUABLE PLAYER!
I'M A WINNER!
MOST VALUABLE PLAYER!
I'M A WINNER!
AND TO MY ARMY...

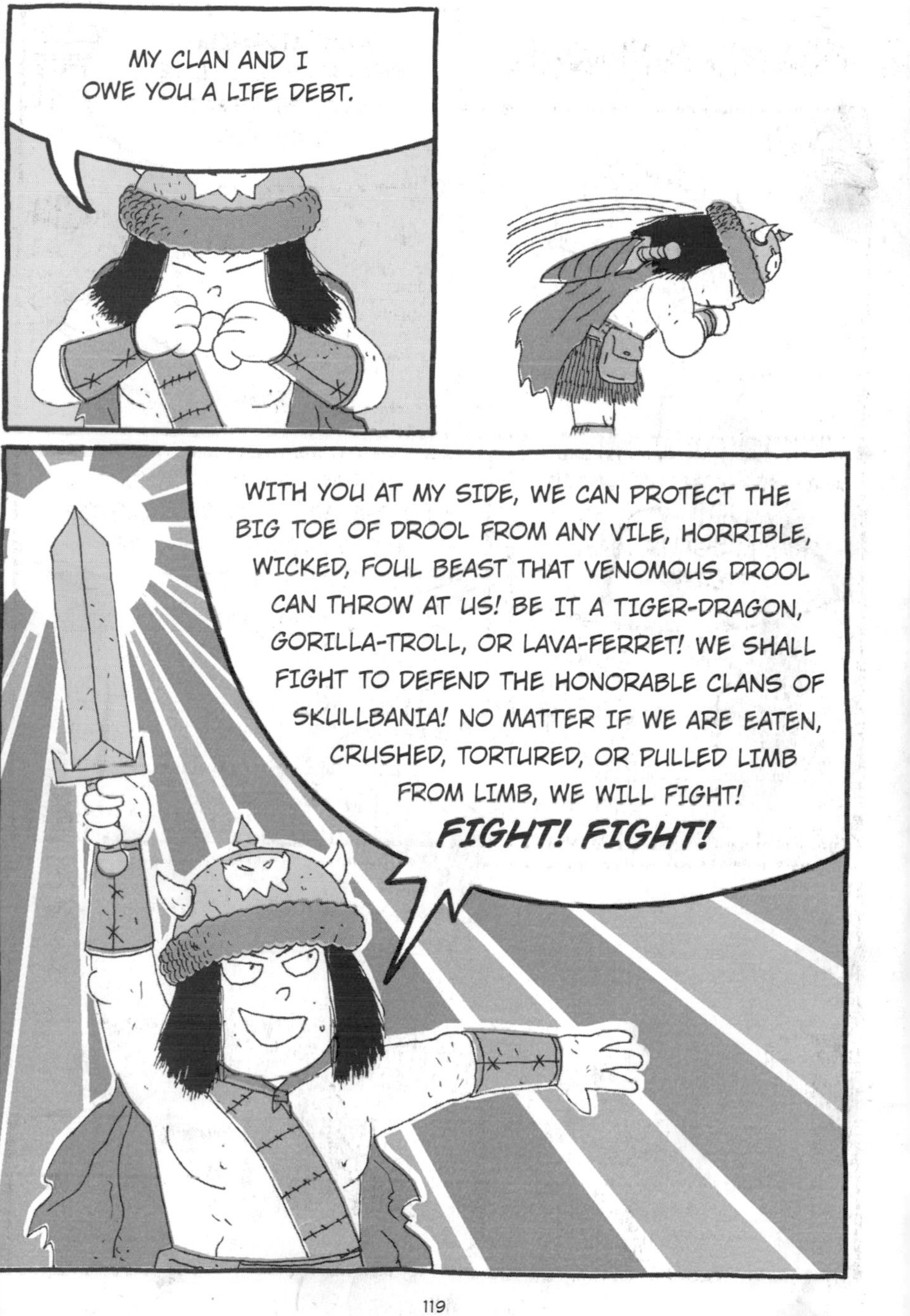
MY CLAN AND I OWE YOU A LIFE DEBT.
WITH YOU AT MY SIDE, WE CAN PROTECT THE BIG TOE OF DROOL FROM ANY VILE, HORRIBLE, WICKED, FOUL BEAST THAT VENOMOUS DROOL CAN THROW AT US! BE IT A TIGER-DRAGON, GORILLA-TROLL, OR LAVA-FERRET! WE SHALL FIGHT TO DEFEND THE HONORABLE CLANS OF SKULLBANIA! NO MATTER IF WE ARE EATEN, CRUSHED, TORTURED, OR PULLED LIMB FROM LIMB, WE WILL FIGHT! FIGHT! FIGHT!

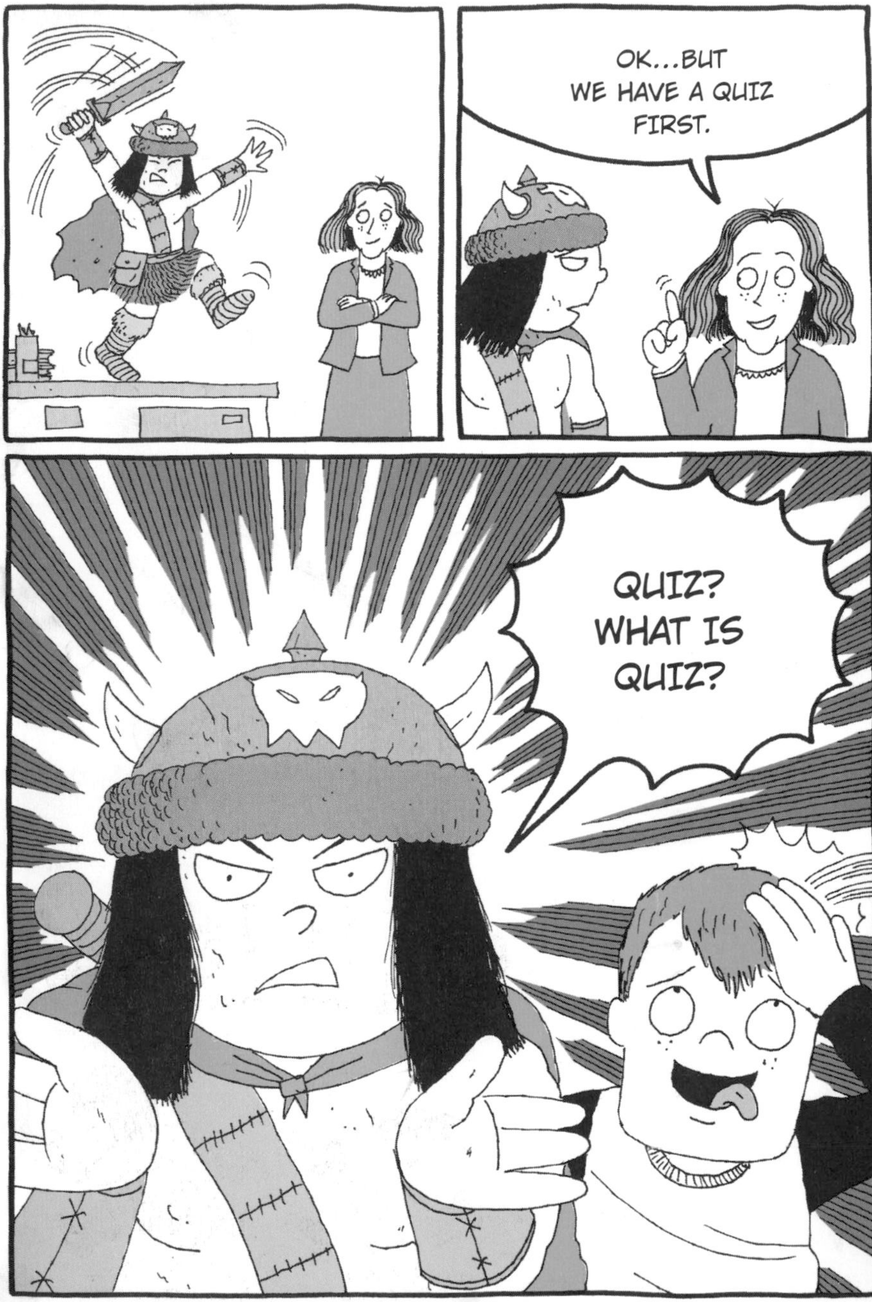
OK...BUT WE HAVE A QUIZ FIRST.
QUIZ? WHAT IS QUIZ?